Croatoan

J. OLIVER GLASGOW

Social Media:

Like this novel on Facebook
http://www.facebook.com/CroatoanNovel

Follow and tweet on Twitter
@JOliverGlasgow, #CroatoanNovel

Post your support
http://www.goodreads.com

DEDICATION

A wonderful amalgam of tough-as-nails moxie, mixed with undeniable goodness…thank you Carol Grimmett Kennemur, and Andrea Casson-Galiano for inspiring the main character in your own special ways.

CONTENTS

ACKNOWLEDGMENTS

Many thanks to Liz Morgan for the book cover design, and to Lori Michelle Miller for the additional editing. I couldn't have done it without you!

1.
12.19.9.11.6.09; 19 CHEN, 1 CIMI — DEATH

October 1, 2002, 2:05 a.m. EST

Nobody heard the eerie soft clacking of talons on the rooftop overlooking the darkening alley as she glided toward the man below. The earlier rain had left behind a deceptively clean and glassy sheen on the neglected asphalt upon which he walked, glossing over the oily grit and grime that made up this septic part of the city. Dark shimmers reflected the soles of his perfectly appointed Italian shoes, as the object of her immanent lust walked directly up the narrowing passage, seemingly oblivious to her piercing gaze as she stalked his echoing footfalls from above. Even now as she shifted shape to something more or less like a human, her thirst was building with every palpable pulse from his more than visible lifeline.

Those of her coterie had ways to measure the life experience of their prey. One's victim, if weak in the ways of truly living life, might prove little more than a mere transient fix that sustained life but for a short while. However, some of those plump from the risks and rewards of continually pushing their lives to the brink could yield a banquet of stored events and knowledge, providing dizzying heights of sustained satiation.

And this one…this one was reading off the charts.

Though she tried to suppress them, Salindria's fangs refused to behave. They betrayed her hunger for him, for the aura of life that radiated from him with a high voltage hum. Her biggest challenge would be just to *wait* for the reward of patience as her mentor Gallendon had taught her. And this cache of delight was proving more than her young willpower could resist as one of the recently Turned.

Salindria had been mindful of the checklist—he was alone; it was past

2:00 a.m., and the alley had limited exposure to the street and beyond. Not to mention he traveled alone.

Go figure.

A man full of pulse and vibe, walking a New York City alley at this time of night! If it had not been for his immaculate trench coat and near stoic poise, he would have fallen just short of the perfect mark.

And yet, something in the back of her mind seemed to be warning her off. Maybe it was too easy. But as she noticed the blondish-brown sideburns of a groomed gentleman, his confident stride completing his comportment, her tightened breath betrayed this effete caution.

Over the centuries, vampires developed the ability to read their potentials for prana—the life-force that they gained from the feasting. Gallendon had said, "When you feed, make it worth your while. Try to make it *beyond* worth it. Every pulp fiction reader fancies himself another Van Helsing. There is potential danger in every encounter. Try to find the prey that will offer a reward worthy of such a risk."

She was almost drawn to this stranger more for the experience, than for the fact that she had waited too long to feed. Unrest used to be far easier before these complex modern times. Since terrorism had found its way to the American shores, people surrounded themselves in cocoons of safety and comfort, avoiding the fullness found by living on the edge that bolstered their natural prana. They no longer lived life to the fullest. They had become—cautious, guarded.

Yet, this unsuspecting soul had obviously *lived*. His shared experience might even satisfy her sensually—at least in the way her race understood sexuality, than just slake her thirst with his blood that would soon fill her system. She had been taught well by Gallendon, and the essence of the victims' lives was as important as their blood.

This man had both.

As Salindria approached the corner of the rooftop some fifty yards above him, she noticed a slight increase in the tempo of his steps, as if some sixth sense had told him danger was lurking nearby. But this served only to heighten her drive. She loved it when the prey anticipated just a step or two. Her two, sharp, white and stiffening protrusions were becoming obvious in the fullness of her anticipation as they pressed against her generous upper lip. And the alley was only becoming darker and more intimate the deeper in they traveled. She started to wonder if he had taken a wrong turn.

Oh, the poor dear, she thought. "Awh…sorrowful, lost soul," she began to whisper to herself.

What happened next was not the last surprise her final night would bring her, for her prey actually answered, "Sorrowful in little—least of all hearing." He had mimicked her private tone as if he understood she could hear every last syllable. The damp gravel-dust from the pavement grinded under his heels as his planted his feet. The sudden stop punctuating his sentence as well as her surprise.

As she effortlessly lifted up five feet in an elegant but swift arc that foretold of the impending swoop, she said, "What is this trick, sir?" And as she approached his back at a speed that defied common understanding, "I hope your life is as rich as your senses."

Salindria was nothing if not conscious of her appearance. Virtually from the day she was turned, she held tight to the quaint belief that the impact she had on her victim somehow heightened the experience of their final moments. The victims' blood—sweetened by emotion and adrenalin, was considered by some of her race to be an essential element of the gourmet. To that end, she always followed the fashion that mortals ascribed to the darker rivulets of society.

In other words, she dressed for success.

The flittering, expressive whims of this century brought endless surprise to her sense of style. With eclecticism came a swirling collage that allowed a different fashion taste to be sated on a nightly basis. On this particular evening, she had chosen a black, flowing gypsy outfit, of cascading delicate patterns—a perennial favorite for these cool autumnal nights. The corset underneath she wore for her own amusement, perhaps to tease with should the moment present.

She felt the ensemble captured the October spirit that filled her with a certain melancholy, longing for the wistful days of her youth. The laced fringe that webbed from her waist to her wrist extended as she reached for the gentleman's shoulder. This gesture usually began the mind control, the first foreshadowing poison that something was horribly wrong for the victim, much like the paralysis an insect might feel just as the spider makes her first controlling stick.

She felt the fingers of her control pry their way into his mind like an unexpected burglar in the night, effortlessly opening a second story widow from a trellis. They probed as they felt their way around the landscape of his psyche. As she felt for those rare areas of control that made the target completely hers, she noticed the frictionless surfaces of his mind that almost welcomed her touch. Most minds recoiled from this intrusion—throwing up shields in vain attempts to thwart the unwanted violation. Thinking she had found a rare oddity, Salindria purred, "Oh, pet, it has been so long since I found a willing submissive."

With the mind seemingly fully in her control, she willed him to turn to her. For Salindria, at times—the victim's struggle was half the fun. She imagined a psycho-babbling shrink would say she was finding revenge for all the men that had forced themselves on her before the turning. And now that she owned the mental, and what was more, the physical advantage with her abilities, she often played with her prey like a demented cat with nothing but time on her paws.

But a submissive was to be treated with *some* respect. These tortured souls that spent their days searching for the glorious release they *thought* would come in the giving of their life-force to the creatures of the night deserved nothing less than *some* respect. Yes, they were naïve, but the moment could still be a pleasurable one for the taker. Salindria always felt a bit guilty for playing this role knowing that the victim would not find peace but rather pain for their misbegotten desires—but only a tiny bit of guilt. For only *one* draws the benefit from death's dance between two players.

This alley was no two-way street.

The refined gentleman turned in place as commanded, the rasp of his shoes grinding the only sound between them. During this heightened moment, her senses were at their peak. A faint drip from a gutter halfway up the alley seemed like the metronome tick of a pulse. It was in this still moment when she became fully aware of life, or at least what she understood life to be, that the eye contact with her prey meant everything. It brought the stream of timeless existence into focus. She felt every atom of his being in the weight of his gaze. And he had that look all right. Behind those dreamy eyes of his, was a soul that was yearning, albeit mistakenly, for what he *thought* would be the climax of his purpose.

They stood motionless as she took a moment to revel. Without breaking eye contact, she allowed her back and chest to relax as she breathed in through her nose, filling her lungs with billows of cool air, expanding in a slow and graceful sigh. Holding it for just a moment at its apex, she wished she could just float away on the peace that now filled her. She hitched and slowly exhaled while the tingles radiated from her solar plexus to all her extremities. Her fangs felt longer than ever but she no longer attempted to hide her lust. She was in full bloom—and she knew he felt it as well.

As a smile forced the corner of her mouth into a curl, she spoke, "You have waited so long for this moment. Yield to me as I desire."

With somewhat of a confused expression, one that seemed to betray his belief in his own control, he extended his chin out and up slightly to one side. The rumbling of a distant train matched the now audible rumbling of his blood as it flowed through contracting arteries that were virtually bulging in his neck.

Surprisingly he spoke. It took Salindria quite by surprise not only by the mere fact that he *could* speak, but that he did so with such measured control. "I yield, but ask only for my desires to be met in return."

Salindria marveled at this, even though she realized his conditions could only be empty. But she also realized that there must be some area of control in his mind that she had carelessly missed. The moth was paralyzed, and partially wrapped in the silk of her web, yet it could speak.

She concluded with some delight that an exchange with a mentally keen creature such as this would indeed satisfy her for some time to come. Consuming his life may well be the richest feast she had experienced since her turning. On that first time, the feasting had been rudely halted by her master before it could be made complete. But not this time—no, this time she would feel the climax of the exchange, his life to hers.

Realizing the potential of it all, she held herself up for the briefest of moments. Maybe it was a twinge of guilt. Maybe it was her summoning the memorial remnants of her dormant sexuality, but she made a rare decision to at least give this one some false sense that he had been correct all these years in his submissive delusions.

As she moved into the heat of his space, she slid one hand down the front of his pleated, perfectly tailored slacks as she opened her mouth to receive the gift from his neck. And though it may have been centuries since she had done such a thing, the practice was surprisingly fresh and familiar to her fingers. She became suddenly aware of the sensation, feeling the pulse of his erection with her hand as she simultaneously felt the pulse of his neck with her lips. The stereo beats may have even been something akin to sexual pleasure to her, even though she no longer had the capacity for that gift of the flesh.

Still, it was not altogether unpleasant.

Again, she hesitated before piercing him. She took time to savor the pheromone taste of his taut skin and delighted in his palpable and increasing body heat. In this unexpected elation, she was so enwrapped that the warm touch of his one hand to her waist and the gentle cupping of his other to the nape of her neck almost went unnoticed.

Almost.

She gasped as her lips momentarily separated from his neck leaving a telltale press of moisture that betrayed her hunger and her near complete abandonment of control. Still, Salindria was not overly concerned. This mortal could certainly not harm her in any way and was no physical match, but this moth seemed to at least be partially immune to the entangling web of her mental power.

"Yet another surprise, kind sir?" Her dark and soft voice almost sounded stuffy as she spoke around her fangs expressing her cute confusion. It had an endearing quality to it, a quality that invited more than it warned.

He responded by drawing her closer in many other ways. As he pulled her waist in to him, she was suddenly aware that while the front of her hand still caressed his slacks, the back of it was now pressing into her. It became a type of proxy for something more, and she found herself wishing she could experience it all again. As she allowed her weight to shift in his grasp a little, her lips bumped the soft and stretched skin of his awaiting neck, almost triggering a reflexive snap.

As she fought for slipping control, Salindria became aware that the thumb of his right hand was now bracing softly behind her ear as the fingers massaged through handfuls of her flowing, raven black hair, caressing the place where her skull just met her neck.

To be honest with herself, she now even wondered exactly what she intended or even desired to do with this strange situation. But this moment of reflection was fleeting and her unnatural instincts returned. She had a single job to do and had more than paid him for the interesting foreplay. Salindria decided she would mercifully spare him any unnecessary torture. She thought it unfortunate for him that she would still consume his life completely, which would mean a somewhat slow and agonizing experience as he shuffled off this mortal coil.

More's the pity.

So she sloughed off any minor remaining remorse like an old skin and decided to begin the process.

"You go slowly at first," Gallendon had instructed her the night before her turning. "Tomorrow's sun shall be the last that you see with your own eyes, save for the crude, captured artificial and cold images of the artists that pale by comparison. But when you consume a soul, that sun is always the first thing that you see through their memories if you take your time. For them, it is the beginning of their memory; it is their first best god—whether they realize it or not. It always starts with this and proceeds from there."

"Will I feel pain?"

"In the turning, yes. But in the consuming of others? No. The pleasure is not only in the satisfying of the hunger—which is only base sustenance, but also in the living of their experience. And that sun is always right there at the start," he said, brushing her hair from the tear tracks on her cheeks.

"I'm not sure I understand," Salindria heard her own voice quiver in this far away memory of the centuries-old preparation.

"There is no *understand*. Not now. There is only accept or reject. *Understand* is for a later time. The important thing is to feel the sun tomorrow. It will be your last sun regardless of the choice you make—death or un-death. You are too far gone now for any other path."

"I'm not sure I can do this thing you ask," she said looking up at his endless eyes—that face she had trusted since the early days at the orphanage. He had visited her in the vestibule on those nights when she tried to remember her birth parents and prayed to God for their return. He would go there, yes, but daren't go further inside. There she lit the candle that would burn down to a nub long before her hopes were ultimately snuffed like the fragile flame.

He laughed softly at her. She was so ignorant. But they all were. Even he was at one time. "No, dear child. It is not something that you *can* do. It is something that you *will* do, should you choose this path before you." The soft words stood in stark contrast to the chiseled features of his alabaster skin, the severe and graying hairline that enhanced the natural stretch of his face down to his strong chin.

"But how does it work?" her voice nervously revealed a certain curiosity that exposed more desire than revulsion.

"As the pulse is felt in the lips, your teeth open the path for their life to flow into yours. No sooner does their life touch the tongue than you see beyond seeing. Their entire life unfolds before you. Their feelings, their experiences, and knowledge are transmuted to you as they are peeled away from their very soul.

"And as these are removed, they feel the first of the physical pain that will bring you triumphant joy. For these experiences are as much a part of their flesh and bone as is the blood that issues forth from them."

She was surprised to feel her pulse quicken a bit at the thought. Perhaps she had a darker spirit than she had first imagined. Perhaps all that selfless sacrifice that had held her at the orphanage for seven years past her legal age to leave was nothing more than bitter spite.

It was now beginning to dawn on her, on the eve of *her* last sun, that perhaps she had stayed in this place she had abhorred only until she found the strength to seek her revenge on the society that had made her—that had made so many like her. Perhaps this growing desire was just her first idea of power beyond this life, which had thus far been thrust upon her for the sins of her parents, or of this blasted country and time. "Please continue," she bade him.

"You are no longer frightened?" he asked as he noticed the tapering of her tears.

She shook her head quickly as if to say "no" without leaving his gaze.

As he continued to stroke her shimmering black hair, he said, "I knew you were strong. I knew you were meant for us. Ah, well. Then it shall be. But I continue only at your behest, young Salindria. The next stage, the baser things are extracted: their strength, intelligence, stamina, and drive. The very building blocks of their existence are pulled from their subconscious as your hungry mouth pulls harder at the thicker substance. Then finally, the foundation of their soul is consumed with the matter of their marrow. It leaves one quite…satisfied. Quite…complete…as complete as the life-giver's termination. It is the beginning of a new you."

"So everything becomes ours?"

"Not quite *everything*. There is the seed that only belongs to the *others*. It taints them and so we reject it. But most everything else, yes. You see, you change with every taking. You are enhanced and greater than you were before. They continue in you, as you increase in knowledge more than they could ever imagine." His words trailed as softly as a lover slips from between the sheets after one last warm embrace. "But first—always the sun…"

"The entire process happens much more quickly than the experience seems. And most have a tendency to rush clumsily through it, clods that they are. I tell you now and ask you always to remember it." To this, she nodded quickly like the little girl looking up at her favorite schoolmaster as she received the finer points of a grand lesson. "You must steady yourself. Just before that moment of impact, you must allow yourself to breathe. Breathe like you would if you knew fate and heaven were going to allow you to see the sun for only one last time. Breathe as though you could stop the flow of time and yet allow the flow of life to continue."

This time she nodded more slowly as if she really did understand perhaps for the first time. She broke her gaze, wondering if she could ever bear to part with the mystery and majesty of his voice.

And now, in a dark alley, both centuries and miles away from the man she saw as her savior, as she held this unusual find in her grasp, she nodded slowly with the memory, allowing her lips to brush softly again on his extended neck.

And she breathed, once more to see the sun.

At first, it started as a slight, innocuous pressure at the top of her neck. She had just begun to hold her breath to stop time and to still her soul when she felt the odd, sliding sensation of something thin and fibrous extending from the tip of gentleman's middle finger which was still pressed firmly into the base of her skull. Something like a needle swiftly pierced inward and upward towards her unsuspecting and defenseless mind. Just as the shocking pinch of pain injected into her surprised realization, *there* was the sun—an explosion of brilliance in her eyes, more dazzling than she had ever encountered.

She gave herself permission to exhale, for she could do little else, making full ready for the taking, when she realized that her body no longer yielded to her own command. In fact, now that she thought about it, she did not actually remember biting him.

Breathing in was useless as well, her body refused to accept any more direction from her mind. And in her growing panic and rush to free herself, the super nova in her mind's eye faded and she found herself face to face with her victim. Only now, *he* was smiling—smiling more wildly than anyone or anything she had ever encountered before.

"Awh…look at you…" he said in mock care like a master might say to a disobedient puppy. "You were about to do something naughty, weren't you?" This he stated more than questioned, maintaining a slightly patronizing tone. He paused between each sentence as if he could hear her part of the conversation. Someone watching the transaction might actually imagine hearing her replies. "What's that?"

What's happening to me?

"Wow! Check this out. Your neurons are jumping like crazy."

Who are you? How can you do this?

"Yes, Ma'am. Your brain is a regular old Sparky." At this he allowed a private chuckle.

I will kill you!

"Tut, tut, luv," his words curled around their lilt. "Do you have any idea how long it took me to first find you and then to bait this trap? Such hatred should diminish in your realization that all this attention is for little, ol' you." His eyes darted up and down, surveying the finer features of her face.

Salindria could feel the panic rising in her. It was the claustrophobic panic from her childhood when the nuns in the parish orphanage would restrain her. She had only meant to seek her parents. She knew if she could get outside, she could find them. It was that cold, hard, horizontal wooden box they called the *politeness bed*, where they taught unruly girls the high calling of their daily manners—taught them or drove them insane. Either way, they ridded themselves of the immediate problem at hand.

She had not felt this panic in decades, centuries, certainly not since she had been turned. The turning had liberated her. And now, in this three-story alley, black as pitch, staring into the eyes of a mad man, she could feel those oaken planks pressing in on her once again, the violent convulsions rising from deep inside.

"Well now…if I didn't know better, I would say that every fiber of your being wants me to let you speak." This, he said in a more feigned sentimentality, his words stroking her like a parent stroking her long tresses. "But can I trust you? If I allow you to speak, would you be our Little Miss Manners?"

Salindria started at the mention of the name. She wondered how this beast, this cold bastard, could possibly know the special phrase Sister Theresa saved for that moment where she teasingly let a smidgen of light and fresh air seep into the punishment device, not so unlike a coffin. They would allow you to *think* it was almost over, and then slam the portal shut leaving you to, "…meditate on your sins and the liberties you lose when you embrace them. Sin, after all, equals death!" As she thought this, she could almost swear she saw his lips move with the words as they were played out again in her mind. It was like watching a horribly twisted ventriloquist act.

Despite her mental anguish, she felt a relaxation in his control. She knew this was her moment. Something bizarre had her—something extraordinarily bad, and she surmised that this might be her only moment to strike. This freak could have no concept of her power, mental or physical. He would rue the day he had violated her in this most intrusive and garish way. And now, in his vain ignorance, he had made his first misstep. He had given her back just enough control. She would not tarry for another opening. Summoning all the repressed hatred from her childhood, all the physical strength from the current panic in her system, and all the supernatural power from her bottomless existence, she welled up to scream, kick, shout, and strike.

However, all that emitted from the mouth of the volcano, from the pressured magma and the welling explosive force, was a feeble and very defeated whimper. She found it took everything she had, and all that managed to escaped her was a simpering, "Why?" and she began to sob.

"Oh, sweetheart. Oh, baby. The only 'why' is the seed you are going to share with me. You see…you are *very* special." As he drew her closer, her somewhat restored breathing allowed her to smell the sweetness of his breath. It was less a pleasant odor, as it was the sick, sweetness that often accompanied slightly spoiled meat. As she sensed all, she felt her mind's defenses begin peeling away, one layer at a time.

"You see—a human seed is so often flat and uninteresting. One life can only store so little. But you—look at you. That seed you are about to willingly give me has been just aching to be shared for so very, very long." This, he now said in an intense whisper. The moment was becoming more and more intimate as she felt him truly penetrate her mind.

The ringing in her ears was barely audible at first but seemed to crescendo with each passing second. And as it increased, the tunnel of her vision narrowed, surrounded by a light grey haze. Eventually all that was left was the image of his face, and then finally, just his eyes. Remarkably his voice still could be heard clearly above all else.

The grip of his right hand now constricted, and she could feel the tip of his middle finger pulsing, just there at the top of her neck. Beyond any doubt, she could actually *feel* the filament that protruded from his fingertip, piercing the soft flesh, and finding the crease between skull and upper vertebra; that anterior opening that leads up to the cerebral cortex. Even in those areas where she had no nerve endings that could alert her to pain, she was still *aware* of its presence—right down to the synapses, the gaps between neurons that allowed him to jack into her being, controlling her like some crazed puppet master.

In that moment, before her non-existence began, and what she knew of life ended, she became aware of concepts flashing in sequence. Images, first were recalled, then viewed, and then discarded like so much chattel. Salindria watched in her mind's eye as he was rifling through her memories like a thief flipping through secret files in the dark. She marveled at the experience as she virtually lived each vivid memory and thought.

And then, the parade of images began to slow.

She realized he was *not* randomly channel surfing, but rather traveling in a most direct line towards some macabre destination. The photoplay became more intense and more intimate with each passing frame. And now, they were no longer events or memories, but more fully realized philosophies, complex and complete tangles. Oh, and they were terrorizing. To her horror, they were increasingly dreadful, cursed things that she would not ordinarily have fathomed.

With each passing step, her emotions increased. The realities in her mind became whole, intricate models, and they were so heinous that she could not believe they were springing up from her own psyche.

She became aware of something else…for the first time in centuries, she was becoming aroused in the flesh. That part of her, once thought of as extinct, was now blossoming. Energy was radiating in waves, and she found herself marveling at the intensity of his stare. His presence actually had weight to her. And in it, she found a new desire swelling—just like certain strategic tissues. There, she even felt the warmth that could not possibly be.

Here he stopped short, the cruelest of teases. She was finding that she actually *wanted* to share herself with him—the monster! As much as she could not understand it, she now wanted him to partake of her. She knew the next thing he touched, the next place he visited before her eyes, would be the before-unknown center of her being. But she did not want him to merely take it, like some bumbling teenage virgin boy. Instead, she found herself wanting to *give* it to him. He had exposed something in her that she did not know existed, and for this sweet favor, she now yearned to share it freely.

She heard his voice from down the far, distant tunnel. He spoke with comforting authority that gave her the security that only came with experience. He was no fumbling novice after all, this phantom. She was in the hands of a master. He smiled one last time to her and said in a purposed voice, "From the bud issues forth the bloom."

Salindria felt both release and explosive pain. The last thing that passed through her flickering mind was the image of slaughtered orphans. Innocent children were slung in the reckless abandon that could only be the result of savage and yet cunningly executed violence.

The one singular act of revenge she saved to one day commit against those she blamed for her blackest of pains was here, now implemented in her mind against the very ones she held most dear. She wondered at the paradox and the fact that she could have *ever* devised this most hideous of all acts in her mind.

And then, she was aware of nothing.

The lethal fiber retracted back into the tip of his finger as he carelessly dropped her now limp and truly lifeless corpse to the shimmering asphalt. Looking up as he breathed in, the just visible light blue sparks danced around his body as the charge of her life-force made orbits around him before crashing into the atmosphere of his body.

And then he shuddered.

The hidden desire that was her seed now perpetuated his immortal soul, becoming the drive for the machine that was this physical existence for him. He decided that taking her form would not be necessary for this Mission. So he allowed *that* moment to pass.

The mindless and savage slaughter of innocent orphans, once her darkest of denied temptations, would now be his new charter; his new lease on life. *Yes, this shall sustain me,* he thought. *And this one won't take years to accomplish. No, this Mission can be done swift-like. Then I can rest for a while. And this will fit so nicely into His plans.*

Danreck Porter rubbed the tip of his middle finger. The surface was now smooth to the touch, his horrible hair-like probe secreted away, secured back into its hiding place. He allowed for only a precious moment in the afterglow. There was absolutely no reason to take risks by dallying here. With one last glance at the vampire corpse that had once carried for centuries all the knowledge and experience that even now was augmenting him, he turned to make his way back out of the cold, dark alley, back into the cold, dark reality of the existence immortal.

Her seed was now his. It would make a fitting enough bridge over the chasm of non-existence until he next served the Cause.

2.
12.19.9.11.12.1875; 5 YAX, 7 EB — TOOTH

October 7, 2002, 4:30 p.m. EST

"I just don't understand why we couldn't have flown there, C.J."

"Ned, why don't you try just sitting back and relaxing?"

Casper James was the kind of graying, stern and stolid figure that would seem more at home on a Montana ranch, with two mature sons fixing split rail fences, than here, behind the wheel of a white Lexus 430. The car wistfully kicked up leaves as it hugged the curves on the Blue Ridge Parkway heading south, the sun cutting slants through the tree line as it set in the west.

After a little pause, and speaking as if a great idea had just popped into his head, Casper said in a slight and seldom exposed Texan accent, "Just watch nature." He remembered his mother saying the same thing to him during their long cross-country jaunts back in his youth and impatience. The irony brought a thin smile that curled the corner of his lip.

"Nature is fine," Ned Smarny said in the patronizingly submissive way that an upwardly-mobile junior speaks to his boss when he wants to transform a perceived admonishment into an agreement. Almost sounding like it was *his* idea from the start. "It's just that I wanted to spend my time at the Center learning as much as I can before my next assignment. They really have cut down on our time in between, you know."

Ned sat back, content that he had just successfully converted a point in the negative column to a one in the positive in his boss's mind.

The shafts of golden light seemed to strobe between the shadows cast on the windshield as the mountain road curved to the left and then opened to the right. The turn exposed a previously unseen dark mouth stretching

13

open to gobble them up. It was the entrance of yet another relatively short tunnel that cut through a portion of the mountain that did not allow for straight passage when they formed ages ago.

Ned noticed the beige rock cut in squares that lined the arch like jagged, grungy teeth, the vibrant green moss pushed up against them like decades of decay as they reflected the glow of the afternoon sun in fall. He congratulated himself in executing his director's most recent request—he had watched nature. *Far Exceeds* would be the rating on his next quarterly review.

Then all went black save for the few ancient looking incandescent lights that lined the ceiling of the tunnel like some unfinished dot-to-dot picture. As they soon emerged back into the late afternoon light, he allowed himself a sigh in the boredom that now so quickly followed the completion of his last assigned task from Casper.

"Look, Ned…you want to spend time at the Center, right?"

"Right."

"So you can learn more from the Codex, right?"

"C.J.…" Ned said in an imploring tone.

"Ned," Casper said cutting off his attempted objection with a constructive, "There is more to life than the Center, the Codex, and your next assignment. Did you ever stop to think that you may become better at your work if you slow down and learn more from the world around you?" With this, he gestured out over the steering wheel where his palms were draped, using the fingers of both hands to suggest the vista beyond their windshield.

"Sounds like some holistic mumbo-jumbo *they* would preach," Ned crossed.

"Keep your enemy closer," Casper retorted.

"Sun Tzu," Ned rebutted.

"And sometimes you have to stop and eat the pecan log," Casper concluded. The debate was over and Ned felt he had somehow lost without really understanding it at all.

"Who said that?" Ned asked.

"I did," Casper chuckled, "just now."

"I'm sorry, C.J. I don't follow you."

"You don't have to follow me. You just have to let me pull over up here at this store." Casper said this as he indicated with his index finger a small, white cinderblock building about 300 yards ahead. The sign, bounded by a fading border proclaiming the virtues of Sprite in the mass-produced colors and fonts of an age gone by, spelled out "Little Mountain Convenience Store."

Ned sighed again.

"Look, C.J. we are never going to make it there by nightfall if you keep stopping." His open frustration with his boss was almost spilling over the border into insubordination—though Casper never paid any attention to such things.

"Have you ever really *had* a pecan log, Ned? I mean, I know everyone that has traveled in the Southeast has *seen* one, at least on a sign. But have you ever actually tried one?"

"Oh my god, you're serious aren't you?"

"I never joke about pecan logs."

Ned found himself rubbing his temples, as he begrudged, "No, C.J. I have never had a pecan log before."

"Then it's settled," Casper said in an almost overly pleasant voice. He supposed he got that from his mother as well. He always was able to sound cheery even when he was saddled with a Gloomy-Gus, or in this case, an over-worked agent whose increasingly heightened sense of duty or drive was getting him noticed, yes, but also might land him in an early grave without some kindly intervention. That very intervention was Casper's mantle to bear—and the reason he had brought Ned on this trip.

Small rocks and limestone gravel popped and sputtered from the tires as they gave slightly while Casper steered the now decelerating carriage onto the low-budget parking service. He glided up next to the aluminum-framed glass doors, applying just enough brake to stop safely without any noticeable lurch.

Casper had a habit of seemingly escaping from a car and standing by an open door just as it stopped—an act that revealed his own impatience with certain transitional events in life, often leading to his own frustration, as passengers in the car almost seemed to move in slow motion to exit. He often felt compelled to toss in a, "Well, here we are," just to get the others moving from their seemingly frozen states.

Casper glanced inside the car and saw the thin, well-built, nicely dressed agent just sitting there. He stretched out the stiffness in his legs and lower back as he grunted, "Well, here we are."

As if on cue, Ned opened his door and stepped out. If Casper was going to make this pit stop, Ned thought he might as well not drag it out by inaction. There may even be a way to get some productivity out of it, if he could just think of a topic to discuss. He started searching his mind for some subject that would prove beneficial to him as well as make him appear top-shelf in his superior's mind. A cowbell with an attached jingle bell clanged against the glass as the door swung open. A man exited the store carrying a brown paper sack in the shape of a six-pack. He nodded as he passed Casper and Ned.

Ned asked, "How did we get here, C.J.?"

Casper thought of responding, *"By car, you dumb-ass,"* but caught himself while catching the door as it was swinging closed. Holding it wide he said,

"Charles Dawson died last week, Ned."

As Ned accepted the gestured, "*After you,*" from Casper, he attempted to feign surprised sympathy for the passing of someone he didn't really know. "I am sorry to hear that."

Ned attempted a modification in tone but it still came across as forced.

"Yup. It is always a shame to lose them, especially when we just really got him firmly on the reservation—if you'll pardon the expression."

Casper nodded at the old woman store clerk that Ned either missed or did not deem worthy of his attention. Casper allowed a respectful, "Ma'am," as he passed by.

Ned paused just inside to allow Casper to catch up with and ultimately pass him. He really had no idea what exactly it was they were looking for, but did not want Casper to know that.

"Actually, C.J., I am not really sure who that is." Ned fell back a little to follow Casper's lead. "I mean, I know we are encouraged to mingle and cross-train at the Center," and this next part he lowered his voice, "but the Order does stress that we won't know all the other Agents—only those in between at the same time. Parity."

Casper's expression remained unchanged as the patient, old warrior advanced down the second aisle. He said, "Charles was a good man. Any good person should be mourned. But in our business, that never happens." Then a look of recognition snapped on his face as he turned to his left and hunkered down to the next-to-the-bottom shelf. "Ah…here we are. Golden treasure."

His hand reached out to a row of stacked cellophane-wrapped confectionaries, six inches long and a little bit more than one inch in diameter. Snatching up two in one hand, he nimbly tossed one to Ned while maintaining the possessive grip of a five-year-old on the other. "Here you go, Sonny Jim," he said as he in one fluid motion, stood up, and turned to the cooler section that lined the back wall.

Ned glanced at the pecan log's surface through the clear plastic. A crumbled, jagged brown surface that looked to be rather unforgiving to the roof of one's mouth was waiting patiently underneath the red letters, *Patty's Pecan Log: The South's Finest!*

He looked up, and realizing he was falling behind, quickened his pace down the aisle illuminated by rows of exposed florescent lights. There was something about small independent stores, dirty tiled floors, and bright lights from an unnaturally low ceiling that always gave Ned the feeling of 2:00 a.m. no matter what time of day it really was. It didn't help that the only view to the outside world was provided by two, old cigarette ad-covered glass doors on the other side of the store from the coolers.

Casper fully intended to purchase a Sprite. *Those signs really pay off from time to time*, he thought to himself. But as he opened the cooler door, his gaze fell on something he had not seen in quite some time…an R.C. Cola. "Holy cow! Would you look at that?"

"What?" Ned asked as he caught up with his one-time mentor, and now close friend—maybe the only real friend he ever had. He was clueless how much he alienated his peers by exuding the very behavior he thought would draw people to him.

"An R.C.!"

"R.C.?"

Casper took two out and passed one to his junior saying, "Royal Crown." He stared with anticipation for the certain recognition he expected from Ned's face. He was disappointed as his associate blinked, and then blinked again. "You really have no idea what that is, do you?" This was more of a statement than a question. "Wow…you really need to get out more, Ned," he said as he moved past him and back up the aisle to the register.

Ned stood there for a moment looking at the two strange objects in his hands—presumably, a cola and a snack—wondering now what Casper was really trying to teach him, if anything. He had been around this elder statesman of their trade long enough to know that he did nothing without purpose. There were many times where the weight of a seemingly passing comment from Casper would not ring true until days later.

Ned began to walk briskly up the walkway now aware of ambient events that had previously gone unnoticed. The realization of the footfall echoes was now married with the visual recognition of items inventoried on shelves. He noticed bread, and snack cakes next to a section with batteries and mousetraps. All of the clatter-trap, meshed with the sound of *Slurpee* machines, tumbling in anticipation of the next indigent boy that would come through the glass doors with bare feet and three shiny quarters he had found under the steps of his cabin.

And there was the faint smell of day-old doughnuts barely noticeable over the fresh urinal cakes wafting from the now ajar door to a dark room off to the side.

Ned found himself wondering if this race was really worth saving. But to his defense, and credit, he had been under an enormous amount of stress lately with a series of assignments that seemed to only increase with intensity over the past year. And he was one of those actively engaged to do that very thing—save this race from *them*.

As he approached Casper who was now paying the lady at the counter for their items, he overheard their conversation. The old woman was just finishing her sentence, "…not like him. You notice people. I like a man that can make eye contact with a stranger."

"Well, thank you ma'am. I'm just happy to find these rare treats."

"Them ain't so rare. You can git 'em most everywhere from the top of the Ridge on south." She added a gesture, asking him without words if he needed a sack.

Likewise, he refused the bag with a nonverbal gesture, as he chuckled, "Well then I reckon we'll have to stop often as we travel south until I'm finally satisfied."

As she laughed in a polite reply, he said, "Thank you and have a great day."

There was an old-fashioned bottle opener just under the countertop. It was recessed, and contained the aging, bottle-top artifacts of so many thirsty customers. Casper extended his R.C. bottle, and swiftly jerked it down, which produced the escaping air sound that coincided with the metallic tinkle of the cap falling in amongst its newfound friends. Ned looked at his bottle and asked, "Casper, don't they just twist off?"

"Yes. If you have palms made of steel. Otherwise, you may want to save yourself the co-pay and use that," Casper replied with a broad smile.

Ned followed suit with the bottle opener and then trailed Casper through the still open door.

Daylight slapped their backs as the door slapped its metal frame. They heard the muffled sound of the jangling bells. The woman storeowner shouted out a pleasantly authentic, "Y'all come back, now!"

Walking towards the car, Ned spun around and looked back, halfway wondering if her words were a call for immediate action, or if they were simply a standing invitation. He realized it was the latter by observing Casper, who was now virtually bounding for the car with all the enthusiasm of a shoeless boy with a brand new *Slurpee*. And so he continued to the car, too.

They were both about to get in when Ned spoke to Casper over the roof. He felt this technique always provided some distance to ask a difficult question while allowing the other person time to formulate a reply while getting inside, starting the car and buckling up.

"Where does the money come from?"

To this Casper halted and that look of newfound joy left his face. It was replaced by a look that was both practiced and purposefully difficult to read. He did not get in the car, but rather held Ned up, giving his response, now—over the car.

"Ned, life is a giant dot-to-dot. There are the points that mean something. They either change our direction or reaffirm that we're traveling on the right path. And there are the lines that we draw between them. The lines are just as important as the dots. And what is more—the act of *drawing* the lines is where the real experience of life occurs."

"I don't follow you."

"You don't have to follow me, you have to just get in the car and join me in drawing the lines." He said this while raising both hands up over the roof, waving an R.C. cola in one and a pecan log in the other as if to say, "*I got mine!*"

Casper got in, started the car, and buckled-up while Ned was left to formulate his thoughts. He soon joined him sliding in, closing the door and then trying to figure out how to both hold his items and buckle-up without getting condensation from the cold drink on his dry-clean only slacks.

Somehow, he managed.

As they continued on their winding journey, Casper expertly opened the wrapper on one end, and peeling it back like a banana, revealed the end of pecan log for a quick chomp.

Ned opened his wrapper completely, discarding it in the door pocket. Now holding the naked pecan log in his left hand, he cautiously drew it up to his mouth to take a bite.

He halfway expected it to taste something like a crunchy version of a pecan pie, but was surprised that instead of the jolting crunch of a bar completely made of nuts, his teeth sank slowly through a gooey center. He now realized that his jaw would get more of a workout than it had bargained for, as his teeth became a set of factory sprockets bogging down on the tar of a saboteur. Pulling the bitten-into pecan log back from his face he looked at the previously-hidden white center, and asked around the chewy blockage jamming up his mouth, "What is the white stuff?"

This came out "Wha i-na whie-nuff?"

"Nougat."

"Whadth thnat?"

"I don't think anyone actually knows for sure."

Noticing that Casper was not speaking with a pronounced speech impediment, Ned now said, hoping for a helpful suggestion, "thith nuff id snicky."

"That's what the R.C. Cola is for."

Ned took a sip of the Royal Crown and noticed right away that it was far more acidic and sweet than any of the major brands he had tried before. The sticky nougat virtually dissolved in his mouth upon contact with the icy liquid—not completely disintegrated, but reduced enough to allow his teeth to do their better work. He marveled at the salty-sweet combination that would surely send a diabetic to the hospital.

Dangerous stuff, this.

After swallowing, his now-free tongue made the trip around the surfaces of his teeth checking for the almost certain damage he thought it would find there. It stumbled across a half masticated pecan wedged neatly between two molars and delighted in having the new hobby of first freeing it from its bondage and then reveling in the new, added flavor as he carefully finished chewing it up before sending it home riding on the rapids that were another swig of cooling cola.

Casper looked over at Ned. He looked like a man who was putting together his first canvas lawn chair without instructions. The fingers of his left hand were glistening with stickiness and the front of his crisp, ironed shirt was covered with the little boulders of a pecan landslide.

Ned wiped the remaining wetness from his lips with the back of his hand so as not to soil his cuff or sleeve. Casper found himself wondering, *What is Ned short for, anyway?...Nedward?...Nedson?* and with this private amusement, he allowed himself to exhale a small quiet laugh through his nose, at his colleague's expense.

Speaking now with a clear oral pathway Ned said, "I think you may be on to something here, C.J."

Casper chortled, "Yup. I think you're right," and then in a completely different tone and tempo he said, "Farmers."

Ned paused just before another excursion into the violent act of eating a pecan log and pulling it just a little bit away from his face he asked, "What?" And then took an even larger bite than before.

"Farmers, Ned. You asked where the money comes from. It started with the colonial farmers hundreds of years ago. Mostly tobacco."

Ned moved the freshly chomped portion to one side of his mouth and speaking as best as he could between chomps, "But that was about the same time the first of the Croatoan showed up. Are you trying to tell me that the backwoods farmers figured the whole thing out before modern science? What did they use, divining rods?"

"You shouldn't mock that which you do not understand," the sage admonished. But now in a more supportive tone continued, "Farmers are different than in your estimation, Ned. They are studied businessmen in both that time and this. But especially in those days, they were the wealthy and educated European aristocracy relocated here in the new world to build even more wealth and power. And you know very well *they* didn't just show up 400 years ago. They were just reintroduced to the race of men. It was a mistake we humans avoided for nearly six centuries, but this time it was epic. The farmers of North Carolina not only recognized the problem, they also knew how to test for *agents* and how to fight the spread."

Looking through the fire that was the color of the trees in fall, Ned gazed at the distant farmland that was stretching out to the east making a patchwork quilt of old-world hues that blanketed the flat plains disappearing on the far horizon. He was just finishing with another bite; his jaw now becoming sore from the battle, as he was beginning to rue so hastily opening his wrapper and discarding it. He would have liked the chance to save the rest of this treat for later. Having no other resort, he placed the remains of the pecan log on the wrapper in the door pocket and made a later-to-be-broken oath to himself that he would remember to discard it at the next gas station.

"How would they come by such knowledge?"

Casper had long since finished his snack and was casually taking sips from his R.C. in that enduring way that older gentlemen acquire. "It is widely thought that most of them were also Freemasons and keepers of odd knowledge. But 'how' is not nearly as interesting as 'why.' There were slaves in the South—even back then. But the learned and scholarly landowners knew what a liability it was to have a person's will stolen from them through slavery's loss of self. If you want real productivity, you have to find a way to make a person *want* to work for you. They must see some stake in the endeavor. Not only was there a problem of wills with slaves, there was also the language barrier and the learning curve."

Ned stated, "But they still needed man-power, right? I mean, carving out a new agrarian society out of a wilderness without modern equipment is no small undertaking."

"Right. So enter the indentured servant: usually European, usually spoke the language, having a desire to come to the New World, and seeing a chance to pursue their dream legally after say, ten years of backbreaking work. Putting off an entire segment of your life in order to realize the free pursuit of your dream was the very beginning of the entrepreneurial spirit in this country. Its very soul still vibrates here to this day.

"But rumors of a super-race of murdering beasts lurking in the forest, ready to snatch out of your head the very thing you most feared, and yet desired to accomplish in the darkest part of your soul? I think that would cause a little crimp in the sign-up lines, if you catch my meaning. I don't think tens of thousands of dreamers would continue to look to Carolina if they ever thought that the boogey-man, to end all boogey-men, was creeping around just behind the next tree.

"The tobacconists were afraid not only of losing their recruitment pool, but worse, that the shift of momentum would move to neighboring states like Virginia or Pennsylvania where competing fledgling industries like mining were taking root. The move of the power base would take not only workers, but also jobs further north and that would mean delays in building cities and much-needed infrastructure.

"So the Order was established and whole tracts of land were set aside to support our efforts. The Codex was birthed from any of the rare and ancient tomes they possessed that pertained to the Croatoan—including the test to identify agents and the chemicals necessary to keep them...viable."

Ned questioned, "But surely they no longer have a need for indentured servitude? Their industry is beyond mature today and their market secure. Why would they continue to fund something so expensive as this when there is nothing to be gained financially?"

Casper shot a glance at Ned with the raised right eyebrow of almost stunned worry, "Because, Ned...there are some things that are maybe even slightly more important than profit—say, like the continuation of humanity?"

Ned allowed the fizz of the last gulp to dissipate in his mouth as he pondered this thought. Finally, in a reverent low tone, "Jeez…and I thought the fact that smoking kills you was the best kept secret of the tobacco industry. Now I find out that the bastards have been secretly *saving* lives, and protecting mankind for four hundred years."

Casper allowed the silence that ensued. The slight roar of wind and road created the perfect white noise to foster a deeper thought in his pupil. He understood the valuable purpose of quiet time. There was no need to force the discussion to continue. Further, he had always felt it a weakness of the mind to desire constant aural activity. People that could embrace thoughtful silence were often more secure in who they were and did not require the affirmation of chit-chat to maintain self-worth.

The fiery opus in the western sky was beginning to give way to calmer shades of a pink and purple rondo as the two agents began their descent from the mountains. Soon they would be on the more mundane four lanes of straight and disinteresting interstate. Casper often wondered why people preferred them. He speculated that they were more interested in the dots than drawing the lines.

At length, Ned asked, "So why are we headed to Georgia? I have never heard of two agents going on an assignment together. And besides, the last time I remember you leaving the Center was when you and Ben recruited me."

Casper decided the time was appropriate. "The things I told you a little while ago, the answer to your question, all of that is a matter of secrecy to be maintained at the team-lead level or higher."

Casper chose at this point to stop talking again to see how Ned's deductive reasoning was coming. Ned looked up from his own shoes with the realization crossing his face like the darkness that was now crossing the land to their east at 1,038 miles per hour, bringing with it a spectacle of stars that would soon be their canopy.

"I'm not!"

"You are!"

"No way."

"Yes way."

"Oh man. Thank you, Casper! Thank you!"

"Don't thank me, take a good, hard look in the mirror sometime and thank the person there that is staring back at you. I think he had a bigger hand in this than I did."

"I don't know what to say."

Casper laughed heartily, "Well, that's certainly a first. If I had known it was going to make you speechless, I would have applied for your promotion years ago."

"Well, where do I begin?"

"Why don't you begin by reaching on the back seat there and grabbing that blue folder? It's the dossier for your first team member."

Ned wasted little time in unbuckling his seat belt, and half-climbing over the gap between their seats, he reached for the folder. Retrieving it from a stack of three folders, he returned to his seat and began flipping through the documents found inside.

Casper now spoke as the doting parent, "Buckle up. Safety first."

"Oh yeah," Ned allowed, as he took the annoying time to refasten his seat belt.

Ned clicked on the passenger-side map light and began going over the notes on the first member of his new team. He felt pride as he noted each positive attribute and the plans to coach each weakness. He was looking at the diamond in the rough and realized that he, the jeweler, would ultimately be judged by the polished product, as much as the gem would be itself. He had no idea he was learning about the person that would ultimately bring an end to both the Order and the Cause on December 21, 2012 at 8:04 p.m., precisely as the Mayans had foretold centuries before.

But that would not happen for another decade, and much ado until then.

"Andrea B. Ellijay," he spoke, almost in a whisper.

"How's that?" Casper asked, not quite hearing his words.

Now louder, Ned said, "Andrea B. Ellijay. What does the B. stand for?"

"Beulah," Casper replied.

"You have got to be kidding. What kind of name is Beulah?"

"The kind given by a father whose wife died in childbirth in order to honor the family matriarch. It was her maternal grandmother's name." Then leaning over and in a confidential tone he added, "It's an ancient Southern term. It means Beautiful Land and is sometimes used as a euphemism for Heaven."

"It says here he died shortly after her death. It says suicide." After a thoughtful pause, "I thought the Order didn't allow histories of mental illness."

"They don't. But it's not mental illness. It's simply a matter of not being able to carry on after your mate dies. Not being able to cope is more mental frailty than mental illness."

"But what kind of person could turn their back on an infant? I mean, she was raised as a ward of the state in an orphanage for crying out loud."

"There is more to the story than simply that. If that had been all, then she would surely have been adopted. Newborn infants with no family rarely make it completely through the system—they are too valuable a commodity. Someone would surely snatch them up. The adoption waiting list is so long."

Casper spoke as an authority on the case, as if he had been following it from afar for some time. Ned asked, "When did she flunk the test?"

Casper spoke directly in a correcting tone, "She tested *positive* three years ago when she took her physical after completing her law branch's Officer Training School."

"How did she come to your attention, C.J.?"

"The Order has been following candidates since the beginning. The practice has changed little in the hundreds of years that it's been applied. At my level, we are required to follow sometimes as many as fifty prospects at any given time. Usually they are all in the same region. It's not too difficult. We just felt the timing was right to bring Andrea into the fold. All of the elements are in place for her now."

"But what could have possibly soured the well of adoption if not for mental illness?" Ned inquired.

Casper replied by pointing at the pink sheet of paper two back in the stack and tapped its corner. Ned pulled the background report to the front of the pile and read. There he learned that she was from a small community in a county of relatively low population. Everyone knew everyone. Frank and Irene Ellijay were average enough people. Common job, common house, common church, they were unique only by the events surrounding Andrea's birth.

It appears that Irene had been gathering up blackberries from a thicket in the heat of another Georgia summer when a rabid animal, (fox or wolf was suspected), bit her. The odd thing is that it had leapt off the ground and struck at her neck. In those days, the only place to get the shots for rabies were in larger metropolitan areas and the disease was still feared and misunderstood in the more rural regions.

Rather than go into the city and trust the quack doctors, Irene retreated into the mountains. There she found the three sisters of legend that were revered to be a type of local witchdoctor trio. Her husband would have never consented to her going to them, for these women were shunned by the townsfolk and were veritable outcasts from society. Ned found himself thinking *Twice removed: the outcasts of the outcasts*, but kept this thought to himself fearing yet another rebuke from his counselor.

The women concocted a brew from local botanical specimen mixed with some unidentified elements. They told Irene that her body would not be able to *fight* the poison of the disease. Instead they instructed her that the only way to beat it was for her body to absorb it, *imbibe* the poison and use it as something it could ingest.

They assured her that their "medicine" was just such an elixir that would cause the natural process of rejection to reverse and become an assimilator. She was to welcome the disease and make it part of her.

Frank had reported to the authorities during an all too short and purposefully dismissive investigation that the old crones had convinced his wife. She had willingly taken the medicine at every full moon for the last three months of her pregnancy.

When Frank committed suicide some two months after unsuccessfully attempting to cope with his beloved's passing in childbirth, no one within a 100-mile radius would touch the child that was now permanently relegated to the whispers and gossip that would make fast her path as an orphan in modern times. She would be raised with other outcasts, always knowing that she was not actually damaged goods as they were, but rather the unfortunate byproduct of local superstition and ignorance.

"Wiccan," Ned allowed himself to postulate out loud.

"No, no," Casper chuckled. "No such history in that part of the country during *that* time. Sure there were mountain folk, but no pagans had moved down that far south since they were driven out by the great Christian Stump Revivals of the early 1900's. Only in modern years do you get the "X" generation playing with fire that they do not understand. And these ladies were ancient thirty years ago. There is certainly no evidence to support the theory that they were Wicca."

"So she is just one of us. She just tested positive. That's all?"

"Well, a bit more than that. Smart as a whip, good grades, best in class, extremely physical, a keen law officer..."

"And she is cautious," Ned concluded the list for Casper.

"A trait we all had before the conditioning, I might remind you."

"Then she'll be difficult to recruit?"

Casper looked at his young friend and comrade, reached up and turned the map light out, "No. I placed a call to the Governor." He leaned back in his seat and silently told himself that there would be no more lessons tonight. Ned had plenty to take in as it was. They would stop soon and sleep. Then tomorrow, they would approach Andrea.

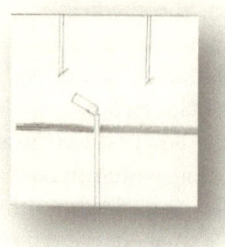

3.
12.19.9.11.13.5625; 6 YAX, 8 BEN — REED

October 8, 2002, 1:30 p.m. EST

Crossing the Avenue of the Americas from the West Village, Danreck Porter pulled the collar of his trench coat up to protect him from the autumnal wind as he made his way to Washington Square Park. He was hoping to catch Josie before she left for her next Mission. From the national news last week, he suspected that he had a few more weeks.

His last religious experience with Salindria had left him unusually buoyant. He had found some surprisingly interesting happenings as he explored each nook and cranny of her existence, assimilating the burgled knowledge into his own.

Of course, with every existence there are certain universal truths that cannot be denied. But mostly people are made up of the observations that are subjective, personal. Most people make the mistake of formulating opinions based solely on their own understanding gleaned from individual point-of-view experiences, and then build a framework of actions and decisions upon them. They mistakenly assign to these personal conclusions, the moniker of "Truth".

Humans that only have a life cognizant of seventy-two years or so, and only the ability to comprehend through the span of one singular existence, rarely require the forced, objective comparison of two conflicting opinions in one mind, both standing juxtaposed to a standard of real truth. So, they would never have to learn a technique for the resolution between the three. When confronted with input in direct conflict to their personal understanding of truth, most people either change their once fixed opinion based upon the new data, or they stubbornly hold on to their original

26

formulation and live in denial.

Real truth rarely enters into most people's largely subjective comprehension of the world.

The Croatoan term for such necessary resolution is Reconciliation. It is a proper noun to them describing a formal process that has been perfected over time. The more mature their latest harvest, the less Reconciliation is required, because observations and conclusions of the harvested tend to be closer to real truth. This distillation of truth, and its distillation from subjective opinion, makes for a race of philosophers and debaters—but not in the classic sense.

They do not spend hours arguing over novice philosophical debates like "whether the spoon exists or not," but rather, they string together Truth postulates to formulate conclusions delineated from theories.

Danreck was pleasantly surprised that as he explored the added neural pathways and bridged synapses acquired from Salindria, that he could spend less time Reconciling and more time just exploring.

She really had her shit together, he found himself thinking.

He approached an open-air gathering of tables and chairs, as the noon sun made a nuanced transition to afternoon, ushering in a slightly lowered temperature on the winds. The yellow glow that was unique to Washington Square Park at this time of year, made the coffee temperature against one's palms just right for sitting and talking until the coolness finally pricked one's attention and urged a natural conclusion to discourse, at which point people left to find the warmer climes of their apartments or town homes.

Here, he spied his mark. Josie was unmistakable, sitting and staring out over her cup at the park and life beyond. He sidled up behind her diminutive form and in a prankish way touched the back of her neck saying, "Zap!"

Without moving she coolly said, "Anyone else would have been dead in one second, Porter. But I am generous and will allow you to live this once."

Taking the seat opposite and feeling free to talk for there were few people here on this weekday afternoon, "How are you Josephine? I read the paper last week and know how your work has been. But how are *you*?"

"Comme çi, comme ça. Can't complain. And you?"

"Simply wonderful," he stretched the word *wonderful* to its breaking point. "Thanks for asking."

"Oh, you *are* on a Mission."

Danreck shot a comical and mocked sense of shock from his face as he said, "And just how would you know that?"

"I can smell it on you!" she said laughing in her slight way.

He had always loved this part of her charm the best. She had the ability to not quite give you enough of anything. She would reserve just enough of her attention or reaction to make you come back for more. He realized this was how she *believed* she maintained control, but it was studied and practiced—honed to a science. And he found it most pleasant.

Miming a sniff at the air, he proffered, "And you, my dear are *not* on a Mission."

"Oh, you can *smell* that?"

"No," he said laughingly, "I know your kill was just last week and you're still recovering." He allowed himself to appreciate the pleated schoolgirl tweed skirt and matching solid sweater. A look she could pull off with her eternally youthful twenty-one years of age.

It was her turn to react with a facial smirk as she brought her cup up for a sip from the steam-emitting surface. "Your prana is off the scale, Porter. I'm jealous."

Her hair was straight, jet-black, and shoulder-length. But it was her olive skin accented by her eyelids and lips that were more of a shade of brown than of pink that won his favor. He allowed himself a short wondering journey as he breathed a somewhat private sigh. Then more seriously he said, "And I need your help."

"Tell me about it," she said now in earnest.

"After your recovery, which should be complete when? In one more week?"

She nodded her affirmation.

"I need you to take a woman."

"Kinky," she said in a faux slyness that she knew would not be taken seriously.

"She needs to be high up in the media, preferably TV—network if possible."

"…and?" she said, raising an eyebrow.

"And she has to be a Girl Scout. We need one with a false sense of honor. You know…Truth, Justice, and the American Exposé."

"Ok, so you think she might be driven by the opposing desires to use her power to harm someone falsely?"

"One can hope," and then after a slight pause, Danreck added, "And at the very least, you might get a lesbian fling in the Poconos out of it."

Ignoring this last dig, she answered the bigger point to his request, "You have *got* to be kidding, Porter! I mean, any semblance of *truth and honor* have been driven out of a person in the media by Columbia *long* before any of these bleach-blonde bimbos make it as far as the regional desk."

"World class pessimism, that is," he said as he allowed himself to steal another glance at those eyelids and lips, "and one of your more enduring charms. But you must allow yourself to bend like a reed for the Cause, Josie."

"You must really think this is big, Danreck."

"Not big—the end of their silly little Order. I think we can force the agents out into the open once and for all with this one—especially after your stunt last week. And then they'll be compelled by their own law or guilt, or both, to disclose the cure to the human race."

"All I did was perpetuate the myth. Hacquee asked that we leave certain *signs*, so I left certain signs," she said dismissively.

He helped in the conclusion, "Especially after 9/11, it won't take long for Homeland Security to put it all together—I mean the part of it that is not in the control of the Order. I have noticed that even though they've been able to suppress most of their existence with crafty clauses in the Patriot Act, there are still small pieces of it getting out through blogs and whacko forums. Even the name "Order" has surfaced a few times in some circles—thanks largely now to your work."

"It's only a matter of time," she agreed.

"Less than eight years, if you ascribe to such Mayan things," he supported.

"I've been meaning to ask, where does that crazy date come from?"

He offered, "The only reason you're not aware of it is that you were one of the first of the Thirds. The Legacy-Bringing was not part of your siring. All of us Seconds have it drilled into our core from the sharing, from the very beginning."

Appearing somewhat hurt she said, "My having been *born* into the Cause makes me no less of a sireling than you."

He found himself in what he felt to be the wholly unnecessary business of comforting her—an irritatingly necessary act that he had predicted would be required. It was one of his chief objections when Hacquee introduced the theory of Thirds to them a century ago. "I didn't mean it in a bad way. You Thirds have certain benefits in the way you were created. Certain skills we Seconds have to spend decades perfecting are a mere act of instinct for the Thirds. But there are certain tradeoffs as well: like the knowledge we get automatically in the sharing. You have to learn over time. But, it's not like you have to worry about the constraints of time. Time has no meaning for us undead. In the near centuries, you will know as much as we do about our history."

"If we have centuries left," she pouted.

"Ah, now you bring us back to your first question. The date of which you speak is the end of the Mayan calendar. The Maya were one of only a handful of civilizations that hold to the idea that there are cycles to the Earth's existence and that December 21st, 2012 marks the end of the present cycle that began some 5,100 years ago.

"But it's more a matter for the paranoid prophets of doom to scribe on their Internet sandwich-boards as they march up and down in front of the cyber cafés crying, 'The end is coming! The end is coming!'" This last exclamation he acted out in an overly dramatic voice—his right hand over his heart.

They both laughed.

He continued, "The unnerving thing is that over the span of that time, the Mayan calendar has only been off by thirty seconds at the most. Not bad for a race which had a classic period only lasting 750 years or so in the middle. It is probably due to the fact that they discovered the number zero before any other culture…if you can ever discover such a thing."

"How do you know so much about them? An interest of one of your harvests?"

"No—more from the sharing. The Maya were the bridge from the Egyptians to your father's creation by the Paspahegh Indians in 1590.

"Some believe as I do that our true beginning was ushered in when the pharaoh, Menes, first started trade with the Minoans. It's difficult for even the skeptics of history to deny that the Mayan calendar started in 3001 B.C., the year that Menes unified Northern and Southern Egypt into its first dynasty. No small coincidence there.

"After all, 'Croatoan' is nothing more than a rough English transliteration for the Egyptian word from that first dynasty meaning, 'one born from Minoan and Egyptian lineage—combined.' Phonetically, it has a common cousin in almost all of the Southern-tracked cultures as Egypt spread through the colonization of its first dynasty.

"For example, we know that the Egyptians had a colony in South America. Even the humans have discovered this. It's where the Egyptians got their cocaine. The colony was more than likely the Atlantis of which Plato speaks. But when the first Egyptian dynasty fell, the colonists were cut off from their African motherland financially. The following flood from an inland lake probably drove them north and added to the Atlantis myth."

"They moved north to become the Maya," she speculated.

"The very same. Of course something mysterious brought a catastrophic end to the Mayan civilization, and over the following centuries, they trekked even further north, evolving more than likely into the Aztec, who also came to somewhat of a sudden end. That was most likely due to the Spanish, but there were some other unexplained elements at play as well."

"Seems like something ghastly always follows our lineage," she speculated.

Danreck continued, "From there we can trace the Pueblo and others as they branch east in North America and become possibly even the Cherokee. And all languages, from the Atlantians on up, have this phonetic concept for us—Croatoan.

"But they preserved more than just the word. All of them maintained the ritual which originated with the science of Pharaoh Menes. They passed down from the Atlantians in South America, through the Maya, all the way east to the Paspahegh Indians near the outer banks."

Josie seemed disinterested with this level of detail in exposition and brought the subject back to the area of her interests, "Tell me about when you met my father."

Danreck looked up. He stared at the contrails in the powder blue sky overhead. He always marveled at this shade of powder blue, which could only be enjoyed in an October sky. But now, he marveled at how this mighty nation trembled slightly at the white lines drawn in the sky over the tops of skyscrapers simply by the actions of nineteen insane men some thirteen months earlier. Those lines crisscrossing high overhead connected the dots of so many interests and so many lives. The irony of how those nineteen changed the face of the geopolitical landscape versus how nineteen not-so-unlike men and women did the same thing some 310 years ago in Salem captivated his attention now.

Still looking up, Danreck recited:

O Christian Martyr Who for Truth could die
When all about thee Owned the hideous lie!
The world, redeemed from superstition's sway,
Is breathing freer for thy sake today.

"I'm sorry. You lost me, Porter. I asked you about my father?" she reminded him.

"Yes, Josie. John Greenleaf Whittier wrote those words inspired by your father's actions in my hometown of Salem." With pained memory, his gaze slowly returned to her face as he continued, "Nothing about that tragedy was inevitable.

"Some think it was only an unfortunate combination of an ongoing frontier war, economic conditions, congregational strife, teenage boredom, and personal jealousies. But in truth, from someone who was there, it only needed a simple spark to ignite that tinderbox of fervent religious Puritanism. Left alone, none of it would have ever happened.

"You see, your father had been wrestling for 100 years to perfect the ability to sire. He was, and remains the one and only *First* Croatoan of our generation. But immortality brought loneliness as its boon companion for him—much like that of God. Hacquee's Cause demanded more troops in participation. But whenever he attempted to sire during the sharing, things went horribly wrong and it ended up in a cascade failure like it did so many times before in history—feeding in upon itself, like the serpent snake, Ouroboros, eating its own tail, until it destroyed dynasties, civilizations, or in your father's case, even the lost colony.

"It just so happened that he perfected this ability in 1692. It took a bit to get it under control, but Salem survived...and so did we." There was coolness about his voice that matched the air around them.

Feeling the moment getting a tad heavy for even his taste, he immediately brightened it with, "Oh, you should have seen your father, Hacquee, in those days. He came dragging into town with Tituba, a female Indian servant brought there for the employ of Sam Parris, the new minister. He was passing himself off as—are you ready for this—'Indian John'—the famous lover of Tituba in all the Salem stories."

She smiled.

"Now *that* is original," he editorialized.

Then in a little more serious tone, "He had met her in Barbados. She was an Arawak from South America and so she knew of his legend long before meeting him. Violent was their first attempt at creating a Third." He measured Josie's response at the mention of her long-dead half-sister.

Seeing no visual cues to stop, he went on, "She was mortal, but they both loved her dearly.

"I was actually his second Second, if you pardon the pun. The first one he sired was a strange, shadowy man. Hacquee never tells us his name, and even today he does not speak it. But they are inseparable." Danreck throttled the jealousy he felt rising in his throat and continued, "The amazing thing is that with the two Croatoan in the town, one siring others, and with all the vampires in the form of animals, both real and projected that were naturally drawn by the multiplying prana, the whole damn trial thing *still* would never have occurred if it weren't for that bumbling preacher, Parris!

"His daughter, Betty, couldn't help getting sick that winter—no more than Tituba couldn't help practicing her medicine to save her. I always thought it was a wonderful twist of irony—the vampire familiars roaming the town in the shape of dogs, and Tituba making witchcake of the girl and feeding it to the vamps."

He laughed out loud, "She was using their presence to identify the one who was afflicting the girl! That's using magic against magic for sure."

He allowed his own jovial laughter to die down and was pleased to see she had joined in a little, no matter how reserved. It was good to see Josie laugh. She asked, "What's witchcake?"

"It's a mixture of rye and Betty's urine, cooked and fed to a dog, in the belief that the dog would then reveal the identity of Betty's afflicter."

"So what happened?"

"Well, Hacquee found the culprit…and killed him. He harvested him."

"Who was it?" she asked, not wanting to invest the time to read to the end of the mystery. She desired the proverbial peek at the last page.

"It was Parris!" He exclaimed.

"You mean the preacher would want his own daughter *dead*?"

"Not dead, just sick. You see, Parris had secretly purchased Tituba to be a concubine originally on Barbados. Then later he got married to someone else. After his wife gave birth to Betty, Tituba developed an unnatural affection for her—almost as if she were her own. Meanwhile, his wife became jealous of her own daughter. Parris had said that if his wife didn't back off, then God would surely do something horrible to Betty."

"So he made her sick," she said in disgust.

"I really think the man was mad. He would've made a hell of a televangelist today," then soberly, "except that for all his faults, Parris actually did serve God in his own way."

"What?"

"He saw God in everything! He did have this knack of bringing out the best in you. He really made you feel *connected* to God."

"So when my father harvested him…"

"Hacquee took on Parris's form, which accounts for Indian John's mysterious disappearance in all the Salem legends and lore, and he acted out the seed. He saw Satan in everyone. He used his powers to bring out the worst in everyone."

"My God!"

"In his frenzy, he beat Tituba until she confessed to being the first witch. Her confession and accusation of the next three or four really got the ball rolling. It became a runaway freight train that couldn't be stopped until it burned itself out—nineteen hung and one squashed to death before Hacquee was able to bridle his blood lust.

"Parris was replaced as minister of Salem village by Thomas Green, who devoted his career to putting his torn congregation back together."

Josie allowed the tide of this new perspective to wash over her. "Sometimes I'm amazed at what we find in the hearts of men."

"Yeah. Thank God we didn't burn any of them. Those of the supposed "witches" that were sired Croatoan just waited to be taken down from the gallows and buried. Later they would crawl out and walk off. Some of them still carry the scar around their neck to this day."

"No way, Porter. You *are* pulling my leg."

"You know George Burroughs?"

"Of course."

"…and?" he asked, with one eyebrow raised.

After a few moments of reflection, enough to add just the right amount of comic timing to her conclusion, "Oh my god! The turtlenecks!"

"Well, *now* you know. He left for a couple of decades, but then came back to settle down in Brooksby Village posing as an Indian. Hacquee had shown him how the water there had a special property that helped in the tanning process of animal skins. George was able to teach the technique to the Whiteman demonstrating his worth to the community—turned Brooksby into the freakin' Leather City.

"No one ever questioned his name as being from the Salem trials. They all thought it was a coincidence of a chosen Christian name," he said laughing again. Then in a distant voice, almost like he was making a mental note to himself, Danreck added, "I'll need to include George. He would be perfect for the pickup I need."

A small squadron of pigeons landed on the ground a few tables over and started moving in their school-like manner, bobbing and weaving together in a way that reminds one of fish. The two Croatoan allowed the conversation to take a small breather as Josie collected her thoughts for another round of questions.

"You were around when my father was created, weren't you?"

"Oh, no…almost 100 years later to the day."

"But you are one of the few that knew him in his early days, right?"

"Well, you have to keep in mind that he spent a great deal of time on his own until he perfected the siring process."

She attempted to project the seriousness from her face that the question she was about to ask would require in order to elicit a solid answer. She had asked it many times before and to no avail. People would always put her off, not wishing to discuss it with one as *young* as she.

She knew that Croatoan are a proud people and do not like their sense of order disrupted. Everything used to have a clean pecking order until the Thirds showed up. So the Seconds took special care to not share details with them. It was their way of maintaining some power through ignorance.

But Danreck really didn't worry about such things. In the current scheme of things, he was as close to second-in-command as one could get. Well, at least as long as Hacquee's shadowy companion remained.

"You want me to tell you about your father's creation?"

She nodded emphatically.

"Ok, here goes."

He took a big breath to be overly dramatic, held it a second, clapped his hands together as he exhaled a laugh, "There really isn't much to tell."

"Porter!" she said in an imploring turn, now running her bottom lip out in a mock pout that matched her mock school-girl skirt and sweater ensemble perfectly.

Laughing even more, he said, "All right, all right. Do a man a favor. I'll tell you; just don't use 'the pout' anymore."

She affirmed with a nod and he continued, "It's unclear to me whether the Paspahegh were completely your father's tribe, or if the remnants of his tribe merged with them later. All I know is that they were an amazing society.

"They had this wonderfully unique religion that taught a precept that was beyond communal. You see, they were taught, like many tribes, that there was no such thing as ownership. That concept, in and of itself, is commonplace. But *why* they believed it was solely remarkable. They observed, like anyone with half a brain, that when a person dies they leave all their shit behind."

They both said in unison, "You can't take it with you."

"Boom," he added in a dry voice as punctuation that meant, *"There you go."*

He continued, "And so...if one developed an attachment to an item, say a bow, then when one died, he or she would miss that bow in the afterworld. Observing that no one had ever come back from the dead, keep in mind they missed the whole Jesus/Lazarus thing," at this she snickered a little, "to say, 'Hey! Where's my bow? I really could use that thing over there you know.'" Porter continued through her snicker, "They formulated the belief that people would terribly miss the things that they felt they owned here in life.

"So the idea of spending an eternity longing for something you could never possess again was considered the worst form of hell to them. Therefore, they developed a way of living where you would never have ownership of anything. Everything had a use or a purpose. You used it until that purpose was satisfied, and then you moved on. No one owned items, or people, or even land.

"However, they also understood the immediate need of the tribe's survival. If a threat was presented, they would develop an equal defense to protect them from it. So when they fought, it was only to defend the existence and continuation of their tribe—never for land, or territory, or possessions. They would rather let someone steal from them realizing that it would be the thief that would end up in hell, and not the victim.

"But when they were living near the outer banks of North Carolina and saw the White settlers setting up shop on the island across the sound, and more importantly their ability to use guns and build protective structures, they felt they needed an adequate defense. The wise old council of elders met and reflected on possible solutions for many months.

"The idea of retreating deeper into the countryside came up on many occasions, but they noted the Europeans' large vessels and felt that they could stalk across any terrain. Finally, a plan was hatched to simply scare the settlers away. All they would need was a warrior mightier than anything the Whites had ever seen before.

"One of the elders remembered a ritual that had been handed down from time out of mind. All they knew were the steps, the formula, the chant, and the name Croatoan.

"Some other Indians had used the word without understanding its source or its meaning. They simply knew it as something mighty...something beyond them. And they would ascribe it to regions sometimes out of defense, as if to say, 'Don't go there. It's a dangerous place.'"

But Hacquee's tribe maintained all the customs and rituals from their past. They were the freaking Harvard of Indians." She smiled as he made a goofy face with this.

"They chose the mightiest warrior—your father. Hacquee's name meant, *where the river branched*. It was akin to Indian words like Acqueednuck. His tribe believed in cycles of life like the Maya believed in cycles of the planet. There were three stages and a person could be renamed at each cycle. The mother gave a child a nickname as an infant. The father gave a child a name when they matured and excelled in some particular skill. And finally, the chief named an adult when they accomplished some great act as a warrior.

"One time when their tribe was threatened, Hacquee split an enemy war party in half and weakened them. He stood in the middle of a charging line and killed the center man dividing them into two groups. It was easier to surround them and finish the fight. Later, the chief said Hacquee stood like the rock at a point in the shore that splits a strong river in two. He was considered their greatest and bravest warrior.

"According to their understandings of the process, Hacquee was to be made 'like dead.' They had no concept of undead, so they thought he would probably just face death like a peyote-enhanced fast in the wilderness.

"I don't know too much about the ritual. His own memory provided to us in the sharing is either spartan or guarded in this. But what I do know is that they gathered herbs and ingredients for months. They also had to capture a live wild boar on a hunt. Simply keeping such a beast was dangerous with their limited technology and architecture. A baby was required, sired by Hacquee. The ritual would have to be performed the night of its birth. And finally a metal blade was needed.

"The tribes of that time mined copper as best they could from the earth. Warriors often wore a necklace with one bead of copper for each wife they had. They were allowed to marry as many women as they could support. So it was no problem really for them to hammer out a blade in the shape handed down to them for generations. But since copper is fairly pliable, the base of the wedge had to be thicker than one might expect. And, it could really only be used in the one ceremony. They attached a special handle that would allow two full-grown men to bare down on it.

"The day the baby was born, they began a late afternoon of celebration, calling forth the spirits of their dead. They danced and prayed in earnest until the stars filled the sky. Everyone felt a sort of electricity in the air. As the evening progressed, they started the chants the elders had taught them—chants not heard in ritual for some 840 years. The Egyptian syllables were meaningless to them, and felt awkward to their mouths at first. But as the frenzy increased, they became smooth and fluid.

As he continued, Danreck's focus became distant and his words increasingly rhythmic, almost as if he was describing events unfolding before him.

"The men of the tribe strapped Hacquee to a flat stone that was something like a table. They paid close attention to the binding around his right hand and wrist. A board was placed below his right middle finger, and his hand was secured palm-up. The board had been hollowed out to catch the blood in a trough. They then poured the medicine that had been cooking for hours down his throat. He drank it willingly in big gulps.

"They were ordered to dip the baby in the river no matter how cold it was and then tie him down on a flat board and safely secure him with thongs. The board was placed so that his and Hacquee's heads would be together. As this was happening, the spasms from the medicine started overtaking Hacquee's body in jerking convulsions.

"The umbilical cord was still fresh, for the birth had happened late in the day and it had been stored in a skin filled with the mother's blood as the elders had instructed. It was stretched out and placed between them.

"The drums and the chants were reaching a fevered pitch as the witchdoctor began his incantation. The two warriors chosen to bear the blade came forward and they carefully aligned the blade to the tip of his middle finger by the jumping light of the fire, interrupted by the passing shadows of the dancers.

"While this was happening, a warrior had been told to bring the wild boar forward. He held out a long, thin lock of hair from the boar's shoulder, wrapped it around a hewn stick and rolled it up, locking it in place. It took two others to hold the boar he now straddled. There, he awaited the signal from the witchdoctor.

"What followed happened in fast succession as orchestrated and practiced. The witchdoctor was virtually screaming the incantation as the din from the fire-chanters nearly drowned Hacquee's death-throe cries of agony from the medicine now coursing like lava through his veins. When he arched his back nearly stretching the ties to their breaking point against his chest, the witchdoctor held out his right hand.

"The hunter pulled the stick up ripping the lock of boar's hair free. He separated out a single hair with the bloody follicle still attached and handed it to the witchdoctor while the boar's cries joined the cacophony. Then, all at the same time: the hunter sliced the squealing boar's throat, catching the flow in a cup, the two warriors bore down on the blade in a rocking motion against the tip of Hacquee's middle finger, splitting skin and bone, and the witchdoctor passed the boar's hair horizontally all the way through layers of umbilical tissue like stitching a needle through cells and liquid. Stem cells from the umbilical tissue adhered to its follicle.

"As he carefully positioned the base of the hair in the breach of exposed bone, the hunter mixed the boars blood with that caught from Hacquee's finger, and the two warriors moved into position over the baby's throat with the blade. The witchdoctor first bound the split finger, pulling it tight. While the hunter held it that way, the witchdoctor made two crude stitches in the tip.

"They all waited in the climax of the chants for the death stroke. It was only a matter of seconds before Hacquee screamed a cry to the heavens and was momentarily loosed from the bonds of his body. As he screamed, the warriors made their expert cut in the infant's jugular while making the chittering, ye-ye-ye war-cry. The hunter gathered the blood from the child in the mix and then brought the completed elixir to the witchdoctor. Holding it up above his head so all would know the moment of the spirit passing was about to happen, the drums sounded a final *bang*! And all was silent—save the crackling of the fire, and the sighing of the breeze.

"He slowly brought the vessel down to Hacquee's lips and poured a mouthful to the brim. He forced the mouth shut and tilted the head to force the liquid down. As instructed in the ritual passed down through the ages, he balled his two hands up with interlaced fingers in a large fist and struck Hacquee on his chest with a mighty blow.

"Hacquee coughed and sputtered. And then he breathed in through the gurgled sounds in his throat. After swallowing once to clear his pathway, he breathed in a huge breath, and released a primal scream that echoed for an eternity down the fields. Then he fell silent. He was in what we now know as a coma, but what they called the sleep of the dead."

Blinking, Danreck regained eye contact with Josie. With all the composure of an ancient soul, he now continued with a tone of voice that was more here in this world, instead of one reporting a story 412 years old, "He's the only one of us that has ever seen his own seed, you know. During the forty-eight hours he was away on his sojourn, and while the baby's soul blended with his, becoming more than just alive or dead, he went to that place none of us can go. He peeled away the layers of his own psyche and stared at the one thing he suppressed the most—the one act he would deem most heinous by his own understanding of the universe at that time."

"What is it? What is his Mission?" she asked. Danreck noticed for the first time that she was asking him through tears. He had no idea how long she had been crying.

"Oh, honey...none of us know that. We can only guess from his actions."

"What happened next?" she asked with every intention of learning all that she could while the words were flowing.

But already Danreck had noticed that the chill was pricking at the nape of his neck and the base of his calves, reminding him that this conversation was finite, and that there was warmth by his penthouse fireplace calling his name. Without wanting to go into the whole story, but not wanting to rudely shortchange the twenty-one-year-old girl that was now crying at the newly learned truth, he tried to modify his tone as to elicit a change in tenor. He wanted to bring this to a close as quickly as sensibility would allow.

"Oh, it was a pretty wild tale—sort of tragic in a way, when you think of it. I mean to say, more in the classic sense of a Greek or Shakespearean tragedy, rather than something morose. The tribe sent him to the island to simply frighten the colonists away. They had no idea that Captain White had returned to England for supplies. They also had no idea what your father had become—though he knew…he knew.

"He found a colonist, a woman that believed in dreams. A frail woman that believed that dreams were the private, secret prayers we usher up to God. She believed in praying in a closet as the Good Book instructs. And she took it literally. In her mind, there was nothing more sacred or reverently private than the dreams of others. When your father took her, he had a hard time controlling the power of her seed.

"As she died, he felt the instinct to take on her form. He was amazed that he could look so much like her and seemed to know her language and mannerisms as well. I won't bore you with the details, but with nowhere to go and no ship with which to leave, one dream led to another to another.

"His purpose, what has become our Cause, devoured the whole island. It just so happens that the last person taken had a dark desire to destroy all that he found dear. So Hacquee returned to his tribe and destroyed what he could before the remnant escaped.

"They made their way north and settled in with the Powhatan. It's still unclear to me if the remnant made up all of the Paspahegh or was just a band of nomads that merged with them. That practice was common in those days. But they were so disturbed from what they experienced that they never really fit in anymore. It was their kidnapping of the English outside the fort at Jamestown that escalated a tense peace into all out confrontation. The English wiped out the Paspahegh as a symbolic gesture to the others. There were no eyewitnesses remaining that could ever tell history about us."

She had finished wiping her tears away as neatly as the English had wiped her ancestors from the land that they loved. But in a final twist of irony, she began to see the English not as the protagonists that had come spoiling for a fight, but as an intricate piece in a puzzle that was influenced at a global scale. If she was going to continue to blame the English, she had better pony up and blame the Egyptians, Atlantians, Maya, and her own tribe of origin in the mix.

Maybe it would be best just to destroy it all. The Cause sharpened to a new, focusing clarity in her mind now. Coolly she concluded, "When do you need me?"

He matched her tone, "Six more days for your recovery, then say…one week to get into position. How about 19 Yax, 8 Cimi?"

"The twenty-first? Why Porter, how romantic—a full moon!"

"You are a quick study, Jose."

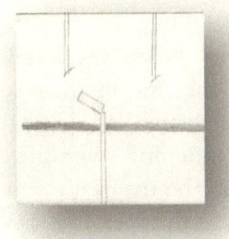

4.

12.19.9.11.13.₆₈₇₅; 6 YAX, 8 BEN — REED (CONTINUED)

October 8, 2002, 4:30 p.m. EST

Running always cleared her mind.

The numb spot had returned just over her left knee, but she hoped a good workout would make it go away again. Yes, running would help. As she ran past the reeds that marked the beginning of the town proper, she wondered if it really mattered that a wolf ran alongside her. She wondered if it really mattered that she was the only person that even saw it.

The constant soft slapping of her soles against the pavement drove away the pain from the constant hard slapping of her soul against reality. As she ran along the picturesque and winding streets of Blairsville, she avoided the fallen leaves on the wet pavement as best she could. They would become the banana peel in her comic fall in autumn if she was not mindful of them.

She thought about her real fall from grace and favor. Did she really make a mistake? She supposed the Georgia Bureau of Investigation would be happier with her if she had just given in and died. Funny how those that fight the monsters in the movies and win always end up looking like lunatics in the eyes of the crowds they save. *Honest, he was a werewolf before I shot him with a silver bullet!* or *That pile of ashes was really a murdering blob before I guided it into those power lines!* She felt the anger well up at the unfairness of it all.

Yes, running would help—slapping her soles instead of slapping her soul.

She supposed that those who lost to the monsters looked worse than lunatics…they looked dead. She guessed in the grand scheme of things, a live lunatic was better than a dead sane person.

As she rounded the corner of the fort at the center of town, some of the nice people of her newly adopted home waved. They were called J.C.'s, a local fraternity of do-gooders that more often than not spelled it out "JayCees," in order to avoid being confused with the Carpenter from Galilee. When they weren't meeting in their secret lodge, practicing their secret handshakes, and telling secret lies about the women they met at their last convention, they were watching over the fort here until the magical month of October ushered in the magical event for which the town waited the other eleven months out of the year.

The fort was a bonafide, honest-to-goodness fort. Made up to look like one of those you might see in an old rerun of F-Troop on TV Land. The J.C.'s had cleared a square city block, and had erected the fort years ago. They lined the inside walls with kiosks, and had a great courtyard for pole climbing, tug-of-war, limbo contests, and such. She had used one of the limbo sticks to end a battle with a bad-guy just two weeks earlier. The investigation still continued...as did her obligatory suspension-with-pay until it was completed.

She ran *slap, slap, slap*.

The people here now knew what had happened. There was no need to convince them, as there was no need to tell them to keep their secrets. The North Georgia Mountains held their secrets just fine without needing any schooling from a citified teacher. She had developed a kinship with them by simply looking in their knowing eyes. No one had to tell her they believed her. She simply knew it by the *feel* from them.

Still she did not know if these gents she now ran past were smiling and waving because they admired her bravery and skill, or that they were admiring her navy blue gym shorts with the white piping which pushed up the gathered waist of her grey sweatshirt, GBI printed in large, plain letters across the back. But then again, in the grand scheme of things, did it really matter? Being admired here was better than being considered a freak down in Gainesville.

The GBI encouraged the idea of their agents living in different communities within the jurisdiction they served, but no one in the eighth district lived this far north. Andrea thought she wouldn't have ever come this far north if it were not for the once legend-come-lately reports that streamed in at the last full moon. The Bureau always got crackpot calls on full moons, but not from up here, not in Union County. No, the mountains held their secrets well.

So when the calls did come in, she took them seriously—even though no one else did. Her comrades-in-arms didn't care about these people. They joked about the benefits of thinning out the gene pool here. Just thinking on it made that anger well up again.

Slap, slap, slap.

But now—she was renting a small white house with a nice front porch big enough for two rocking chairs. Nice neighbors living on either side brought her things. Things a "single woman would need until the right man came along—" blankets, preserves, and sorghum. It may not be the way of the rest of the world but it was theirs and Andrea found it very charming, looking past the modern call for political correctness in all things.

Sorghum was the black gold of these hills. It was the reason for the event; it was responsible for the fort that the J.C.'s built. The bumper crop in these parts for centuries had been sugar cane. Pure, north Georgia mountain sugar cane has some special properties. Among them is the sap. If you grind the cane up in a mill and drain off the sap, you can cook it until it becomes molten green lava pouring slowly down a cooling trough like the flow from a martian Mt. Vesuvius. At the end of the trough, the J.C.'s captured the rich ooze in ready jars and capped them. As it cools, the molasses turns the dark black that signals to the tongue a bittersweet paradise, which would later be poured over hot, buttered biscuits and then devoured.

Every year, the farmers bring the crops to town here in a parade dappled with high school marching bands, floats with the prettiest teens, and the J.C.'s riding their go-carts and mini-bikes making the crowds laugh and cheer. Then they all turn into the open gates and march into the fort where the cane is cooked while people shop the crafts that were carefully made during the other eleven months. Everyone would munch on the fresh fried pigskins and crunch on the cinnamon almonds while choosing between the hand-carved monkeys or the woven-back cane chairs.

Andrea had been able to witness the events every Saturday for the last two weeks, and looked forward to the next two weekends. The events lasted all month and she really wanted one of the quilts she had seen. These people were so kind and those sworn to uphold their safety had been so cruel.

Slap, slap.

She made her way around the block and then began the final climb back up the sloping hill to her new abode some three blocks up. This last stretch was tough, and she always had to really turn it on to keep her momentum to the very end. She was so intent in her workout that she was completely unaware of the five or six J.C.'s that had filed out into the street to watch her final push. But she needn't have worried…they were watching her back. If their wives had been present, they would have easily been able to explain that they were just making sure the new girl made it home safely.

As she approached the tall hedge that separated her house from the neighbors, Estelle caught her attention. The septuagenarian motioned from her own front porch. Andrea spied the frantic waves just before clearing the hedge and was not quite in eyesight of her own house yet. She made an arching curve to the right and into Estelle's pecan strewn yard and then up to her porch, "Yes, Estelle. What is it?" The words were nearly panted as she bent over to stretch out while she awaited the elderly woman's reply.

The old woman was at that age where she no longer looked like a pleasant grandmother. She had blossomed into a full-fledged busybody. She was the kind of woman that started every conversation with, "Now I'm not one to gossip, but I heard Maydelle say..." and finish most every one with, "Bless her/his heart." That was the punch line that allowed for even the most tainted words to cross one's lips.

Andrea was mostly able to control the laughter when this happened, but it usually at least forced a cute smile on her face—one that could almost be taken for happy interest in the conversation.

Estelle's house was also white, but the old-fashioned, wavy, thin siding was streaked blackish-grey from age. The railing and front door were white wrought iron with a thin coating of moss on all the northern surfaces. And the east-facing porch was made from a large slab or poured concrete set atop a cinder-block base one step up. There was just enough room for a glider-swing. Estelle must have just stood up, for the glider was still swaying gently to a stop as she was now perched on the step, hanging ten and leaning over in an obvious effort to keep the next comment completely confidential, "There are men at your house."

"What?" Andrea said, looking up now with a little more interest.

"Those men, two of them, they are at your house!" she said in an impatient whisper as she pointed towards the hedge that ran the length of the border separating their yards.

Andrea's head was clearing with each gasp of fresh air. There was plenty of that here, good and crisp. She looked from the lady with the distraught face over to the hedge and back. "Oh, probably someone from the office," she said in a dismissive tone.

"Well, they ain't from around here. That's for sure."

Andrea marveled a moment at this simple logic and the care that it revealed in her neighbor. She replied in as comforting a voice as possible (this time *using* the smile that had sprung up), "Ok, Estelle. I'll be extra careful. And I'll call you if there's any trouble."

"Do you want me to send Buford over to take care of them?" She was talking about her husband—a farmer for fifty years that had retired on subsidies and purchased this palace after selling the farm to a conglomerate whose legal department would be able to work the system for cash without growing a single crop, all while the land value increased over the years.

Some system, that is.

"No Estelle, it simply wouldn't be fair. There are only *two* of them."

Estelle looked at Andrea in a puzzled way for a moment and then getting the joke, she waved her hand in a dismissive gesture and said, "Oh you!"

Andrea walked briskly to the end of the hedge and then acted out a little spy scene all for Estelle's entertainment. As she was sneaking around the hedge, she was expecting to see a GBI car in the driveway. It was about time for I.A. to make their appearance. She really didn't look forward to their version of Twenty Questions. When she cleared the branches, she saw the car. *What have we here?* she thought. It was *not* GBI issued. The white Lexus 430 was extremely out of anyone's price range, but more importantly, way out of anyone's class range in District 8.

Now she was beginning to think that there might be something to Estelle's concern. She glanced back and saw the matriarchal figure still on point. Andrea raised a finger to indicate she wanted her to wait around a moment.

Then Andrea came around the hedge directly, with purpose. There were two men on the porch, long trench coats, talking to each other in quiet tones. The older one had a folder under his arm. They looked official enough, but not Mormons, not Jehovah Witnesses. As they turned towards the sound of her voice she said, "You gentlemen lost?"

"No ma'am," the older one said with a pleasant enough face. Andrea felt he was missing a Stetson to tip. "Andrea Ellijay?" he asked.

As she walked in somewhat slow steps diagonally across to her porch, she said in an exaggerated southern accent, "Well, now you fellers have me at a disadvantage."

"Please forgive the intrusion. I'm Agent Casper James and this is Agent Ned Smarny. We'd like a moment of your time, if we may."

Andrea raised one eyebrow. They seemed harmless enough. Even though they were packing, she detected no malice from them. She figured they might be from the state office. She gave both of them a quick look-over taking in all her training allowed. The younger one was projecting what she called the California look. She halfway expected him to mime a pistol shot while clicking his tongue, followed by saying some stupid one-liner pick-up. But he just stood there with GQ polish, very controlled and self-confident this one. She decided he needed a little deflating before she approached in her sweaty state.

"Smarmy?" she asked, intentionally mispronouncing it. She had heard it correctly the first time.

"Smarny," he flatly corrected. She detected a slight twitch at the corner of his mouth.

BINGO! First shot, she thought.

As she now picked up the pace, she kept her eyes on them as she shouted over the hedge, "It's ok, Estelle. They seem harmless. But if I don't call you in a little while, phone the troopers...or better yet, send Buford over here with his ugly stick."

"I assure you, ma'am, that will *not* be necessary," Casper said with a pleasant smile.

As she reached the step and stopped to re-tie her shoe, she said, "State your business, Mr. James."

"We'd like to have a word with you…about your future."

"Oh, God, you are Mormons."

Casper let out a warm laugh. This definitely was not a GBI man. He was *way* too sincere. Ned, she was not so sure about. But Casper did not fit the profile at all.

She stood there and noticed neither one said anything else. They just smiled at her. Casper gave a slight nod of recognition. He was studying her.

She came to the conclusion that these two were the genuine article. They were trained extremely well. They weren't giving anything away and they were waiting to see what she was going to say next. Interrogators are taught that silence is your partner. People abhor silence. They will often speak to start a conversation back up, and that is when they say too much. The direction they take on a blank slate indicates which direction you wanted to follow.

Feeling a bit put off by what she perceived to be time-wasting games, she pushed past them and opened the screen door and then the large, solid front door. She stepped onto the hardwood floor allowing the screen door to slam behind her, the spring making the all-to-familiar creak as it pulled to.

Leaving the front door open, she crossed to the large terrycloth towel waiting for her on the floral print couch; she picked it up, and dried her legs off. The numb sensation was still there over her left knee. She had first noticed it about the time she had her physical after completing her Officer Training School three years prior, but she did not have time to worry about such things just now. She wrapped the towel around her neck and started drying off her face and the edge of her hair. They stayed politely on the front porch. After a few awkward moments, she said, "Well just don't stand out there like a couple of statues. Come on in."

They wiped their feet on the mat, opened the door, and stepped neatly inside, but only two or three steps before stopping. "Look, I filed my report. The guy is dead. The state is a better place for it. The end," she said as she retrieved her sweat pants from the back of the couch and slid them on. "There really isn't anything else to tell."

"We're not here for an investigation," Ned said.

"Ok, you boys aren't Churchers, and you're not GBI, so I suggest you give with the details before I holler out that door and fetch Buford over here."

Casper stoically said, "I'm afraid that any more beatings from an ugly stick and my partner here would just be no good at all." He was able to say this without cracking a smile, but Ned did shoot him a scowling glance. "But I will come right to the point." Casper shifted weight and relaxed his stance. And now he smiled, the warmth was tangible, "We are here to offer you a job."

It was her turn to be stoic. She tried to put it all together in her head: Agents, unmarked expensive car, nicely dressed, she was on suspension, they did not call first, they didn't say much, they were offering a job, and this one here seemed genuine enough. She thought of rational things to say or ask. Finally, she decided on continuing the conversation with, "You can't afford me."

Ned took a step forward and said, "Starting pay is $125,000 per year plus expenses, full medical and dental, matching 401K up to the legal 7%, continuing education, and a progressive vacation and holiday plan."

She had meant it as a joke. But they were offering more than double her current pay. Andrea began to speak, stopped, thought some more, then continued to speak in an aggressive tone, "Look, you haven't even told me who you work for, what the job is. You walk right up to my house, seem polite enough, come in here and make some crazy-ass offer without the slightest interview to a woman you don't even know."

Casper had glanced down at the hardwood floor during this. Andrea thought he looked to be taking his lumps but he was actually admiring the craftsmanship in the interior of this house. You just couldn't find the patience in today's contractors to build a floor like this anymore. When she finished her brief tirade, Casper looked up in a slow and controlled motion, made eye contact and said, "We know you killed a vampire two weeks ago and that no one believes you."

"Ok, who the hell are you?"

"We are here to offer you a job from people that believe *in you*."

Andrea noticed the stress on the words "in you" and it threw her off a bit. She abandoned the next question she had prepared, and the plans to throw them out. Instead, she chose to think on his choice of words. Before she could formulate a new stratagem, Casper continued in a calming voice, "May we sit down? We'll be happy to explain it all."

It was then that Andrea realized her forgotten manners. She invited them to take off their coats and stay a while, asked if they would like something to drink which they politely declined, got a bottle of water enhanced with electrolytes and climbed into her oversized, overstuffed chair opposite the couch upon which they were now sitting. She left the front door open. The grey day outside was cool, but not enough to warrant cutting off her lifeline to Buford.

The whole time she was thinking about how to respond. She wanted to dismiss them as quacks, but they had known about *him*. More than just knowing, they appeared to believe it to be true. She could always sense when someone was putting her on, and these two were true enough.

More importantly, she really wanted someone, *anyone* to believe her. She sat there quiet for a moment, her feet tucked up under her in the position she used when she wished to look outside and ponder things. She sipped on her water—the two of them sitting on the couch, hands in their laps, politely giving her the time she needed.

Putting it all together, she mistakenly concluded, "So you boys are Feds then?"

Casper replied, "Not so much Feds as a special investigative agency under the Interior. Our jurisdiction is decided in a case-by-case manner with special consideration from the courts. In our order of things, we can sometimes act internationally. Ned's group concentrates on the East Coast and mostly the northern part of that."

"So you are a specific crimes task squad?"

"Not so much specific crimes as specific *interests*. We are working to disrupt, and one day hope to end, a long-standing group of, well, terrorists. And we have made great strides in the past year or so."

"Terrorists. In America. So you're after Islamic fundamentalist cells?"

Ned answered this one, "Not exactly."

Andrea allowed herself to pause. She had made two incorrect speculations so far. Whether they admitted it or not, this *was* an interview. And whether she admitted it or not, she *was* interested, if only somewhat. She knew that incorrect speculation in an interview could be seen as a weakness.

So she fell back on her training. She remembered an exercise their GBI captain, Bob Guthry, had taught them. He would pose a mystery and have the class ask only questions that could be answered with a yes or a no. He called these "closed-ended questions." It would take the class sometimes thirty or forty questions to solve the *who-dun-it*. Then he would pose another mystery and allow them to ask open-ended questions. All it would take was the first officer with half a brainstem to rub two brain cells together and ask, "Who-dun-it and how?" Bob would then meticulously explain the whole scenario in detail.

The point of the exercise was to drill into the officers not only to ask open-ended questions, but also to see a red flag when an answer came out as an affirmation or a denial. It signals that you just asked a closed-ended question.

She had just asked two of them—bad form.

She thought her next question through as well as she could, and then asked, "What is the goal of your organization?"

Casper allowed a semi-controlled smile to wander across his face, but he yielded the floor to Ned. He knew Ned was spreading his wings for the first time and saw this trip as much a test for Ned as he saw it for Andrea. Ned answered, "The group we are after has been around for a long time. They have spread across the world with the movement of the population. For their own survival, they remain extremely covert. They have only made one slipup in centuries that alerted the world to their existence in a meaningful way."

It was now Ned's turn to ask a question, "What do you know about the word *Croatoan*?"

The word at first seemed only just *familiar* to Andrea. She knew she had heard it. But then the hallways of her mind made a connection to a cluster of memories she had not accessed in some time. The revisit to this wing of her thoughts brought pleasure at some indefinable level. She spoke as she remembered, "Me and a few girls from college took a Spring Break trip to Cape Hatteras. We had a lot of fun exploring the area. It seemed somewhat mystical to me."

"How so?" Casper said gently urging this exploration of rediscovery.

"Just the juxtaposition of all these unusual historical events. One day I am standing on Killdevil Hill above Kitty Hawk imagining I'm there on the day the Wright Brothers flew, and the next I'm exploring lighthouses and forts from a time when new settlers had to protect themselves from other new settlers.

"I remember we went to a musical about a colony that Sir Walter Raleigh started on an island. He had gone back to England and found another captain to continue the work, a Captain White, I think." Casper nodded as she continued, "He brought two loads of colonists back over and went back for supplies. He wanted to stay, but felt he had to go back for one more load. When he returned the whole colony was gone, vanished.

"The historians spoke of it in the same spooky reverence as so many other mysteries—almost like they found half-eaten dinners left and chores undone. They try to spook you with phrases like 'no one really knows for sure what happened to them.' I almost expected one of them to say," and here she stuck out her hands, wiggled her fingers, and made a scary ghost "Oooo," with her voice.

She finished the history portion of her interview with, "All that remained was a single word carved on a tree," and as she was about to say the word, she suddenly recalled the original question and its relevance to this conversation. "So the Croatoan are your terrorists?"

Ned continued, "I don't think they see themselves as terrorists. I believe they see themselves as elitists that have a common goal. They just don't realize that a troublesome side-effect of that goal would be the destruction of everything we know."

"That's some side-effect," Andrea said in an effort to sound like she was joking. But she really didn't feel much like joking. She still had not figured out if these two were recent escapees from the P-Wing down in Hall County, or if they were legit. "Look. I don't know if I want to become Scully and join the X-Files. I have enough problems here at home with the simple stuff."

Casper said patiently, "Please allow us a little more time, Andrea. No one is asking you for a decision now. And we really have more to say before we get to that point in the conversation. If we are not keeping you from something more important, may we please continue?"

There was something comforting in hearing this man speak her name. It was almost like a favorite uncle picking you up when you had 'skint' your knee. Just the sound of the voice could take more sting out than any medicine. And she found herself wondering what she had to do that was more important. All she had to look forward to tonight was a hot bath, some frozen dinner, and a tepid show or two on TV.

"All right," she said slapping the arms of her chair in a gesture that showed definition of purpose to stay put for a while, "Please continue. I will listen."

"This next bit may require you to stretch your understanding of the world a little," Ned said and paused in a way that indicated he expected a confirmation before he continued.

The first thought that flickered in her mind was the feeling of the limbo pole rough in her hands. It was heavy and solid. And then the image came to her of *him* in the rain, in the middle of the night, out in the courtyard of the fort. She saw the twisted image of his face in the flashes of lightening as he approached her with the strength to rip her limbs out. She had seen him do it just a few moments earlier to a local deputy.

She, by instinct more than knowledge, raised the pole to a chest-high level like a javelin and as he approached in his rage, she thrust the point into his chest at the center. The memory of it was still tactile. Her fingers remembered how the pole resisted a little at first, like it was going through a layer of thick papier-mâché. And then it gave for about a foot and hit more resistance like before. She drove it through and felt his weight collapse backwards like some sick, perverted fulcrum driving the point down into the ground.

She could feel his feet kicking in frail flurries at her shins with the lightweight impact of the dying. She could hear his screaming just barely audible over the cracks of thunder that surrounded her. His deteriorating hands clasped the pole in a vain effort to remove it from his shuddering body. One of them brushed against the front edge of her left hand in a leprous, glancing blow. The feel of the now rotting flesh brought a rise in her gullet. She had to suppress the urge to vomit.

As the screams died off, the image in her mind was now replaced with the sight of a very real Ned sitting across from her awaiting her affirmation,

"Oh, believe me Agent Smarny, I think I can stretch it a bit."

"Good."

"Before we continue," Casper interrupted, "May I use your facilities?"

"Oh sure, just down that little hall at the end." Andrea gestured to the hall behind her.

"Thank you my lady, you are most kind," Casper said with a little grunt as he got up and crossed the room to the hall.

Ned cleared his throat and sat up a little towards the front of the couch. "The Croatoan touches the victim at the base of the skull. Then a sharp, nerve tipped proboscis is protruded from the tip of the middle finger."

Andrea took this in and, true to her word, she allowed her understanding to stretch a little. But she was extremely skeptical. "Proboscis?"

"It's like the hollow tube a butterfly extends to collect nectar and then retracts. To be honest, we have other names for it, but they are somewhat unique to our work and scientific. They don't really help much in explaining it. You can use the word filament if you like. It taps a specific nerve at the base of the cerebral cortex that allows the Croatoan access to the locked box."

"The locked box," she echoed.

"Yes. It's the center of one's psyche that drives our ability to think in abstract ways. Therein, the Croatoan finds the one secret that all of us carry at our core. We all have some dark, unspeakable desire that cannot be acted upon. This desire is based on the controls of one's psyche, which are largely shaped by the societal environment of that person."

"I'm not sure I'm following you."

"It's ok. This *is* strange. I find it strange telling it and I work in this field every day. Let me try it this way—everyone in every society has some concept of right and wrong. They teach this to infants with the first concepts of language. As a person's mind develops, it takes these core values and builds from them a belief system. It is a framework that allows us simply to function. Without it, we would be vegetables.

"At the center of this core is some thought, some *sin*, if you will, that is thought to be the most heinous or reprehensible by that individual. We are drawn to it like a young child is drawn to touch the eye of a stove. We have no real understanding of the consequences, so our conscious mind protects us from it; buries it way down deep in our psyche. It's like the grain of sand in an oyster; the muscle moves it out of the way and coats it with a smooth, hard shell to protect the oyster from its irritation.

"Just like that, our mind takes this one horrible temptation and buries it, protecting the host from ever acting upon it. But its presence, and the conflict to keep it hidden, is what sparks imagination, random thinking, and ultimately our ability to abstract thought."

"I think I understand." Andrea hated to admit it, but she was finding the conversation interesting, stimulating. More importantly, this part of it made some sense to her.

Ned continued, "So…this locked box, or *seed* if you will, changes from person to person."

"How so?"

"Well, if one society is taught to embrace a particular *sin* and another society shuns it, the sin is most apt to be captured to a seed by a person of the latter."

"Can the seed change?"

"Yes, but not that often. As a person matures, they start to understand that there are things that may be considered worse than the core of their limited understanding in their immaturity. So naturally their seed would mature and adapt to their larger understanding of the world around them."

"The Croatoan first expose this seed and then remove it from the host."

"But that would do some damage, wouldn't it?"

"It kills the victim and gives extended life to the Croatoan. The even worse part is that the Croatoan is then driven to act upon that seed. It is driven to carry out and execute the secret desire of the victim without remorse, without regret."

At this, they heard the flush from down the hall. Andrea half-shouted over her shoulder, "Jiggle the handle, Casper. Old plumbing." She heard the handle jiggle and then the tap run. She logged an entry in her mind that he washes his hands. That's a trait you don't witness often in these parts…demonstrates manners.

The old door creaked and she heard footfalls as his approaching voice at first boomed and then lowered as he drew near, "The Croatoan are real, Andrea. They are nasty and they are dangerous. In short, we need your help. We will give you all the training and resources to be successful. What do you say?"

What would she say? This was all so sudden and new. Her mind was following, but the universe had seemingly changed without regard for her inability to absorb. And now, this relative stranger was asking a trial close of her without giving her a moment to gain her bearings.

As Casper crossed to the couch, the phone rang. Andrea got up in mid-thought and walked back to the open counter that separated the ancient kitchen from the little eating area. If it were not for the bedroom wing with the bathroom at the end, this old house would be what they called a shotgun house in these parts—just an open room straight back with rooms separated only by changes in flooring.

"Hello?" she answered. Then Casper and Ned heard without eavesdropping, "Oh hi, Bob! How are you?" She was twisting the loops of the long cord around her finger as she listened, "That sounds serious, Bob.

What's wrong?" She glanced at them and then down at the kitchen floor. She was trying to find privacy in lack of eye contact. "Bob, this just isn't fair. I'm a good cop. What are they asking?"

She turned her back on her company and stared out the back door twisting the long phone cord around her body in a macro example of how she had been twisting the coils around her finger. "So they aren't even asking?" Then after a short pause, "I see...ok...well...I guess there isn't much more to be said." She reached for box of tissues on the counter, pulled one out, and balled it up in a clenched, angry fist. "I will look for your package, Bob. Yes. I'll fill out the forms. Do I at least get a reference?" She turned in such a manner as to untwist herself from the cord as she untwisted her life from the GBI. "Yes, Bob. Thank you for trying. I hope to see you again sometime." She nodded at the last, "Yes Bob. Me, too. Soon. Bye."

They all stayed that way for a while, all of them exactly where they were, all of them motionless, all of them pretending not to know what the rest of them knew—what they were all thinking. Then Andrea broke the silence, and through a few tears she said, "Is your offer still open, Casper?"

In the most genuine and sincere voice she had ever heard in her life, Andrea heard Casper say the string of words that would usher in the last stage of this life for her, "You know it is. You can always count on me, Andrea. I will never back down in covering your six."

In some degree of regained composure, she smiled and wiped her face in a discrete gesture. She thought about drawing this out. She did not know these two from Adam. But the offer seemed real enough, and this would be too elaborate to be a cruel hoax. Besides, her life-plans were somewhat flexible at the moment. If this did not turn out well, she could always bail and be no worse off than she was right now. After a moment of consideration while they patiently waited for her next she said, "Thank you. When do I start?"

"When can you be ready for a move?"

She laughed in the spasmodic way people do at the end of their tears when someone says something ironic, "I never really unpacked here. All of my things are in a few suitcases and boxes in the bedroom. All of this," she gestured around the room, "comes with the rent."

"That explains the taste in interior," Casper said smiling.

"Or lack thereof," she countered. And they both laughed at this. Ned even gave a polite smile.

Casper crossed to her with the yellow folder he picked up from the coffee table. "Here Andrea," and as he handed it to her, he continued, "You will find everything in there: plane ticket, itinerary, the phone number for movers with an account number if you need them, your address at the Center, all the necessaries like W-4's. Just fill those out during your flight if you like. And finally, contact information for me and Ned if you have any more concerns.

"Ned will be your boss. You are joining his team. Ned reports to me. Any questions should go to him first. But I am always available." Then he reached out a hand and shaking hers, said, "Welcome to the team!"

After she said her thanks, Casper turned around and said to Ned, "I think we should be going now, Mr. Smarny," he gestured at the door.

Ned looked at Andrea and said in a business-polite way, "Welcome to my team. I look forward to working with you soon. Let's hook up at the Center on Friday, say after lunch. Take the time between now and then to travel and get situated. If you have any questions, don't hesitate to call. It's a satellite phone so you'll have no trouble reaching me. We will issue you one like it at the Center."

Ned nodded as he turned to leave. She said her goodbyes in that southern way that often goes on too long. People in the south can easily tack on a good hour to the end of a conversation by simply saying bye. The two agents got in their car and drove away.

Andrea turned around to face a room that didn't belong to her, looking at furniture that didn't belong to her, and contemplating a life that didn't belong to her—the state had seen to that. From the very beginning of it, this state had made sure that nothing belonged to her. She had rented her life from the great state of Georgia. But now, that was going to change. Now she was going to get the hell out of here. Now, for the first time, she was going to *own* her life.

At least, that is what she thought.

As Casper and Ned made their way out of town and turned onto a highway that was large enough to be an interstate, but still allowed cross traffic, Ned said, "She accepted a lot faster than I thought she would."

"I told you I placed a call to the Governor."

Looking out the window while contemplating Casper's words, Ned noticed an unexpected turn. "You just turned south?"

"Yes I did."

"But aren't we going back to the Center?"

"Yes we are."

"But south?"

"It's the fastest way to the Atlanta airport. Grab that other folder in the back seat, would ya?"

Ned once again reached back to the rear seat and grabbed a green folder, the only remaining one. Turning around, this time he fastened his seatbelt before opening the folder. He found a plane ticket. It was a round trip from the Center to Atlanta and back again in his name. "You had me a ticket the whole time?"

"Yep."

"Why a round tripper?"

"Wasn't sure I would be able to tolerate you the whole way." And with this Casper chuckled to signal it was a joke. "When you get to the Atlanta airport, make sure to tell the ticket agent that you decided to rent a car to drive down. Tell them you were dropping in on accounts along the way. The TSA are being real assholes about security these days. With any luck, there may even be a cavity search."

"Hey!"

Laughing in a much heartier way now, Casper continued, "And while you're flying the friendly skies, I'll be munching on Appalachian cuisine and enjoying the quiet ride and terrific view."

Ned gave this some thought. He found himself beginning to question the fast-paced life of modern travelers that he had so easily embraced over the years. The thought of spending four hours being harassed in an airport, so he could fly four hours shoehorned in with smelly strangers, sharing germs, only to spend four more hours being harassed in yet another airport did seem to be fading in the popularity polls of his mind. Maybe Casper was right after all. But Casper's team was already established and could pretty much do without their leader for little while. Ned had much work to do back at the Center to get prepared. He found himself bracing for what he now saw as the necessary evil of a flight back. And he found himself to be just a bit jealous of Casper.

5.
12.19.9.11.15.8125; 8 YAX, 10 MEN — EAGLE

October 10, 2002, 7:30 p.m. EST

Actually, it had been more difficult for Andrea to say goodbye to her neighbors than she thought it would. She had only lived there two weeks or so, and was now leaving them. But she guessed there was something about acceptance or unconditional love that makes you closer to people than you might normally become.

The farewell on Estelle's doorstep had been particularly painful. Buford had given her a bear hug worthy of the nearby Blood Creek mountain bears. Estelle had given her a box filled with preserves for which Andrea was extremely thankful. She had thought that there was nothing quite as good as pear preserves on a hot buttered biscuit. Just saying goodbye to those two had cost her about forty-five minutes on the taxi meter while it sat idling patiently at the road, waiting to whisk her off to the local rental car agency per the plans.

Long Southern goodbyes—taxi drivers are used to them.

The moving van had arrived as ordered, and professionally packed her things in a timely manner. All of it was a little alarming in its efficiency. She didn't have that much, but they were sharing the space in the truck with another move, so she didn't feel too guilty for all the fuss over a few boxes. In the end, she had even decided to ship most of her suitcases as well. She figured she might as well take as little as possible for the Atlanta airport security to complain about.

They had even provided a car rental with all the plans in the itinerary. Everything she needed was there and nothing was left undone. All she had to do was open the folder, spot the next item, and do it. By the end of

Wednesday, the paper was filled with red check marks save for a few items at the bottom to be done on Thursday.

She had wondered what would have happened if she had needed more time to decide. She gave some thought to how they were so sure she would accept. But this thought passed quickly into the realm of discount. She arrived at the answer that they must have meant business. All or nothing— "Take it or leave it."

The State of Georgia had made it extremely difficult for her to "leave it." But there was still something about the implicit surety of the itinerary that bothered her at a subconscious level.

After picking up the reserved rental, her drive to Atlanta had been nice. The car was not quite as nice as Casper's had been, but still the Sebring had probably been the best one available at the local rental agency. One thing was for certain—her new employers did not seem to monkey around with second best.

A couple of times she had felt the distinct impression that she was being followed. But those bumpy thoughts and the bumpy thoughts of leaving her newfound friends and home seemed to dissipate as the hilly mountain roads gave way to the smoother, flatter winding valley roads of Cherokee County.

By the time she made it to I-575, the gentle swells of the hills were only a small reminder of the mountains in the rearview mirror. As she passed through these parts, the color line blended into the green trees that were still a few days ahead of the autumn color front. In the south, the color band sweeps slowly across the landscape like a line on a weather map, converting the green forest into a blaze of yellows, oranges, reds, and browns.

An eagle soared out over the colors using the carrier winds to wing his way to the greener hills beyond. Andrea saw this as a little metaphor from nature telling her that she was transitioning from her tumultuous past into a green, lush future. Little did she know that nothing could be further from the truth.

The rental included curbside drop off, a rarity at the Atlanta airport, and she was virtually swept through the process as if she were a VIP. The only reminder she was one of the teeming masses came when she wedged herself in with hundreds of other people and rode the underground train to the terminal. She concluded that only here in the Atlanta airport could you find people who didn't believe in bathing, crammed right up next to people who believed in cooking with curry in all dishes.

But all of this drifted away as she felt her first class seat slip the surly bonds of earth. It was almost as if gravity held the monster of her past as it was forced to relinquish its hideous grip on her soul. She imagined the scrunching of the landing gear folding neatly up in their wells as the claws of her history losing their hold on the plane. Then there followed only the rushing sound of the wind and engines.

She had gone through the folder while in the air, as Casper had suggested, and found many forms with little red tabs attached to their corners. These she filled out with the care of a new hire wanting to get everything letter perfect. She was surprised to see a medical form that asked for even more detail than the average new patient form at a general practitioner's office. She filled it out, but really didn't understand why that was necessary. She figured she would find her own doctor once she settled in at her new home.

Finally the jet landed in Virginia and she transferred first to a puddle-hopper and then finally, to a helicopter. This last was particularly amazing as she found herself sailing along the topology of a state ablaze with autumn. The bladed craft was mimicking the shape of the terrain below, giving her the most amazing panoramic view of the interior of the state.

As she approached the Center, she noticed a car gliding up to the landing pad to meet them. *These people really have their act together,* she surmised.

After a few kind words to the chopper pilot for the fun ride, she turned to meet a woman for whom she would develop a continually growing respect. The lady introduced herself as Victoria. Andrea had mistakenly assigned her the role of executive secretary for Casper in her own mind. She would later wonder how she could have ever ascribed that position to Victoria. But for this moment, the job of secretary was the cubbyhole in which she best fit. So there she was put.

Victoria had led her around the grounds, which looked more like a quaint Ivy League college than an agency. The buildings had obviously been there long enough to earn historical markers, but at the same time presented the impression they would find such ornamentation gauche.

The need for medical records became obvious as Andrea was led into a building that seemed better equipped than most small hospitals. The medical staff was courteous and seemed to be an intricate part of the goings-on around here. Andrea almost didn't mind the battery of injections. They were all described as inoculations like one might expect before going overseas. They told her that they wanted to get this part out of the way so that she would not be bothered once she got her first assignment.

Finally, she had been shown her townhouse that was in a fairly large complex adjacent to the Center. Yes, it was fully furnished, but they assured her there would be no problem swapping anything out should she wish to make her own purchases. They also told her that she would be able to find her own home nearby if she liked, but that the Order really encouraged on-campus housing for the rookie year.

Andrea had wondered about the word *Order,* and it had raised her

58

curiosity. But her conservative nature prevented her from asking any straightforward questions about it just yet. She just filed this away with all the other information she was gaining by the minute.

Andrea had found this technique of learning the best for her. When she was faced with a stream of new information, she would accept everything at face value and consider it true unless otherwise proved false. And any new word was assigned a generic label of noun or verb until its real meaning was revealed to her.

Victoria had left her at her new home with a suggestion that she should visit the research center that evening before calling it a night. She was given thorough directions.

And now, Andrea found herself standing at that destination, staring at a building that appeared to be more of a chapel than a library. In the pale light of evening, just after the sun leaves a faint blue ribbon behind as a nightlight for the rest of the darkening sky, she saw the spire of the clock tower some three stories up. She allowed her gaze to move down the front of the building to the two large white doors at the top of some steps. She was about to head up the steps and into the research center when a voice near her feet startled her.

"Good evening, Miss."

Andrea was so taken aback she sucked a breath in between her teeth. Taking a small hop back from the sound emanating from just off to her side, she looked quickly down to its source and saw a man in a grey set of coveralls kneeling in a flowerbed to the side of the steps. He was looking back over his shoulder, his feet hanging out on the sidewalk. He looked as if he had left them there so someone could pull him out should the bushes decide to eat him for dinner.

"Oh," she said, still in a voice of surprise. And then with more control, "How do you do?"

The man chuckled a little, "I do fine. And yourself?" His eastern European accent was diminished with time, but still very much a part of him.

"A bit bewildered by it all. But I *do* fine, thank you." Actually, she was telling the truth. She had not felt this good in years. The numb spot over her left knee was even gone.

"You are new here, no?"

"No. I mean, yes!" she corrected with a giggle at the flipped negative.

The elderly man that still looked young for his apparent age stood up, dusted himself off taking great pains to wipe the dirt from his right hand, extended it in a show of friendship and said, "Sorin. It means sun."

Taking his hand and smiling, "Andrea. It means…Andrea." They both laughed at this.

"What is your last name?" the groundskeeper asked.

"Ellijay."

"Ah...Cherokee. Um...'Where-the-rivers-merge', no?"

"Wow! Do you do parlor tricks?"

"I used to bend spoons, but then could never find anything to eat ice cream with, so I gave it up."

Sorin made himself comfortable on a concrete bench beside the sidewalk as Andrea pulled her notepad up to her chest like a schoolgirl on her first day in a new high school. She found herself wondering how this quaint old man could have this effect on her.

In an effort to continue the conversation, and maybe even make an acquaintance she sputtered out, "Gaelic."

"Gaelic, what?" Sorin asked.

Andrea felt as awkward as she imagined she looked. She tried to pull herself out of this feeling and get the conversation to someplace it could sound more mature. She thought that even the weather would be a better topic than the way this had started out. Sorin looked patient enough with his request so she continued, "Gaelic. I mean, I am more Gaelic than anything."

"Ah, but there must be an Indian in the woodpile somewhere," he said with a twinkle in his eye.

Blushing a bit now, she said, "Well, yes. I mean, I was always told that I was at least part Cherokee. People that knew my mother and father say my paternal great-grandfather was Cherokee. But I never put much stock in it. I always thought my kin selected the name when they settled down near the Coosawattee." Then after rocking back on her heels she added, "Sure is nice weather this evening."

She was wrong—talking about the weather was worse.

Looking up, he allowed a few glances in either direction. She noticed that his hair was mostly grey, but that randomly dispersed through it were single strands of jet-black. He looked back down and regaining eye contact said, "That it is! It seems that blue ribbon up there is only displayed this time of year. It is almost like nature is putting a bow on the gift of autumn."

Then with more purpose he said, "So...you are the new Agent."

"Word travels fast."

"In these parts it does."

"So, you understand the work we do?" she asked, hoping that she wasn't engaging in discussions of a sensitive nature with someone that was not privy to the content.

"Understand?" he snorted a short chuckle. "I'm not sure anyone here really understands the work that is going on, or what they are up against. But I do have some degree of knowledge. No one is allowed to work for the Order unless they have some idea what is going on."

She wanted to ask about that word now, *Order*. But she was afraid they expected her to already know about it. Again, that conservative layer rose up like a blanket and smothered a perfectly logical question before it was uttered. She chose instead to say, "You must be very special then."

"Not really, just a gardener of sorts—with a really great gig. Keeps me off the streets."

"So what advice do you have for a new rookie?"

"Read."

"In there?" she motioned up the steps.

"Read everything you can *about* everything you can. It's all connected, you see."

"What's all connected?"

"All of it. Everything we see, hear, and learn. All of it has something to do with one of the Factions."

"Factions?" she heard herself ask the question before the blanket could stop it.

"Basically 'them', 'us', and the other 'them,'" he answered.

She blinked at him.

Realizing he had lost her, Sorin continued, "Basically the three camps. You know about one, the vamps. But then there is the Order, of course. That 'them' would be us. And then there are the Croatoan. It's all in there," he said, thumbing a gesture over his right shoulder.

"Read," she concluded.

"Aye. Read."

"Anything else?" she asked, smiling the best she could, hoping to warm up the ending of the brief encounter with the first person she had met on her own here.

"Understand the seed. That part is a little trickier than all the rest," he said as if he were talking to someone that understood it all.

"The locked box." Andrea said this as a student might answer a question—wanting to sound sure of the answer in front of the professor and still asking with her eyes for confirmation that it was correct.

"Yes. You would do well to learn about that first."

"Well perhaps you could illuminate it some for me."

Now it was Sorin's turn to think about his reply. He looked like a workman sizing up a piece of lumber before using it for some important purpose. It was almost like he was trying to figure out if this little fish was worthy of the effort involved.

At length he pontificated, "It is essential for every sentient to have such a seed. It is a captured and forbidden desire."

"It changes, right? I mean after the person's understanding of their community's ethos matures?"

"A person's seed may change over time as a person's society changes. But in most cases, the concepts surrounding the forbidden desire are deemed to be so heinous, that they are ingrained in the collective psyche of the community. It would be rare indeed for such a conclusion by a group of people to evolve to the point where first it is tolerated and then embraced by the very same society within the span of a single generation."

"Can you give me an example?"

"Tell me your thoughts on enslaving minorities to work on your plantation down home."

Andrea got a shocked look on her face and nearly gasped, "That's horrible!"

"Right. But your ancestors may not have thought so. In fact, the transition from acceptance to repulsion has taken decades or even centuries for most of the cultures on earth. Some cultures that are fully aware of our history here, still embrace slavery in their own land, even today."

He allowed her to take all this in a moment before continuing, "I have always found it interesting how self-deprecating America is on the whole subject of slavery when they actually led the world in its emancipation. Sure it was horrible, but shouldn't the first civilization in modern times to voluntarily rid themselves of slavery be entitled to some sort of kudos?"

"There are some folks from my neck of the woods that would argue over the word 'voluntarily,'" she replied in an effort to seem quick. They both smiled a bit.

"So there are. And so the society continues its slow progression towards changing its ethos. It certainly doesn't happen overnight. Do you now see my point?"

She nodded slowly as she mulled this over in her mind.

"So in most cases, the seed a person captures as they mature really never changes all the way through their life."

"Ok...so I am still confused. What is it exactly?" She now was a little less self-aware and really wanted to know some answers to the questions that were swimming around in her head.

"Did you ever take any computer programming?"

"A little in college. I really enjoyed it," she answered.

"Tell me about random number generators," he requested like a dean at an aural exam.

She gave it some thought and then, "Well...it's important for a computer program to be able to generate a random number. It's used in varying a choice each time through a decision. For example, if I wrote a computer game about the United States, I may use a random number generator to select your starting state by picking a number between one and fifty. Then I would take the gamer to the matching state. That way he would get a different state each time."

"Very good," said Sorin, "and so the pattern of that list of numbers would be all mixed up, right?"

"Right. So it might be something like 27, 13, 42, 3, etc."

Sorin shifted his weight and then asked, "And what would happen if I exit your game and come back again later. What will the pattern look like?"

"Won't it be different every time?" and then she started to remember, "Oh wait...I remember doing this. It was the *same* every time, no matter what I tried. It would repeat the same sequence of random numbers: 27, 13, 42..."

"Did you ever figure out how to break that problem?"

"Yes..." the look of recollection was genuine, "You had to *seed* the random number generator. If you passed in a different number, the series would be different each time. So if I passed in a 7, the series would be something different than if I didn't pass any other number in."

"And if you passed 7 in every time?" he quizzed.

"Then *that* series would repeat. So we would use the date and time of the current moment. That way the seed would generate a different sequence of numbers each time."

Andrea was pleased with the memory and liked the easy way that Sorin was smiling. He then formulated for her, "The seed in your mind is like unto this. The desire to do the worst thing imaginable is in constant conflict with your obligation to suppress it, control it. Your brain is a series of neural pathways that create thoughts, ideas, and dreams, even visions out of sequences of electrical impulses. Without a seed..."

"They would just repeat," she concluded for herself, "The numbers may be different—number by number, but the sequence would be the same each time."

She watched him watching her. She knew he was sensing the tumblers clicking in her mind. Finally she asked rhetorically, "That wouldn't be much of a life, would it?"

"It would be no life at all," he agreed.

"That thing is pretty damned important, isn't it?"

He allowed a furtive pause and then, "It *is* life." Then he added, "Guard yours with yours."

Her right hand instinctively slipped around the back of her neck in what must have been a reflexive act. She was both guarding it and massaging it with the tips of her fingers at the same time. Her fingertips needed to be convinced that there had been no entry there. A little unnerved, but trying to hide the shiver that coursed through her, she recovered enough to say, "I will. And thanks for the warning!"

"That's what old friends are for!"

"But we are not old friends..." she reminded him with a half-smile.

"...that you know of," he corrected, "but we will have a chance to be if you just remember that lesson."

A question had been standing at the ready in her mind during this entire exchange. She really wanted to know how a gardener knew so damn much about things. She would have just blurted it out, but she realized that it would not be socially polite. Once again, her conservative nature would prevent her from seeking an answer to an immediate question. In her experience, these things always worked themselves out. The answer would come about in time and she would not be seen as a nosey busybody.

She appreciated the warmth with which the lesson had been given. She made a body language movement to signal she was making her exit, "Indeed. I'll be mindful. But for now, I really need to get to my reading. So I must make my exit good sir."

He excused her with a polite, "Have an enchanted evening, my lady." He performed a pretend royal bow, waving his arm in horizontal circles in front of his face as he moved downward.

She laughed and started up the steps. As she opened the door, she turned to see that Sorin was already back at his work in the hedges. She really felt good at making this new acquaintance. This sage did feel like an old friend somehow. She hoped everyone she met here at the Center would click so well. Turning into the open door, she left the encroaching veil of night on the doorstep and walked into the rich brightness of the research center.

The interior seemed almost to be one large, open space divided into three levels with a grand oval opening in the middle. The upper two levels looking down on the first through ornate metal and carved wood railing, were accessible via black spiral staircases on the left and right side and a rather wide staircase at the far end. Signs were posted at the base of each of the staircases stating in simple terms that the upper levels were reserved for people of team lead rank and higher.

The first level seemed to be divided up into departments of information that wrapped all the way around the floor in a semicircle from left to right: National Government, Foreign Governments, Terrorists, Legends, Croatoan, and Statistical Analysis. Each section had high sets of bookshelves wrapped around waist-high tables. Each table had a rack on it. The racks were stuffed with packets of stapled paper reports, usually five to ten sheets each. They looked like reports typed up for school credit. Andrea noted that some of these reports were also stacked neatly on the tables. At the end of each island were rows of filing cabinets terminating with a computer and microfiche machine.

With a little investigation, Andrea concluded that researchers worked in a particular area. They worked up a report on some current subject of interest and placed the most recent findings out on the tables. As the reports became older news, they migrated to the racks. Then after some time, they made their way into the filing cabinets, and then finally onto either microfiche or computer files. She also noted that certain authors seemed to work solely in a particular area of interest with few exceptions.

She spent a little time at each section starting on the left, working her way clockwise through the room. She read a few briefs on national affairs, updates on foreign countries, and situational updates on terrorists. Andrea felt she could probably spend hours on this subject. It was all so fresh on everyone's mind after 9/11. The things she read there were certainly *not* in the mainstream media. Some of it was exceptionally scary.

As she made her way across the back of the room, she saw a giant bookcase stretching the length of the back wall with sliding ladders. Tables were at its base, making instant reading easy. The books housed there looked quite old and they were protected by a halon fire control system. The curators seemed to be far more concerned about the safety of the books than they were about the general welfare of those nearby when disaster struck.

There was a sign across the top that read "Codex" in big print. Andrea allowed herself to first thumb down a row reading the arcane titles on the spines of these tomes. Then selecting one quite at random, she thumbed through its pages. This particular book described metallurgy and crafting by early Native Americans. It was replete with detailed descriptions and drawings from the time. Placing it back in its home, it slid together comfortably with the others as if the shelf had been custom built to accommodate exactly the width of all its combined volumes.

Moving further to the right from the Codex and back out to the station area, she came to the section on Legends. Here, she found articles on things one would expect to see in an old black-and-white movie. But they were written in contemporary terms with current dates. She was more than a little disturbed to spy a report in the rack with her name on it. She snatched it out and started reading it. It was written by a researcher whose name appeared on many of the documents here, Leeza Banes. Ms. Banes had captured the entire event that happened in Blairsville roughly three weeks earlier.

Andrea felt a little flush as she read as much as she could stand and glanced over the areas that brought memories back that were too disturbing to revisit just yet. But it was *all* there. It could not have been documented more thoroughly if a reporter had been on the very spot as it happened. The most chilling thing to her was the date. Andrea felt someone walk across her grave as she noted that the date of this report was the very next day. She had not even begun her own report to the GBI before this complete and detailed account had appeared here on this table.

She blushed and glanced around to make sure that the building that had seemed empty when she entered was indeed *still* empty. She breathed a sigh of relief when she saw that no one had joined her for the moment.

Deciding it better to return this report, she carefully slid it back in with its cousins and patiently patted it down until its edges aligned neatly with the other reports. She did not want those pages to draw extra attention from passers-by.

Just as she was about to make her way to the next section, another report caught her eye. This one was more recent. It appeared to her that just nine days earlier a vampire had been killed in an alley in New York. Deciding as it was getting late, she pulled this report to review later that evening. The one thing that did manage to catch her attention was that the analyst believed a Croatoan had killed the vampire. This intrigued her enough to take a copy.

Moving on into the Croatoan area, she realized that at the volume of reports and books here, she would need to spend weeks, hell—months just to learn enough to be any good at this job. Sifting through the most current reports, she found one that drew her in. She remembered Casper had told her that Ned worked the eastern seaboard, but mostly the northern part. There was a report of two Croatoan meeting in broad daylight in a public area in the heart of New York City. Apparently, this was a rare event based on the language of the report. She felt this might make good companion reading to the one she had already selected, so she pulled a copy of this one as well.

Now walking with the two reports under her arms, she made her way towards the front door past the last station on the way out. Andrea had absolutely no intention of stopping by the Statistical Analysis station. There was nothing that bored her more than numbers. But then, she second-guessed this conclusion. "Maybe I can find something that will help me sleep my first night here," she mused softly.

Again there was one report that caught her eye, but not because it had anything to do with her new career. Here was a report referencing her home state. The report was interesting enough. It was a list of websites whose overall hit-rate increased within a general geographic area.

In other words, hit-rates went up and down all the time, but if the hit-rates for say a drycleaner, school, police station, and apartment complex on the same block all went up at the same time, it would be statistically interesting. It might indicate an interest a person or a group of people have in a particular area.

This report stated that of the top ten shifts in network traffic, number eight was in the Savannah area. She had known a boy from the Bethesda Orphanage there. Andrea had been temporarily placed in a Baptist Children's Home in Baxley and occasionally they would take the girls down to Bethesda for a mixer. She had always loved Savannah, the old charm of the city made it like unto New Orleans for her. Wren had been his name. It was a childhood crush that had driven a few letters, but then waned as she moved back up to the state-run orphanage in North Georgia.

Andrea grabbed up this third report, tucked it up under her arms neatly with the others, and made her way directly for the front door. She was a little disappointed when she stepped outside and did not see Sorin climbing around the hedges. It was later than it felt, and she guessed he had gone off to prowl wherever it was that people like him prowled in towns like this. She pulled the collar of her blazer up around her neck to shield it from the drafty night, or so she lied to herself. Subconsciously, she was fighting off a giant case of the heebie-jeebies and a monster lurked behind every shrub.

She made her way across the quad towards her townhome on the other side of the campus. She took some comfort in seeing sets of couples or trios talking under lampposts or sitting on benches. But somehow, it made her feel lonelier at the same time. Even though these were her new colleagues, she was still a stranger in a very strange land. She looked down at the path directly in front of her feet and quickened her step.

There was no wolf jogging at her side this evening, and she desperately wanted the comfort of a locked door at her back.

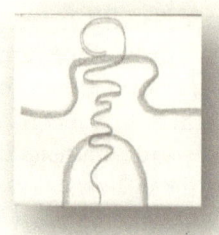

6.
12.19.9.11.16.22917; 9 YAX, 11 CIB — SOUL

October 11, 2002, 5:30 a.m. EST

"Go figure," George said to himself as he fought off the sleep that was trying to overtake him. "Mr. High-And-Mighty, Danreck Porter gets the big plan and I end up talking to myself on Interstate 55 all the way from one shit-hole to another shit-hole. Come on Georgie! Stay awake, damnit!"

George Burroughs had grown accustomed to talking to himself. It was something he did even *before* the Salem witch trials. Hell, it may have been the reason he was *in* the trials to begin with. One thing Puritans didn't like was a person that thought out loud. George slapped himself on the cheek as he felt his rental for the fortnight creep over the white lines a little.

"If it's one thing I can't tolerate it's driving all bloody night. Wake up!" This was followed by another slap. This one was hard and stinging to his right cheek.

He had already played the radio too loud, stopped for bad Mexican food, and citrus soda (a heartburn combo sure to cause severe enough pain to ward off the sleepy-monster), turned his heater up to the point of burning his shins, and now, he had turned the air conditioner down to the point where his teeth were chattering despite his turtleneck sweater. He had lowered his windows to boot.

But the last slap had done the trick. "Almost to Jackson you son-of-a-whore!" he yelled. "Damn. Memphis to Jackson! I feel so Presleyed! Damn George. You always could find the verb in a noun."

George Burroughs was a slightly overweight, pale Croatoan. People would not describe him as "fat," but he was thick enough that he might be considered husky. It didn't help that he always seemed to buy his clothes maybe one size too small. They would cling to his form allowing one to see exactly how much of him there was. He would buy large. Extra-large would be admitting he was over the threshold.

Even with his immense knowledge gained from centuries of harvests, he still played the pratt to the others. He always came off as bumbling even though he had never failed to execute a single step in the Cause.

He had always hated the Memphis airport for the most part. It always seemed to be midnight there. Jets came in and out of that airport at a faster rate than any other. It was like an airline salad shooter. It was also moist there. The humidity was always so far off the scale that the pinkish streetlights gave off a familiar halo. It had always reminded George of swimming in an overly chlorinated pool at night and then driving home. Everywhere you look—halos.

The dampness in the air also did not help his eternal pageboy haircut. The strawberry blonde hair draped down straight and fine. In this air, it took on an oily texture and became flat. He always had to pull it back behind his ears like some comic stooge.

The one part he didn't mind about coming here was how the Interstate actually ran under the taxiway for the jets. If you slowed down enough, chances were good that one would drive right over your head. There were not even any railings or fences to obstruct your view. It was almost like you could reach out and touch them they were so close. George liked to pretend it was a freak Interstate where jets drove around town like cars. It was always great fun for him…for a few seconds anyway.

"Dear old bossie-wossie sure would be pissed to the umph-degree if you screwed the pooch and crashed your car right now," he continued to yell at himself. He shook his head until his cheeks flapped making a slapping noise, and then recovered his focus by blinking his eyes.

"Hold out, Ace. You're almost to Jackson you bastard!"

George had gotten the call three days prior. Danreck needed him to do a specific job. It had to be done cleanly. He had to take the highest precautions. It had taken him and a team working for the Cause a solid day to do the research on the Internet, then a day to get ready and leave.

"No real worries mate. Go over the plan again. That will jazz your brain. The trucking company is in Jackson. The fertilizer is in Meridian. The drop is in Savannah. Cake."

He strained a little. He thought he was seeing spots. But it turned out to be an unfortunate swarm of insects that had the added bonus of poor timing. He turned on his wipers and washer, but that only made matters worse for a moment. The smeared mess obscured his vision so badly that the warning grooves in the breakdown lane announced he was off course. "You big dummy!" he yelled as the adrenaline helped him revive a little. He slowly pulled the car back into the lane.

"Leroy Hoffman," he said in disgust. "Leroy-fucking-Hoffman! Out of all the piss-ants in the world, I have to be *Leroy* Hoffman for a week! Damn! Danreck owes me big time for this one."

George remembered his history. He remembered how this country had changed over the past three centuries. The railways made a huge difference in all the ways of life. They used to ship everything, even fuel, for thousands of miles. But that had all changed with World War II. "This is the hardest it has been for me to stay awake since that time in 1943. Man! Now *that* was a party! One harvest and we all stayed hopping for eight fucking years."

In WWII, the federal government had put limits on how far fuel could be shipped by train in the U.S. It was considered a huge hindrance by the oil tycoons. They needed to get gas to the stations all over the country and the government had seen to it that it was going to be a right pain in the ass to do it.

One man, Billy Thackston, saw the hassle as an opportunity. He had picked Jackson, Mississippi partly because of its prime geographic position between the two ports of New Orleans and Savannah, Georgia, but mostly because his company had shipped him there—a final insult to an illustrious career.

You make money for the man, and the man sends you to Jackson.

So this one entrepreneur took the last energy he had and founded a trucking company just far enough inland that the trains could not carry the fuel any farther without risking federal intervention. Thus the Natchez Trucking Company was formed. Thackston connected a network of southern cities with trucks. All were strategically located where the rails could legally continue the passage of fuel to the center of the Eastern U.S.

Natchez was an old and trusted courier. It always had the best licenses and contracts. After the Oklahoma bombing incident in 1995, they were one of the few trucking companies whose fertilizer credentials were reviewed in moments, and reprocessed to continue without interruption.

"Leroy, I'm coming for you!" George cried as he stuck his head out the window for a moment, hoping the blast of cold air would shake off the heaviness in his lids.

His plan was simple enough. Leroy worked for Natchez. He made one route, two times a week. He drove from Jackson to Savannah picking up the fertilizer in Meridian every Tuesday and Friday, and drove home after swapping out trailers at the shipyards for his load du jour. George would harvest Leroy, take his form, and wait until the night of the twenty-first to act out Leroy's seed. Then he could take back his own form and drive the rental back to Memphis, this time after some good sleep.

Meanwhile, he could operate the rig and get Danreck his precious cargo. If all went well, they could skim enough off the top—over three loads, that no one would be the wiser. In the end, Leroy would be blamed for his crime, and his disappearance explained as escaping the long arm of the law.

"All will be great except having to make this damn run three times as Leroy-for-the-love-of-god-Hoffman!" George switched the air back to heat. He was freezing now. When he looked up, he was ecstatic to see the faint blue ribbon appearing in the eastern sky. Somehow, he always thought it was easier to stay awake on the road when there was a little light in the sky.

George strained to see an approaching street sign. "Fifteen miles to Jackson. Hot damn, you old fool! You made it!" The temptation to just chuck the whole thing and go down to New Orleans for the weekend was intense. But there was a job to do and Danreck was pretty important to Hacquee. And Hacquee was more important than George's relaxation this weekend.

As he approached the northern side of Jackson, the signs for the seedier side of the city came into view. There were plenty of places for "gentlemen" (as they who pay for such entertainment in these parts are called) to find solace. Adult bookstores with live entertainment were adjacent to bars with "real girls."

"The first place I see with imaginary girls, I'm stopping, George Burroughs!"

Once he made it past the Interstate 220 bypass, he started looking for exit 102. Natchez Trucking would be only two or three blocks to the right. It was still fairly dark. "Looks like your timing is still perfect, eh George?" he said as he turned on his blinker and decelerated for the exit to the right. Turning on to E. Beasley, he made his way to the point where the road turned into W. Beasley. There at the place where the road crossed the Illinois Central tracks, he found his target. "Ok, George, now we need to find a nice place to park this car for a few without suspicion if we can help it."

Driving past the company lot a few blocks down from the tracks, he found what he was looking for: a storage rental facility. He pulled in and parked his car to the side of the main building. They were not open yet, but that was ok. Leroy would be back to clear things up in a little while.

George got out of the rental car and stretched the kind of stretch that ends a four-hour trip in the middle of the night. Throwing on a windbreaker, he walked briskly the few blocks back to the trucking company's employee parking lot.

"It's been years since I flattened a penny," he said to himself as he crossed the tracks. He remembered a time when he would regularly go out to the Hudson, Pelham & Salem line at the turn of the last century and flatten coins on the track. Laughing to himself he added, "They still think it was the fault of the crew on #137 for that head-on. Wow! Was that ever a show! Boom! Crash!" Still chuckling he recounted the six dead on the HP&S in 1903.

But he had a job to do and Leroy had an appointment with his own fateful penny at the end of the line. So George cleared his head and kept on walking. As he approached the parking lot, he found a perfect place to wait. To the left of the pavement, riven with fissures where clumps of grass sprouted out like so many tiny green volcanoes, he spied a Dipsty Dumpster. The employees were filling in the row near it now. It would supply just the cover he needed.

It only took about five minutes for his mark to show up. "Timing still perfect, you old fart," he muttered to himself. Leroy Hoffman pulled up in a butterscotch golden 1972 Oldsmobile Cutlass Supreme. George felt car names should be demoted over time, and that this one barely warranted the title of Cutlass Mediocre at best. He tittered to himself at the thought as the large, Black man opened the door with a rusty squawk.

As Leroy got out of the two-door coupe, he pushed the door past the squeaking place in the middle where it always seemed to want to hang, and with some force—he slammed it shut. *I'll have to fix that when I get back,* George thought to himself as he headed across the twenty feet or so that separated him from his mark.

Leroy was just turning to head towards the lights flooding down from the large grey sheet metal building on the other side of the parking lot when he heard a friendly enough voice say, "Leroy? Leroy Hoffman?" from behind. Turning around he saw a stranger approaching, but he didn't look like the homeless riff-raff that frequented the area up and down the railroad.

"Who wants to know?" he smiled as he asked, stopping in his tracks.

"I'm George. George Burroughs. I'm starting today. Frank said you could show me where the lot manager's office is." George was getting close enough to strike, but didn't want to take any chances.

"I'm afraid I don't know a Frank," then turning to his left, Leroy pointed to the end of the building and continued, "but Sally's office is just over…" It was the last words his body would ever allow him to speak freely, and some of the last words Leroy Hoffman would ever speak at all.

As he was turning to the left, he felt a stinging sensation at the top of his neck. This was followed by the warmth of someone grabbing his left arm with a full hand at his bicep, turning him around in mid-sentence. Leroy felt the motion of his body. His legs were moving, but seemingly quite on their own. A voice, soft and comforting in his ear told him as he walked towards the dumpster that, "Everything is going to be alright friend. We just need to talk for a few minutes over here about some business."

Once they got behind the large blue dumpster, George continued in his congenial tone, "Here we are, friend. This isn't so bad, now is it?"

Leroy knew things were bad wrong. He could sense that this wouldn't go well for him. He had always been a fighter and he was not about to give up now. He tried to shout out for help, but had absolutely no control over his own voice. He also realized he was completely cut off from any physical movement except breathing—which he continued to control. It was as if his brain had somehow been isolated; he was left alone only his thoughts of escape and panic welling up inside him. The strangest part was that he could still feel everything. He was not numb at all. He could feel the pressure on his neck and around his upper arm. The Earth was still a firmament under his feet and gravity still had its precious hold on his soul—at least for the moment.

"Oh man, your thoughts are very busy in there. Quite a surprise, that is. I had expected somewhat *less* from the namesake. I guess I owe you an apology, Mr. *Leroy*. My stereotypical ideas of a southern trucker with your name just flew out the old proverbial window for me." He chuckled a little.

"Tell you what I'm going to do…I'm going to let you talk some. But keep in mind that I am completely in control and you are not going to be harmed in any way. You won't be able to scream or anything, and I need to be prompt at my business here. So make your conversation count. You ok with that, Leroy?"

"Yes," Leroy said. It was like cool ice on a hot summer's day.

Just being able to talk after totally losing all abilities reminded Leroy of the old spiritual where rich man Dives said, *"Dip your finger in the water come and cool my tongue 'cause I'm tormented in the flames, man!"*

With direct purpose, Leroy said, "Jesus, help me."

"Oh He will, friend. I know you two are close. That's a good thing." George had already begun his trip to the center of Leroy's psyche. "It gives me great satisfaction to know that you have made your peace with our Maker."

Shaking in an effort to gain a little more control, Leroy said with some considerable consternation, "He isn't your Maker. I know who you are." Leroy's eyes were starting to have a difficult time staying focused. They would roll back every few seconds or so and then snap back into proper alignment as he struggled to free himself.

In a calm and cool voice, George answered. "Oh come, come, friend. Haven't you heard the good news? His Father is everyone's Father! He knew us long before even His own Son walked here." George was already finding the sweet spot. "It may surprise you if you actually knew who I am, or was. But to be honest with you, I have some difficulty concentrating in my new line of work when I'm being reminded of my old line of work."

Shifting his weight a little, George continued, "So, my friend…how about if we give you a really pleasant send-off? Wouldn't that be lovely? How's this?"

At that moment, Leroy saw a fireworks display explode on his vision. There was a warmth that coursed through his body. His eyes became distant, unfocused as his shaking calmed. "Oh, my," he said.

"Yes. Oh, my, indeed," George echoed.

"Is it heaven?"

"No, not quite. But that will come soon enough. We have a little unfinished work to do yet, Leroy."

As George drove hard for the core of his inner workings, Leroy began to see the images form and flicker past his vision. They became grittier, more hedonistic as they progressed. Leroy felt his body turn around slightly and could barely make out that he was now face-to-face with his assailant. George's right hand was now cupped around Leroy's neck supporting his weight with super-human strength, while drawing him in with his left hand, which was now around Leroy's bicep.

"Well, Leroy," George cooed in his ear as they were now cheek-to-cheek, "You are not so much the saint after all...are you?"

Leroy was confronted with dark thought after dark thought. Now his mind-play was taking almost solid form with motion. And he was more experiencing them than seeing them. It was like a big fantasy world with which he could actually interact. He now stepped freely into that world drawn by his own desires.

"Yes, Leroy...that's it. Amazing, isn't it?"

"Oh, yes. Oh, yes," he said over and over softly, moving his head back and forth. George allowed their cheeks to rub a bit. It was bringing some comfort to Leroy and that would make things go a bit faster.

"You see, Leroy, this process you are experiencing is special. Very few get to enjoy it. You will experience great satisfaction and release as you die."

Leroy was fully cognizant that his attacker had just said, *"die"* but he was welcoming this entire experience now. He could actually smell, taste, hear the events unfolding before him, and he knew them to be from the darkest reaches of his own mind.

"Good. You know it to be truth. Share the truth with me, Leroy. The truth shall set you free and you will be free, indeed."

The images were now moving so fast that they blended into a river of emotions and feelings.

"It works this way, Leroy. This experience is beyond sexual in its extremity and pleasure. The process can be fully comprehended by you if you cooperate."

"No fight here, man," came his answer, soft, but clear. The sun was beginning to warm the sky with a sherbet orange overhead. It became the pastel backdrop for the realization of Leroy's deepest and blackest desires.

Moving into Leroy's center, George continued, "You are doing beautifully, Leroy. You should be proud of yourself."

"I'm doing good?" Leroy asked with a genuine desire to know George's approval. Nothing meant more to him at this moment in time.

"Oh, yes Leroy. You are doing quite well. The intimate sharing of the most private and closely held of all your secrets is a joyous happening to be revered and respected by all of us. It is a religious experience for us. It is coveted and lusted after by some of the greatest of all the creatures on this planet. Your vampires cannot even duplicate this—though they really wish to. They envy you, Leroy. They wish they could be here right now. They want this."

And at that moment as George harvested Leroy's seed, Leroy felt a wave of pleasure and release flow through his body and soul. He let go of everything as his soul flew into oblivion.

George stifled the primal scream of exuberance as the energy coursed through his body. It came out as a low, guttural growl. Images and memories flowed through his brain with amazing speed, finding homes among the neural pathways. They were neatly arranged with like knowledge as George began the process of Reconciliation.

It was about then that George felt the moment of change come on. He welcomed it and gave license to his form. The process was fairly swift as he grew in stature and build. Brown skin replaced fair and all of his body hair changed. His face felt a little foreign to him, as did the toughness of his skin. Looking at his arm still supporting Leroy's dead weight, he realized that the shade was a little pale, but it was close enough.

George came to the conclusion that Leroy's seed would be a tidy thing to deal with on the last Friday night of Danreck's Mission. In fact, he concluded that it would be much easier to take care of Leroy's seed than it would be to take care of Leroy at that moment. The front of Leroy's pants was damp. He hated it when that happened. No doubt about it, old Leroy had shot his load.

Given the current circumstances, George reckoned he would need to employ an old Croatoan trick. Since he had not retracted his needle-like appendage from Leroy's brain, he was still "jacked-in" so to speak. Simply reversing some electrical pulses, he manipulated the motor neurons in Leroy's body to react as if George was a puppet-master and Leroy was a marionette. It took a great deal of energy and would leave a Croatoan drained afterward, but it was better than carrying a dead body across a parking lot full of witnesses.

George half carried and half prodded the lifeless Leroy across the lot to his car where he opened the door and with some effort had Leroy sit down in the passenger side. To an onlooker they would have looked like two twins, one rubbing the other one's neck as they crossed the pavement together. George hurried around to the other side and quickly drove off the lot and headed back towards the storage place.

In an absent-minded gesture, George rubbed at his own throat under the collar of his turtleneck with his hand. It always felt good to feel the absence of the scars there. At least his neck was nice and smooth for a while.

He turned into the storage facility with his Cutlass Mediocre. This time he pulled right up to the front door. There was an Open sign, the type of which he had seen at the warehouse discount stores many times. George got out and made his way inside. There was a sleepy looking Black man behind the desk.

"Hey, Leroy my man. What's up?"

"Not much Digs. My old lady threw me out a few weeks back and I need some space if you follow me." It always amazed George just how easy it was to assimilate information from a fresh harvest. He instantly knew everything about this man. His name was Digs, or at least that was his nickname. He went to high school with Leroy at Lanier—Go Bulldogs, Sick'um! He even knew that Digs had a penchant for White women, something about which his wife had absolutely no clue.

Digs rebuked, "Shit, that's old news. Everyone knows Thelma threw you out. She makes sure of that. I've just been wondering if you had anything to store anyhow."

"Funny man. What do you got that can store say 10 by 15?"

Digs looked at a chart under the desk, "Number 28's open."

"Cool, my man. How much you need?"

"Fitty square and it's yours for the month."

"Shit, I need at least through November. You're not gonna jack me around middle of next month are you?" George did a good job of feigning hurt.

"No way, my man! The boss won't see this hit the books 'til November first."

"Extra ounce in it for you on my next run," George threw in. He didn't *remember* that Leroy ran drugs, but got the impression that they joked about it a lot.

Digs threw a key over the counter and said, "Get some sleep, my man. You lookin' a little sick-like."

"Will do. Thanks, Digs."

George went out and got into the car and drove it back to his parked rental. Getting out, it was a simple matter to lift Leroy up and move him to the back of the rental. Then he drove the rental down the rows of white buildings looking for number 28.

"Ok, George, er...um...Leroy...let's see where we live for a bit." George seemed to regularly forget who he was playing. Most of the time it didn't matter, but sometimes it was embarrassing when someone called him by his harvest-name and he didn't respond quickly enough. He slowed as the numbers approached 28.

"26...27...28! Here we are! Your new home for a couple of weeks,

Leroy." George got out and unlocked the storage unit. He removed Leroy's corpse from the back of the car and laid him across the center of the back wall. Then he carefully backed the rental in right up to the corpse. Anyone checking the space may not *see* the corpse right away in this position. And he hoped the cooler temperatures might prevent them from smelling the corpse as well. But he really wasn't that worried about it.

He reached into the glove compartment and pulled out a sealed packet with a padlock wrapped safely inside.

Closing the overhead door George locked it tight. Then with nearly all of his superhuman strength, he ripped the packaging open on the padlock. He wondered how mere mortals were able to open these packages on their own. He giggled with amusement at the thought of them trying and then giving up with cussing disgust as they yelled through their homes for the location of the only pair of scissors. He imagined that this caused at least a few coronaries per year.

George carefully threaded the padlock hook through the holes in the metal brackets, heard and felt the satisfying click as he locked it. Then whistling to himself, he made his way back to the Cutlass. No one was around when he got back. He didn't think anyone would be. Digs was lazy. That's why he was working a morning shift at a storage facility and Leroy had a nice trucking route. When he made it back, he climbed inside and casually drove off the lot with all the confidence in the world. This would work because George Burroughs was really good at his job.

Pulling into the parking lot of Natchez, George parked as close as he could to the parking place that Leroy considered to be his lucky spot. Funny how wrong we can be about such things. One's luck may be another's coincidence. He got out of the Cutlass and made his way to the tongue-lashing he knew he would get from Sally.

He no sooner opened the door to the abutment built on the north side of the larger building that was Natchez Trucking Company than the flood of words hit his ears as the flood of light from the hanging lamps hit his eyes.

"Damnit, Leroy! You're twenty minutes late!" Sally scolded.

"Sorry, I had to take care of some business."

Sally Frostwork looked more than her usually perturbed self, "Your business *is* our business! We have a trucking line to run."

"Damn, Sally, that's just cold. After all these years of never being late a single time…"

"Look, Leroy. I'm sorry you and your old lady fell out. But this is a line…and the line has to stay on time!"

"You know I can make up twenty to Meridian. No sweat." George flashed her that winning Leroy grin.

"Damn Leroy," she said in a lower tone, "You know I can't stay too angry. But get the hell outta here already, would ya?"

"Just give me my board and sword, and I'm a gone motherfucker."

Sally handed him a clipboard with multiple sets of official documents and a ring with keys on it. George turned on his heels and made for the door.

"Whoa, whoa, whoa, hot shot! One more thing…" she called after him.

"Yes, Miss Sally?"

"Your pickup is on the Tybee side of the harbor this time—a loaded down reefer. Just avoid the forest fires and you should have a safe trip."

"Oh, I can assure you…there is absolutely no chance of that. Fires are un-cool bad."

She flashed him some dimples that told him all was forgiven with his tardiness and he opened the door and started whistling. George noted that he had never really enjoyed whistling before. It was an annoying habit he would need to break after this Mission. But for now, he would allow it to continue.

He had picked up his load of fertilizer in Meridian and was halfway to Birmingham on Interstate 20 before Agent Ellijay made it to Ned's office for his requested meeting. Looking down at the cuffs of his pants riding high over his ankles, he figured that he would need to stop and buy some better fitting clothes.

He now knew, thanks to Leroy, of a place in Anniston, Alabama, between Birmingham and Atlanta on Interstate 20. It was a nice small town with a mall just off the interstate. No one would suspect a trucker stopping to stretch his legs while he did a little pre-holiday shopping.

Besides, they had the most amazingly bad Mexican food there. He could pick some up right there at the exit as well. That and a citrus cola, and he would be finer than frog hair split three ways the whole trip to Savannah.

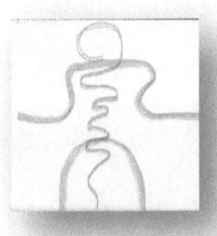

7.
12.19.9.11.16.5347; 9 YAX, 11 CIB — SOUL (CONTINUED)

October 11, 2002, 12:50 p.m. EST

Andrea stared down the long quad where sidewalks crisscrossed from building to building making abstract geometric shapes out of the landscape at the Center. The triangles were broken up by the occasional circle wrapped tightly around some water feature.

People walked along the paths to their various places of interest. Andrea's place of interest for the moment was the administration offices for East Coast Affairs, also known as the Buchanan Hall. It was the third building down on the right as she walked from her town home towards the research center on the opposite side of the quad.

The day was pleasant and bright and she had slept well after a good dose of statistics as a nightcap. She had spent the morning reading introductory material left for her through her mail slot—she guessed by Victoria.

There was one white paper that talked about how Agents were supposed to get to know other Agents when they were at the Center. But it stressed that no Agent really knew how many others there were. This was for the sake of what they called "Parity." Andrea thought it might be to keep people in line, for she would never know who was watching.

Among the other items was a reminder card to meet Agent Smarny at Buchanan Hall room 229 at 1:00 p.m.

Somewhere around 10:00 a.m., she had to drive the unexpected deliveryman back to the car dealership from whence her company-lease had arrived. She had left her Jetta with Estelle and Buford. They had a daughter moving home after a bad divorce and could benefit greatly from a good used car. She figured she would take her small savings and transfer it up to the Center, then go buy a new, used car once she settled in.

The salesman at the dealership explained that the lease was temporary, six months at most, and that he would be happy to help her pick out a new model once she felt at home here. It was standard policy for the Center to supply leased automobiles for the first six months. She had driven back in her new off-white convertible simply happy as a clam. It seemed life had really taken a turn for the better.

As she walked along the sidewalk in the shade of large hardwoods spread out to give plenty of room for growth, and yet, still provide a canopy that was over 100 years old, she mused to herself that life just couldn't get much better than this. Her reading the night before and this morning had been extremely interesting, if not a little difficult to believe, but other than that, these surroundings seemed perfect for a fresh start.

She carried her articles in a manila folder that she had found in a writing desk at her new place. All of the articles and some paperwork she had questions about were stuffed to overflowing. On the other side, she had her black Sak purse slung over her left shoulder.

And now, at nearly 1:00 p.m., she found herself standing at another set of stairs, looking up at two new doors to open. Buchanan Hall was solid brick like all the other buildings here, distinguished only by a slightly different shape, a different style of gables, and the name plaque at its entrance.

She took a deep breath, steadied herself to meet her new boss, looked down and brushed a small wrinkle out of her best navy blue skirt, and with all the determination of a proud Ellijay, she marched up the stairs and straight through the door.

She was so determined to have the right body posture and aggressive attitude that she didn't even notice the man running towards the door from the inside, and the collision was a cascade of papers, folders, and a sack lunch making up the sum total of what they both had been carrying.

"Oh, crap!" she said with an aggravated voice.

"No harm, no foul," came a friendly voice as she stooped picking through the mess to find as many of her papers as she recognized. Looking up she saw the dumbfounded eyes of a person not quite ready to admit to himself that they had a vested interest in helping clean up this mess. "Happens to me all the time."

She said in a gradual crescendo, "Well it doesn't happen to me all the time, and especially not five minutes before my first meeting with my new boss, and there *is* harm, and there most certainly should be a foul!"

"Guilty. I will go to the penalty box for two minutes and feel shame."

She stopped with her hand on some papers of hers and thought that line was actually kind of funny, but she refused to dignify it with laughter. Still she could not think up a witty enough retort, so she just continued picking stuff up and simply said, "Well just don't stand there, help me!"

"Gladly…let's see…I think that's my apple," and he stooped to pick it up. Holding it, he looked down on her and said, "There…now the way is made clear for you to find the rest of your papers. I'll get whatever's left."

"Oh, thank you very much!" she said as she pulled up what she thought were the last two pages of her various debris. "All done. You may have the floor," she said as she pushed past him.

Laughing, he replied, "We will have to do it again sometime! Aren't you the new girl? I'm Scott."

"Not if I can help it." Then turning and softening a little she added, "I'm Andrea, Scott. Nice to meet you. But I really must be going."

She turned and nearly collided with a bust of a rotund and bald old man with a large handlebar mustache. It was perched upon a large marble pedestal. She pulled up short just in time before playing the Pretty Paper Pickup game all over again.

"Don't mind him. He's just Bucky. He sometimes runs into people like I do. But you get used to him…and me." Finishing picking up his spilled items, he called down the hall as she had already corrected her course and was now moving swiftly along the ornate walls sided with paneled wood, "Nice to meet you, too!"

She gave no reply so Scott turned and made his way out the door and into the bright midday sun. He could still hear her heels echo as they clicked up the stairs to the second floor when the door closed softly behind him. Then to himself he added, "Not a bad day! Bumped into a pretty girl and Banachek is back in the states—life is good!"

Turning the corner at the top of the stairs, Andrea started looking for 229. It was with some frustration that she realized it must be completely on the other end of the long hall. No one seemed to be stirring, so the clip-clop of her heels announced her presence to every open office she passed along the way. Face after face looked up from their business to see who was moving in such a rush in this hallowed hall.

At one point she looked in a darkened glass of a closed office that offered somewhat of a reflection and she saw that a wisp of red hair had escaped the merciless hold of her hair spray and barrette to swing recklessly down in front of her face. *Oh, great! That helps a bunch!* she thought.

She felt like the wanderer in the desert who stumbled upon an oasis as she stepped into the cool air of room 229. The office had little décor at all. At first she figured there must have been a recent move for her new boss, but later she would find that it was just his taste. "Less is more," he would often say to her. The office was ringed with dark grey wainscoting, trimmed with a functional lighter grey at a chair-railing height topped by a picture-less stark white all the way to the ceiling.

There, positioned at the mathematical epicenter of the room behind a 1959 Government Issue rounded grey metal desk was Ned Smarny. "Welcome to my new home away from home," he gestured to one of two standard No. 38 black chairs with casters parked in front of his desk as he mocked standing up a bit. "Please have a seat, Andrea."

As she was making her way to the seat (she had always taken the seat on the right on such occasions) she heard him ask, "So what do you think of the design?"

Nodding as she looked around just enough to make sure her eyes had not played a joke on her brain, nope...the room was still just as she had seen it, she said, "It's very...institutional?"

"I prefer the word spartan. 'A clean room makes for clean thinking.' Got that from the *More Habits* book. It's a great read, don't you think?"

Lying, she said with a face that matched the room, "Oh yes...great!"

Changing the tone and direction a little, Ned asked, "So what do you have there?" He pointed at the folder of askew papers in her lap.

"Oh, this? I did a little studying last night at the research center."

"Impressive initiative. Anything good happen in the last forty-eight hours?"

She sorted through the mess and found the three reports. They were now riddled with highlighter marks and notes made in blue ink. "Yes, I think I have found something here." She placed the first report on Ned's desk facing him and with some excitement started her well-rehearsed presentation, "Ten days ago, a vampire was killed in New York City. Local authorities think it was a drug addict that unfortunately hooked up with some satanic cult. They claim a blood sacrifice was responsible for the seriously low blood levels found in the cadaver."

Ned made a happy sort of smirk trying to look duly impressed as a new boss.

Placing the next report on the desk, tiled over the first so some marks from both were still visible, "And here, two of these Croatoan thingies were seen in a public gathering spot in the Village during broad daylight. From what I gather that is highly unusual behavior."

Ned nodded an affirmation and gestured for her to continue without interruption. She thought he was saving his congratulatory comments for after her presentation.

Placing the last stack on the desk, she concluded, "Lastly, this report shows that the *number one* location for Internet local cross-referenced searches for sites with contiguous geographical locals is..." she paused for dramatic effect, "New York City!"

She sat back a little and waiting for the big smile to cross her new boss's face.

"...and?"

Realizing he wasn't making the connection, she concluded further, "…and…there seems to be a lot of activity in New York."

"…and what are we supposed to do about that?" he asked with a voice that suggested he needed yet another conclusion.

Andrea controlled a growing frustration. These guys were supposed to be the best of the best, "…and…we should go up there and bust someone, you know…arrest some bad guys!" She hoped this would make her new boss happy.

Ned took a moment to let things settle a little before he responded, "Rule Number 1."

"Excuse me?" Andrea asked sincerely, as if she had not heard him correctly.

"Rule Number 1. Never outshine the master." Ned waited for a flash of recognition and clearly not getting one out of the confused look on her face, he continued, "It's from *48 Rules to Power*…you know…Greene?" Still nothing. Ned always found it hard to believe that upwardly mobile people had not read all the same authors. And he had an even harder time believing that there could be any kind of professional *other* than upwardly mobile. Then clearing his throat and continuing, "You haven't read it?"

"Well, Agent Smarny…"…"

"Ned," he said.

"Ned," she said through her best first-day smile and blinked a few times. "To tell you the truth, Ned…I just haven't ever been one much for 'self-help books'."

Now it was Ned's turn to blink.

At length, he asked, "So how do you shape your future? How are you planning to climb Success Ladder?" He pantomimed a little ladder climbing.

"Well…to be honest…um…I've always sorta believed that if a person works hard, and excels in what they do…that it all sort of works itself out. You know what they say, 'The cream rises to the top!'" She smiled.

"Um…yeah…ok…maybe that is something we can add to your work plan for the year. Yeah…that would work. We can read some management books together and think about ways to improve your career prospects. Then we can use the results as part of your year-end evaluation. What do you say, trooper?" He had that used car lot smile on.

Not wanting to get off on the wrong foot, though she had some concern it might be far too late for such caution, she nodded, "Ok…we can try that."

Ned re-gathered his initial point, "Now, as I was saying…'Never outshine the master!'"

"*48 Rules*," she quickly said in a voice that was perhaps a little too strong for the size of the room.

Ned blinked.

"Right…*48 Rules*. What I mean is…I appreciate your effort, but you are still new here. Let me see if I can guide you a little bit, young padawan."

She shifted her weight and kept that winning smile up despite the inner fight to now engage this man in open combat.

Guiding, he said, "First off, we do not 'arrest' anyone." He made little quote marks with his fingers. "We are an investigative branch. We investigate. That's it. If something crosses legal lines, we notify local authorities."

"Got it," she agreed.

"And if we did 'arrest' people," yet another set of quotes, "who would we 'arrest' in this case?" She did concede there were no concrete leads. But she had speculated that the Agency had a list of all the bad guys and knew their whereabouts. Ned had just taken a test from her and hadn't even realized it. She had an answer to a question she didn't even have to ask.

She also had become convinced that if he did the little finger quotes thing just one more time that there would be at least one concrete lead after the bloodshed here.

Ned said, "Finally, let me ask you a question…what is the date on the Statistical Report?" It was a rhetorical question. The date was on the corner facing him in plain view. She let him answer it. "October 10th…for the past month…which just happens to have included the first anniversary of the largest hostile terrorist attack on U.S. soil in history." The weight of the point and the truth of it knocked the wind out of her sails. "Don't you imagine that maybe a few people in this great wide world were accessing information on all kinds of disparate sites located in New York City during the past month?"

"Good point," she conceded.

"But still you are showing the right initiative. Just not the right action."

"I'm sorry, I don't follow you," she honestly asked again.

"We don't need people to do research, formulate opinions and theories, and then come begging for direction from a superior."

"Well, I can't just go jump on a plane and fly to New York."

"That is precisely what you can do. I have been known to engage on far less information than what you have there. I want to work on that area first. From your files and what I see in you now, you may be too conservative for your own safety and need to learn to follow your instincts more."

This lesson was the polar opposite than the one she was expecting to receive. She had made a bad conclusion based on misunderstood data and her boss was riding her that she *didn't* start a land-war in Southeast Asia over it.

"Ok…I will try to do better."

"You will fail," he said matter-of-factly.

"What?"

Doing his best alien voice, he quoted, "This is why you fail. Do or do not. There is no try."

"Yes, master," she mocked. Andrea felt all off-balance. This was not going well and she just wasn't really able to find any traction with this new boss. It seemed like any direction she attempted was completely wrong.

"You really need to lose the conservative, cautious-cop bit. In this business, you are either sharp or dead. To be frank, it almost prevented us from approaching you."

Andrea took this as genuine concern and advice and forced her mind to receive it. After a bit, she asked, "Ok…when do I start my orientation?"

"Orientation?" Ned asked this as if she had spoken a foreign language. Then with a look of sudden understanding, "Oh! Orientation. Right."

With this, Ned turned around to the grey cabinet that ran the wall behind him. In a fancier office, this might have been called a credenza. He opened the cabinet and pulled out a small box. He then spun around and placed the box on his desk and started rummaging through it pulling items out one at a time and placing them on the desk in front of her.

"One identification badge in wallet. By the way that is recognized at a federal level by all law enforcement agencies. One service revolver with silver bullets."

"Did you say silver bullets?"

Looking up at her, he deadpanned, "You have to ask?"

"No," she replied with a quick shake of the head that also suggested he continue.

"One stun gun, one corporate gold card—for expenses only, one satellite phone, and one assignment folder with your first assignment information inside." Ned took the now empty box and placed it on the floor. While they continued to talk, he took out a sticker from his desk and wrote "Trash, Basura" on it. Then he applied the sticker on the box and moved it next to his waste can. Andrea noted how coldly efficient this man was.

Looking at the items displayed before her, which were waiting for her to pick them up and make them a new part of her life, she asked, "That's it?"

Ned looked up from his label-making with a determined look that communicated a growing impatience. "Andrea," then a slight change, "May I call you Andrea?"

"It's my name."

"Fine." Now back to the original timbre, "Andrea…we don't hire rookies. You were selected because you had all the abilities necessary already. I trust that you will do the right thing."

"Ok…so I just go do whatever is in that folder?"

"Don't worry. I'm going to give you some instruction. I just didn't want you to expect a classroom with rows of desks and initiates running around in jumpsuits and baseball caps."

"Understood," she said in an effort to get the conversation going again.

"The silver has been known to work on some legend type suspects in the past. Either way, it works on normal suspects as well. Better safe than sorry.

"The satellite phone works as an IP phone when you're near a free hotspot or WiFi, a cell phone on both analog and digital SS7 networks, and as a satellite phone with GPS. Its wings open up there by pressing the two small yellow buttons with your thumbs," she had picked up the phone and was doing this as he was speaking, "and you can use the split keyboard on the wings for text messaging.

"All of your contacts are already programmed in. You can get help on any functionality on the view screen there. It also carries your agenda from your assignment folder with to-do lists that can be checked off as you go. These are automatically communicated back to the Center so we can keep up without formal reports during an assignment.

"And the assignment?"

"Did you get your car?"

"Yes."

"Good. All the information is in the folder there. You're going to find some *real* information on the bad guys. But I am afraid it might not be quite as glamorous as you may think. History question: Do you know how they finally got Capone?"

"Are you telling me the boogeyman files taxes?"

"Cute. But close. There is an account that was opened in a bank in Peabody, Massachusetts a long, long time ago. The money sat idle for decades, just drawing interest. At the beginning of this week, someone requested an ACH transfer out of that bank."

"ACH?" she asked.

"It stands for Automated Clearing House. It's the transfer rules that have been in place for banks for decades. It is how one bank sends money officially to another bank."

"Like a wire transfer?"

"Similar, but still different. Fed Wire Transfers involve...well, the Fed— where ACH is more like a contract between two banks."

"Where did the transfer go?"

"Now *that* is precisely what you are going to tell me on Sunday."

"But that would require a court order," she observed.

"It's in there. Follow the directions in your folder and drive to the airport. It's really more of a small landing field not too far from the Center. Look for the hangar that belongs to Steven Knight of Knight-Flight Charters. He is an old friend to our Agency and will always take care of you, no questions asked.

"Charter up to Peabody and serve the papers. The bank is open on Saturday from 10:00 a.m. to 12:00 noon. So you have plenty of time to get up there today and spend the night. Find the bank and serve the papers. It may take them a week to ten days to do the research, which is stupid because all it takes is a few keystrokes, but that is the rule-of-thumb judges follow and allow. The fax number they should send the results to is on the order. It will come to your email account in a special fax folder, which you can access from the PC in your townhouse.

"Any questions?"

"Yeah, hundreds...but I'll try to figure them out as best I can. One quick one, though...stun gun?"

"Oh, yeah!" he replied with renewed cheer as if he had just remembered something humorous from his past, "It's set at a different amperage and frequency than the normal ones. It doesn't really hurt most people, but it plays hell on the nervous system of a Croatoan. Seems like there is something having to do with energy in the way they work. One good zap and it wrecks them up—almost as bad as fire."

"Fire?"

"The only way we know of to kill them," he said plainly.

"So they really are supernatural?" she asked.

"Hmmm...I'm not so sure I would use the word 'super.' It's too metaphysical for my taste. They are definitely natural. But at the same time, they are extremely strong, live a long time, and have very unpleasant ways of killing people from the evidence left behind."

She raised an eyebrow, "Care to share any more?"

"Agent Ellijay, this is the way we operate. New recruits are to be given assignments, and then come back here to the Center. You learn as you go, between and during your assignments. It prevents one from becoming obsessed with the subject. I have provided quite enough for you to be successful. Just return here after serving the papers with your soul and body still in one piece. I look forward to reading your report on Sunday. Please drop it off here any time."

Andrea took that as her awkward cue to leave. Being exceedingly glad she had brought her Sak purse, she gathered up the ID, stun gun, and service revolver with the phone and placed them inside. Then she collected her reports, placed them back in her folder, which she cupped in her left hand with the assignment folder. She then stood. Ned did his little polite half-stand as she turned to make her way out.

As she reached the threshold he said, "Best of luck to you, Ellijay. Welcome to the game."

"Thanks for having me," she replied, not quite sure if she should turn completely around and look him in the eye. She chose to just keep on going.

As she clip-clopped down the still, stoic hall, the realization of the meeting came crashing down. Her thoughts rose up noisily, *New job, great pay, awesome bennies, great new home, fascinating things to learn...and a complete gimboid for a boss. He is the biggest smeg-head I have ever seen in my life!*

She could sense her blood pressure was rising with the volume of her inner monologue, so she tried to bring it back down a level as she brought herself back down a level on the stairs, *Ok, it's like I always told Terri on the GBI: All work sucks. That's why they pay you. If it didn't suck...they would charge admission and call it Six Flags.*

Feeling somewhat better as she hit the main floor, she noticed an office on the left with the name Casper James stenciled on the door. Her heart dropped a bit when she saw that the lights were off and the door shut tight. She made for the exit and as she passed Bucky's head, she reviewed some notes in the folder detailing her first assignment. Pushing the front door open, she concluded out loud, "And this sure as hell ain't Six Flags."

Thoughts swirled as she made the brief walk back to her townhouse. She could maybe get past this first impression of Mr. Smarny...though it would be difficult. He *had* shown an interest and *did* seem sincere a few times.

Fighting for a piece of her consciousness turf was the feeling of being completely unprepared to handle the assignment she now carried in her arms. Another Sumo wrestler attempting to take center ring was the thought of how crazy all this was. She would have written the whole lot of them off to the funny farm had she not been able to still feel that limbo stick resist a little as she penetrated the creature's heart. She could still smell the tainted odor that escaped.

As all these thoughts joined in a giant tag-team main event, she did not even realize she had crossed the quad, made it into her townhouse, placed her keys on the hall stand, made her way upstairs, and was now standing in her bedroom cluttered with unpacked suitcases and boxes. She stared at the bed. The only thing she had managed to unpack was her overnight bag with jammies and her toiletries.

"The one thing I have unpacked...and now I have to pack it up again."

She started to cry.

She spoke out loud really hoping someone was there to answer, but desperately knowing that there was not. "Is this right? Is it right to birth a child into this world knowing that they could lose everything? Is it fair that I have no one to talk to?"

She was outright sobbing now.

"How am I supposed to do this job? Who am I? Van-Fucking-Helsing?!"

Her fists were clenched to the point of pressing little smiley-faced purple dimples across her palms—a twisted, anti-metaphor. Her sobs were at their peak as she felt that tremendous shudder that signaled to her that the tantrum was nearly over. They passed quickly after she turned eight or so in her first foster home.

As she sniffled, she grabbed the bottom of her sleeve with her right hand rubbing the moisture from under her nose and eyes in big swipes as she picked up one item after another and virtually threw them into her overnight bag.

This activity went on for about ten minutes with frequent interruptions to make a trip to the bathroom to pick up yet another unpacked item and throw it back into the pack. With each item, her sorrow diminished. With each item, the need to do this job increased.

At last, she had an overnight bag ready to go. Her face was relatively dry, albeit a little red and chafed.

Andrea carried the pack down to her car, and after making sure the townhouse was duly locked, she jumped in and started the engine. Thinking twice about it, she decided to lower the top. This of course would require a sweater to go with her white blouse, so she went through the trouble of stopping the car, going back inside, getting a navy cardigan with white stripes on the cuffs and hems, coming back outside, and locking up like a good girl. She jumped back in and adjusted the heater to moderate the slight chill in the air.

It was nearly 5:00 p.m. when she made it to the airstrip. It was small, yet functional. The northeast to southwest smart runway would allow pilots to take off and land with the least amount of crosswind for these parts. Four hangars lined the northwest side of the strip. The second of these had a logo of a large, black knight in armor in front of a rising full moon.

"Clever," she said aloud as she pulled into the small parking area next to the hangar. She took a moment to put her top back up, get her bags, and lock up the car. Then she went around to the front of the hangar where she entered the door to the small office on the side. The door chime announced her presence to a bright looking man in his fifties standing behind a counter. His salt-and-pepper hair was accented by the pair of aviator sunglasses on his face that always had a way of "just looking cool" to Andrea.

"I should take up flying just to get to wear the cool glasses!" she said.

"Oh, thank you. I've had them for years."

"I'm Andrea Ellijay. I'm from the Center and I would like to charter a flight to Peabody Mass, if I may." She said this as she extended a hand from under her overnight bag strap in a good-natured show of friendship.

The man did not reach out to shake hands at first. Then he shifted a little and said, "Oh, yes. The new agent," now he reached out to grasp her hand missing a little at first, but finding it ok after that. "I'm Steven Knight, the proprietor here. We were expecting you. The Center calls ahead most of the time—especially if the assignment has an itinerary. But it's hardly necessary, we are wired in…so to speak."

He gestured over his shoulder to a computer on a desk against the far wall. Andrea noted that in front of the keyboard running its length was a flat bar that was four inches deep. Its surface was comprised completely of small silver pins that could rise and fall independent of one another. Further, the screen was displaying text only. There were no windows or fancy graphics. She realized from all of this that the bar was a brail encoder and that Mr. Knight was blind.

Now speaking with a slightly louder voice she said, "Great! When can we leave?"

With a visible grimace on his face, he chuckled, "Blind people hear fine, you know. You don't have to shout."

"Oh, sorry."

"Quite alright…happens all the time. You know…I've always wondered if people squint at the hearing impaired while communicating in sign language." This he said dryly, but they both ended up snickering a little at it.

"Mr. Knight?"

"Steven."

"Steven. Well met, sir," she said rather formally.

"Well met, indeed," he replied with a little bow.

"When does your chariot depart for Peabody? And if you don't mind me asking…"

He interrupted her, "Right now. And no, I am *not* the pilot." Then he continued after she stopped giggling, "Although I guess I could be…You see, even though I probably wouldn't pass the FAA physical…technically I still have my flying license. I just can't get insurance. Now if you wouldn't mind signing a legal waiver…I could probably do it 'by feel' if I could just get someone to yell Left, Right, Up and Down! You game?"

"You know…I'll have to take you up on that very tempting offer some other time. But for now, I think I need to be getting to Peabody."

"Very well. No problem." Then he pressed a button on the phone system in front of him and said, "Tim, Ms. Ellijay is ready to depart." Then back to her he said, "Tim will take your bag for you."

And as if on cue, a tall, kind-looking man came through the door behind Steven. Andrea was only half relieved to see that he was not carrying a white cane because it really wasn't expected. Tim said his salutations to her and after the introductions, politely asked her to follow him out to the Gulfstream G-450 now ready on the tarmac. As she was leaving, Steven called after her, "I'll keep an eye on your car for you."

"Very funny," she said back to this most charming man.

"You're right, I'll probably take it for a joyride. I'm kind of wild that way.".

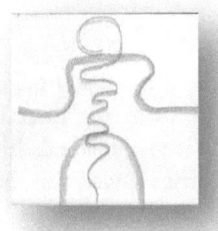

8.

12.19.9.11.16.7917; 9 YAX, 11 CIB — SOUL (CONTINUED)

October 11, 2002, 7:00 p.m. EST

While the Gulfstream G-450 knifed its way through the clouds towards Peabody, Massachusetts, down below and not too far to the west in upstate New York, a silver coupe was knifing its way through the fog and mist along the curvy roads that traversed a heavily wooded area where large mansions were set far back from prying eyes. Danreck was relaxed and listening to his favorite CD—*Stan Kenton Cuban Fire*. The band was just hitting the hottest part of *La Suerte De Los Tontos*. He had always loved that era. Kenton was so ahead of his time.

Danreck got a mental image of dinner jackets and pocket squares—those thin handkerchiefs that were pressed sharp for looks only. Angled shoulders, thin lapels, and a cigarette held coolly by a hand bedecked with just the right touch of gold were fashion icons lost on this eclectic age of junk-dressers. He remembered the time he watched this very band play this very number and the lady in the deep red velvet dress shared herself with him before sharing her *self* with him.

Things were going well. His Mission was coming together nicely and everything was right on schedule. He could make this one appearance required by etiquette and be back home before midnight. Best of all, the groundwork so tirelessly laid to expose the Order was going to finally pay off. This was a mid-election year, after all. There would be senate hearings and congressional subcommittees set up for months on end trying to get at the bottom of this. Most importantly, the serum would be public and the Cause could finally move forward in a *big* way!

He blended with the contour of the touring sedan's seat as he accelerated slightly with the music's climax. The timing of it could not have been any more perfect for as the song relented to its conclusion, his destination came into view.

Danreck turned onto the drive that led a short distance up to two very sturdy looking private guards at a substantial gate. As one of them peered through the dark windshield from his post inside one of the two brick keeps that were sentinels to the entrance, he waved to "drive on" after recognizing the guest. The other guard was busy opening the large, black, wrought-iron gate.

It was another minor journey just covering the distance from the entrance up to the main house. As he approached, he marveled at the sight of the manor. It was relatively plain, but stately and large enough to be deceiving in size. Danreck pulled up to the main turnaround and motored down as he exited the car. Making his way across the cobblestone park, the doors swung open for him from atop the five sculptured-marble steps.

As he approached, the man holding the door said, "Good evening, Mr. Porter. Good to have you back at the estate after all this time."

"Thanks, Vincent. Good to be back."

"Begging your pardon, sir, but Vincent was my father. I am Dalton."

Smugly, Danreck said, "Then it has been a long time after all." And he did not even break his stride as he crossed the threshold and entered the main hall.

Due to the darkness of the hardwood shadows in the early evening, the inside was ablaze in the golden yellow light cast by the five main chandeliers. The rich, dark, wood furniture and the marble floors made for a scene just perfect for a fancy party where guests spent entirely too much time getting dressed for the occasion. But tonight, there were only a handful of people milling around various parts of the mansion.

Danreck cut through the main hall and up the east wing to the suite at the end. He pulled up short when he stepped through the main doors only to find the second door to the main study shut tight.

"Hullo, Danreck!"

Danreck spun around and spied an old friend sitting in a large, wingback chair in this antechamber. "Harlan Banachek! As I live and breathe," then an aside, "as it were. How are you my old friend?"

"Not so old these days. I feel young like I did in 1932!" Harlan stood and shook hands with Danreck, a gesture that became a warm hug with slaps on the back. "And I understand that you are partly responsible for this!

"He is busy just yet—a tribute to your recent work. He is in there with *him* again, his faithful number one. They seem very intent on spinning out all the possible threads from your latest task. Please, sit with me old friend and catch me up some."

"Catch you up?" Danreck moved to a chair beside Harlan and they both sat down. "Catch *me* up, is more like it! I haven't seen you since…"

"Munich. The end of it all."

"Now *that* was a Mission!" Danreck said as Harlan pulled out a thin, silver cigarette case and extended it open to him. It was his trademark Treasurer Cigarettes. With their silver foil-wrapped filters and watermarked paper, even aficionados knew them as posh. A single pack sells for as much as two cartons of the finer brands. They both took one of the long elegant cigarettes and held them while Harlan deftly closed the case with one hand and slid it back in his jacket pocket.

Harlan knew that they were two of the few Croatoan that had conquered their innate fear of fire. Danreck had even developed a notoriously perverse enjoyment of it, living dangerously with its play. Knowing Danreck was always equipped with some trinket of interest, he asked with the slightest of accents that matched the slightness of his frame and the thin mustache that was only just now coming back into vogue, "Do you have a light, Heir Porter?"

"But of course, my good man!" Danreck said with a weighty British accent as he produced a Tiffany lighter and ignited first Harlan's and then his. The top of the lighter made a tight click sound as he closed it and placed it back in his pocket.

"Europe has been so bland since then. The cold war was just that, my friend—cold. So much boredom mixed with angst, grey mixed with concrete and steel. Sometimes I could swear that the Iron Curtain didn't fall, but just rusted away from the blandness of it all."

"But you got a lot accomplished, my friend."

"Yes, but most of it was in the 40's. The rest was some long kind of anticlimactic letdown. I would have sworn that that crazy-ass Pollock Croatoan would have had Hacquee in position to finish our Cause by 1945."

"He was not counting on the U.S. getting in on the action—at least not yet. He was close, that is for sure."

Harlan took a deep drag off of his cigarette. At the end of it, there was a little wisp of smoke that escaped his mouth and disappeared into his nose. Then he slowly let out a long trail of smoke with a contented sigh. "These things will kill you, you know."

They both laughed at the irony.

Then Harlan asked in all seriousness, "What do you think happened to him? I mean, I really can't understand how the ending was ever able to come about."

"I think he was just what you said—crazy."

Both of them let that word hang in the air with the smoke.

Then after a moment, "I suppose you could be right, dear friend. That would explain the command to burn them both."

Danreck nodded slowly. Harlan then asked, "Do you think she was insane as well?"

"Not likely. He shot her in the head, first. But that would have just slowed her down a bit. I think it was just to give the soldiers time to light the fire. He shot himself as well, maybe to avoid legends forming around the process of their consumption."

"You are probably right."

"You know the one part that really blows my mind?" Danreck asked.

"Every pun intended?"

Danreck chuckled, "Yeah…every pun intended."

"Good. I hate to see a good pun go to waste."

"You and me both, friend," Danreck countered.

"What, Danreck? Tell me what blows your mind." Harlan made a gesture of a two-finger gun like a Derringer Saturday Night Special pointed at his temple as he mocked the recoil from a shot, all the time his cigarette burning between extended fingers. The trail of smoke that followed his hand made it all look eerily too real.

"The world never figured it out," Danreck said matter-of-factly.

"How so?"

"You have a young, idealistic, vegetarian oil painter…an artist for Christ's sake!…who *loves* his own Jewish grandfather dearly. Then boom! You get the Beer Hall Putsch."

Harlan added, "He even changed his name from Schickelgruber!"

"You have to admit, *that* was a smart move. Hard to get all worked up with fear over a Schickelgruber."

"Jerge Stromduski was an unappreciated genius," Harlan postulated.

"You can say that again, brother. He invaded Poland first!"

Harlan had a melancholy look slide across his face, "Good times. We were all very, very busy for a long, long time. I remember being drunk with all the souls harvested. But look at my manners. You have driven a long way. Would you like a beverage?"

"Sounds delightful. I believe your favorite was Scotch?"

Harlan stood and crossed to the small but well-stocked bar on the other side of the large French doors that were the main opening to this room. He quickly found two tumblers and used the tongs to neatly place three cubes of ice in each glass with three distinctive clinks. Then quietly poured the Scotch, all the time humming a soft version of a popular song from Germany during World War II.

"I remember that tune," Danreck said.

"Yes. Those were good times, indeed. We were permitted for a time to practice our craft in broad daylight. The world thought nothing of it. They all just accepted it as part of the evil they were fighting."

Danreck allowed himself to wax philosophical for a moment, "You know, there are humans today that honestly believe that none of the atrocities ever happened. I think that is a tribute to the fact you just pointed out. The entire world watched as we openly played with their secret desires. And now looking back on it, their inaction would bring so much guilt, that the mere thought of it makes them want to wish it all away."

Harlan agreed with the conclusion, "Better to wish something away than bear the burden of guilt. It is their way in all things."

Then Danreck chimed in, "Denial…it's not just for breakfast anymore."

"It's what's for dinner!" said Harlan, and they both had a healthy laugh.

They both were a little bothered by this thought for a while. Harlan sipped from the tumbler and Danreck now smoked in a way that would have made the bandstand envious. After a nice pause in the conversation where ice drifted into the sides of glasses and more thin cirrus clouds were added to the upper atmosphere of the room, Harlan interrupted the peaceful silence with some ominous news, "Francois is dead."

"No!"

"Yes—only last week. I am surprised you have not heard.

"Well, I have been rather busy, and that is news from Europe. How did it happen?"

"He jacked into a short-circuit. Some tart from Whales. It went horribly for him according to her account to the police. But since there was little evidence that remained, they chalked it up to a bee sting for her and yet another probably-fabricated tale of spontaneous combustion for one of those unsolved legends shows you Americans love so much."

"To Francois!" Danreck insisted as he raised his tumbler in an outreached salute.

"To Francois!" Harlan echoed and clinked the extended glass. They both took a sip from the Scotch, which was just now hitting that perfect temperature where the flavor is smoothest.

Harlan quizzed Danreck, "Do you remember when Francois got into that whole first dynasty kick?"

"Funny you should mention that, I just spoke of that to Josephine not three days ago."

Harlan continued without breaking thought, "He really thought he was on to the whole Pharaoh Menes's alchemic formula from the Minoans. He really pissed off Hacquee as he went on that tare around Europe after the war, breaking into all those museums trying to piece the puzzle together."

"He was afraid Francois would draw too much attention to the Cause," Danreck defended.

"Please…the whole of the human race hasn't figured out anything about us for four centuries. How would a little crazy serial looting tip them off to anything?"

"It was just such clumsiness by those idiot vampires at the Lyceum Theatre that turned a whispered superstition into a best seller for that sickly Irishman, Stoker. Hacquee was right to be guarded and we have remained in the shadow while humans make millions off of their vampiric tales and legends," Danreck continued to defend.

"Well, I found the whole thing so amusing. Especially when Francois found himself locked in that first dynasty sarcophagus in Munich," Harlan reminisced with a telling grin.

"I was not amused."

"You didn't *look* amused then, either. There you were, trying with all your might to open that lid from the wrong direction! You thought it was some sort of amazingly clever engineering when the whole time it was a simple matter of leverage."

"Who ever heard of a sarcophagus opening from the right side? Besides, I eventually *did* get it open!" Danreck said with a visible pride.

"Ripping off the bolt mechanism at the seams as you did so is the opposite of clever. I remember just standing back and laughing!" Harlan chided.

"It was messy," Danreck confessed, "and it was clumsy. We had to kill that guard, remember? A wasted seed and needless attention drawn to the Cause." Danreck was beginning to feel a little miffed at the memory of it all.

"Well we were all three already on Missions," Harlan gave by way of an excuse, "It was a free-for-all at the end of that war," Harlan reminded Danreck.

"And in the middle of it all, there was Francois trying to unlock the secrets of Minoan alchemy. It was silly and reckless."

"But amazingly fun to chase him like a rabbit across the continent for those four months," Harlan sighed, "Munich brought an end to the party."

"And now some 'short-circuit' from England has brought an end to our rabbit," Danreck mournfully added.

Harlan continued with disdain, "The bitch still doesn't know she is a carrier."

"They seldom do. I mean, if they have enough symptoms to *know*, we would never attempt to harvest them to begin with. No, my friend, when this kind of tragedy happens to one of us, the harvest-target never *knows* they are a short-circuit."

Then with some sense of cruel revenge, Harlan said, "I guess the joke will be on her in another couple of years. Francois went quickly. Hers will drag out for painful years."

"That is not enough consolation for me, Harlan. We must eradicate this plague from our destined harvest so the Cause may be made complete. If it weren't for the Order and those damned vampires protecting them we would have finished the task centuries ago."

"Fuck the vampires," Harlan said flatly.

"Indeed." And they made another mock toast as they continued.

Harlan said, "They are just jealous of our ability to harvest. They have attempted to develop it for many years now in Europe, even calling it 'Sharing' but they have to do it with other vampires and it is only a baser form of sex to them. They hate us for it and use the Order in a vain attempt to thwart our efforts."

"The interesting thing is, I don't think the Order even knows they are allies," Danreck speculated.

"Of course not! The vampires play far too much the erudite to actually *admit* that is what they are doing. They see the human race as so much cattle, herds that must be maintained and fed, kept happy so they may feast on them as they wish. It is only this strange sense of husbandry that gets a select few of them involved in the first place."

Danreck agreed, "They see us as the predators attempting to thin out the flock." Then turning a sinister eye towards his old friend he added, "but the farmers don't realize we predators like *them* just as much as we like their cattle!"

They both grinned and nodded.

"I both love and loathe to harvest vampires," Harlan said.

"You are right, sometimes their Mission can become long and intricate—they have lived so long and know so many different temptations and morals," Danreck said.

"But what a payoff! Their life's experience is deep and their seeds are powerful." Then Harlan turned more towards Danreck by shifting in his chair, "You, my friend lucked out."

"Luck, hell! It was skill!" Then lowering his expression and dipping his head into a scowling glance from left to right, "The mighty hunter, drifting through the dangerous streets of New York searching for his next prey…"

"You are too much the card, Danreck."

"The Ace of Spades, baby!"

"No, old friend…the Ace is in there," Harlan gestured towards the closed doors with his cigarette. "You are the Joker!"

"Well, this Joker tied into a sweet seed this time: plenty of life, a Mission that fits into our Cause, possibly the end of something that has plagued the dear humans for centuries, and I can pull the entire thing off in what? Two short weeks!"

"That is why I am here," Harlan said.

"Oh, really? But I told the Cause that I had enough help. Everything is in order."

"No, my friend. Not for *your* Mission, for *his* campaign that will follow.

Our leader has everything in place: The congressman that will introduce the sets of legislation, the FDA that will fast-track the production, the pharmaceutical companies that will ramp up the fastest cooperative venture the world has *ever* seen and the insurance and medical networks that will see to it that our Cause will be prepared within two years to begin our dream. We should be able to be complete it in only five or six more years after that if all goes well!"

"I had no idea so much was in the works. I love the company we work for," Danreck smiled.

"I love the work!" Harlan said in a way that would complement Danreck's sentiments. "Josephine was an inspired stroke, if I do say so."

"Thanks," Danreck answered with some humility.

"Was it political?"

"I never discuss politics at the office," Danreck sidestepped.

"Very clever. But your choice of her...why?"

"Well, the timing was right, and she was in the neighborhood, so to speak."

"You are a brave man, Danreck."

"To be honest, Harlan, I really don't see why so many of us Seconds have such a hard time involving the Thirds."

"Because they are his children? His direct heirs? I would imagine that might have something to do with it," Harlan proffered.

Danreck countered, "That's bunk. They are Croatoan. We are all part of the Cause. They will benefit as much as we will from its successful completion. Why should they be allowed to just go around the world harvesting at will and taking little one-offs that don't amount to anything in the grand scheme of things? They should at least contribute. The thing that is stopping them is knowledge. We Seconds must take on the responsibility of mentoring these."

"Bah!" Harland said with visible disgust, then whispering as if to prevent his words from traveling into the soundproof chamber next door, "They are nothing but a bunch of spoiled brats waiting for us to do all the heavy lifting."

"That is precisely what they will *become* if we don't engage them," Danreck said in a helpful tone, "But for right now, they are actually hungry for the knowledge we have from the Sharing. You should try to sit down with one sometime. It is actually quite stimulating being able to openly share some of our locked legacy with a fellow traveler."

"It seems dangerous, and especially with young Josephine. She is one of his favorites. You take a considerable risk, Danreck."

"Nah," Danreck said dismissively, "she will be fine. And what is more...he will see it as his daughter contributing to the catalyst...the beginning of the end as it were."

"Ah...so it *was* political," Harlan said in a 'gotcha' kind of way.

"I told you, I never talk politics at the office," came Danreck's poker-faced reply.

"I am glad to hear all is in order," Harlan said as he helped change the mood and direction of the conversation a little bit.

"You remember George?"

"George Burroughs?"

"Yeah...he harvested and took on the form of a trucker from Mississippi named Leroy!"

They both laughed at the Yankee playing a southern trucker.

"I wish I could see him. I will have to rub that in at the next Gathering."

"You do that. But he has pulled everything off splendidly. The first two barrels will be placed in position in about six hours. Christov will have the fuel in a safe place on Sunday, and Monday Isidora will have the rest of the catalyst items stored separately. We will stagger the remaining shipments over the next week until all is in place for the big show.

"I have the Southeastern five coordinators in place to watch over everything. But we found a basement with a back entrance directly off a little-used road that is perfect. It looked like it has been unused for decades."

"Who will be there to set everything off?"

"Oh, I will light this fuse. You know I have to do that," Danreck said as he tapped his own temple with his index finger indicating to Harlan the seed that was driving all of these events.

Just then the two large doors swung open. "That would be my cue," Danreck said as he stood, placed his drink on the table and stubbed out his cigarette. Smoothing his tailored slacks down a little, he said, "Hi-ho, hi-ho!"

"Good luck to you, Mr. Porter. I will see you after you recover. Do well, old friend!"

"And also with you, Mr. Banachek," Danreck said in a mock of the Catholic salutation.

Harlan saw Danreck step through the two open doors as he crossed to the shape in the shadows. As Danreck approached the great seat on the slightly raised platform, the lighting over his head cast a stark shadow on the floor. Harlan saw those golden glowing eyes widen in the darkness as Danreck kneeled. Harlan could still faintly hear Danreck's words as they echoed across the hall, "Hail, the beginning of the mighty rivers that bring us all eternal life."

Just then Harlan saw the two doors swing closed, guided by some unseen hand. They shut with a click that echoed through the halls. He swizzled the remaining small pieces of ice, took one last sip of his drink saying a quiet, private toast, "Until we meet again, *mon ami*." Not realizing that his toast would never come to fruition, he stubbed his cigarette out in the ashtray, and made his way rather ungracefully to his room in the west wing.

9.
12.19.9.11.17.2083; 10 YAX, 12 CABAN — EARTH

October 12, 2002, 5:00 a.m. EST

A great deal had happened to her since her last run. She worked for a different company, lived in a different city, and was now some eight states away from where she last laced up her running shoes. The old elevator sounded a ding as it slowly moved down from the fifth floor to the forth.

Andrea braced herself against a rail, stretching out her calves as she spoke to herself in the twilight silence of the ancient hotel. "Nice and easy…stretch and breathe. Plenty of oxygen to cut down cramps." As she inhaled through her nose, the pungent hotel elevator deodorizer stung the back of her sinuses and she tasted the mildew as she exhaled. It wasn't a dirty hotel. It was actually pristine as well as antique. It was just something she always noticed about elevators in hotels.

Ding.

"I wonder if they get a bulk discount buying from their bathroom scent people…" she mused during the next exhale. She marveled at the real wood finish on the inside of the elevator and noticed the crafted, inlaid floor as she shifted her weight and started working on the other leg. Inhale.

Ding.

"Hopefully somebody will be up. I suppose someone always has to be at the front desk." Andrea then inhaled as she looked up and noticed the Art Deco lamps that adorned the crown molding. "Crown molding in a fucking elevator. Shit." Exhale.

Ding.

The doors slid open with some degree of rubbing and friction. She stepped out into a lobby that was plush. Hell, it was downright opulent. She

101

had noticed the historical marker outside as she arrived the night before. She was impressed with the first forty-seven historical markers she had seen on her short trip from the nearby airport to her lodging for the evening. But somewhere around forty-eight, she had lost interest.

The night before had been relatively uneventful. The pilot known to her only as "Tim" had stayed at the airport. The flight had been chartered for two days by the Agency and he had told her that it was company policy since 9/11 for the pilot to stay with the plane on short trips.

The taxi ride was swift and smooth except where they had crossed the HP&S tracks. Quite some bumps were had there. But then the taxi sped back up and arrived swiftly at the hotel. She had marveled at what a mandated fare from the airport could do to driver's motivation.

She had stopped at a wine store next door and picked up a red zinfandel and a cheap corkscrew. "Expensive wine and a cheap screw," she had flirted with the clerk, "but never the other way around." Having checked into a room on the top story, which for this relic was the fifth floor, she had found her way out onto the classic balcony and drank her well-chosen vintage out of a standard-issue hotel plastic cup.

Hotels this nice usually had the small glass tumblers in the room but Andrea was in the habit of using the plastic one found near the vanity. From her borrowed past she felt more comfortable with things that were disposable. It is what the world thought of her.

She sat there for most of the evening playing the perfect gargoyle as an entire universe of life that was alien to her mogated like ameba in clusters of two, three, or more on the quaint streets below. All the happy couples…all the happy friends.

"Here's to a life that is yet to be. Here's a toast to a life that wasn't," raising her glass she said to the crowds below. No one returned the salute. The drab tone in her voice was more of a moment of uncharacteristic self-pity than anything. She was actually quite happy. She just felt a little off kilter from all the change. The loneliness was creeping back in. Loneliness was that bastard that seemed to have the key to her soul since memory out of time. Usually, she would just wrestle it to the entrance and show it the door. But this particular night, she welcomed it in like the old friend that it was and invited it to warm its cockles by the fire.

As she sat there pondering the deeper questions of life in a clean, white terrycloth robe with a big "W" on it from the hotel, she circled the tip of the middle finger of her right hand around the rim of the plastic cup as if it were the finest crystal. As she felt the moisture from a drop of wine that her lips had left behind, she thought again of Wren. She wondered if he had found his own way out as she had. She hoped so. She hoped he had found a nice, Christian woman and settled down. He deserved that. But at the same time she also selfishly hoped he hadn't.

The thought did cross her mind, and she almost did try to call him. But where to begin was the problem. She had no idea where to start looking for him, or if he would even remember her should she call, or even what she would say should she actually find him. She practiced a few lines out loud like a schoolgirl, her words falling harmlessly on the revelers below, losing their verve as they drifted down.

She also lost *her* verve. This night would be a necessary solitude for her. She actually appreciated the richness of her stillness. But even so…a seed was planted in her mind.

She noticed now as she crossed from the elevator to the clerk that the concierge desk seemed somehow lessened with the absence of a well-dressed, professional-looking woman behind it. Now it was just a cheap imitation antique desk with a paper name card—"Patsy." The night before, it had added an air of sophistication to this historically listed building. Now it sucked the very life out of the pre-dawn lobby. Andrea figured that everything looks different at 5:00 a.m.

The clerk at the front desk was certainly different. He was a gawky and gangly twenty-five at best. Straight, bowl-cut, greasy blond hair accented the nose that was far too large to feel at home on such a skinny face. Andrea was having difficulty deciding if his red vest made him look more like an escapee from the Icecapades or a violin player from a Greek restaurant that was down on his luck. She was just pondering this when his words startled her back into this dimension and universe.

"May I help you, Miss?"

"Sure! I have a few questions."

"You are in luck. I have a few answers."

Smiling, she said, "Good. I hope they fit. Shall I go first or shall we play Jeopardy?"

"Ummm…you go first."

"What is the correct answer to my first question for two-hundred, Alex."

He looked at her with a blank expression on his face. But after a few moments, he inanely said, "I'm sorry, I don't follow you."

"It's ok. The studio audience got it. My first real question: Is it safe to run here?"

"Oh sure. Not much happening this time of day other than some garbage pickup and delivery traffic," he answered without emotion or perk.

Andrea noticed the dark rings under his eyes. She thought it more a permanent feature than from the hours he kept. "Ok. Second question: Is there anything interesting to do in Peabody until around 10:00 a.m.?"

He perked up some and stuck an accusatory finger at her, "Aha! I can tell you are not from around here!"

Andrea quickly retorted, "What gave it away? My accent? Coming in by taxi last night? Staying in a hotel? Ah…I have it," she snapped her fingers, "it's because I just asked you what there was to do around here until 10:00 a.m.! You *are* sharp!"

The playful expression on her face softened the verbal assault a little. Looking back on it later, she was worried she had overdone it with the sarcasm.

"No…" he curled his voice a little for emphasis, "It's because you called it 'Peabody.'"

Andrea blinked.

Taking his cue that she was clueless to his point, the clerk continued, "You see…people from around these parts call it Peab'dy."

This last he pronounced much like you might say "pea bidet" or puberty if it were spelled "pea-b-dy." None of the syllables had a particular accent and the "ah" of the "o" was distinctly missing. The end result was a word uniquely Yankee and very much Massachusetts.

"Peab'dy," Andrea repeated flatly.

"Yes. We can tell the strangers from the locals by their saying Pea-BAH-dy. Stands out wicked pissa."

Her tongue made an audible tick from the roof of her mouth as she got it in position to echo, "wicked pissa."

"Ayuh."

"Ok…I will try to fit Peab'dy in between the 'y'alls' and the 'aints' and no one will suspect a thing."

"Plenty to do."

"Pardon me?"

Now it was his turn to switch on the sarcasm. Speaking slowly as if to be understood by a foreigner, "There…is…plenty…to…do…" he noticed the flash of foreboding doom cross her face and decided to pick up the pace, "around here until 10:00 a.m. It is Saturday so most of the shops will be open at 9:00. But until then, there are some early bistros and coffee shops along the Avenue there." He indicated the road outside the door. Looking that way, all she saw was dark on the other side of the glass.

"Great! Last question: Which way to the Peab'dy Savings and Loan?"

"Three blocks up to your left. Then if you take my advice, you will cut right through a narrow lane two blocks. When you come out on the high street cut right again and come back one block. It will save you a trip around the square that way." He smiled as if he were glad the test was over and he felt he had passed. Now he could go back to his life without having to be quizzed for a few more hours. If he were lucky, the next shift would replace him before anyone else threatened to expose his severe lack of everything cerebral.

Andrea stepped towards the front door, this time at a much increased pace—nearly a jog. She would change to a full run as soon as her laced-up running shoes hit the pavement. "Thanks for your help, Peab'dy," she called over her shoulder.

"Don't mention it," he said as the door closed behind her. Then he concluded to an empty lobby, "…at all."

The soles of Andrea's shoes began slapping the sidewalk keeping the familiar time with her breathing as she reached her target pace. But there was no need for her to clear her mind this time. She was focused on the job she needed to do, light work though it may be. All the other problems disappeared with the stroke of the governor's pen in Georgia four days earlier. That is, if he even had to sign anything.

The brick buildings were only interrupted by buildings sided with whitewashed wood as she moved down the road at a fairly stable clip. The pre-dawn air was a chilly fifty degrees or so, but her own furnace inside was already being stoked from the friction of movement and increased circulation. She slowed only at the end of each long block for just enough time to check for any traffic on the little side streets before crossing to the next corner.

It wasn't the grey wolf running alongside of her that bothered her. She was used to him. She was actually more at ease with his return. It was his absence at the Center that was a little unnerving. He would come and go out of her life occasionally for long periods of time, but his disappearance in direct relation to her sudden move from the state in which she had spent her life was disconcerting.

Now his presence beside her was actually comforting.

It was more in the way he kept looking back over his left shoulder— that, coupled with an uneasy feeling something was wrong, was what bothered her. She remembered once hearing that talking to a running partner was a good technique. If your words became broken or jerky, you were overdoing it and should slow down. So she would, from time to time, talk to her running partner as she did now, "What is it, boy?"

She took a moment to look back as she ran. Her heart skipped a step when she thought she might have seen a figure there, ducking in just at the last intersection. An alkali taste formed on her tongue from the sudden presence of adrenaline in her system.

"Probably just a garbage man."

The wolf looked up at her with a wrinkled brow and then straight forward as he continued to trot.

"What do you care? You wouldn't help anyway."

She spoke indirectly of the night she killed the monster in the fort. She had not quite been alone that night, but she might as well have been for all the good her running buddy did her. He had just sat and watched like a paying member of an imaginary audience, though intently he had watched. But that is all and nothing more.

With no response she said, "That's what I thought."

For safe measure, she crossed the street to the right side. She would be turning right in another block and a half anyway. At least that is the story she told herself for this seemingly random move. It had nothing to do with being unnerved or even scared, and certainly wasn't because she was a compulsive jaywalker.

She had no sooner crossed the next street at the end of the second block than the wolf looked back and allowed a low whiny sound escape from his throat. It reminded Andrea of the sound Lassie made just before she told June Lockhart that little Timmy was stuck in a well…all in one sing-song bark.

Andrea looked back and saw the figure again. This time she got a good enough look to make out a dark jacket with a hood and dark slacks before he ducked into the next street. With no way of turning back safely, and not really knowing the area well, she said, "Looks like we are in for a little wind-sprint training, Skyking. I hope you're up for it!"

And with that, she torqued up the pace a few notches. She almost heard someone's foot scuff the ground in the way it does when they move suddenly to a run from standing still. But her high school track coach had taught her well enough to know that looking back would only slow her down at this point.

She was making the right-hand turn onto the narrow lane and could see the lights from the high street two blocks away. The "lane" was a long, blacktop road that was really little more than an alley littered with three or four dumpsters where side doors allowed for quick disposal of trash from the local shops. She was halfway down the first block before her eyes adjusted somewhat to the reduced light.

Andrea thought she might have heard echoes of footfalls behind her, but her own fast steps where making enough noise in the confined space that it was difficult to tell. *I have no idea what one of these Croatoan even looks like!"* she thought, *"…and me without my stun gun!*

It was even worse than that. She felt practically naked in her running shorts and shirt. "Not even a goddamn photo ID for them to identify me with at the morgue!" she said to the wolf that now had to break from a trot to an open gate just to keep up.

Just then the echo from the other footfalls phased with the sound of her own feet, causing them to fall in between like some sort of grotesque Reggae beat. *Oh, great! I'm going to die a hideous death and my last thought is going to be Bob-fucking-Marley!* This thought seemed to have inspired her legs that were just now starting to burn from oxygen deprivation. They responded by quickening their pace to a fight-or-fly level.

Andrea had definitely chosen to fly.

She crossed the alley at the halfway point to the high street and nearly twisted her ankle in an unexpected dip in the road. It was as if the very earth had reached up and bit her heel. Shards of pain ripped up her leg, but were met by a stubborn desire to keep her soul, spirit, and body united for a little while longer. The next few steps were a little bit slower as she faltered in an effort to remain upright and in motion.

She could feel his breath on the nape of her neck. He was definitely closing. She picked the pace back up despite the shock of electric pain on every other step. *At least it isn't broken. I wouldn't even be upright if it were,* she thought.

It was here that Andrea's thoughts turned for a perilous moment upon her own "seed" for the first time. *What desire would he take from me? What horrible thing lies deep in my id? Am I really capable of something horrible?*

For the first time ever, she was aware of an answer to an inner-monologue. Four simple words from a before unknown voice wafted into existence almost audibly between her two ears from the very center of her brain, "You have no idea."

Just then, the feeling of immediate doom left as she felt she was gaining some ground in her desperate escape. The lane became somewhat brighter bathed in both the light from the street just ahead as well as a noticeable shift in the color of the sky from pitch to an oily blue. She also noticed that her pace was now uneven as she began favoring the hurt ankle. This change in tempo exposed the telltale steps from the continued chase of her pursuer.

With one final push for all she was worth, Andrea steamed the last fifty feet of the lane to the corner in an effort that would make John Henry proud. The pain was now so excruciating that it was all she could do just to look up, squint her eyes and pump her arms for all they were worth. The victory tape of her freedom and safety was across the running track of her destruction.

It was then that she remembered more coaching advice: *Don't stop until you are fifteen feet past the tape.* The whole of her body was on fire and stitches of cramps were forming in her ribs. She broke the tape and continued to run in an arch to the right so wide that she went out into the street. A not so friendly delivery truck almost finished the job her pursuer started but was able to swerve and skid to a stop before doing any real harm.

Two burly men got out of the large red truck slamming doors behind them, "What the hell? You retarded or something lady?"

Andrea made it over to the building on the right and leaned against the bricks as her lungs protested her last burst. Both men had made it over to her before she could get the spasmodic gasps even under control enough to grunt monosyllabically, "It's...just..."

"It's just what?" the other man questioned.

Holding on to the building with her left hand, and using her other to point back over her shoulder in jabbing gestures towards the lane, "down…there…"

Both men looked back. The first one stepped out into the street and down towards the lane while the second one stayed with Andrea. The first one called back, "What? What's down there?" His voice revealed a growing frustration and anger.

Andrea put her hands on her hips and raised her shoulders to give her rib cage more room to pull in the now slower and larger shipments of air to the cells that were screaming their demand to the much reduced supply— respiratory economics.

She stepped over to the lane, favoring the ankle. As she cleared the corner, it became immediately apparent that the lane was empty. There was no sign of life, or even undeath there.

Now with some more control and trying to cover her embarrassment, "That…is one spooky alley!"

"Look, lady. You haven't seen spooky yet. Try jumping out in the fucking street again and I'll show you spooky!" Then with somewhat of a lessened edge, "Hey, you gonna be alright?" She nodded without speaking, allowing the circulatory supply chain to catch up with the needs of its customers. He and his partner turned and headed back to the idling truck. She could hear him say, "Fucking broad nearly got herself killed and we would be filling out forms for weeks!"

She looked down at the wolf. They hadn't even noticed him. Nobody ever did.

After a few moments, she started off to the right towards the bank. The light of the new day was breathing bravery back into her legs while her lungs were breathing in enough oxygen to break down the lactic acid that was causing the muscles around her ribs to burn.

After passing the bank, she decided to go back a different way. She figured if she just kept going straight, she would eventually be able to turn right and head back around to the hotel. But the clerk had been right. She found herself in the middle a large public square with decorative hedges and walls. It was a good two to three blocks longer this way, but that was ok— gave her a chance to work out the ankle.

Still, the whole way back she could not shake the feeling. She was definitely still being followed. It was only when she was back in her room behind a locked door with her stun gun and service revolver that she felt a little safer.

She prepared and turned on the two-cup coffee pot at the little vanity just outside the bathroom near the front door and made her way across the room with the ice bucket that was so cheap that virtually nobody takes them home as souvenirs. There was still some pain in the left ankle from the twist and she could tell that stiffness was starting to settle in.

An imitation antique Queen Anne chair was her throne, a TV remote and satellite phone her scepter and staff, and the hotel ice bucket filled half with ice cubes and half the watery remains from the ice cubes the evening before became her ottoman. "I am Queen Andrea of the Ottoman Empire!" she said with a flourish as she lowered her throbbing left foot into the bucket dipping the bend of her heel in first until the back of her calf and her toes were resting on either side of its rim.

She pointed the remote at the TV and said in a persisted regal tone, "Bow before me slave and do my bidding," then clicking the power button, "Turn on, I command!"

The cyclops obeyed. With a soft snap of a spark from its innards it awoke with a blink of its one electronic eye. The hotel menu came up informing her that she could watch cable, current blockbusters, review her bill or watch the best in tasteful adult entertainment.

Andrea was just wondering if there was such a thing as tasteful adult entertainment when she lowered her mighty scepter and proclaimed, "Turn to something of quality and entertain me, naïve!" With this, she clicked the up-channel button. A network morning show came on. The perky anchorwoman was just reminding America how good she looked vs. how bad they looked.

"You can't get good help these days," she said and then dismissively, "Silence, you beast!" and she pressed the mute key.

There was that twinge again. This time she acted upon it. Picking up her staff, she punched in the numbers 912-555-1212. She raised the mighty staff to her ear and awaited the prompt, "What city?"

"Savannah."

"What state?"

"Georgia."

"What listing?"

"Wren Carmichael."

This was followed by a series of bleeps and bloops that let the listener know that Ma Bell had not hung up on them, but was at that very moment busy trying to look the number up based on speech recognition software that allowed them to lay off another 600 employees just three years earlier.

"Please wait." Followed by more bleeps.

"Good, my southern drawl is keeping at least one more operator on the payroll," she said to her imaginary court.

"One moment," came a friendly female voice on the other side of the connection. As luck would have it, the operator had a clear southern lilt to her voice. Then, "I'm sorry, ma'am. There is no Wren Carmichael listing in Savannah."

"Could you try a broader search please?"

"The system automatically checks the whole area code. That is all of the southeast third of Georgia. Can I help you with another listing?"

Andrea hated to admit it to herself, but it was so good hearing a friendly voice with a southern accent that she didn't want the call to end. Finally, with some reluctance she answered, "No. No thank you."

After thanking Andrea for choosing her local phone company the operator hung up and moved on to the next idiot that could not be recognized by the software. There was a little homesick sadness when Andrea realized it was no longer *her* local phone company after all.

"I guess he found a life and moved on…" she informed her courtiers.

Her ankle was getting good and numb, nearly as numb as the space between the anchor lady's ears. Andrea marveled how she had just transitioned from interviewing the Secretary of State to now asking questions of a chef demonstrating how "working moms" could fix a three-course meal for their family in only fifteen minutes after work.

"This bitch hasn't cooked a homemade meal in twenty years!" Then to the cyclops, "I no longer need your services, off with your head!" and she clicked the power button silencing the helpless creature for the time being with her whim.

Andrea lifted her ankle out of the briny deep that was now her hotel ice bucket and gently set it down on the floor. There was no sudden shock as she put a little weight on it. The twist had been relatively superficial. But to be safe, she would take it easy for a few days.

As she was getting up to make her way to the bathroom to wash off her nighttime film and put on her morning face, she noticed again how good she actually felt. The only numbness was her left ankle. All the rest of her bits felt pretty ok, actually.

She paused at the little vanity outside the bathroom and poured one of the two cups-worth of coffee into the plain white mug that was waiting for the Queen to give it a task. She sipped the java easily as she eased her way across the tile floor. One wet foot promised to add insult to injury should she take one wrong step and slip on the slick floor.

Short work was soon made of the shower and application of all the socially required appliqués. In a mere sixty minutes she was complete, sitting back on her throne, and now staring at the one remaining unequipped shoe dangling from a tie held by her left hand as she sipped again at her coffee with her right.

"Ok, friend…this can either go easy…or this can go rough," she said in her best Clint Eastwood. "What's it gonna be, punk? Well, huh? Do you feel lucky?" Then as if her experiment in channeling was complete, she continued in her own voice, "Why do they always have to be pumps!?"

Easing the toe in first and gliding the heel up to the flat of the sole, she gently started pushing the strap through the clasp on the other side. "There, that wasn't so bad, now was it?"

She stood up and eased pressure back on the ankle. It still hurt some, but it was not the explosion she was expecting. Andrea even thought she would be able to walk to the bank. Checking over her entire list, which included her complete outfit, needed papers, and a purse with ID, a stun gun and pistol, she made her way across to the door.

She had just opened it and was staring at that little plaque of fire instructions and other legally mandatory content that always graces the peephole on a hotel door when she realized that she was indeed staying in a hotel room and was just about to leave without her passkey. She went back over to the dresser that looked exactly like the one they show at the end of those game shows when a contestant doesn't win the car, and picking up her passkey, she slid it into an inside pocket of her purse.

When she made it to the street, she decided after only a moment of consideration to take the long way and go through the park square this time round. She might check out the lane on the way back if there were enough light and population milling around to be safe without backup—always the conservative when it came to such things.

Now it was time for her to get psyched up. The little-known secret about women in law enforcement is that the sexual liberation movement of the seventies is nowhere near the goal of "equality regardless". There is still plenty of inequality out there to go around. By this point in history, political correctness had just put a friendly but deceptive face on it. It was definitely still a man's world. And nowhere was this more obvious than when a lone woman officer of the court served some sort or order to a man.

But Andrea was used to this. She could argue her way or even bully her way into accomplishing her task. But businessmen had been the worst. She usually liked to take a side of beef along with her for masculine support. In her mind, one woman couldn't change the whole world in a day.

The only problem with this line of thinking, she was wrong.

But for now she started coaching herself as she approached the square, "Don't take *no* for an answer. Look them directly in the eye and demand to keep their eye contact above your blouse-line. Be professional and courteous, but still strong."

Agent Ellijay repeated this litany over and over as she gathered up her sterner stuff for the approaching encounter behind the bank door she now approached. She took one last inventory of all the required accouterments and then with a reinforcing inhalation, she grabbed the door handle and stepped inside with the poise of Buford Pusser.

A lady behind a desk saw her approaching and looked over the top of her black-rimmed glasses, "Hello. May I help you?"

Flashing her ID she said, "Yes, may I speak to the branch manager, please?"

"Certainly!" the smartly dressed lady stood up to her fully unfolded six-foot height. Yet she seemed to give off an air of unintended brutishness. Andrea figured she was actually ill at ease with her own stature and wanted to come across as friendly. "May I tell him whom is calling?"

"Yes, Agent Ellijay…. Andrea." The left corner of her mouth perked into a protocol smile as she raised her eyebrows to communicate that it was not a negative visit she was making.

"Very good, Agent Ellijay. I will see if he is available." The lady was already moving to the back office suite with a grace few tall women can pull off effectively. Back in Andrea's area of the country, they would have called her "big-boned."

A few moments later, she reappeared from the office with a gentleman in tow. He was extremely short which juxtaposed to her model height made for an almost comic picture. Andrea realized she was visualizing them as lovers and wondered if he would need a stepladder. She almost lost her composure as they approached.

"Agent Ellijay, I am Stan Geller, manager of this branch. How may we help you?"

Here it goes, thought Andrea and then pulling the court order out of the folder and extending it along with her ID to him she said, "I need to serve this court order…"

Fully prepared to go further with her explanation, Mr. Geller interrupted her and said as he was glancing over the document he had taken, "No problem. Let me look over the particulars."

Continuing as if she had not been heard, "It covers an account from which an ACH transfer was recently made."

"Right. I see that. Should be no problem. It all looks extremely standard."

Still on a roll and building up to win the coming fight, Andrea continued, "All of the information is there and has been authorized by the proper authorities."

Mr. Geller paused as if he realized that she had not heard him. After a moment, he looked up at her and smiled. Handing her ID back to her he said, "Yes, Ms. Ellijay. It all looks in order. I believe we have ten days to satisfy your request, the fax number is there, we should have no difficulties meeting the requirements by then."

Andrea stopped while all of this caught up with her. She figured that maybe it was the region she had worked in that had the difficulty. She was certain that there had to be even more places that did not take a woman with a badge seriously. But these people were courteous and respectful. Now she needed a graceful exit realizing that she had ramped up maybe a bit too much. As hard as she fought it, a faint blush crossed her cheeks.

"Thank you Mr. Geller. We appreciate your cooperation," was all that sprang to mind in that time, that and then just standing there for an awkward moment.

"Is there something else we can help you with?" he asked in a polite hint that they wanted to return to their work.

"Excuse me?" she said almost absentmindedly.

"Perhaps you would like to start an account with us?" the tall lady asked.

"Oh, no. Forgive me. I have a lot on my mind. Thank you both for your cooperation." And then as she turned to leave, "My card is stapled to the top. Please feel free to call me if there are any questions."

Andrea made her way back outside with the dazed feeling that she had just driven a nail in with a sledgehammer. The memory of how the stake gave inside the monster's chest came back to her. She wondered if she would ever be able to outlive the haunting of that moment.

Standing in front of the bank for a little while, she realized that her assignment was over—light though it was. Feeling a little guilty spending so much money to accomplish what was in her mind such an inane task, she decided to get a better look at that lane. She turned left and started heading up the block to where the truck drivers had seemingly saved her life by almost ending it just a few short hours before.

She approached the spot slowly now, not out of trepidation but because she was using all of her training as an investigator. She took everything in: the height of the buildings, the vantage point offered from windows and fire escapes, the distance a person would have to cover to disappear down the lane. As she moved through the scene where the truck nearly hit her, she could almost *see* flashes of memory particularly when she stood in the same places and especially when she touched the bricks that supported her when she was catching her breath.

She memorized everything. She would be able to relive every aspect of this encounter as she worked out the puzzle in the future. It was one of her skills.

As she approached the lane and rounded the corner to the left, the flashes became slightly more intense as the brightly lit lane currently in her eyesight alternated with the dark images in her mind from the predawn gauntlet she had run. Looking down the lane to the street two blocks away, she had estimated it would be extremely difficult to cover that ground in such a short span of time. "Maybe these bugs have super-human speed...?" she mused out loud.

With a Herculean effort, she started her progress down the lane ironically by commanding her injured left foot to take the first step. It reluctantly obeyed. The right foot was then obliged to follow suit. Along the way, she could make out more details this trip thanks to her friend Sol who was providing the lighting for this scene from a crisp October sky overhead.

The lane was littered with bits of garbage scatted around giving the place that homey touch. As she approached the initial blind spot provided by the first of four dumpsters that made this lane a sick kind of slalom course at 5:00 a.m., a tremor of concern welled up in her. This time being a tad better prepared, she moved her free hand that wasn't holding the file folder down into her purse.

Her hand investigated around insider the handbag while her eyes continued to investigate down the lane. It stumbled across a half empty pack of gum, her checkbook and ID, and then fell directly between the butt of the service revolver and the handle of the stun gun. This time, it knew what the threat could be so it grasped the handle of the stun gun and extracted it from the dark den that was her purse into the light of the lane.

She continued her trek imbued with the mental strength that she would have the upper hand on any encounter here. She now became interested in the culprit that had bit her ankle. A depression was there in the alley that crossed the lane about fifteen feet in front of her. It looked like an innocent pothole, but she could now pick it out in a lineup if need be. She started to walk past the corner and out into the alley to nab the suspect pothole and interrogate it when something suddenly nabbed the wrist of the arm that was holding the papers from the bank.

She was spun effortlessly around and came face-to-face with a man wearing a navy jumpsuit complete with a hood pulled over the crown of his head. "You made a mistake coming down this way again, didn't you pet?"

Andrea's mind was awash with so many things. The papers fluttered down to become part of that homey look with the rest of the trash. His grip was severe on her left wrist and she felt pain there. Instinctively she raised the stun gun to the open side of his neck and pressed the button for all she was worth. A loud crack was sounded, as a visible blue spark was emitted from the two probes touching his skin.

"What the fuck?" he yelled as he recoiled a bit. His arm came up in a broad swing that sent the stun gun sailing down the closed-off alley to her right. As he backed up pulling her with the grip that had not relented one iota, he maneuvered them out of sight of either street and rubbed the side of his neck with the back of his free hand. It was holding visibly now a .22 pistol.

"What would a Croatoan need with a piss-ant .22?" She asked, more to herself than to him. She was putting it all together. Here was a stalker that had chased her but couldn't catch her at full sprint, had a .22, and was not affected much by the stun gun so he must be human after all.

"A what?"

His gun hand was still up at his neck. With the sudden realization that this was no supernatural creature, her years of police training kicked in. Andrea flipped her hand around and clutched his wrist in a death-grip. Almost by instinct, she dug her nails into the top of his arm, deep into the soft skin between the two forearm bones. She clutched it as hard as she could.

Something happened then that would not be understood by her for years to come. There was a charge that really didn't register in her mind at the time. Everything was happening so fast. But as her nails and fingertips made contact with brutish thug's skin there was an immediate flood of strength to all her limbs and his leverage felt somewhat diminished to her. It was if she had stolen something from him. Andrea Ellijay had increased and the assailant had decreased.

She pulled down hard feeling his weight give to the pressure to his side and as he shifted weight, she used his wrist like a fulcrum to deliver a high kick to his head. Her aim was a little off and she caught the top of his gun arm.

Always has to be pumps, she thought.

But the action had been enough. He was on the ground still holding loosely to her wrist. The blood and pain that was emanating from his own wrist was enough to take his mind off the death grip a little. His elbow had pulled back to catch the impact of his fall but that being done, it was now free to come back and shoot this bitch in the head.

Andrea saw her one opportunity exposed in the fall and she took it. Coming down with a force aided by both gravity and the leverage from her hand she drove her knee into the side of his head. His neck muscles gave to the blow, and for a moment, his head moved with her ramming knee until it met resistance from the pavement on the other side. There was a sickening kind of thud.

He was out cold. He might be dead. His consciousness was robbed from him like Andrea's breath had been robbed earlier when this alley had been a dark scene of terror to her.

Slowly standing up having been released from her unfortunate assailant, she shook her head as she looked down at this petty excuse for a man, "Oh you piece of shit. You worthless piece of shit. You picked the wrong fucking lady this time!"

She stood up and with all the effort of any good Southern Belle she straightened her dress and hair. She was fully prepared to send another stinging blow to his head from the bottom of her pump, but that would not be necessary. He was still out cold, but she had been able to make out that he was in fact still breathing.

Andrea walked around picking everything back up into an orderly cargo. When done with that chore, she picked up the satellite phone and dialed 9-1-1. A friendly enough voice on the other side of the phone answered, "Yes, Agent Ellijay. How can we help?"

She was a bit taken aback. This was definitely not your run-of-the-mill cell phone. "I have a suspect down. Unconscious. He was attempting to attack me. Looks like a mugging or a rape attempt. I suppose we need to roll a car," she said, not knowing if this operator would understand specific codes so she stuck to plain English.

"I have your 20 just off of Winthrop Lane. We will have the locals send a car. Is the suspect a threat to you in any way?"

Looking down at the sprawling motionless bleeding lump that was her assailant she said, "No."

"Then protocol suggests that you stay there until the blues arrive. Identify yourself as needed."

This was slightly cryptic to Andrea but she thought she understood. She also wondered at the matter-of-fact way the operator handled the call. There was no sense of urgency or curiosity if this were one of those Croatoan or not. Andrea supposed that if it had been, the call would have gone a lot differently. After considering a thousand questions to ask, she settled on, "Is there anything else?"

"Will you be ok?" the operator asked.

"Yes. I think so."

"Good. Call us again if you need us."

Before she could say thank you, the call was terminated. A short while later Andrea could make out the faint sirens calling in the distance. They arrived soon enough accompanied by two of Peab'dy's finest.

She handled it like a normal mugging attempt to avoid delays and gave them her phone number telling them that she needed to leave town on business. They asked if she could come back to testify if needed and she said she would.

The report was taken, the arrest was made, and the alley was cleared of one very large piece of trash within an hour. He started to regain consciousness in the back of the patrol car and immediately started the muffled screams for a lawyer and his rights.

Andrea returned to the hotel, packed, checked out, and made her way to the airport by midday. She was on the steps up to the Gulfstream when she stopped. Tim asked if she was all right to which she replied, "Just a little something I have always wanted to do."

She took off her pumps and shook the dust from her shoes. Then turning, she boarded the jet. It would be years before she saw this town again.

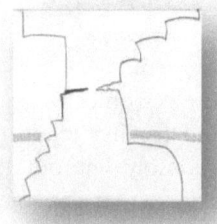

10.
12.19.9.11.18.₄₁₇; 11 YAX, 13 ETZNAB — FLINT, KNIFE

October 13, 2002, 10:00 a.m. EST

Andrea was just putting the finishing touches on her report. It was easy enough once she found the PC that she understood to be *somewhere* in her townhouse. It was in what she thought was a guest bedroom but as it turned out, was a study with a nice little desk, PC, phone, and plenty of office supplies.

The computer had surprised her a little. It was fully configured with the best and latest software. But what really impressed her were the templates that were easy both to access and use for the many tedious things like Expense Reports and Action Reports that she routinely had to complete.

She found a report template for Assignment Briefs and followed the wizard as it explained each step. Most of the values were already populated. For example, when she got to the section on location, Peabody was already filled out with flight times, accommodations, and all. It seemed that the template was tied into all sorts of backend systems such as scheduling. The only real effort was the prose descriptions of events and that was really not all that difficult.

She had found the study the night before as she looked around the house for something suitable for soaking feet. Just after discovering the study, she had found a container in the hall closet that was perfect. The Epsom salts she picked up at the drugstore on the way back from the airstrip the night before worked wonders in the hot water when all was mixed with the missing ingredient of her sore left ankle.

This morning she had felt much better and even now as she put the finishing touches on her report, the ankle was being used to rock her gently in the desk chair. She clicked the *Next* button and was asked if she wanted to file her report electronically. There was a list of names already populated with Casper James and Ned Smarny.

"This is too easy," she observed.

She wondered if she filed electronically would she be able to still print out the report. Ned had asked for her to drop off a copy at his desk on Sunday and she wanted to comply without taking anything for granted. Risking the worst, she checked *Yes* that she wanted to file electronically and clicked the *Next* button.

The subsequent window asked if she wanted a print-out, and how many. With a little relief she entered a *2* and clicked the *Next* button. The printer whirred to life and printed out two clean copies of her report. These she gathered up and placed neatly in a file folder ready for the short walk to their destination in Buchanan Hall.

She took a moment to gather all the articles she had been squirreling away from the research center and placed them in neat stacks down the left side of her desk. Each one had a title sticking out about an inch on the top so she could put her fingers on them quickly.

One last task she wanted to do before she wrapped things up was to find the fax controls. There was a folder in her email labeled Faxes. By right-clicking it, she discovered a menu with options. There Andrea found the item she was after. It was a selection to store faxes or print them out when they arrived. She selected to automatically print them out and then chose her printer as the destination. "That simple, that easy!" she said.

Andrea was ready to jump up and run the reports to Ned's office but one glance down reminded her that her feet were still shod with bunny slippers and her body still adorned with a robe—this time not white with a W but a proper robe. "Well then...this won't do for a stroll around the courtyard."

The bunny slippers looked up at her in protest, but she was adamant.

Andrea spent the next hour getting ready for her day and thinking about what all she would like to do. After some consideration, she decided on meeting her obligations first, then running her car out to find a box of "chicken and fixin's" and see if she could get lost and then found again. To her it was the best way to learn new surroundings.

The walk across the quad was a quiet one. At 11:00 a.m. on a Sunday, there was not much life around. She figured some people would probably be at church and reminded herself that she needed to find a new place of worship to do likewise. It was something introduced to her by one of the few caring foster families of her past. Just thinking about the Johnson clan removed any remaining edge off her day.

She did not consider herself a saint by any stretch of the imagination.

But no matter how much she dreaded going to worship beforehand she always felt better afterward. To Andrea, this was all the debate there was to religion. She went because it made her feel better to do so. She had yet to find a theologian or atheist alike that could debate that point.

The process of entering Buchanan Hall went a little more cautiously this time. She eased up on the doors and opened them, halfway expecting a relatively handsome young man to slam into her again and found that she was halfway disappointed when there was no such collision. Stepping down the hallway that was empty as a tomb, she stopped long enough to pay her compliments to Bucky, "Why the hard expression?" she said aloud and giggled to the bust.

"Hello?" came a kind woman's voice from down the hall, which startled Andrea a bit.

"Oh, hi...someone's in here," Andrea answered. She wondered why people always answered, "someone's in here" when they don't know who is asking. To her it seemed the most likely answer when a janitor proclaims "housekeeping" at a bathroom door. It was a mystery to her why society had not found it in everyone's best interest to come up with a standard reply and teach it to all the little school children. Instead, they figure out a proper etiquette for every other occasion under the sun and leave the "bathroom answer" up to people to ad lib on their own. Somehow, "someone's in here" always seemed to fall short of the mark to her.

As she made her way further down the hall to the disembodied voice, she heard it call out in now a familiar tone, "Is that you, Andrea dear?"

It was Victoria and she was in the last office on the right. It was the one marked Casper James. "Yes. It is I," she replied in a dramatic flair as she turned the corner into the room with a big smile on her face.

"Well it certainly is good to see you again. I hear you had quite the eventful little jaunt up to New England. We're so glad you are back and in one piece," she said with more warmth and genuine concern than Andrea had ever heard in her life.

The truth of this hit Andrea and she had to compose herself with a quick clearing of her throat, "Thank you, Victoria. That's most kind."

"Don't mention it, Hun. Just keep coming back like that and we'll all be fine." Then with a hike of her thumb pointing back to the office behind her she said, "He's in there. Go on in."

Andrea had not really planned on stopping in to see her boss's boss. But she also realized that a few industrious brownie points never hurt a new career either. "Thanks, I think I'll just pop in for a moment."

She walked past Victoria, who was returning to her work at a computer terminal. Andrea no sooner crossed the threshold than she heard Casper's booming baritone, "Ms. Ellijay! How good to see you again! Please, please come in and sit down for a little while." He was standing out of respect and indicating a vacant chair.

"Thank you," she replied as she moved around the chair and then sat at his large mahogany desk. She could not help but notice that this office was much more traditional than Ned's. It radiated the warmth of good taste from a bygone era.

Retaking his seat, Casper said, "I hear there was quite a lot of excitement! How's the ankle?" he asked as he stretched to try to get a look at it over the expanse of the desk, but realizing the futility sat back down.

"It's fine! Just call me Hop-Along for a few days."

Smiling a broad one, "I'll do that. I hear there also was an incident after serving papers at a bank?"

"Yes. I was really worried it was one of those Croatoan. I really have a lot of questions and concerns about sending agents out so ill-prepared."

Sidestepping the last, Casper's smile never broke, "Well…there was little chance of him being a Croatoan. But he was certainly not some average thug."

"How so?"

"The police have several positive idents on him now. They have charged him in a string of crimes. Apparently there has been a serial rapist working in that area for some time. He is also wanted in one murder case where they think he got 'carried away'."

The full importance of his words and their meaning hit Andrea like the red delivery truck didn't. "I had gone that way earlier in the morning—on a run. I was almost certain I was being stalked, even chased. If I had known what I was up against in this creep, I would have never been so cavalier in retracing my footsteps."

"I think you may be starting to get the point." Casper was alluding to her bigger question about the Croatoan that he was still sidestepping a little. "Well…besides that Mrs. Lincoln, how was the play?"

"Oh, that. I served the papers. Now we have to wait ten days to get some response."

"They sometimes come in sooner. Be patient," Casper said as a dutiful patriarch.

Realizing she was not doing much politicking just talking about herself, "So, how are things here back at the ranch?"

Casper raised his eyebrows a little and with that smile he was very much the weathered cowboy, "Thanks for asking. Most agents are pretty self-absorbed in their own work. It's like they are all trying to become human sponges. It's nice to have someone take an interest in the old man every once in a while. Actually, we're in a state of some heightened concern. There's not much we can do about it. But something is definitely up.

"Our agency investigates some sensitive issues, as you are now well aware. Anonymity is extremely important. Why…it would have been exceedingly difficult for you just to serve those papers yesterday if that bank manager had been looking over your shoulders for the Boogieman.

"The agency has been around for quite some time and we have managed to stay somewhat under the radar. It was more difficult before the Patriot Act. But since 9/11, the public has been far more interested in catching *them* than they are in catching us."

"I'm not sure I follow you on that."

"Look at the TV shows over the years. They have become increasingly interested in government corruption, exposing Big Brother, how mean and nasty we all are. It has eroded the public's confidence in their duly sworn officials to protect them. They became interested in how bad all the agencies that are there to protect them have become. There are some rotten apples in the barrel and they do need to be cleared out. But by a vast majority, protection agencies are far less corrupt than corporations or small business. Hell, even their bridge clubs and bowling leagues are more corrupt!"

Andrea was a little skeptical on this but she understood how this kind, older man would have a rosy outlook on agencies. He was high up in one and appeared to be the real McCoy.

Casper continued, "Well, just over the last few months or maybe longer…there seems to be a ground swell effort to expose our agency as some ruthless and vile thing. There are discussions on the Internet blogs that name us specifically."

"But surely those that may know about us understand the importance of our work."

"They may be enemies to our work. That is the irony of the modern information age. Blogs are becoming an alternative to what some see as a left-leaning Mainstream Media. In most cases they're correct and the bloggers are intelligent and fairly accurate. But there are no checks and balances. The consensus is based on a preponderance of viewpoint—the pure majority of the moment rules. If a whole lot of different people express the same viewpoint, then…it must be so."

"So if some organization was large enough and patient enough…" she began to speculate.

Casper concluded, "They could start a false rumor and have everyone in the world looking for clues. And once that starts, the witch-hunt is on. The innocent could be tried and hung before Due Process ever got out of bed."

"And presently we are the witches?" she asked.

"And presently we are the witches. Yes. In this case it appears they are starting to lay the ground work for a major conspiracy theory."

"Ah, crap," she interjected.

"Indeed and well put. But I'm not too worried about it. The theory is that our agency has always been a terrorist organization planted as a cell to pull off an act to rival 9/11. All of this would be just plain silly unless there really was some huge act of terrorism. Even then, they would need cooperative access to the mainstream media. The public as a whole are not going to believe a bunch of Internet jockeys that stay up late in their Fruit of the Looms trying to sway public opinion."

Casper carefully left out the part of the theory where the bloggers were speculating that the Order had some sort of cure for a disease and was keeping it from the rest of the world.

"Then there is nothing to worry about," she innocently said.

"Well…there is still some level of discomfort that our agency name is even coming up to begin with. We don't want Fox coming up with a new show about us." And then with a glint in his eye and a wry smile, "Although I think they could probably get Robert Redford to play me!"

She laughed and he snorted.

"Well I really need to be getting this report up to Ned."

"Very good. Keep that man happy! How are things working out with you two?" he asked as she was getting up to leave.

Andrea threw her purse strap over her shoulder and shifted the file folder to her other hand, "I think very well. He strikes me as very…um…professional."

"He is that! Just make sure you don't strike him back! I hear the perp in Peabody needed a few stitches. You are tough as nails, Andrea."

"Thanks for the vote of confidence. Goodbye, Mr. James," she concluded as she stepped out into the hallway waving at Victoria on her way past.

Turning, she headed towards the stairwell at the end of the hall. Her tennis shoes made sure that the upstairs was not so aware of her approach this time. She concluded her long walk down the hall on the second floor only to find her boss's office locked up tight as a drum. The lights were out.

As she examined the now closed door, she noticed a feature she had missed on her first visit. There was a slot there in the middle of the door. Taking the hint, she slid her report into the slot and felt satisfied she had finished the assignment.

Now it was time for play!

She turned to go back down the hall and descend the steps. As she reached the base of the stairs, she was somewhat surprised to see Casper's office closed up and the lights out. "What is it with these people?" she asked and her voice echoed slightly in the hall. With no reply to her question, she headed out into the light of a bright October Sunday and to an afternoon in a park somewhere.

Her day was fantastic as she drove through central Virginia getting a feel for her new surroundings. She had found many things including a Colonel

Chicken, the perfect park, and a dog named Boomer that fetched a Frisbee for her a few times. She had loved his bandana and complimented his owners.

But sundown had brought an end to her day of rest as her car brought her back to the Center. She had a snack of a dinner from the leftovers and a cold one from her fridge. She wasn't really a "beer person," but spending a life in the South trained one to keep a six-pack cold in the fridge just in case an emergency broke out.

In the early evening, she was bored with TV, so she decided to go to the research center and do a little perusing. This walk across the campus was as beautiful as the first and she really felt happy with the completion of her rookie assignment and the relative ease she had in taking to her new life.

She climbed the steps to the library and opened the doors to the first floor of seemingly endless knowledge. There were more people in here than last time. She could see people at all three levels milling around, reading, and carrying on hushed conversations respectful of the needs of others for quiet.

The first two stations to the left, National Government and Foreign Governments had many new briefs, mostly dealing with the midterm elections coming up. The first station reporting on which American groups were trying to affect the vote to their favor, and the second with what other countries were trying to do the same.

Andrea made her way to the third station, Terrorists. Here was another woman busy stacking and sorting briefs in a hurried and mouse-like way. Andrea had quite hoped to make a new acquaintance here and this woman appeared to be about her same age.

"Hi," Andrea said in a lowered, but direct tone.

"Oh, hello. Don't mind me. I was just bringing out the latest brief and will be quickly gone," the woman said with a swift nervous glance over the top of her narrow reading glasses. She was plain looking—the sort of severe but wholesome looks that would have made a killer third grade teacher back home. Yet she had an understated beauty that some African-American women possess that transcends race.

In an effort to restart the conversation, Andrea pressed further, "The latest brief? What's it on?"

The petite woman was even faster in her business now. She looked like she really wanted to leave, but her Type-A personality really needed these stacks perfect before she did so. Her hands were a nervous blur. "Some tractor-trailer stolen. We get one a week."

This wasn't going well. So Andrea thought the direct approach might work better. Sticking out her hand in a purposeful line over the stack of papers that was currently being corralled back into order, she said, "My name is Andrea. I am new here. Not many friends yet."

Taking her cue to stop her current task and show some social graces even though she really longed for the solitude of her research desk, she grasped Andrea's hand and smiled, "Yes. Welcome to the agency. I am Leeza."

"Leeza Banes?"

Now she looked embarrassed as well as mortified. Andrea figured this was the shyest person she had ever met in her life. Leeza looked back to her straightening and answered, "Yes. Leeza Banes."

"I've read your briefs. They are quite good."

"Thank you. Is there anything I can help you find?" It was an attempt to change the subject to one she could control and end.

Ignoring the attempt for a new direction, "I especially liked the one about me."

She stopped and looked up as if there was a little more respect, "Oh, yes. You must be Andrea Ellijay."

"Listen, Leeza. Can I ask you a question?"

"That's what I am here for," came the proper reply. But Leeza hated the fact that her sentence ended in a preposition. She wished she could back time up and correct that. She was just going through the proper rewording in her mind when Andrea interrupted her thoughts.

"You wrote that brief as if you were there that night."

"That is what we are supposed to do with a blue report."

"Blue?"

"Oh. I'm sorry. You are new here. It is a color-coding system that the agency came up with a long time ago. We have three basic types of reports. Tertiary reports based on many second hand reports, gossip, or unreliable sources, but when there are many of them speaking one story to the point where they have some credibility and should be taken seriously. Those are red and are written in the style of an encyclopedia or journal article.

"If we have an eye-witness that is not a trusted source or some second-hand information from a person that *is* a trusted source, that is a white report. We write those in the style of a newspaper article. You know…most important fact first, etc. Nothing can be stated without sighting a source."

"And then there are blue reports?" Andrea guessed.

"Yes, an eyewitness account from a trusted source. Those are written in first person as if from the vantage point of the reporter."

Now Andrea was extremely curious and she pressed, "And a trusted source is…?"

"One that works for the agency," Leeza said in a matter-of-fact tone.

Someone had been there that night when she killed the vampire in Georgia. Someone from the agency had been watching. Andrea got a cold chill wondering if they would have saved her should things have gone badly. She stopped this line of thought before she reached analysis paralysis.

"Interesting…" Andrea said with the best poker face she could muster at the moment. Leeza looked so nervous that Andrea guessed she did not even notice. "So the latest report is on a stolen truck? What color is it?"

"Oh, it's red, just your average story. A fuel oil truck was stolen in Jacksonville, Florida and ended up in Columbia, South Carolina. Some of the barrels are missing but the Department for Homeland Security says that they were probably just stolen for home heating. It's common for illegal immigrants to do this."

"Fuel oil? That was used in the bombing in Oklahoma years ago. Why would you think it was illegal immigrants?"

"Well, they can steal a flatbed, drive to a point along the way and drop off a few barrels, then continue on to some town far away and drop off the truck. Since the trucking company gets their truck back along with most of the load, no harm no foul. And should they get caught, the trucking company doesn't want to spend the time or money to prosecute. To them, the lost partial shipment costs less than the legal expenses."

"But taking stolen property across state lines is a federal offense," Andrea observed.

"Right…and the Feds are pretty busy right now with a small skirmish in Afghanistan as well as a few other things. You will see a rash of these types of crimes through the winter months. That's for sure," Leeza confidently predicted.

Andrea realized she had a wonderful opportunity to make a good friend here, but it would not happen overnight. So she looked for a chance to end this encounter on an up note. "Well, I think I'll take a copy anyway, Scoop! Your work makes for interesting reading. You are very good at what you do."

There was a visible blush under the frames of her glasses as Leeza looked back to her stacks with renewed interest. "Thank you," she said without looking up again.

"You are entirely welcome. One last question…where could I read more on the vampire that was killed in New York several weeks ago? What was her name?"

"We think it was Salindria."

"Yes, that was it."

"You could check the Codex. There is a copying machine there beside it, but those books cannot leave this building. And I know you will be anyway, but please be careful with those books."

"I will. Thanks for the chat. I hope to see you again soon."

This time looking up, Leeza chanced an awkward, "Me too."

And with this Andrea made her way back to the Codex. She searched the shelves with a new interest. There were books on records and information dating back centuries here. Some had clearly been re-bound and there seemed to be an effort to recreate many of the volumes with new, modern covers and spines. These all had the same pastel blue color with gold trim and letters, and were sitting next to their original version. There was a sign encouraging agents to use the newly bound versions where possible.

Andrea found one such book called, "A Vampirism History." She opened it up and found that each name was listed in chronological order— not alphabetically. All events were captured up until 1938, and then a compilation of the modern history of each name up to the year 2000 was listed alphabetically in the back.

Looking in the back, Andrea found several indices including one for national origin, religious faith, and of course an alphabetical listing. She checked the last one to find Salindria's name listed. She flipped to that page and found a relatively short section, really only two or three pages at most. She made a few copies without really reading it and replaced the book next to its antique cousin on the shelf.

She then moved to the next station. There was nothing really new at the Legends or the Croatoan tables. And Andrea felt she would have absolutely no problem sleeping tonight, so she decided to skip the Statistics station altogether.

By the time she looked back to the Terrorist section, Leeza was gone. Andrea had at least planned to wave goodbye. As she stepped through the big white doors into the crisp cool air, she hoped she would be able to talk to Leeza again soon.

Crossing back to her townhouse, she saw the familiar bottom of an older man swaying from under a shrub near a fountain that was lighting up a courtyard section with dancing water. She approached the man from behind and stood there for a moment listening as he was humming softly to himself some ancient tune full of mystique and bravado. She guessed it to be an Eastern European or Russian folk tune.

"It's got a good beat and I can dance to it…I give it a 10," she said from over the papers folded in her arms at her chest.

"Ah! Andrea! Is that you?"

"Indeed, Sir Sorin. Or should I say Troubadour Sorin?"

Turning around and sitting down on the edge of the mulch he rested a hand holding sheers on his right knee. "Happy Flint Day, to you Agent Ellijay."

Giggling, "Flint Day?" she asked.

"Ok…you are a traditionalist. I like that in you…Happy Knife Day." Then in a musing voice he said, "Yes…that does have a better ring to it. Cuts right to the point."

"I'm sorry, Sorin. I have totally lost you."

"It's not you who is lost," he said in a jovial way.

"Then who is it, oh great bard?"

"Why the Maya of course!"

"The Maya."

"You would do well to research their calendar. There are many hints and clues for what you are up against."

"Oh really now…" she skeptically said.

"Oh really. Each day has its own word. Today is Etz'nab." This he pronounced *ehts' nob*. "It means flint or knife."

"And what clue is that supposed to offer me in my quest?"

"Someone or something you care about was cut today. But it works like horoscopes. You could apply that to virtually anything from an aunt cutting her finger to the organization you work for being cut down to size by someone."

Andrea thought for a moment about the bloggers Casper had spoken about.

Sorin continued, "But mostly it is just fun. You would be amazed at what you will see around you if you just start looking. Like the old parlor trick of seeing the number 6 over and over, because all the numbers are there, you are just more aware of and looking for 6."

"Or like me never seeing a white convertible on the road until I own one and then I see them at every corner," she added.

"Exactimundo!" he proclaimed. "You would do well to brush up on your Maya knowledge. They *are* the bridge."

"The bridge?" Andrea wondered why this man constantly seemed to speak in riddles. But she found him charming.

"Between the Egyptians and us."

This step blew her mind and she really was not in the mood for another Discovery Channel special on the paranormal. "I'll do that, Sorin. Thanks for the tip!" She wanted to leave before the subject of crop circles came up.

"Not at all! You be safe, Andrea."

"You as well, Sorin. That hedge looks hungry for charming old men!" she said as she continued to move towards her house.

"Indeed it is…it is good that I am not old!" He retorted and they both laughed.

Sorin went back to pruning under the shrub and Andrea made her way back to the comfort of her warm townhouse. Once there, she slipped the bolt on the front door and once again felt safe.

After popping into her flannel jammies and bunny slippers, she started a fire and curled up in a large wingback chair in the living room. She had Leeza's brief and the three pages copied from the Codex book. The brief had been a bit dry.

She had found it was like arguing with a friend who had told her that their pumpkin bread turned out too dry, and she argued back that it couldn't be. And then she would take a big bite to make them happy, realizing that it was much worse than described. But she would finish eating it anyway to prove her point and support for her friend.

Andrea considered this to be the "polite lie" for which Southerners were so famous.

The second part of her evening read was far more exciting. Andrea read the words captured by a historian in 1938 about a woman vampire that had been highly involved in a political world Andrea did not even know existed. It was not a work of fiction. All of the events fit too neatly into her understanding of the world's timeline. The validity seemed obvious.

This author would start an article from the moment a vampire was "turned"—a term used to describe when they were converted from human to vampire. He would then trace how they had impacted the world around them through their life. And Salindria had been quite effective a few times.

Then the historian would recap anything significant about their years before they were turned. Andrea thought the average reader would find this part boring. Salindria had very little eventful life to mention before that moment. Only that she had been raised in an orphanage.

But for Andrea…this was the world. She had a sudden bond with this creature of the night and a certain sad empathy for her passing. She now wondered how anyone could be so cruel as to end a life such as this. But then, the right side of her brain took over and reminded her of the way the limbo stick had slid sickeningly easy through the chest of a creature hellbent and determined to kill her.

"I guess there are two sides to every story," she postulated to her bunny slippers. One of them nodded in reply.

On a whim, she picked up the phone next to her and called 912-555-1212. This time she asked for Bethesda Orphanage. She wrote the number down on the back of the brief, and immediately called it.

"Good evening, Bethesda. Liddy speaking," came a polite female voice on the other side.

"Good evening, Liddy. My name is Andrea Ellijay. I was a member of the girls' orphanage up in Baxley a long time ago."

"Yes. The Baptist Children's Home," came a knowing reply.

"Yes ma'am. Correct. And while I was there, I met a boy from Bethesda named Wren Carmichael."

"Oh yes! Wren is a wonderful young man. But he is no longer a Carmichael."

"He isn't?"

"No, no. He was adopted and his last name became Busby." Andrea's heart was about to pound out of her chest, "He works here at Bethesda as a counselor now. We are all so proud of our Wren," Liddy said with all the pride of a Southerner. "Would you like his number?"

"Please."

After Andrea entered the number in her phone's directory, Liddy added, "I know he would just love to hear from an old friend again. Would you like me to see if I could hunt him down? I'm sure he is around here somewhere…"

Andrea was not prepared for this. Her bunny slippers were even shaking with a little trepidation. "No, no. I wouldn't want to bother him just now. I'll try to call him at a better hour sometime this week."

"Well, that would probably be best. Would give you two plenty of time to catch up. May I tell him you called, dear?"

"Yes. Please." The words escaped her mouth before she had a chance to take them back.

They said their goodbyes and Andrea spent a good ten minutes just looking into the fire while her heart walked-off the second good workout it had gotten this weekend. Finally, she looked down at her bunny slippers and said, "Well, I guess I stuck my foot in that one."

One of them nodded in reply.

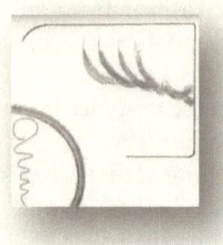

11.
12.19.9.11.19.417; 12 YAX, 1 CAUAC — STORM

October 14, 2002, 10:00 a.m. EST

Jenna Domnanovich had always been an enigma. She was one of the lucky ones in life. While it didn't seem likely that a sixth grade girl would be attracted to playing the tuba, she was and did. Yet it was playing the tuba that set her apart eight years later to win a spot in the national beauty contest representing her home state of South Dakota.

That is just the way the cards fell for Jenna. She would get the best-damned poker hand you ever saw with that one. You wouldn't think a tuba playing blonde land-girl would score big in the eyes of the nation, but she did.

Her love for classic literature and all things old caused the greatest struggle in her life—trying to decide between a major in English or History. Either one would qualify her to draw unemployment upon graduation. Yet, it was her passion to see history preserved that caused her to use her beauty title and smile to attract statewide news attention to a threatened historical site. She won her fight against the big construction firm and the site became protected by law.

She had a pretty good run going at the table of life. One good hand after another...and she never had to bluff. One wouldn't think that an awkward girl from a backwoods family would end up learning the poise and charm necessary to lead people to action, all from trained professionals hired with the single task in mind to get her through a national competition, but somehow she did.

When after graduation, the offers for a literate historian in South Dakota didn't come pouring in, but one offer from a small local TV station *did*, she took it. It was the kind of spot in a market just small enough that the "talent" never got noticed and stayed a part of the local community through retirement. Yet, her constant success with her "Six on Your Side" segment that often championed the small-guy against the large corporate engine won the hearts of many and broke the barrier. She was soon taking up the causes of all the people on a regional level for a network affiliate.

The Dealer was smiling at her with every shingle tossed down. She could fill an inside straight on a dare. You wouldn't think a conservative Republican girl would become the voice for the outcast and downtrodden and do it so effectively that the Nielsen families would find her like they found their daily horoscope, but she did.

And when the global news network that had reigned for twenty years went beyond losing a little ground in the ratings to the new upstart conservative news channel and actually started coming in a distant second place, they needed a fast fix. They scoured the nation looking for a wholesome, fresh, socially concerned ratings-getter that hopefully looked sexy in a one-piece. They gave Jenna Domnanovich that big break into the world market at the tender age of twenty-four. They could already see a reduction in hemorrhaging in the three short weeks she had been working.

All aces with a king, man. You wouldn't think a woman with a hard-to-pronounce last name that *does* play the tuba and *didn't* graduate from Columbia would find a spot at this network, but she did.

So how was it that all of this came crashing to a halt with a single hand of Five Card Stud on a rainy October morning in a dark and cold Atlanta? All the chips were on the table, baby. And the Dealer was looking for a little payback.

The night before the cards shifted, she had been celebrating yet another triumph with her 43-year-old producer, Stan, as they watched the lead story on the Sunday evening news magazine broadcast from the bullpen—*her* story.

"I just don't understand how you do it?" Stan laughed as he good-naturedly slapped Jenna on the back like one of the guys while the rest of the reporters gave a more than obligatory applause. All the reporters, that is, except Jamison Hendry—the ex-shooting star whose flame was now being dimmed in the eyes of others by comparison with this new upstart.

"Do what?" Jenna said with a genuine naivety that made Jamison, who was visibly green as he looked on, sick.

"How you take a report that was hot two days ago but is cold news today and turn it around into something that would stir the consciousness of the country, that's all! You took Jamison's lead from Friday and gave it a tie-in that made it human! It was no longer boring news I didn't care about. It was real to me!"

The commercial break was over and all the reporters and crew that were congratulatory for the moment now shifted their attention back to the anchor as he was leading in the next story.

Jenna liked to like everybody. She really didn't want to find the scowl behind the smile. She liked to think that everyone else in the world was just as optimistic and happy as she. But she also knew Jamison's type. You don't compete nationally in the arena of beauty without understanding that most of the contestants got there using their ugliness. Jamison was just another Miss Fill-In-The-State, only with frost white hair, ice blue eyes, and was X-chromosome-impaired. So she knew what to say in front of him and what to keep hidden.

Once Jenna was convinced that Jamison had turned his back and was trying hard to put the past five minutes behind him, she said to Stan in a hushed voice, "Where did you grow up, Stan?"

"Reseda."

"Did you ever use to go on Easter egg hunts? Big ones where a whole bunch of people showed up?"

"Yeah, a few. Why?"

"In the Dakotas it is different than California. Sometimes the ground is still frozen at Easter. The township would want the kids to have the same fun, but it would be a bit difficult in a frozen flat field. So a farmer would plow a field just for the hunt. The frozen dirt chunks were easier and safer to walk across, I guess."

"Ok...I'm following you..."

"Well, you line up 100 kids at the edge of a field and shoot a starter pistol, how would you go get the most eggs with the prize inside?"

"I would race out there as fast as I could to the first egg I saw and start grabbing them up," Stan logically concluded.

"Right! And so would the other ninety-eight kids. But not me."

"No?" Stan puzzled.

"Nope. I would wait at the starting line. I would watch all the other kids run a quarter into the field. Then I would get to choose as I dashed out after they stopped to pick eggs up. If they missed a lot of eggs, I would simply clean up after them. But most of the time, they would stop too soon. I would race way out past them and have the whole field to myself."

"And that is what you do with the news?"

"Look, we all get here about the same time in the middle of the day. We all get the same crack at the same dailies. Jamison was throwing his weight around last week to get the "stolen fuel oil truck" story because it has terrorist overtones. If I had stopped at that egg with him, we would have spent most of the day scrapping over it.

"Instead, I let him have it and I picked a human interest story. Ma and Pa Red-State don't want to focus on bad stuff on a Friday night. They want to see the new lion cubs born in the zoo while they get ready to go out jukin'." With this, she did a little dance to make a point.

"So I let him have it and he covered it as straight news. I bet most of those that watched it forgot about it before the first slow dance of the night. But what I saw in that story is the plight of people that want to be in this country so desperately that they would break laws to get here and break laws to stay here. These are not the terrorists. These are the people of Ellis Island after they closed Ellis Island down."

"So you take a story everyone was familiar with…"

"And one that has already been legitimized and vetted out by our very own one-and-only Jamison Hendry…"

"And you build on it to make a deeper social point," Stan said.

"That leads off the Sunday magazine. As long as I have the best producer in cable news behind me, we could go all the way. I think it was Ronald Reagan that said, 'There is no limit to what you can do or where you can go, if you don't mind who gets the credit.'"

With a surprised and stealthy face and a finger in front of his mouth, "I don't think you should mention his name…we want our careers to keep heading up!" he said and they both laughed.

While they were laughing, Stan looked at Jenna with all the fatherly love and warmth a person could ever need. She could tell that he really cared about her and that was all the support necessary to make it in this world. It was that kind of concern Stan and so many others showed her on nights like that one that kept her warm on a blustery, rainy and dark morning like this.

Jenna was now standing on the sidewalk outside her Arts District condominium, wrestling with an umbrella that just would not cooperate. Taking instead the side of the wind in this tug of war, she made it two against one. The whole time the umbrella dance was going on, she was looking for a taxi. That was one of the worst things about Atlanta. She estimated there must be somewhere between three and four taxis—tops!

She was hoping for an umbrella defection over to her side so she could make the two-block hike to the MARTA subway station and from there she would be sheltered the rest of the way. But the umbrella did not appear to feel very rebellious against the wind so Jenna decided to chuck the whole thing in a nearby garbage can.

"I guess I can have someone in makeup fix me…nice to have such perks!" she said as she looked out from the awning at the ominously dark sky up above. With a quick wish for luck, she dashed out into the rain, pulling her long raincoat in close to her chin to protect the expensive dress-suit hidden safely underneath.

She stayed as close to the buildings as possible except where the gutters were overflowing thin sheets of water onto the limestone sidewalks forcing her out into the elements. It was at one of these moments between sheltering overhangs that her cell phone chirped to get her attention.

"Oh, great!" she huffed as she pulled it out and made for the closest shelter. Then after pressing the magic button that allowed those using a fancy tin can on the other side of an invisible kite string to send their desires aurally to the tin can held up to her ear she said back into her can, "Yes. Hello," in an extremely curt voice.

"Jenna?"

She knew the voice immediately. It was Jamison. He was particularly bouncy and this made the soaking Jenna exceedingly upset. "Yes, Jamison?"

"You don't sound yourself," he managed in a moment where he sounded as if he cared for someone else before returning the mirror back upon his own form.

I don't feel myself, she thought. But she said, "Sorry, Jamison. I'm caught in the rain and making my way to the MARTA station. What can I help you with?" and then realizing she could add it without being a lie, "I'm almost there and my cell loses its connection in the subway."

"Sorry to hear that, Jenna. I knew something must have been holding you up," he said in an obvious ploy to drag the conversation out.

"Thanks for the concern. What can I help you with? If I miss the next train, it could be fifteen minutes before the next one. You know how those things are." And as soon as she said it, she wished she hadn't. She knew he would delay things even more.

"Yeah. I waited thirty minutes one time. They get bogged down with the weather. More people riding them I suppose. Say...do you think there is an angle there for a story?"

"Jamison. What do you want?" She said as directly as she could without hurting his feelings. She still cared what people thought about her. It was a fatal flaw.

"It's just the dailies," he said, drawing his voice out a little for effect.

"What about the dailies?" she asked knowing he wouldn't go on until she did so. She started looking up and down the street for a taxi. *Why are there no goddamn taxies in the city?*

"Well...there is a story that is available. But it will take someone jumping on the corporate jet and making it to a remote location to cover the Secretary of Homeland Security's reaction to Australia condemning the Bali attacks. It demands immediate attention and I told Lloyd I could do it."

"Jamison, you know it is my slot in the rotation..."

"I know...I know...he is right here and I told him you would want me to cover it. He is excited about your three-part series you are so busy with!" His voice was virtually a used car salesman's with happy enthusiasm.

"What three-part series? What are you talking about, Jamison?" The rain was coming down in bigger drops now and her emotions were crashing down with the same terminal velocity.

"Right! I know! Who would have thought we would become so close in such a short time." Then, he paused as the reality of it all started dawning on her. Jamison was pretending to be having a totally different conversation with Jenna for the benefit of all those around him—namely him. "That's right. I promised I would help you with the series. I can call you from the jet and help you with anything you have problems with…"

"Jamison. This is low even for you."

Acting like she had said something different, something kind, he replied, "Uhuh…Uhuh…well you are so thoughtful for thinking of me," she heard a hand muffle the receiver a little and then heard Jamison say to someone else, "she told me to have a safe trip and stay where she can reach me for help. She's still learning the ropes." Then he said back to her, "Ok. Well, be safe on the road, working on that series of yours. Lloyd said to be safe!"

At this point, Jenna just stood there and listened instead of giving him more opportunity to ignore her and change her words. She could have hung up, but wanted to hear as much as Jamison was willing to say with her still on the line. If she hung up, he could have the two of them engaged and planning a trip by week's end from his side of this increasingly fictional conversation.

Instead, Jamison simply ended the conversation as if Jenna had said yet more pleasantries. "Will do chief. You are the best cub reporter I have seen in quite some time. You keep up that winning attitude and you just might be a lead reporter like me some day." He paused for more of her supposed lines. "Of course I'd be glad to help you out along the way. But I need to dash to the airport. Be safe! Looking forward to seeing that series rough draft soon!"

Before he could hang up, she did manage to slip in a coolly voiced, "I will get even with you when I get in today." But before she could hear his reply, the tin can on the other side made an audible click.

"Now he is telling those around him that we are engaged and the trip is this weekend," she said in a disgusted conclusion aloud.

There was no need to cry. She looked up and the sky was crying for her.

After a few moments of unusual self-pity, she screwed her courage up to the sticking place and said, "When the going gets tough, the tough get liquor!" She joked to keep her own spirits slightly above the flood line in the curb beside her.

With that, she trudged back out from under her temporary shelter and started making for the MARTA station—now only one block away. After crossing the street, she was passing an old store that had been converted into a failed puppet workshop before being vacant for eight months out of the year. The happy months when the national tax preparation firm would be back to offer free coffee in the morning was still another three months and four holidays away.

As she passed in front of the large floor-to-ceiling windows, she turned and looked square at the face of the drowned cat from Dakota that was staring back at her.

"It's going to take more than makeup to fix this," she said as she pulled her wet mop of a hairdo all the way out to the side and let it flop back against her right ear.

For just a moment, she felt the huge invisible tug of her Grandmother's quilt calling her back up to her high-rise condo. *Jenna...it called, Come home and I will warm you while you play hooky!*

"Oh...I can't do that..." she replied to her reflection that was a waif in the window.

Jamison told Lloyd you were working on a series...Just stay home and make one up!

The quilt always did make more sense than reality. It would be so easy to go back now. *That's it. Nice hot soup and a warm quilt made with love.*

"No," she said suddenly as if breaking a spell. "No. I will go to work. There are stories to be told. I'll just straighten things out with Lloyd when I make it to the office and take the second slot if I'm not too late." Turning back to her right she made a determined line for the MARTA station that was just ahead and then onward to the office via subway.

But she would never make it. In the end, Mike Castaneda would handle the story in the second slot.

The walk to the station was a little less than a run making good time. In a few moments, she was pulling her monthly pass out from her press credentials and sliding it through the turnstile. Stepping out of the rain and into the large, concrete slab structure was more than enough to put some spring back into her step.

Passing the posters of Latino women, that looked more stylized American than anything else, proclaiming the virtue of some product in Spanish, she made for the down escalator. A recorded female voice echoed in the dim wash of fluorescent lighting taking away whatever charm there could be found in seventies slab architecture, "The next southbound train is for Airport station. The next southbound train is for Airport station."

"Hold on!" she cried to the open doors that promised to be impatient if she did not hurry. Running across the platform, Jenna just made it inside before the doors slid shut with an unceremonious flam behind her.

Being somewhat observant, she always looked around and tried to make eye contact with everyone on a subway car. This car was not particularly crowded. There were a few people from the local phone company going from a building further uptown to the main building downtown. You could always tell them by their badges with either blue or red stripes down the side. Then, there were a few people that looked like hard-working blue-collar types. Lastly, there were a few young people that looked to be students at the city college.

Two of these were sitting together going over something in a textbook. The third was an attractive, Italian looking girl wearing a black duster coat over an outfit that looked a little like a throwback to the old Catholic Schoolgirl uniforms. Looking back up at an advertisement for a singles chat line, she made a mental note, *Plaid skirt and sweater top. Must be making a comeback!*

Jenna took an open seat before the train lurched towards its destination. Facing front now, she could no longer see all the people behind her. She picked up her PDA and turned it on. Soon, she was engrossed in the meetings planned for today and the rest of the week. The train made stops as she worked deeper and deeper in thought. She decided to move a few things around as she heard the friendly female voice say, "Next station, Midtown. Next station, Midtown." The train had made its stop and was now whisking off to the next.

She continued to work on her schedule until she had enough things balanced that would allow her to accomplish her goals for the week. There were three people she would need to contact at the office and postpone meetings until later. The train continued to make stops. As she was jotting some notes to herself about a conference planned for the Terrorist Alert Level scheme recently introduced, she heard the friendly female voice say, "Next station, Midtown. Next station, Midtown." The train made another stop.

Something in Jenna's subconscious startled her back to reality and she wondered out loud, "Did she just say Midtown again?" Looking around, she saw no one particularly close or friendly to ask. At this stop, a few people got off and a few more got on. She looked at the station but could not make out from memory which one it was. It looked like North Avenue, but the voice said Midtown.

As the train pulled off again, Jenna became concerned that she would ride past her station needed to make the connection west to the network building. After some quick consideration, she concluded it would be better to get off one station early than to miss her station altogether. She had discovered from experience that the next station after the connection was further away and extremely difficult to cross over to catch a train back.

As the train started to slow down for the next stop, she put her PDA away and gathered her things. If she was wrong, it would only be a short wait for the next train—she hoped.

The train stopped and Jenna exited without waiting for the friendly announcement. It didn't always give you the name quick enough to make a timely exit. Standing on the white tile platform, she knew almost instantly that this was the Civic Center station—two stations early. It was the "almost" part that caused her to miss the chance to dive back on.

"Shit," she said to the flam of the doors.

A giggle came from her left as the MARTA train started to pull away. She looked to the left and saw no one there. But the giggle was still echoing.

This particular station was different from all the others. Since it was for the Civic Center, it was a little more formal in attire. Where all the other stations were bland, poured concrete like something out of a bad sci-fi film, this station was mostly made up of clean white tiled walls. It was also roomier than the others. To gain the extra space on either side of the track, architects had incorporated large rectangular columns with rounded corners. They stood at attention in two rows guarding either side of the tracks in parallel lines.

On weekdays, this station was particularly dead. Presently, Jenna was the only person there. Just her and some disembodied giggle haunting around the columns. In an effort to not feel quite so dumb and at the same time acknowledge someone that might actually be there, she said, "What's so funny?"

A fading and warbled reply came back. It sounded like it was being played backwards on a phonograph. "I didn't know you were the type for profanity..." followed by another set of giggles.

Civic Center Station is actually above ground for the most part. The tiled walls on either side are met by large sections of glass. The dark storm clouds outside almost gave the feel of evening. Jenna felt horribly alone.

Getting a sense that the sounds were coming from her left, she decided to walk down and confront them—better the enemy that she knows, than the enemy she doesn't. As she moved down the outside of the columns looking for someone to be behind the next one, she heard the distorted voice say, "What's the matter, Jenna? Never had a fan stalk you before?"

Ice filled her veins. Her adrenalin was pumping, not because the voice knew her name, not even because it used the word "stalk," but because it was now coming from a distance *behind* her. Jenna wheeled around just in time to see the tail of a black duster coat disappear behind a column. Putting everything together, she came up with the conclusion, *There are nuts out in the world that like me as a celebrity. Most are harmless. Some can be deadly. This is the young lady from the train. She is having a college prank with me. I can confront her and maybe break the suspense before the next train arrives.*

She started taking steps toward that gap between the columns keeping mindful of the spaces between them and the tracks. She was not going to allow this trickster to double-back on her again. She was just coming up to the corner when she decided she would turn the tables a little. Jenna jumped the last step and did her best "Gotcha!" pose.

No one was there.

"Nothing to say? Cat go your tongue?" the voice came. This time it was on the other side of the tracks! Now Jenna was getting concerned. She really didn't comprehend how this was all happening. Then on the other side of the tracks, the Italian looking young lady stepped out from behind a column and stood in the gap opposite Jenna. She said with a direct tone that easily covered the distance between them as if she were using some freakish amplification device, "...But you are so rarely at a loss for words, news lady."

Jenna's mind relaxed a little. There was a good thirty feet between them, not to mention two sets of subway tracks and a thin orange rail with the station name stenciled in white lettering. She was just starting to de-puzzle how the girl could have possibly crossed the tracks and the rail when something totally heart-stopping happened.

As the young lady was saying in yet another distorted voice, "Perhaps I can help you find some words..." she visibly rose straight up about ten inches off the ground and hovered. Her arms were at her sides and her palms were extended, stretched out flat, facing down in a parallel line with the floor.

"What the?" Jenna managed. Her own voice sounded like it was coming from someone else. All she knew was this was bad. This was very bad. And she needed to use all the new energy being created by the chemicals in her body to run away—fast!

Jenna turned and started running to the exit just fifty feet away. She only made it two of those feet before a blur terminated with the form of the pretty young lady standing in front of her. She looked maybe twenty-two at the most. Jenna was able to ask, "What *are* you?" Still her voice sounded distant. None of this seemed to actually be happening to her. She was numb from it all.

"I'm Josephine. I will be you. You will be me," the girl riddled as she grabbed Jenna's right bicep with her hand. Jenna struggled to get free and run again but the grip felt more like a solid steel restraint than a flesh-and-bone college girl.

"I don't want any trouble," Jenna heard herself say.

"No trouble at all, sweetie. Like passing a hot needle through butter."

Jenna saw a blur to her left ear as she started to scream for help. Just as her voice was rising she felt something like a bee sting the nape of her neck and immediately her voice stopped cold in its tracks.

Josephine was about her same height and was now pulling her in close to her. Jenna could feel everything but was unable to move a single muscle on her own. Her predator said softly in her ear, "Now hold still and this will go very quickly for you."

Her mind became a humming, pulsing blur. For some strange reason, Jenna started to feel a seductive heat and an aroused dampness between her legs accompanied by warmth rising in her breasts. Flashes and images started unfolding.

She felt like she had only just embarked on a long journey in her mind and in her senses when suddenly a full field of bright pink flashed before her eyes.

The pink field had stars in it and it sizzled with energy. This sudden field of light that reminded her a little of her uncle's flash attachment on the old instant camera was accompanied by a loud popping noise in her ear. Then she heard a crackle and felt her arm release and the pressure suddenly removed from the back of her neck.

Jenna struggled to regain her vision by blinking her eyes as her body mobility returned. She heard moaning mixed with screams as she started being able to make out the form of Josephine falling back from her as if shocked back by a high voltage fence.

Josephine was screaming, "Oh, you bitch! You little shit!"

That was about all Josephine could yell before the screams crowded the intelligible words out of the communication subway tunnel that was her throat. No more word trains would be arriving at the station of Josephine's mouth today. The Scream Express was coming through.

Jenna watched in horrid disbelief as Josephine started lifting up off the ground and while listing a little to the left, began slowly to spin. Jenna became aware that there were now two sets of screams. Her own out-of-body voice had returned to this macabre scene to make it a horrifying duet.

The two women screamed at each other as Josephine's rotation increased its speed. Just then light started emanating from every orifice on Josephine's head. It poured out in straight lines radiating three feet. She looked to Jenna like some sort of hellish lighthouse spinning fast and faster.

The smell of burning flesh started wafting around Jenna and her gorge rose with the now intensifying screams from both of them. Soon Josephine was a bright spinning blur of heat and blue light. Jenna could feel the temperature now actually doing damage to her but was totally overwhelmed with a fear and awe that refused to let her move one step.

With a horrible sound beyond imagination, Josephine was completely consumed in the blaze that was her person. Jenna winced and closed her eyes as the force of the sudden release of pressure pushed her back. Wind rushed around her echoing down the tunnels in both directions being chased by the haunting remnants of Josephine's wailing.

Then there was silence.

When her senses returned to her, Jenna realized she was now kneeling. There was a small patch of dust on the ground just in front of her. The wind of the approaching train blew the dust away as its rumble drowned out her sobs.

The news lady just knelt there and cried.

12a.
12.19.9.12.0.3333; 13 YAX, 2 AHAU — LORD

October 15, 2002, 8:05 a.m. EST

Ned was late for their meeting. Andrea didn't mind so much. She was on time and the professor was late. That was all that mattered in her book. Besides, she had a new hobby of sorts.

While Ned had instructed her to spend this week studying early colonial culture and customs out of the Codex, she had snuck in a few minutes to follow Sorin's advice and studied the Maya. As it turned out, there were a lot of interesting things there.

She had concentrated on the calendar. It had turned out to be so complex and accurate! Andrea had found an ancient book that had picture-words for dates that looked like glyphs. The calendar was actually made up of two sub-calendars.

The historian-writer explained that these twenty picture-words for one of the sub-calendars were the Tzolkin, which represented twenty days. These sets repeated thirteen times to make a 260-day period. Each Tzolkin glyph had a matching word and meaning and all of it together made up one Tzolkin calendar.

These Tzolkin days were then paired with thirteen numbers that would repeat so that they would result in a pattern that was eight days off each cycle.

It works something like our days of the week. It would pair these days with numbers of the month. Andrea learned that there would be 1-Imix (similar to Sunday, the 1st) followed by 2-Ik (just as Monday, the 2nd). When you get to 13-Ben, the next day would start the numbers over again but continue with the remaining picture-words. So it would then go 1-Ix, 2-

Men, etc. It takes 260 days before the cycle gets back to 1-Imix again (13 x 20).

The 260-day period was coupled with a concurrent eighteen-month calendar. Each month had twenty days with five days for rest added. This would bring the total for this second calendar to 365 days. This was called a Haab calendar. If the 260 day Tzolkin calendar is lined up with the 365 day Haab calendar, it would ultimately repeat itself every fifty-two years—a number that has an uncanny parallel to the fifty-year Jewish Jubilee where sins were forgiven and slaves were set free.

With this combination calendar the Maya believed that every 3,600 years, the Earth would renew itself. In this book, Andrea learned that the next cycle would be in the year 2012 A.D. and that some scholars believed that the Maya taught it would usher in the age of the 4th dimension, whatever that means.

She didn't really take any of it seriously, but for what it was worth, she had programmed in these glyph names into her satellite phone so that she could see what day it was to the Maya. She was looking down at the phone now. The name that appeared in the upper right corner was Ahau or Lord.

"Lord, don't let the boss-man find out I've been studying something other than colonial culture and customs!" she said in a melodramatic way.

A voice interrupted her isolation, "I'm sure He heard you. But there is one small problem…"

It was Ned entering his sterile domain to sit behind his desk and pontificate to Andrea. "Do you believe the Lord answers prayer?" he asked directly to her.

"Oh, definitely! I'm still here, aren't I?"

"Quite. But here's the problem. Everyone knows that in the Good Book it says that He answers every prayer. But they presume that means the answer will always be *yes* and if He doesn't answer yes, then they are doing something wrong—theology right out of the pit. But I can think of four ways He could *choose* to answer each prayer."

She asked skeptically, "What would those be? Yes, No, and Maybe?"

"Not quite. You got the first two correct. Yes and No. But He never seems to have difficulty making up His mind so I would think that Maybe is out."

She actually was a little interested in what he had to say. Maybe Ned wasn't all that bad. This was the second time he had her attention and he definitely seemed fairly wise in some things. "Ok, professor…what are the other two?"

"One is substitute," he said flatly.

"What? Isn't that a little jejune for the Almighty?"

"Not really. I would consider it more benevolent. You asked for a fish, He would give you a boat and a fishing pole. You go *catch* the fish."

This seemed to make some sense at a kindergarten level to her. "Ok…and what is the fourth? *Hell* no?"

He laughed. Then Ned said, "No, it wouldn't be hell no. It would be Wait."

"That's it…*Wait?*"

"Right. He waits until a situation becomes so humanly impossible to solve, so miserably screwed up, that when He answers the prayer…there is no way anyone could get the credit for the answer but Him."

"So much for a benevolent God. Sounds a little like parlor games to me."

"Not quite…He could have just said no. If you ask, then that means you are prepared for the fact that the Lord, God Almighty can answer any way He pleases. By merely asking, that means you fully anticipate Him to be free to answer with His *will*. And that is the nature of 'Thy will be done'."

Andrea hated to admit it, but it seemed like this Ned fellow had at least a pretty good grasp on some things. In an effort to lighten the mood up a little she asked, "Is the lesson over? May we have juice and cookies now?"

"Are you asking? Or are you presuming?" He quizzed.

"I'm asking," she dutifully answered.

"Then my answer is no," and with this they both laughed a little. Then a little more seriously, "I have a new assignment for you."

"Really? Already? Shall I go deliver a subpoena?" She said with a little too much sarcasm for her own taste. She wished she could take it back and was relieved when Ned appeared to step right through her point and continue with his.

"A woman was attacked yesterday. The local authorities think she may be having a mental breakdown because there was no evidence of the attack—at least not much to speak of. But we believe she was attacked by a Croatoan."

"But I thought that would kill the victim," Andrea said.

"Not always. And that is precisely why we need an agent to scope it out and ask questions."

"But why me? I mean…I'm still a rookie," she said.

"I told you. We don't hire rookies. You are an experienced agent in more ways than one. We need you to go because it is in your old stomping grounds."

She raised her eyebrows in an effort to say *How so?* without using words. It must have worked because Ned continued, "She's in the downtown hospital in Atlanta, Georgia."

"Oh, Lord," Andrea said.

It wasn't long before she was on another jet. Ironically she was heading back to the home she felt she had left years ago. It blew her mind to realize that it had only been a week.

There were many other people on this jet. It was not a private trip. But as lonely as she had felt on the flight up to Peabody, she now felt over-crowded. She supposed it was the fact that she was heading back to the state she had wanted so much to leave, and all the emotions swirling around it that made her now just want to be alone and look at the sun's rays as they dappled the cloudy mass below her.

The other agents on the plane were swapping stories from the field and helping one another learn. It seemed to be an obsession with them. The way that some had gotten out of their seats and were now sitting on armrests, clustered in a little group talking about their assignments like a coffee klatch gabbing about the latest football game. The jovial atmosphere of camaraderie now repelled her into a dark world of solitude and inner questioning as the sunshine from outside her window ironically bathed her face in light.

One of the other agents bounced into the seat next to her and asked, "Everything ok, Andrea?"

She was a bit startled to hear one of these use her given name. She turned and came face-to-face with the agent that had smashed into her in Buchanan Hall. With the recognition and memory of his name, she said, "It depends, Scott…how fast can you run in this small jet?"

Laughing a little he said, "Oh, that. I'd hoped you had forgotten." Then turning around and looking up and down the aisle as if to measure it for a serious answer he concluded, "Pretty damn fast actually."

Skeptically with one eyebrow raised she asked, "Oh really?"

"Absolutely! I am a strong starter but a slow finisher." He stretched out the word slow and there was a perceptible twinkle in his eye.

Andrea realized, as most women do, that this man-thing was now trying to flirt with her by using double-entendre. Playing it like she did not understand the second meaning because she often found that got her more quickly out of this kind of encounter, "Your high school coach must have loved you as a sprinter." She turned her head back to the window as a clear gesture for him to get a clue and leave.

Persistently he came back, "Actually I was in the band."

Turning back to him with a slightly annoyed look on her face, "What?"

"I was in band. I couldn't be in music and athletics at the school I attended. And I really loved music. So I chose band."

That desire to crawl away in a cave somewhere became stronger now. She thought about saying something short to him and driving him away. But then she realized she needed to think about her future a little as well. Her police training had taught her that no matter how much she may have disliked a fellow officer, she really had no idea when her life may depend upon their action. So she tried to accomplish her first goal of being alone within the framework of this tenet. "That is really cool. I know I would love to hear about it in detail sometime. But you know, Scott…I really have a lot on my mind right now. Can we try to hook up back at the Center for coffee sometime?"

With the twinkle never leaving he said, "Absolute. I'll leave you to your thinking and look forward to running into you again soon."

She was a little startled to find the smile on her face was genuine. She bantered back to him as he was leaving, "Next time yell 'incoming!'"

Turning back to her he said, "Will do."

Once Scott was gone the rest of the trip became one strung-together sequence of events. The world of people around her moved as blurs as she seamlessly landed in Atlanta, got her overnight bag, rented a car, and drove the twenty minutes to the hospital downtown. In her blurry consciousness were thoughts of everything and nothing. More impressions of the past mixed with questions of the future. There was even a small thread there for Scott to occupy.

At the hospital, she used her credentials to make fast work of finding the correct section, floor, and wing for Jenna. But she was stopped at the door when she arrived at the proper location. The attending nurse explained that the visiting hour was at 11:00 a.m.

Andrea looked at her watch and noted that it was already 4:00 p.m. "That's the most ridiculous thing I've ever heard," she said, "What kind of hospital has only one visiting hour per day?"

"I am sorry Agent Ellijay, but it is a strictly enforced policy here. The only exceptions are by court order and with the attending physician's presence. It is a state regulation I am afraid. Please come back tomorrow."

Andrea really wasn't getting this. She had been on hundreds of investigations before and never run into this kind of regulation. "Is the attending physician in by any chance?"

"I believe so."

"May I have a word with him?"

"It is a 'she' and I will see if *she* has time."

Andrea felt a little embarrassment being caught in one of the oldest perceptions of stereotype there was. "Thank you," she said to the nurse as she was leaving. It came out a little sheepishly.

She waited at the large double doors for what felt like a week. The hatred for the way hospital personnel treated the public could not intensify any more for Andrea. That meter had reached and passed its red line years ago and was now planted firmly against the post that prevented the needle from spinning all the way around. If that post ever gave way, her "Contempt for Hospital Personnel" needle would spin so fast that the whole damn gauge would fly to Peking.

Finally, after an eternity of watching the needle chop further into the post out of sheer force, a petite woman from India wearing a white lab coat and obligatory stethoscope came through the doors that looked too large and heavy for her to move with her tiny body. But they virtually slammed open.

Small, but powerful this doctor seemed.

In a competent and more than polite voice she said, "Hello. Are you the agent investigating Ms. Domnanovich?"

"Yes. I am Andrea Ellijay. May I ask you a few questions, please?"

"Certainly." She was looking up at Andrea. Her small wire frame glasses magnified her brown eyes. "But I need to see your identification first. It is a matter of policy."

Scrambling almost instantly in her purse Andrea said, "Oh, I'm sorry. Of course." She brought out the leather case and flipped it open. The doctor held it up close to her face and studied it intently.

Handing the ID back to Andrea, the doctor said, "I am Dr. Patel. How can I help you?"

"What can you tell me about the condition of Jenna Domnanovich?"

"State law prevents me from discussing any details of Ms. Domnanovich's medical condition without her expressed consent."

Dr. Patel's face now showed that she had registered the growing look of frustration on Andrea's face. She reached a hand out and touched Andrea on the arm at the elbow and said in a soothing voice, "But I can give you certain observations on her appearance and general conclusions one could draw from that. Beyond that, we will need to wait until tomorrow."

"That is another thing, why has the hospital instituted this crazy one hour visitation rule?"

Dr. Patel answered, "It is not the hospital. It is just this ward. We do it for the patient's safety."

Andrea realized now where exactly she was, "Why is Jenna in the P-wing?"

Dr. Patel said, "Without discussing things that I cannot, I *can* tell you that Ms. Domnanovich came to us in a heightened state of delusional consciousness. She had redness to her skin as if she were sunburned, some slight bruising around her upper left arm, and she was complaining of a stinging sensation to the back of her neck.

"She was admitted to the hospital. Her harried state and own professed observations met the medical criteria for us to hold her here for 48 hours for observation. We are performing the necessary tests to conclude whether or not we will need to hold her for a longer period of time."

"You mean institutionalize her," Andrea said with maybe a little coolness to her voice.

"I mean commit her for further observation and possible treatment. Yes."

"What were the observations she made?" Andrea resumed her questioning.

"On the surface, and purely as anecdotal information, she claimed to have been attacked by a woman that exhibited properties easily ascribed to fantasy or delusion."

"What tests have you run and are there any conclusions?"

"I am sorry, Agent Ellijay, but I cannot speak on such things without the patient's permission and presence." Then with a look of genuine sincerity, Dr. Patel said, "Agent Ellijay, I think that this woman's condition may be helped by a visit from you. Having someone genuinely interested in you during these moments in life can help a person find a lifeline. I will schedule my rounds tomorrow to coincide with the visiting hour if you wish to come back. I can then discuss some results with Ms. Domnanovich in your presence if she is so willing."

"That is most kind and I will be here tomorrow," Andrea said.

The needle on the gauge had not moved down a lot. But at least it was no longer playing lumberjack against the stop post.

Andrea checked-in to her hotel near the hospital and updated her sat-phone agenda with information. A call to Ned was not necessary and after a nice dinner, she stopped at a small wine shop she knew and purchased the customary bottle to be her companion for the evening.

Once again, she found herself perched on a balcony overlooking a crowded city street with a plastic glass of fine wine, her phone in her lap, and a desire to call an old friend.

With the courage brought by the second glass, she scrolled through her directory and stopped with the cursor pointing at Wren's number. It flashed there impatiently waiting for her to press the dial button.

"Gonna chicken out again, Andrea?" the cursor seemed to say to her.

Her conservative nature that had protected her thus far in life was now bound and gagged in the corner. Her thumb found new bravery and mashed the dial button as if it were sending out the nuclear dawn.

She held the device up to her ear and listened patiently as a phone on the other side of countless switches, routers, and fiber optic cables requested Wren's attention with some sort of annoying audible signal. After the second such signal, Andrea started to become concerned that no one would answer. But on the third signal, there was an interrupting click followed by a voice that could play on a radio program the father of the boy she knew. It said, "Hello?"

Andrea started to speak but the words froze in her throat. Try as she may, they were on strike. The picket line was forming and they were holding up signs saying, "Free the Conservative Nature!" and "We stay gagged while it is gagged!"

"Hello?" the voice reiterated.

Taking a quick sip of wine to wash down the protesting words and bring in the scab workers, Andrea virtually gasped, "Wren?"

"Yes, this is Wren. How can I help you?"

"Wren, this is Andrea…Andrea Ellijay." She was halfway expecting to have to explain who she was. She had been rehearsing this unnecessary monologue for half an hour now.

"Andrea? Liddy told me you called! How the hell are you doing?!" Wren asked with obvious happiness.

"I'm doing great, Wren! How are you?"

"Fantastic! Life is great and the orphanage is as solid as ever."

"Ironic that you are back at the orphanage. I always thought you would take on the biggest challenges of the world!" she said with an obvious tone of friendly respect.

"I am! When I was adopted at eighteen, the family that did it said they saw a great future in me. They wanted to help me with it. So they gave me a last name and an education."

"And I meant what I said to you all those years ago, Andrea. I did want to take on the world. I knew I could make a difference. So I studied for years, got my PhD, wrote some white papers and decided to go to the largest orphanage in the United States to solve some problems using some new models I developed."

Andrea took a sip of wine and asked, "Where was that?"

Wren laughed a little and said, "Why right here, of course! Bethesda *is* the largest orphanage in the U.S.!"

"Really? I didn't know that!"

"Sure, it's one of the oldest as well. We were founded in 1740, well before the country as a matter of fact!" His pride was prominent.

"Gee, I just thought it was a good place to pick up boys," she said and they both laughed.

Wren said, "I was always really glad you and the others came down from Baxley. I have thought about you often over the years, but lost track of you after that last move."

"It was difficult to keep in touch with the people I met. The system shifted me around from place to place and I sort of lost my desire to set down roots. It hurts too badly when someone breaks them off over and over."

"That is precisely what we are trying to fix at Bethesda. Some of the new models are even getting world-wide attention!"

"You better be careful Wren. You will become a celebrity!"

Slightly embarrassed, Wren switched the conversation back to her and asked how she was doing, and what had life dealt to her. She answered, "I managed good enough grades to get some scholarships, worked in law enforcement, even the GBI for a while. And now I work in security investigations."

"Wow! I will have to mind my P's and Q's!" he said laughingly.

They talked on like that for what seemed like only minutes to them, but in the end, it was 1:00 a.m. when they started their goodbyes.

As they were both Southern, well…it took a while.

They both promised to stay in touch and Andrea said she would try to stop in to visit within the next year, as soon as she got some vacation time accrued.

The two old friends slept well that night knowing that someone else in the world shared their own fears and angers from the past and that someone else had made it out of the system and was making a difference.

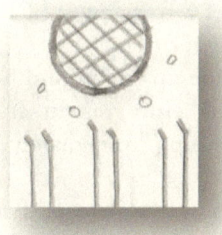

12b.
12.19.9.12.1.₄₅₈₃; 14 YAX, 3 IMIX — WATER LILY OR WORLD

October 16, 2002, 11:00 a.m. EST

Andrea Ellijay had been waiting outside the double doors with a handful of concerned visitors for other patients. She had wondered if anyone else was there for Jenna. Each person had to tell the nurse which patient they were here to visit. She had been a little surprised when no one else said Jenna's name.

Now rounding the corner from the hall into Jenna's room, she found a pretty young woman hooked up to an IV with her covers pulled down to her waist exposing the latest in hospital fashion.

Without any makeup, Jenna's face was noticeably puffy presumably from crying. The grey autumnal light filtered through the cold rain outside was casting shadows across her bed and added zero contribution to the cheerless environment. Andrea realized the only happiness this poor woman would see today would be in her own smile. She put on her warmest face and crossed to the bed.

"Jenna Domnanovich?"

"Yes?"

Extending her credentials, "I am Agent Ellijay. Please call me Andrea. Do you mind if we talk a little while?"

Jenna looked as if she were going to cry again. "You mean someone finally might actually believe me? I am not crazy! I have told them a thousand times!" And then, some tears did manage to escape from their puffy prisons.

Andrea instinctively sat beside her and reached her arms around her to hug Jenna being mindful all the while not to brush up against the IV needle in her arm. "Shhh…There, there. It's ok. We can talk when you're ready."

Jenna reached around as best as she could. She could only manage to grab Andrea by the elbows before the IV would reach its limit. But it was enough for her. She pulled her face into the comforting place in the square of Andrea's shoulder and let a fresh river of tears flow as she rocked back and forth in a gentle swaying motion.

After some time, she came up for air and her nose was in bad need of a tissue. She looked suddenly embarrassed at the dampness of Andrea's shoulder and started apologizing immediately as she looked frantically for her tissue box.

Andrea said, as Jenna found the box and started attending to her nose, "Don't worry about it at all. My shoulder is always here for someone that needs it." Andrea was taking this moment to study Jenna's face. It had seemed like a trick of the odd lighting in this room, but her face did look a little sunburned. Also, the bruises on her left bicep were yellowing a little but were still obvious.

"It was just so horrible. This young woman named Josephine approached me and looked like she was going to kill me. She moved faster than anything I've ever seen and…" her words trailed off as if she felt she had said too much.

"And what?" Andrea pressed.

"and…nothing. I say more and they will put me away. I understand the score and I am *not* crazy. I will figure it all out on my own. It's what I do best."

"I'm sure you will. I will do everything in my power to help you. Let's not worry any more about details from the attack for now. What happened to your assailant? Did she get away?"

"Oh, she got away alright…really far away. I think she's dead."

"How so?"

"Let's just say she disappeared and leave it at that."

"Fine. We can leave it at that for now as well. How have you been since then?" Andrea said in an effort to keep the dialog going.

"You mean besides the obvious?" Jenna said as she lifted her arm with the IV in it.

Letting a little warm laugh escape, Andrea said, "Yes…besides the obvious."

"I have been having these flashes every once in a while. They aren't really memories or events that I know about. They are more like metaphors for innocence."

"I am not sure I follow you."

"Look, the lady that attacked me did something to me. She touched the top of my neck and it shocked me. I don't know if it was a device or what, but since then I have been getting these scenes of innocent things: children, flowers, puppies…you know…innocence. They come to me in single bursts. About the only thing they *have* done here that made any sense to me at all is an MRI and CAT scan. I'm hoping they can find the cause of these flashes."

"And we may just have done that, Ms. Domnanovich," came the voice of Dr. Patel as she entered the room with a clipboard. "You are looking well this morning." Then to Andrea, "And hello, Agent Ellijay. I am pleased to see you are here." Then back to Jenna, "Jenna, I believe this woman can help us some. Is it ok if we speak about your prognosis in front of her? I will need your consent."

Jenna looked at Andrea and back to Dr. Patel, "I suppose it's ok. Am I under any sort of investigation? Are there any legal consequences to any of the information that you will discuss?"

"Not on your part. The only person here that can take any legal action is you at this point, Jenna. We are asking for the sake of your own rights, not for any investigation," Dr. Patel answered.

"Then…it's fine with me," Jenna said.

Andrea was still sitting on the edge of the bed next to Jenna and Dr. Patel pulled a physician's stool up to the side of the bed. She extended the clipboard with a folder on it and used the folder as a slate for an illustration. She drew a quick sketch of two lines with casing around them. The tips of the lines were nearly touching.

"These lines represent nerves between your brain and your muscles, Jenna," Dr. Patel began, using her pen as a stylus and a drawing tool when needed, "These casings or sheaths wrapped around them are fatty coverings called myelin. Myelin ensures the swift transmission of nerve impulses from brain to muscle.

Dr. Patel opened the folder up and showed some images of magnified tissue. It said "Magnetic Resonance Imaging" across the top. Using her pen as a pointing device she continued, "Here on your MRI, we see that the myelin has been damaged from scarring."

"What causes the scarring?" Jenna asked.

"Medical science still does not know the answer to that question. The destruction of myelin seems to be due to an abnormal response of the immune system in which cells that normally protect against illness react against the body's own tissues.

"The net result of this kind of scarring is that body movements may become slow or uncoordinated because signals from the brain to the muscles deteriorate, or arms and legs may feel spots of numbness because sensations from the extremities no longer reach the brain.

"So in your case, we cross-matched these results with those from a Magnetic Resonance Spectroscopy as well as a study of your cerebrospinal fluid, where we found the presence of specific antibodies."

Jenna started getting the look of shocked worry across her face, "What exactly are you saying?"

Dr. Patel shifted her weight on the stool a little and looked Jenna directly in the eye. "From all of the results, I feel confident that we can conclude that you are suffering from the early stages of Multiple Sclerosis."

"What?" Jenna asked. Andrea had found herself almost voicing the same question.

"I am afraid it is true. And unfortunately there is more, but I must be direct with you. Eighty-five percent of those with MS have the kind that flares up and then goes into remission. It can take years or decades for the full effects to appear, if they ever do. But you appear to be unfortunately in the fifteen percent that have the progressive kind of MS."

"No," Jenna said.

Dr. Patel continued unabated wanting to put all the news out there rather than drag it out and make the patient suffer, "symptoms generally do not remit and may become, and usually do become rapidly worse."

"No," Jenna repeated.

"I think you should stay here for the afternoon and then I would like to transfer you to a different wing of the hospital where you will have some more liberties and where you can rest for twenty-four hours. I know this is all a heavy strain and I really feel it would be best."

"What can be done to stop it?" Jenna asked.

"There are breakthroughs every day. We can discuss all your options for treatment at another time. For now as your doctor I suggest that you just spend some time resting. You have much to digest and think about." Then looking at Andrea, "Agent Ellijay, I trust you can stay for the remainder of the hour?"

"Yes, of course," Andrea said in a diminished and distant voice.

Dr. Patel quickly left the room and the two women looked at each other. Jenna started slowly shaking her head back and forth. In a voice that started as a whisper and grew with crescendo, she said over and over, "no, no, no."

Andrea's shoulder again became the willing host as she embraced the sobbing Jenna. Andrea was now aware of the sound of the rain outside. It was falling even harder, as if the sky was sobbing with empathy. As she rocked her back and forth, Andrea realized she was now rubbing her own leg just above the left knee.

The numbness had disappeared just after her new employer had given her a battery of injections.

She thought to herself while this relative stranger was falling apart in her arms, *They picked me because I met certain criteria, they gave me a shot and the numbness went away, they hire us to fight the Croatoan, the Croatoan work on electrical impulses from the brain, a Croatoan died while attacking this woman because of the fault in her electrical system…*

With each passing puzzle piece that snapped perfectly into place, Andrea's rage grew inside her at an alarming rate. She now realized that she also had MS and that the Order was *using* her.

Containing her rage for the time being, she knew that she needed to get back to the Center for some straight answers. Trying to finish up her responsibilities here she said to Jenna, "It's nearly noon. Will you be ok?"

Still hiccupping from the crying session she said, "Yes. My family is coming in from South Dakota later today. This is all just so much of a new world for me. Thank you for being here, Andrea. I'm not sure what I would have done if I had to face that news alone."

Handing her a piece of paper with her satellite-phone number on it she said, "Please call me if you ever need me. I work nationally and may not be able to get here in person. But I will continue to investigate your story and try to help where I can."

"Thank you," Jenna said.

"And by the way…I believe you."

They were trying to say their goodbyes when a nurse came in and shooed Andrea away.

Now she turned her attention back to her own rage. She would feed on it the rest of the day as she made her way back to those she would confront.

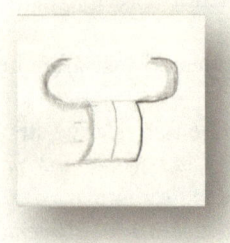

13.
12.19.9.12.2.3333; 15 YAX, 4 IK — WIND

October 17, 2002, 8:00 a.m. EST

Andrea didn't talk to anyone the rest of the day, except a polite thank you to cashiers and desk clerks. She caught a late flight back and stared out the window into black space. The night in the townhouse was spent regimentally as she performed required household and personal hygiene tasks without emotion or comment. Bucky didn't even get a regard this morning as she passed him. All of it, everything was focused into the next confrontation she was about to have.

Many thoughts had been flooding the space between her ears over the last twenty hours or so. They took on the form of nightmares in her sleep. No matter how she sliced it, it still came up the same. There was really no denying it. This was some sort of macabre soap opera that had been going on for a long time, and she was the new cast member—whether she wanted the part or not.

Her rage had been her companion—hell, her best friend for the past day. Now it was heating up and displacing all aspects of her being, including common courtesy. She crossed the threshold of Ned's office and was ready to begin her soliloquy—"Ode to a Manager I Wish to Kill," by Andrea Ellijay, Esquire.

As usual, the other actor in the scene had obviously missed his cue. The seat behind the grey desk was as vacant as Andrea's missed expectations. The engines were on full boil, but it wasn't time to pull out of the harbor yet. She had no alternative but to plop down in one of the two seats and turn the temperature down to simmer. Her sigh was the whistle releasing a little pressure before the boiler seams popped. Andrea was more than a

154

little miffed since her initial salvo across Ned's bow would not carry quite the same punch now.

There she waited in the same universe as in the hospital the day before—the universe where time only seems to exist for those who are waiting. The ones for whom they wait have no clue of the mini-torture that the waiting endure.

Just then, the torture-master came in and made the circuitous route around Andrea and his desk to his chair. His stride and posture suggested he had just won a scratch card lottery or something. He was absolutely nothing short of chipper. Placing a file folder down in the exact center of the barren desk, he took his seat neatly and folding his fingers in front of him he said, "Agent Ellijay! To what do I owe the pleasure of this visit?"

Andrea looked up at him with the slightly deranged eyes of a woman possessed and said in a threateningly low tone, "How long have you known?"

Ned said flatly now matching her tone but still managing an irritatingly chipper edge to it, "From the moment your dossier hit my hands." He opened up his hands for a moment and demonstrated. Then the church of the two hands folded back up again holding their own private little meeting.

"So you people know I have this…this…"

"Disease? Yes. We know."

"And you didn't tell me. The only one that really matters in this…matter!" She was getting frustrated. She wanted to nail this guy like Perry Mason and the words were picking up their picket signs again. Only the stupid words were making it through the line this time. But her face more than made up for the missing words. Her face convinced Ned of the severity of this exchange.

"It is protocol, Agent Ellijay."

"What the fuck kind of protocol is that?!" Her voice was now exposing the anger that had raged in her. She could not believe how coolly he was reacting. She hated to be in a fight with a person that thought they had the upper hand and could not be hurt by her words. Her body urged for physical violence, but her consternation kept it at bay.

"It's the kind that has kept our agency viable for centuries."

"You mean you have been emotionally raping people for centuries? Oh! That takes the cake!"

"I know you're disturbed right now, Ellijay. But that's no reason for hyperbole."

"You start talking to me like a goddamn human being or I am going to start disturbing your face with my hyperbole."

Ned adjusted his posture as if he realized this was going to be a little more of a challenge, but he wasn't giving up yet. "Your weakness is your greatest strength."

"What in the hell is that supposed to mean?"

"We hunt Croatoan. We are looking for a way to eradicate them from the planet. What is a weakness to you…destroys them. You should look at it as a blessing in disguise."

She was within inches of jumping across the desk and eradicating one more jerk from the world. "Well then, I guess I should be doing handsprings around your office! Let's throw a fucking party!"

Ned took a deep breath and tried a different tact. "I understand how you could feel that way. Many of our agents have felt the same way. But they have found that our medications have kept their disease in check while they lead fruitful lives pursuing a cause in which they really believe. This has been our way for hundreds of years.

"You have seen some of what these monsters can do to people. Jenna Domnanovich will have to deal with this the rest of her life. But at least she *has* a rest of her life. Most of their victims die on the spot, Ellijay. They don't have a chance to struggle through their own challenges for decades like Jenna will have."

To Andrea, this was just simply rationalization—the kind she felt the whole country was addicted to. In her mind, people rationalize things all day long instead of facing them head on. She ignored the comments he meant to be noble, but that she ascribed to being more ignoble and went straight for the point that mattered, "You mean to tell me that you have been able to keep Multiple Sclerosis in check for hundreds of years?" She was at the bursting point.

"Actually," he said in a trump voice, "We can cure it."

Throwing her hands up in the air, she slammed them down on the arms of her chair and at the same time standing up, "That tears it!" she yelled.

Andrea Ellijay walked out of Ned's office and virtually stomped her way down the hall, down the stairs and first floor hall, leaving a wake of profanities and obscenities to splash into the open offices along the way like little eddies. She really didn't care at this point how many people she disturbed with the sound she made in the hall this time. She wanted the whole bloody world it get a whiff of this.

Marching past Victoria's protests, she went straight for the doorknob and said as she burst into Casper's office like the very wind, "What the fuck is going on here, Casper?"

She looked down and saw a petite older lady in the chair in front of Casper's desk. She had obviously barged in on some sort of meeting, and it didn't seem to be with another agent. Casper stood up and with the manners of a genteel patron, he said, "Agent Ellijay, this is Anne Waldrip. Anne, this is Andrea Ellijay, one of our newest and…more enthusiastic young agents."

Mrs. Waldrip stood up and Andrea could see when she grabbed her four-footed walker cane that she was slightly beyond older. The frail woman collected her shawl in a proper clasp in front of her and extending her hand out she shook Andrea's, "Oh my. How pretty you are." Then looking back at Casper she said, "Kinda reminds me of me when I was young." Casper was standing at a proper attention, hands folded in front, and nodded with a little polite laugh. Then back to Andrea she said, "My dear, you obviously have more important matters to discuss with Mr. James than I. I will make my apologies and exit presently. But keep that fire in your belly," she said poking a twisted finger at Andrea's gut. Then pointing back to her own she said, "I know I still have mine!"

She hobbled out of the office with all the dignity of royalty and closed the door. Casper cleared his voice and said, "Now, Ms. Ellijay…Andrea…please, sit down. I have a feeling I know why you're here."

The wind had been let out of her sails a little by the unexpected encounter with Mrs. Waldrip, but now the Nor'easter was beginning to come in again with all of her fury. Setting her jaw and her disposition, Andrea prepared for round two. And just as she was about to launch off, Casper interrupted her, "Individual purpose is like an iceberg and words are the tip. Our own control is the sea."

Andrea blinked.

"What does that have to do with the price of rice in China, Casper? I don't even know what you mean."

"It's like this," he said as he sat back in his large black leather chair and looked up at the ceiling while he formulated his words. "A boyfriend asks a girl, 'Are we ok?' and she replies, 'Yes, why would you say such a thing?' But at the center of his purpose are questions of his own security. He obviously cares a great deal for the girl whether he tells her or not. He has picked up on something she said that has shaken his foundation and he is wrestling with his own conscience. She on the other hand at the core of her purpose has met her own needs for security and social stature by having the obligatory date for the dance. She has proven to her peers that she is desirable to the point that a boy has committed to see *only* her and no one else. Any additional work required would simply be bothersome. She feels crowded by his constant need for validation.

"And yet the only tip we see of the iceberg is 'Are we ok?' and 'Yes, why would you say such a thing?'"

"Casper, I have a disease that countless thousands have suffered from over hundreds of years. Your organization can detect it, treat it, cure it and you have kept this from the world so you can play cops and robbers with monsters. And you are talking to me about high school melodrama?"

"Just so." His gaze had been redirected back down to her now as he drove the point home, "You're seeing the tips of the icebergs and not understanding the depths of purpose underneath hidden by the controlling sea of the Order, the Cause, and the Covens."

"Ok…Mr. Cousteau…take me under the surface and explain to me what you mean."

"There is a delicate balance between the three factions. The agency you work for is known in some circles as the Order. It is a name that goes back a long way before we had a Federal system. The Croatoan serve something they call the Cause. It is still a mystery to us. All we have to go on is the trail of corpses that they leave behind like some sort of sick who-dun-it. And the vampires and Wicca now live in fractured collections of Covens that are a mere remnant of their once great nation-states.

"The only thing that is keeping this delicate balance alive long enough for the Order to find and understand a weakness in the Croatoan is the disease, Multiple Sclerosis."

She was following, but voiced her concerns, "I still don't see how purposefully harming fellow human beings could serve any greater good, Casper. I'm just not buying it."

He answered, "When a Croatoan attempts to harvest a person with MS, the short circuit in the neural pathways causes a type of feedback loop. Instead of discovering the individual's seed, their own seed is revealed to them. It causes a cascade failure of their entire central nervous system. While something like this would be a mere blip of amperage in you or me, when the supernatural power of a Croatoan gets crossed over on itself? Well, it's like the electrical grid in Cleveland blowing up—they all but spontaneously combust."

Andrea recalled Sunday afternoon documentaries on the subject of spontaneous combustion but had always chalked it up to another Yeti or Loch Ness Monster. The thought that all those cases could have been Croatoan tapping into MS victims gave her a cold chill.

Casper continued, "If we wipe out the disease altogether, then the Croatoan would have nothing to fear. There would be no natural enemy for them. They would be at the top of the food chain. And we would come in an unfortunate distant fourth behind the vampires and Wicca."

"So the fear of tripping over a person with MS…" she began.

"Forces them to work cautiously and slowly," he concluded for her. "We must be given more time to understand them. The Codex you have been reading is the sum of our knowledge and we feel we are getting closer to a solution. There are breakthroughs every day."

Andrea noted with some irony that the same sentiment had been spoken to Jenna Domnanovich just twenty-four hours earlier.

They didn't go down any better this time.

"I say let the whole world know everything. Then we could all work together and stop this madness."

"There are some that think *that* is precisely what the Croatoan have in mind."

Now she was confused again. "What do you mean?"

"Some of our top minds believe that the Cause of the Croatoan is being driven by a desire to make all of this public. We know their leader only as the Warrior. We believe he was a member of a Cape Hatteras tribe before the colonists came. The tribes of that area believed in the preservation of life and the denial of ownership in all things. His seed then would be..."

Now it was her turn to conclude, "To kill all life and own all things."

"Even to the ultimate destruction of his own kind," Casper cemented the point. "So the Warrior wants to force the Order to be exposed and the remedy to be made public. He wants its distribution to the masses to flow."

"But if everyone knew of their existence..." she postulated.

"They would still wipe us out. The whole of the human race would be nothing but a speed bump on their journey to destroying the whole planet."

"But that doesn't make any sense whatsoever," she protested.

"Madness rarely does," Casper solemnly said. Then with a sigh and a slight change in direction, "So our job is still before us. They are crafty and strong. They have been using this new age of political correctness to their advantage."

"How?"

"By infiltrating the ranks of socially conscious organizations. Those that stand for guarding our civil liberties or protecting the ethical treatment of animals, one and all are becoming puppets for the Warrior. They have been stepping up their efforts for years now to expose more and more of what they call corruption in government agencies hoping to bring us and our knowledge out into the light."

"So what you are saying is that the very organizations that profess to exist to save us..."

"Are really hell-bent and determined to destroy us by remolding the country into their own image. And they are more than willing to receive any power, no matter how dirty, to gain their will and way in America."

"But that seems like they would ultimately become the very corruption that they claim to hate," she observed.

"Look, you're going to need to learn a simple fact if you're going to survive at this level. All of us: you, me, Victoria, the President of the country, one and all care more about ourselves than we do anyone else. I care more about my Order than I do about you. You care more about your disease than you do Jenna's. The cold hard truth is that if someone came along that actually did care more about others than himself, we would either worship him or nail him to a tree."

As she contemplated this last, there was a soft rap on the door and it opened enough for Ned to poke his narrow face in a little, "Ok if I join you

C.J.?"

"Come on in, have a seat."

Ned came in, taking obvious pains to be respectful of the ongoing conversation.

"So I am cured now, right? No more MS for Andrea?"

"Not quite," said Casper. "We give you just enough of the cure to keep the disease in a frozen state. It allows you to live a normal life, and yet, will still prove lethal to the Croatoan. That way you will remain useful to the Order for most of your adult life."

"That is simply cold."

"That is simply business, Andrea. The two edged sword for you is that if an agent elects to 'come in from the cold' so to speak. They lose their ability to acquire the drug."

Andrea was horrified at the matter-of-fact tone in Casper's voice. Her delusion that this was a sweet old cowboy was completely shattered. Trying to find some point that would allow her some leverage in what was fast transitioning from a negotiation to a talking-to, "So what if I just go public myself?"

Moving a little in his chair signaling with his body language that he had won before any other words were spoken, Casper said, "There have been more than a few Indians that have tried to leave the reservation over the years. That's why we have the Cavalry. You will have noticed by now that we encourage agents to talk to each other here at the Center but no agent knows who all the other agents are. If the Order is threatened, the Order shall be preserved."

Now Andrea understood the iceberg she was on. It ran deep and was treacherous. Yet, it gave her a quality of life and an opportunity to do some good in the world. She could stay and submit, leave and keep her mouth shut and watch helplessly as her body dwindled away, or she could leave, talk, and die.

Now it was Casper's turn to slap his chair arms as he got up. "I need to run to a meeting. You two are welcome to use my office to discuss the decisions facing our Agent Ellijay." Making his excuses, he left the two there in their chairs and closed the door behind him.

Andrea was staring off in space, running all the thoughts and their ramifications through her mind. She hated feeling trapped, and if this wasn't the largest bear trap she had ever seen, she didn't know what was. At length, Ned broke the silence, "Andrea."

She turned and glared at him. The stare was piercing.

"Andrea. You must understand. These are high stakes we are talking about. We need your talent. We see in you a different level of ability than any agent we have recruited. What can I say to ease your situation at this time?"

"Tell me it's all a dream."

"It is not a dream. It is a nightmare. And for what it's worth, you are not alone in it. We are all here, right along with you."

"Look, I am the one with a disease that is being used," she said as she was doing a pretty convincing job at keeping the tears in their prison cells. This warden was tough, but the inmates were restless.

"Yes. But you are not the only one," he said with a tone of voice that was very nearly considerate.

"Oh yeah? Like who else?"

"Like everyone here. We have all gone through this moment you are now facing. It is the final stage of our recruitment process."

"You mean to tell me that everyone in the Order..."

"Has MS. Yes. It is *the* prerequisite. You would not be here today if you did not have it. Neither would I."

The enormity of this thought and its greater meaning was starting to hit Andrea. She now saw this organization as the most twisted, horrifying bastardization of a purpose she had ever known. Now staring directly ahead to the vacant chair that to her represented her captors she said flatly, "Bastards."

"One and all," Ned agreed. "But you will see in time that there was no other way."

I will see in time that the Order is made to pay for their sins, is what she thought but she said, "We will see. We will see."

It was then that she realized that she was her own iceberg. That she had dangers of her own and they all lay quietly submerged below the surface of her own control. And in her mind, the Order was the Titanic. There and then, a thought in her mind started that she would find her own solution to this trap. She would stay and submit long enough to find an option beyond leaving-and-suffering or leaving-and-dying.

Ned said with some of the returning chipper spring in his voice, "That's a good teammate. I have an idea. Why don't you take the rest of the day off and think things over. You can resume your research tomorrow. I'll be available if you have any questions for me."

Looking blankly back at him, the iceberg exposed only the tip of the threads that were being constructed under the surface, "I think that is a good idea. I'll do just that."

"Fine. Fine," and patting the back of her hand, "We will always be on your side. Just let me know if there is anything I can do for you."

"Oh, I think you've done more than enough for me today. Thanks Ned."

They both got up and made their way out. Victoria was gone and they both quietly exited into the hallway and went their separate ways. Andrea headed back to her townhouse.

There was much to think about.

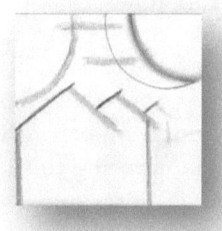

14.
12.19.9.12.3. 9167; 16 YAX, 5 AKBAL — NIGHT-HOUSE

October 18, 2002, 10:00 p.m. EST

The faint lighting in the near total dark was barely a sheer, pale blue, doffed by other skyscrapers as they reflected the month's growing moonlight into Danreck's perch on top of the city. It angled in like rays underwater, filtered only by the laced curtains that decorated the sides of the huge floor-to-ceiling windows. The spaciously open living room was designed artistically to perfection with just the right mix of deep crimsons and navy blues. Small statues and images from around the world easily put its price range far out of reach for the most discerning of collectors.

As he walked around, he gained comfort from all of the souvenirs from his global travels that spanned hundreds of years. Often he would actually purchase an item from a master, sometimes even before he would drive them mad—or even better, harvest them and live out their darkest desire.

He had plans for this evening, but presently, they were preempted by three separate phone conversations. The first of which was occurring at this very moment as he spoke directly into the privately scrambled line, serviced by a small and rare device wrapped around his right ear. The only person that could hear at this point was his guest in the bedroom chamber next door. But he didn't think she would mind too terribly.

"Yes, Christov. I am planning on being there as the corn gives way to the snake."

The low, soft voice of a man driven by a purpose replied in his ear, "We will have everything you need in the two storage bays. Are you sure you can find them?"

Gazing down upon the city, he saw the red beacons flashing their warnings to approaching planes. There would be no such warning for what would take place three days from now.

"Yes, Christov. I will be able to find everything just fine."

"If you needed us to stick around..."

Danreck knew that Christov was simply looking for an excuse to keep Isidora and himself at the location to watch the events unfold. But to be honest, Danreck didn't feel like listening to the two of them squabble. It always seemed that no matter what was going on, those two would want to fight about something irrelevant regardless of how they jeopardized the Mission.

"You needn't stay. I trust that the two of you have far more important things to do. I really thank you for your assistance in this matter."

There was a soft moan from the other room. Danreck felt it was probably not out of alarm. His dancer was probably only starting to act upon the impulses he had planted in her mind before leaving to make these calls.

"It's really no problem, Danreck. We have plenty of time to stick around. It will be no bother at all."

Danreck walked over to the coffee table and selected from a tray an expensive foreign cigarette that had been laced with a potent narcotic. Taking his time to savor the moment, not rushed at all by a subservient on the line awaiting a reply, he slid his hand deftly down into his silk smoking jacket pocket and expertly extracted a single match. He struck it with the tip of one of his slightly elongated nails—nails so hard that they could easily cut deeper than flesh, and had done so in the past to prove their worth.

Still without replying, he slowly placed the cigarette in his mouth, and with the other hand lit it. He took a slow drag in as he extinguished the match and said into the phone, "No, Christov," then exhaling slowly, "You two leave town tonight. The corn and the snake will bring another day. George and I will handle things from here."

"As you wish, Danreck."

The phone did not click signaling a hang up from Christov, as custom would dictate. Danreck was more than a little perturbed by the insolence. He held out his left hand with the cigarette between the two middle fingers and slowly stretched his arm out to its full length. Then he slowly moved it down, like a leaf falling first left and then right. He watched the trail of smoke that was left from over $500 worth of substance just burning away.

"Was there something else, Christov?"

"It's just..."

He had now brought the cigarette back up and watched as the trail played with the angles of light streaming into the living space. It gave curves of randomness to the lights authoritatively straight and rigid lines. He saw in this a metaphor for their Cause.

Drawing in another drag, "It's just what?" Then he exhaled again.

The voice came from a slightly more distant range to him. "We were wondering…"

His patience with these two was at an end. He knew what Christov wanted to hear. He only hoped that it would finish the call. In his mind, high-maintenance should have been preclusion to membership. "You both did fine, Christov. I'm thankful to you both and if this is a success, I am more than certain that both of you shall be rewarded."

"Thank you, sir. We are very pleased that you are happy."

Still there was no click. There was another soft moan from the room beyond. Danreck really felt that these two should be taught a remedial course in protocol. He hated to be required to terminate calls to those beneath him. But there was other business that demanded his attention, and time was moving on. "Goodbye, Christov. I will be in touch."

And with that, Danreck Porter terminated the call. The words left a bad taste in his mouth. This present problem he remedied with another puff from the party favor of the rich and not-so-famous.

He crossed to the base-station for the device in his ear. Soft cushions of fiber woven by a Chinese artisan hundreds of years ago massaged the spaces between his bare toes.

The Oriental people really had this stuff figured out, he thought. This was followed by another thought, *It is now politically incorrect to call people from the Orient…Oriental. Go figure.*

Danreck spent the next several moments wondering what the politically correct would call the Croatoan. "Differently-abled?" he snorted. "Weakness-impaired?" he chuckled. After some considerable thought, he settled on "Illumi-naughty!" and he laughed out loud. "Fucking humans. This calls for a drink!"

Danreck poured a glass of thirty-two-year-old Oban Scotch. He held the glass in his left hand while he accessed George with his right. The number was already set in speed dial.

He pressed the button and took alternating pleasure from the glass and cigarette. He fully intended to add a third pleasure to this little tryst, but she would keep until after his phone business was complete.

"Hello," came a husky, ethnic voice from the other side of the connection.

"George?"

"Danreck! Good to hear from you, brother."

George's southern accent was noticeable. Danreck smiled as he took a drink and crossed to the window on the far side. "George, I'll not keep you."

"Ain't a problem a'tall."

This was almost too much to take. "George, you really must stop."

"Stop what?" Even this was as dripping with accent as the trees around George were dripping with Spanish moss.

"I wish you could hear yourself. You are positively hysterical!"

"Paybacks are a bitch," and then, just for spite, George threw in, "y'all."

"Really, George. Please cease and desist. I need to talk business for a moment."

"What up, dog?"

At this, Danreck went ahead and had a good laugh with a friend he had known for centuries. He was never really quite sure if George had forgiven him for the scar permanently worn around his neck. He had, after all owned one of the sets of hands that helped make it.

Recovering his composure a little, "George, how did your travels go today?"

"Is your side covered?" This was a little agreed upon question that allowed them to confirm a secure connection.

"Scrambled if you are."

"I'm in Savannah now. The fertilizer is in place in the basement...all of it. Are we a go without media coverage?"

A rueful smile crossed Danreck's taught face, "Oh, there will be plenty of media coverage. We'll just have to push a little harder to get them to connect the dots. Our plans to pursue an insider were a big gamble from the beginning. We still have a good foundation."

"How did the other two fair?"

"You mean Rosencrantz and Guildenstern?" Danreck asked with more than a bit of cynicism.

"The very two I had in mind," George confirmed.

"Their shipments are in storage. But we need transport. Any luck with a cover story or are we just going to execute with some possible heat at our backs?"

"Damn, Danreck...you know how edgy I am about this whole thing. We ain't talking about a little bon fire here. This is a huge risk to you and me. I don't want to miss the party at the end of the world. And now you're using metaphors like 'heat' and all..."

Danreck was slowly pulling a match out of his pocket. "Sorry, George. I understand all of our aversions to fire." The head erupted with the loud fizz of a high quality match as his nail scraped across it. The smell of sulfur mixed with the other aromas, the rush from his own survival instincts tingling through his body.

"Was that a match, Danreck?"

"Why yes it was, my southern friend."

George let a whistle escape from his large teeth and the gap between them. "Danreck, you are one twisted mo'fo'."

"What I do in my off-time is none of your concern, George. Now about that transport..."

"Oh yeah. Right. Actually I have some good news."

Danreck was looking down at the match as it burned dangerously close to the tips of his fingers. The heat was becoming for him a delicious and excruciating pain. The fear in his heart challenged his own control as it burned closer and closer. "I'm all ears," he said in a patient and seething voice.

"Well, my Saturday pickup was delayed by the security warning."

"But it stayed at yellow..." Danreck said. With the last syllable, he blew extra air out, thus destroying the enemy that threatened his existence, as it turned wood to ash. He realized that in a short while he would destroy a bigger enemy that threatened, and this time it would be wood and the bodies of orphaned boys that turned to ash. He reveled in the comparison.

"But the mere fact that they thought of raising it to orange delayed several shipments in the harbor. I can't pick up my load until Monday. So I can easily be here for you tomorrow night."

"Bloody marvelous," Danreck said as he slowly spun the now extinguished ember between his thumb and forefinger. "Perfect. Everything is working out better than I expected."

"Well...almost everything..." George was alluding to the loss of Josephine. Rumors had already circulated, caused a sensation, been confirmed and the loss mourned. Danreck was ready to move on. Ready, that is except for one more piece of unfinished business. But that would be the next call and not this one.

"Yes...it's a shame that we did lose young Josephine," Danreck lilted his voice.

"What are you talking about? She was one of those fucking thirds!"

"Now George, you know that is no way to talk about our brothers and sisters."

George very nearly exploded, "Damn bastard-steps if you ask me!"

There was a certain amount of hatred and distrust among some of the Seconds. George was not leaving it up to ambiguity about which side of the rack his hat hung.

"Peace, George. We have work to do."

"Sorry, boss."

There was that accent again. Danreck almost started laughing anew.

"Look, when you get back home, people are going to pick on you for weeks with that accent."

George started thinking about the racial condition of the times. He had been a northern White man in a southern Black man's skin for nearly two weeks. He had seen the way some people treated others just because of their outward appearance. To be honest, it was really not that much better up north. But now it was different. He had seen the clouds from both sides. Disgusted, he said in his best Yankee accent, "I know. But what am I supposed to do about it? If it's one thing they can't stand down here, it's an uppity niggah."

Danreck was just about to take a puff from his cigarette. But when he heard this he just froze for a moment and said, "Don't lose yourself in the part, George."

Shifting easily back into the voice of his victim, "Hard not to. There are some things I would do for my harvest regardless of what the seed mandated. But in this case…it's a happy convenience that both happen to be one in the same thing."

Danreck asked, "What are your plans after we are done setting things up Sunday night?"

"Gonna kill me a White woman!"

"Is she that bad?" Danreck asked.

"Aren't they all?"

Another soft moan drifted in from the other room, this time followed by a little laugh and then another softer moan.

"Well, Danreck? Aren't they all?" George knew what Danreck was playing at. It had been his warm-up tradition for decades.

Holding the glass up to his mouth, Danreck could not decide whether to concede to George's jab or take a drink. He decided he had to say something or lose face, but didn't want to walk into a trap. While his lips were still on the rim ready to take a sip, "I refuse to comment on the grounds that I need a drink." At which point Danreck took a small sip.

They both laughed.

"Nice to know some things never change. Are you going to do something mortal and messy tonight?"

"No…" Danreck drew this out. "I think I'm going to throw this one back in. When I'm done, she will find herself back in front of the video rental shelf with a small case of déjà vu. She is far too talented and besides, I have two tickets to see her show on Broadway next week. It would be a travesty to cause the wasting of my own hard-earned money!"

They both howled with laughter.

At length, Danreck returned to business, "So your Mission only requires the death of a woman? Is that back in Mississippi?"

"Yeah. I need to head back as soon as I can and get this over with. I may not even pick up my load. It would be a good cover. Leroy gets distraught while waiting for a delayed cargo, decides to head home and off his estranged wife. Then he takes his own life—all very tidy. She really hurt Leroy. His love for her runs so deep that this seed is nearly blinding at times. She's a real bitch."

"What then?"

"No plans."

"Then it is settled. Once you feel more yourself, head back to Memphis and fly up to New York. I'll put you up here for the two weeks while we both recover. That will give you some time to lose the accent before you head back to The Hub."

For just a moment the clipped voice of old George was back, "You know Peab'dy is nowhere near Boston!"

"Very good my old friend! But it would do you well to bury that accent for a couple more days."

Again returning to the drawl, "Yeah…a Yankee may not go down well in some of these parts." And just like that George had wrapped himself back in the cloak that was Leroy. "Sounds like a plan. I'll join you in New York for the recovery."

"Ok. I look forward to it," Danreck confirmed.

"Yes sir. I'll see you tomorrow with bells on and fare thee well." And with this, George terminated the call.

"Now that's protocol! I must get him to teach that to Tweedle-Dumb and Tweedle-Dumb-ass."

Danreck went to the bedroom door and opened it a crack. There, lying in naked repose across the royal blue satin sheets of the large hand crafted poster bed was the star of one of Broadway's hottest dance shows in years. Her writhing and moans were swells upon the sea of her ecstasy. Only the slightest touch of redness at the nape of her neck suggested these actions were not the effects of some new designer drug.

He took a deep, quick, but full breath in through his nose, warming the air before it filled his lungs and then breathed out in the slow satisfaction of his little work of art. The happening would begin soon.

But first, there was one small piece of unsavory business left requiring his attention. He moved in a blur back to the bar and punched the button for their lord and master, bringing an end to his procrastinated.

Before the connection on the other line even rang a single time, he heard the click of an answer.

There were no words spoken. There didn't need to be. None were required. He was in the proxied presence of his king. The breathing was all he needed to hear. It radiated power.

"I am in your presence, master. No others matter to me. You are the point where the rivers branch. You bring us eternal life with the waters that flow. I thank you for the gift of the Sharing."

There was no reply other than his master's continued presence.

Sweat from the sides of his glass were beading up and collecting near its base. He watched as a drop relinquished its grip on the bottom edge and freefell to the top of his bare foot. There it splattered into so many fractured droplets. These would wait patiently in their final resting place, until a combination of ambient temperature and the basic atomic properties of atmosphere would cause them to rise up into the air, to the great collecting place in the sky, where they would join with the souls of all the other drops of water that had found their way to the end of their cycle only to return to the collective.

Danreck wondered if *he* would ever return.

"I am sorry for your loss, master."

Only breathing. Nothing more. Another drop decided to end it all and hasten its own return to the collective.

Danreck wondered if he would remember his existence here on Earth. Croatoan gave little thought to the concept of passing, generally speaking. Given the degree of severity in which the present moment was incased, he only felt it understandable for his thoughts to be turning so.

Danreck now walked along the windows, along the expanse of the scenic overlook—content in the silence while he formulated the rest of his report.

"Our plans have proceeded. The Cause shall be served."

Danreck heard a short blast of air. It gave him the distinct impression that Hacquee had just huffed through his nose.

"I assure you master, the end result shall be profit from the plans."

Now there was the voice. The voice that sang to every fiber of his existence as it spoke directly to his soul. The power resonated in his being, the words low and controlled, *"Your* plans..." echoed in his mind for a moment, "...killed my daughter." The last was flat and abrupt.

"Yes. I know."

Rather than attempt to chatter away an explanation, Danreck knew that his words must be measured and purposed. It was not swiftness that Hacquee required. Nor was it voluminous content.

Danreck reached the far corner where the glass from one wall came to an apex with the glass from the other wall. With no visible brace blocking his view, he felt as if he were at the corner of the universe and the expanse of the city stretched out from under his bare feet. Here the dampness on his right foot would begin its rapture and ascension.

Danreck longed to leave this world with it.

"I called her in before her time of recovery was over." Danreck halted. That tiny *mea culpa* would mean he was not trying to deflect blame. He watched, as the city seemed to undulate and breathe to the sound of his master's ventilation.

Danreck placed the cigarette to his lips and took a long, slow drag softly letting it out over time.

He continued, "I have always felt the rift between the Seconds and Thirds must be healed. Her willingness to serve and her noble sacrifice will no doubt help to bring this about."

A soft, playful giggle floated out of the bedroom. Danreck ignored this and focused his attention on the immediate business. Perhaps he shouldn't have procrastinated with this call.

He turned and started walking towards the other side of the room. The cigarette needed to be snuffed out. He realized this was yet another word-picture for the end that sometimes seemed so close he could taste it, yet he knew would never come.

"There was, of course…no way for us to know that the newswoman carried…"

"Enough!" came a boom in his ear. The explosiveness of his rage impacted Danreck's body even though he was not physically present. It was the order of a king. It was the commandment of nobility. The power and authority were innate.

Danreck stood perfectly still—not flinching, not breathing. The trails of smoke wafted from the now lifeless butt in the ashtray on the table in front of him. Time was no more and the universe had halted.

"I want them to pay." The quiet words echoed in their quest for a resting place. There was none for them. These kinds of words never find peace. They wonder through our world as disembodied purpose, given life by those that mourn.

Solemnly and without excuse, Danreck answered them, "They will, Hacquee. They will."

Feeling the imminent need for reverence, Danreck set his glass on the table and kneeled in place on the carpet. There in the middle of this blue on black scene he repeated in a hushed respect, "They will."

Danreck's breathing matched that of Hacquee for a while. With head bowed and in devout contemplation, "Their pain *will* be complete."

Now with focus of vision, Danreck slowly raised his head to level, looking straight ahead, he continued, "I will bring them destruction for the insolence of their existence!"

Looking up, beyond his own existence, he said in his own verve and strength, "I will destroy their displaced sons, bringing honor and clarity to our Cause!"

With this, he let out the resonating roar of a warrior. When he was finished, the hushed silence moved back in like the fog after a passing car. Now there was only him. Now there was only Hacquee.

With the correct protocol, Danreck concluded the call. "I will serve you to the realization of your vision, Hacquee." And with that, he hung up the phone.

After some time to meditate, he got up off his knees and took several cleansing breaths. His mind was now calm and relaxed. The drugs and alcohol had certainly begun to lay their foundation.

He moved into the bedroom with the swift silence of the wind. The dancer would only remember the next several hours in dreams over the next several years.

15.
12.19.9.12.4. 4583; 17 YAX, 6 KAN — MAIZE

October 19, 2002, 11:00 a.m. EST

The past forty-eight hours had been like living in an altered state for Agent Andrea Ellijay. She supposed the emotions were a little like being thrown off the Twin Towers, having enough time to contemplate your tragic ending on the way down, only to be snatched back up by a bungee cord near the bottom. Then lowered down and released, you are safe and looking back behind, you see that the buildings are no longer there.

None of the others had bungee cords.

She wondered how it was that so many had to suffer horrible endings brought on by such a terrible disease, and she would be sparred as long as she played their game. To her, the Order seemed the perfect mad scientist. She was just concerned she was becoming the monster.

She did as she said—going back to her research the next day. But somehow, colonial practices and customs were not quite as interesting.

She did have one chance encounter with Scott. She was crossing to the research center on Friday when he pretended not to see her, and acted like he was going to *accidentally* bump into her. "It only works once," she said.

"But today is Two-for-Friday! We give you two helpings!" and he mocked a bad Chinese accent.

"I've never heard of Two-for-*Friday*," she said skeptically.

"It honorable local custom."

They both giggled a bit, but when they were done, she looked at him. She could just feel her eyes saying, *"...even you?"*

His eyes were clearly saying, *"...even me. I know what you're going through."* But he said nothing about it. What he did say was, "Are you getting settled

173

in?"

"I guess you could say that. I'm still mostly packed. It takes me a while to actually believe a new place is home."

He looked at her with just the right touch of warmth and said, "I think you just need the right meal."

"Oh really?" she said halfway laughing. She knew an approach when she saw one, but this time didn't really mind. She would say yes to a date—there was something in this man that seemed beyond the norm.

He assured, "Really. If you have a meal at the right place, it helps you get grounded faster. It was in a psych study I read in college."

"Well...what would be good?" she asked. She thought she might as well make it easier for him.

"You might want to try driving out old Highway 38. There's this great Mom & Pop place called the Sideboard Café. You'll love it!"

Her crest fell a little. He didn't seem interested in being anything more than a friend. But at least she had that. "I will do that." And she screwed on the best smile should could.

They said their goodbyes, which are much quicker this far up north—maybe not as fast as in New York, but still pretty fast. Andrea made her way to the research center.

She was interested in little there. Each station seemed to be about the passions of others. Nothing really hit home. The only thing that did seem to catch her attention was that raising the terror level to orange had been considered due to an increase of chatter, but in the end, the new Department of Homeland Security had opted to just increase inspections of inbound freight to harbors along the eastern seaboard.

Andrea spent some time at each place and read over all the latest research. But what was really going through her mind was her own situation. Every single standard emotion was present.

Hell, Scott had probably read a case study about *her* in college.

At first, she had denied any of it was happening. For about half the day after she left Casper's office, she had simply pictured herself as an Agent that needed to be about the business of the Agency—that simple, that easy.

She even went home and started unpacking a little. She tried to do the actions of the job, checking her email and printer tray for any sign of the fax from the bank in Peabody. Nothing had come in yet.

But soon, the denial turned to anger. She started packing things up. The anger fluctuated between rage and resentment. One minute she was angry at the Order for bringing her into this mess, and the next she resented being used by them. She even resented her own body for doing this to her. At the height of it, she was blaming her own frail mother and quitter father for making her this way.

She very nearly had the entirety of her worldly belongings in a bag, box, or suitcase by night's end. She was tired. It is probably how the stub of a candle must feel…burned down and used up.

Eventually, she found herself sitting on her bed pulling things out of boxes and then putting them back in. She became of two minds and they were bargaining. She would pack one thing and then unpack two. She would make a deal to unpack only the essentials, but then opted for only bringing out the items that could be swiftly packed again regardless of need.

The whole time, she would tell herself that she would stay, as long as they would yield to her demands to cure her completely. All sorts of debates were staged in her mind between her and management. All of them ended with her triumphantly convincing them that *they* really needed her and that *they* would have to cure her to keep her.

But eventually, the futility of this in the stark light of reality became too much for her to tolerate and she ended up broken and spilled out on the bed, sobbing over her half-packed, half-unpacked life.

It was there that she cried herself to sleep.

Presently after the chance meeting with Scott she found herself still depressed and in the research center looking over documents she didn't really care about, wondering what she was going to do. Picking up a book to look as if she was doing some work, she made her way to a table and sat down. Looking at the open tome, she aimlessly flipped the old yellowed pages as she began searching for some resting place for her tired mind.

The words passed through her subconscious without ever taking root. All that mattered to her was coming to an understanding of the puzzle she was in.

The Order wants me to hunt Croatoan because I carry the one weakness that will kill them. If I don't agree, I end tragically. If I do agree, I may still end tragically, but I may also help the whole world rid itself of a blight that could kill it.

Croatoan hunt vampires and can kill them with apparent ease. If we kill off the Croatoan, then the whole food chain moves up a notch. And I know how that one goes. Same shit, different day.

Vampires hunt humans—which brings us back to humans in the Order that hunt Croatoan.

Then out loud she concluded, "Well if that ain't the damndest game of Rock, Paper, Scissors I've ever seen, I don't know what the fuck is!"

This proclamation of the pure truth tickled her a little even though it was immediately followed by a series of very loud shushing noises from others doing research.

Things had just settled back down to quiet when her satellite-phone started ringing from her purse. Looking around embarrassed expecting another volley of shushing fingers, she quickly pulled it out and answered it. She felt a little stupid when it kept making the buzzing sound. It was then that she realized it was not an incoming call, but a reminder of an appointment on her agenda. She was to report to the Medical Department for a scheduled meeting at noon. The warning gave her fifteen minutes.

On the way to Medical, she started thinking over some of the research she had done. Andrea found it fascinating that some of the people that came to the colonies began to dislike or even hate the very things that provided them their dreams. They had the freedom in an environment that would sustain them, and yet had disdain for the lack of some of the things that kept them chained.

Once in the Medical Department, Andrea thought the nurse's questions and the entire visit were just a follow-up to her first. She figured that the doctor would come in and go over some of the results from her physical a week earlier.

"Well, Agent Ellijay...how are we this morning?"

The doctor was a distinguished looking gentleman. He had a little salt in the pepper of his once black hair. And there were two Hollywood dimples that guarded either side of a large warm smile. Pins only wished they were this neat and laces could not hope to be any straighter.

Andrea now only saw him as the final embodiment of the Order's grasp on her life. He was the kind face that would administer the harsh truth through his treatment. He was both her liberator and her leash. "I don't know...do you have a rat in your pocket? Or are you just suffering from Multiple Personality Disorder?"

With hands in the pockets of his spotlessly white lab coat and with equal glibness, he retorted, "I never suffer from it...I enjoy every minute!"

"Could you bring out the nice one?" she shot back.

"Ouch. Tell you what...I'll pull my talons back if you pull yours back," the doctor offered by way of a deal.

"Isn't that our standing little agreement?" The surliness dripped from her lips.

The often polite and always congenial doctor opted past the obligatory rolling stool and pulled out a desk chair from the counter that ran along the wall of the operatory. He flipped the chair around with the nimbleness of a dancer from the old black-and-white movies and sat in it backwards, wrapping his legs around the back of it in a casual pose. He had positioned himself at a lower angle below her as she towered down from the examination table.

"Andrea. You and I have only met, so there is no reason for you to trust me..." he began.

"I don't care if we were life-long chums, there still wouldn't be a reason for me to trust you," she said. But some of the fight was gone from her voice.

"Granted," he said flatly. "But doctors make hundreds of choices every day that seem to go against their ethos of *Primum non nocere*, or 'First do no harm.'"

Now a little curious, Andrea asked, "What do you mean?"

He answered like a friendly professor or mentor, "The phrase *Primum non nocere* doesn't actually appear in the Hippocratic Oath, but Hippocrates probably did say it. Something like it is captured in his writing. But doctors do harm every day. We do it to prevent greater harm."

"Like when a person takes chemo," she speculated.

"Precisely. And in your case, and in the case of everyone that works here, we use a stabilized state of harm to prevent greater harm...namely death...namely your own.

"I realize you're going through an internal struggle right now. You see a group of people forcing you to stay in a state between well and sick in order to gain from you the service that they want. I would feel the exact same things in your position."

Andrea did not interrupt this time. She would let the doctor have his say. Regardless of his intent, or whom he worked for, he was at least shooting straight with her—and *that* was refreshing!

After a carefully measured silence, he continued, "But if I were to cure you completely, it would be similar to overdosing you on antibiotics over a long period of time. It would certainly cure what ails ya, but eventually your own natural defense would erode to the point that you would have no protection at all against the next biotic you encountered and something simple would kill you.

"What you carry inside you is acting like just such a natural defense against an occupational hazard that you will encounter on a daily basis here and I would be crackers and one quack of a doctor to rid you of it!

"So I want you to keep that in mind while you make your decisions in life...for they are *your* decisions to make, Andrea."

A quiet moment passed where neither of them spoke, neither one moved. A bird was chirping just outside the window and Andrea knew that in the near future the birdsong would depart this place for the cold season. She wondered if it would ever return.

Still staring out the window, she broke the silence "So it's like corn,"

Now it was his turn to not quite know what to say, "I'm sorry, Andrea...what about corn?"

"The colonists that came here wanted freedom from everything that they saw as oppressive. One of the things that was used to keep them oppressed was food...you know...staples."

"Yes, the thought of leaving something that sustains you for the unknown keeps a lot of people bound in situations from which they wish to escape. It takes a great deal of courage to actually make that first step," he agreed.

She continued, "...and what they found here waiting for them was the one thing some of them would come to hate—corn! It provided for them a way to survive in their new freedom, but at the same time they hated it because it was not what they had known for their whole lives."

He said, "Yes...I could imagine it might get old surviving on something you hated."

"It drove some mad," she said as her gaze returned to the window and her hearing to the nearly extinct birdsong.

At that moment, as if by some macabre direction from an unseen producer, the door opened and a nurse came in with a tray. The nurse had a mustache and the tray had a white covering. Both acted as a form of protection from unwanted contact. Placing the tray down on the counter she exited.

"Andrea...we want you to stay with the Agency. I want to keep you well and whole. Please let me administer this booster. It will tie you over until you finish making up your mind on things."

"How long will this one last?" she asked.

He was getting up now and carefully placing the chair under the counter. "Each shot will extend the life of the treatment. It builds up in the system in a series of half-lives. The first is shorter than the second, and so on. Eventually we will be in maintenance of once per quarter...every three months."

"And this one?"

"We will either need you back here in two weeks or the Agency will ask you to leave." Then turning back to her from the tray he was preparing, "...and I hope to see you here for your next appointment."

Andrea breathed in the humiliation of her decision as she first stood, then turned toward the table, and pulling her jeans down halfway exposing her rear-end she held on to the table. She didn't want to see the needle.

She didn't know which was worse—the quick sting to her butt or the sharp sting to her ego. Andrea had born more than flesh to these people. She had bared to them her weakness. This took away more than they could ever give back.

She pulled up her jeans with what was left of her dignity, and thanked the doctor for his genuine concern and ability to tell the truth. Then she made her exit and decided to try to escape from all this for the rest of the day. As she left the building she wondered if all that was left to her was a half-life.

The quad was paying its last respects to summer and was already traversing the barrier to autumn. The chill in the air made it just unpleasant enough for people not to be outside for the simple pleasure of being outside. Everyone here was out because they had a purpose for being so and they were quickly moving toward getting that purpose accomplished. Very few people were sitting on any of the benches or at any of the water features.

So it was with some surprise that Andrea stumbled across a huddled Sorin sitting on one of the benches beside a huge tree. The base of the tree was so large two people could not wrap their arms around it and touch fingers.

Andrea walked up and placing her hand on it she said, "I bet this old tree has some stories to tell."

"That makes two of us!"

Plaintively Andrea scolded a little, "Oh, come on Sorin…you are far too young to be so dowdy!"

"But I am not so young as to be knavish either."

Andrea felt a question resurface that her conservative nature had killed before. Now it would appear to her that the new management of her current circumstances had fired her conservative nature. She wanted to hope that it would find gainful employment somewhere else, but truth be known she really didn't care.

"How do you know so damned much?" she just blurted out. With some surprise, she thought that she needed to get used to this new lack of filtration before opening the floodgates next time.

She expected him to ask for clarification, but he didn't seem to need any. He looked at the old tree and said, "I have been around a while. I like to observe things. It's my hobby."

"So you have been around the Order a long time," she guessed.

"Oh…long enough, I suppose. But what I am really interested in is finding things. I like helping others find things."

"I lost my car keys once…can you help me find them?"

He patted the empty seat next to him and asked her to join him. She sat as he continued, "It is not the whole of you that is lost. That is not the problem or challenge you face in your first weeks here.

"It is that there are aspects of yourself that you have never known at all that bothers you."

He looked back at the old tree. Andrea spent some time looking as well. The simple truth was much like this tree—surely there, and had been for a long time.

"I am afraid of what I am becoming," she said in a still, small voice.

"You are afraid of what you already are; you have always been. You are only now finding these things out, but they have always been there."

A bird flew into the tree, but its song had been silenced by its own instincts. The presence of the bird without the presence of its song was somehow disturbing to Andrea. The sound of the wind in the woods to the East and West of this place made a hollow, soft roar that varied pitch as it navigated the hills around the Center.

"That's what I liked about Michelangelo—he never made a sculpture. In his mind, he only knocked away the bits of rock that were *not* the sculpture. The work of art was always there before he even began his work."

Andrea wondered if that is what she was…a work of art waiting to be uncovered. She felt that acceptance of her current situation would be tantamount to self-betrayal and not some clever metaphor by a charming, old man attempting to flatter her and make her feel better.

"Those are stirring words, Sorin," she said at length.

"Not meant to be," he said abruptly. "I'm saying that I see a potential in you that you don't even know exists. I am not trying to build up your ego…I am trying to scare the holy bug-shit out of you!"

He turned his gaze to her. "You haven't learned how to deal with incorporating newly discovered truths about yourself. You must learn how to absorb them, assimilate them into your own understanding. It doesn't get any easier from here. No matter what path you take…stay or go…you will discover more new things about yourself at an alarming rate.

"I have watched you mope around here for the last twenty-four hours and have a pretty good idea with what you are dealing. I have seen it many times before. The real secret is that you have already made your decision. You just have to uncover it, accept it, make it the proper part of your 'self' and move on.

"Believe it or not…everyone in the world goes through this stage at your age. There is nothing supernatural about it. Those that do not learn the technique fall desperately behind and spend the remainder of their days bitterly watching those that *did* learn get placed on boards of directors or promoted over them."

He looked back to the tree and said, "Only in your case…working here in this chosen field…the penalty is not bitterness in old age…it's not ever *having* an old age with which to be bitter."

She looked down at the fall grass under her white canvas sneakers. Her pigeon toes had been digging little circles while Sorin talked. Now a single tear fell in the middle of one of them like the first tributary opening up into a little man-made lakebed. Others soon joined it.

Sorin did not stop her. She was not sobbing or heaving. She was just quietly releasing the pressures that were held behind the spill-gates of her acceptance. She had uncovered another bit of who she was. She was now teaching her mind to learn the process of assimilation.

Andrea hoped that Sorin was wrong. She hoped there wasn't more of her there to discover. But one thing was certain, if he was right…she didn't want the next time to be so painful.

And she figured he probably was.

Eventually the silence had to be broken by one of them. Sniffing a little, she wiped her top lip with the palm of her hand in the tomboyish way a girl orphan picks up when she has to grow up tough. Sorin found it cute and endearing. She said, "I think I will stay for a while."

"Good."

The silence returned as an uninvited third party to this discussion. It had been dominating the conversation a little so Andrea interrupted it again, "And I think I will act on things a little more directly from now on."

"Good," he repeated.

"And I am doing it because I *want* to do it and not because someone is forcing me to do it."

"Very good."

"Thank you for the kind words since I have been here, Sorin."

"Andrea...Ms. Ellijay...You have a big future in front of you. It's not lurking out there somewhere on the horizon. It is entering the stage from the wings and is waiting on its cue from you. Your decision today prepares you for its next line. It will take everything you have learned and even some things you have not in order for you to tame it and make it part of you.

"Are you ready to take on what will come your way?" he asked.

Breathing in sharply through her nose while nodding quickly in short little nods, "I think so, Sorin. I think so."

"Good. Then relax now while you can. You have had a rough time lately."

"I think I will," she said as she got up off the park bench and touched the tree one more time at its base. "Thanks for the time and the kind words."

As she said this, the bird in the tree took wing and flew off. It didn't sing but rather chirped a rapid, harsh sound that was more of a warning call as it sped off to the south.

Andrea made her way back across to her townhouse and went inside. It somehow looked different...smaller.

She decided to go for a drive in the afternoon. But this time, her day was not a postcard as she drove through central Virginia. Colonel Chicken just didn't seem to hold any appeal. And there was no dog by the name of Boomer at the park fetching a Frisbee for her. She missed his bandana.

In the end, she settled on making a grocery run for a few things she needed for her new home. After lounging around a little, Andrea decided to pick up her date for the evening. She went into her kitchen and selected a nice Pinot Noir, and headed up for her bedroom to search the old classic movie channels.

She was so completely and utterly tired of everything, and so wrapped up in her own world, that she didn't even notice the fax lying in the paper tray of her printer as she passed the study.

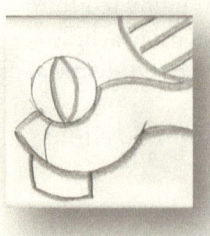

16.
12.19.9.12.5. 4167; 18 YAX, 7 CHICCHAN — SNAKE

October 20, 2002, 10:00 a.m. EST

The first thing Andrea felt the next morning was the pleasant pressure of her smooth flannel sheets being weighted down by the fluffy overstuffed comforter. Soft new pillows supported her head. All of it made for a cloud in which she could slowly regain consciousness and lull her into a false sense of security.

Her yawning mind became aware of the light of a picture-perfect day outside giving her eyes the misimpression that all would be well. The glossy streams of autumnal brightness rayed down from the October sky in yellow, white, and blue ribbons like some fall festival tickertape parade. The morning light had joined in with the bed linen in one giant charade.

She breathed in and stretched having the co-conspiring air send precious oxygen to cells at the farthest reaches of her extremities that were hungry for breakfast. They would use this airborne element to trigger the breaking down of small, soluble food molecules as they began their daily grind of producing energy for their benevolent despot, Andrea.

As she flung her legs out over the edge of the bed and used their weight to fulcrum her torso up, she allowed her messy hair to catch up with her head and slowly fall into place. She sat there alternating the small kicking movement of each foot as she scratched the back of her head and stretched yet again. The final confidence tricksters in the quartet were her bunny slippers looking up patiently from the floor, ready to once again make her tootsies all safe and warm.

These she slipped on, and after a pause for the cause, she stumbled downstairs to the coffeemaker in the kitchen. She flipped the switch and began the Morning Coffee Lean, where she summoned enough patience to wait for the carafe with auto cutoff to display enough of the magical elixir to sustain her ongoing waking-up effort. The countertop was the best supporting actor in this scene.

Eventually she had enough java to get her through the rest of the period where the coffeemaker would bubble, burp and fart out the rest of the pot. Wrapping both hands around the slightly oversized mug using it to warm the insides of her palms, she allowed her bunny slippers to escort her back up the stairs in a soft shuffling way.

Her only intentions were to read some of the news services online and not take this day any more seriously than she had to. Unfortunately, she would fail miserably at both goals.

Taking a moment in her bedroom to slip on a nice, soft terrycloth robe, which made her pleasant morning as complete as it gets (isn't it funny how a Johnny-come-lately robe can try to muscle in on the action of a successful con after all the hard work is done by the quartet of the bedding, pillow, slippers, and coffee?), she then shuffled into her study and plopped down in her office chair.

Still waking up a little, she shook her mouse to likewise wake up her computer. If she wasn't going to get to sleep any more…then buddy, it wasn't going to either!

As the screensaver exited, the monitor made a slight crackle as it changed back to the default resolution for the system. The display slowly woke up, as she had done not five minutes earlier. She thought, *and man built machine in his own image. Thus was it spoken, thus was it done!* She giggled a little, wiggling her toes in each slipper making the bunnies do a little happy dance.

She sipped her coffee.

As the monitor was slowly glowing up to full brightness, she swung her chair back and forth a little. It was on one of these swings that something ominous first caught her eye, something that would be the unwelcome harbinger in an otherwise pleasant morning—a foreboding sentinel that had betrayed the other five con artists and would bring reality back into the harsh light of day.

There in the paper tray of her printer were three sheets of paper.

Still maintaining a grip on the pleasant morning in her left hand that was her cup of coffee, she extended out her right to grasp, and in so doing receive the darker day that was to come by retrieving those pieces of paper.

At first, nothing seemed out of the ordinary to her. She was actually pleasantly surprised it was the fax from the bank in Peabody. It had come in three days early!

The first page was just the cover sheet. It had all the usual and customary legalese on it. Flipping to the second page, she started reading the particulars while she still sipped on the hot cup of coffee. Nothing seemed that unusual. It was an account summary. It was meaningless details like the kind of account it was, that it had been opened in 1954, and was the property of one George Burroughs.

She was a little disappointed. Ned had seemed to think this would be a serious lead to something and all she saw was more like a trust fund or a side account saved for a rainy day. As a lark, she opened up an Internet browser and entered the name George Burroughs with quotes around it.

She had learned during her GBI training that putting quotes around a set of words in a browser search would force the search engine to return only matches for those exact words in order. So instead of thousands of responses, one may only get forty or fifty. This would save some time as an agent poured over leads.

She clicked search and got back 3,080 matches.

She blinked at the monitor in disbelief and the monitor stared back at her without emotion. Realizing that she must have made a mistake, she brought the search window back up and re-entered the name George Burroughs. This time she took extra pains to make sure the quotes were present. Clicking the search button, the results came back the same. There were 3,080 matches to the name.

"Must be a popular fucking name…" she mused.

Clicking down the first items in the list, which would be the most viewed, she was intrigued to discover that a George Burroughs figures prominently in the Salem Witch Trials. "What a damn coincidence!" she thought out loud. But as she clicked down jumping ten, twenty, even fifty links at a time, it was turning up that all of the results were about the same George Burroughs.

She turned her attention back on the document at hand and flipped to page 3. Here she discovered the details around the ACH payment that had started this whole thread. The details presented a story of types. George Burroughs had opened an account with $100,000.00 in Peabody in 1954. Then suddenly this year, he transfers $9,999.00 to a regional bank in the Southeast United States. Andrea was familiar with this bank, they advertised a great deal in Georgia. The specific branch number was listed on the page with the other information.

In a short amount of time, she had the Internet search back up and had located that branch number for that bank. The branch provided a complete list of services including an ATM and was located in Savannah Georgia. It would be exceptionally easy for someone to gain ready access to cash without being questioned in the slightest.

Something about this thought sparked a connection in her mind. Andrea sat back in her chair a little bit. "Ok…that's too much of a damned coincidence!"

The stack of articles and briefs she had pulled from the research center were fanned out in a neat vertical row, as if she had been playing Solitaire with them on the left side of her desk. The row had grown over the last week as she added documents of interest.

She traced down the row until she found the title, "Croatoan in Colonial Times." She flipped through the pages at a quick clip and found the item she was seeking on page seven. She grabbed up a pink highlighter pen and pulled back up the bank fax beside the article. She circled the name George Burroughs. Then she switched to the article and circled the sentence that stated that the Croatoan were suspected in having something to do with the Salem Witch Trials.

Then she went back to the fax and circled the destination of the ACH transfer and circled the bank and branch number. Hitting the print button on the web browser she printed the page from the bank branch locator and circled the ATM and the location of Savannah.

Next, she thumbed down the fanned out vertical row of briefs and found one of the first ones she had ever read. It was about a Vampire dying in New York. She circled the sentence about the suspicion that a Croatoan was involved and placed that find on the growing stack of coincidences in front of her.

She pulled the three pages on Salindria from the book, *A Vampirism History*, and found the section on her upbringing. She circled the fact that she was raised in an orphanage and added it to the stack.

Andrea returned to the arrayed list of source material and pulled the statistical report on Internet traffic patterns. Number eight was Savannah! Thus, was it circled; thus, was it added to the stack.

Without realizing it, her work had increased with speed and fervor. One may even have called it bordering on a pitch. Regardless of the description, Andrea just knew that she was on to something. And this time she didn't give a flying diddly-shit what Ned Smarny thought.

She recalled what Casper had said about the blogs, suggesting that a pseudo governmental agency, namely the Order, was secretly involved in terrorist activities. She scanned down the dwindling pile of source material on the left and found the report on the Fuel Oil shipment. It was stolen in Jacksonville, Florida and found in Columbia, South Carolina. She circled this and went back to the Internet.

Pulling up a mapping program that allowed grandparents to enter their home address and then enter the new address of their grandchild so that they could print out directions and become hopelessly lost on the way to the party and miss the blowing out of the candles, Andrea entered Jacksonville and Columbia. After the map was generated on the screen, she printed a copy out.

Tracing a straight line from Jacksonville to Columbia took the pink highlighter pen right through Savannah.

"Fuck," she said as those two artifacts now joined the swelling majority in the center of her desk.

Then with a look of dazed, flabbergasted shock at the reality of it, Andrea hypothesized, "Salindria was an orphan. A Croatoan harvested her seed. All this activity around Savannah…and the largest orphanage in the whole damn country is…"

Without completing the sentence, she was up and running. Her bunny slippers were taking the brunt of the punishment as she dashed through the house preparing to leave.

It was amazing to her how many times in recent memory she had thrown things in an overnight bag. But she didn't want to get caught without a change of drawers. Andrea decided to pack for three days.

She had a pretty good idea what she was going to do. But even if the hunch was wrong, she was going to see Wren again after all these years and that was important as well. While she made a whirlwind of getting ready and packing, she sorted through the details of her plan.

First, she would not inform her bosses. They had complained that she had been too conservative and she wanted to prove to them, as well as to herself, that part of her was not just bound and gagged, but had also been fed to the fishes with her pride.

Second, she would not inform Wren. She realized there was a risk that he might be away, but he had been there the previous Sunday night. So, it was as good a gamble as any. The main thing she was avoiding was wholesale panic by hundreds of people.

She had often wondered if a person had a time machine, how they would best prevent 9/11. She imagined a person could try to prevent thousands of people from going to work or to evacuate them earlier. But she really guessed one would take out the source. Kill nineteen men and 9/11 doesn't happen.

She was planning on taking out the source.

Third, she would not involve any local authorities. She tried to imagine how that call would go, "Yes, officer…these thought-leaches attacked a vampire in New York and well…" That was futile.

She dashed out to her car and threw her bags into the back. She didn't even lock up. She really didn't care about that right now.

The trip to the airstrip was a blur. She was going through a mental checklist. It never dawned on her that all the items on the list were of the offense type: gun, badge, stun gun, gold card, etc. Things that were omitted included: warrant, itinerary, permission, bookings, notifications, even locking her townhouse.

The bunny slippers would have to fend for themselves.

Pulling into the second hanger at Knight-Flight Charters, she grabbed up her stuff and ran inside. Steven Knight was there at his post behind the counter, "May I help you?"

"Yes, Steven…I need a flight to Savannah."

"Ah, Agent Ellijay! This is a pleasant surprise. I was not aware we had a booking to Savannah. Let me recheck my flight plans." He started turning to his computer on the back wall.

"No need to check it, Steven. There are no plans. I am working on a last minute case."

Spinning back around, he had a slightly grim look on his face, "That's what I was afraid of. I didn't think we had it booked and we are fully chartered today. I don't have a jet left that hasn't already been engaged."

"Crap." Andrea took a moment to think. Then, "Don't you have anything?"

"Well…your best bet to make Savannah by tonight would be to fly out of Richmond. I do have a small one-engine plane, and Phil is here. He's a mechanic and a damn good pilot. But he is not commercial. He hasn't gotten his 5,000 hours in yet. If you fly with him, he could get you to Richmond, but it would be as a passenger and at your own risk."

"I trust you, Steven. If you say he can do it, I will fly with him." Pulling out her gold card, she added, "How much do I owe you?"

"Nothing. I can't take your money on this one. This is Phil flying you as a friend. Period." Then turning to the microphone, he said back over his shoulder, "Hold on a moment."

He called Phil in. Phil looked to be in his upper twenties, but was balding prematurely. Andrea noticed that he made up for the lack of hair on the front and top of his head by growing it long on the sides. She figured he was getting ready for the comb-over stage. He was tall, but not tall enough for his weight to be proportional. And the one-piece jump suit always had a way of either really working to make a man look handsome or really making him look awful. There didn't seem to be an in-between.

"Phil, could you fly Ms. Ellijay up to Richmond and direct her to the terminal there? It would give you a few more hours towards your goal and I will buy the fuel. You can use the Comanche in spot 27."

Phil was wiping grease from his hands with an old, red rag, "Yeah! You bet!"

Steven proceeded with the introductions, "Phil Davis, meet Andrea Ellijay. Andrea, Phil."

They both shook hands and Phil directed her out onto the tarmac.

Andrea had never boarded a plane by stepping up on its wing before. But the Comanche wing had a wide strip of black grip material similar to sandpaper. It was no problem at all to follow Phil up the wing and then down into the five-seater. She got to sit in the copilot seat and that was a new adventure for her. Her bags were the passengers in the back three.

She said to Phil while he went through his preflight routine, "It's a little like a nice-sized sedan with wings and two steering wheels."

"Yokes."

"What?"

"They are called yokes, not steering wheels," Phil answered and by way of demonstration he grabbed his and moved it back and forth. The yoke belonging to Andrea moved back and forth at the same time.

"Do I need to know any of this?" she asked.

"Nope. But I will be glad to explain anything you want to know. It's about a ninety minute run to Richmond and that can either go quickly or slowly depending on if this is your first time in a private plane."

Andrea decided to take the ignorant route and just observe this flight.

They taxied out onto the runway. Andrea noticed things she had never seen before. It was such a different experience at this vantage point. The tiny little white stripes at the end of a runway were actually *huge*!

Phil halted the craft and went through some more checks. She had always wondered why planes stopped just before takeoff. Now she was seeing it all up-close and personal. After Phil had finished all the checks including revving the engine up and down which caused the pane to buckle and jerk against its own brakes, they proceeded out onto the end of the runway.

Phil was busy talking to the small two-story tower, which was little more than a ladder with a shack on top of it, while they started rolling free of the controlling brakes.

Andrea felt free of her controlling brakes.

In this small plane, it didn't feel like the craft was leaving the ground. It felt more like the ground leaving the craft. It was as if the earth just fell away and the little plane had to struggle in small swoops to catch enough air not to plummet into the murky depths.

Soon the landing field became a patch and all the patches then became a quilt. It reminded her of the quilt she had received from her neighbors back home.

She was leaving all her security behind in this bold move to hopefully save her neighbors. That was what she had to believe to press on.

The trip was indeed short. Phil had learned the trick of adding in the ground-time on both ends of his flight-time. The actual time in the air was little more than fifty-five minutes. By 1:00 p.m., Andrea Ellijay was standing in line at a ticket booth inside the terminal proper.

She selected an airline based in Atlanta. She had heard on the news that they had been having the toughest go of it after 9/11 and thought she would throw a little business their way.

"How can I help you, today?" the bright, young lady asked at the counter.

"I need the quickest flight to Savannah, please."

"Ok…just let me check." The ticket assistant clicked her long nails across the keys.

Andrea looked down at her own nails. She never seemed to be able to get them much more than a quarter of an inch out from the tips before they were breaking on guns at the firing range or stair rails as she chased some bad-guy. But she wondered if she could stand them long. If they grew out to the point she wanted, and they clacked like that on keyboards…it would drive her nuts!

Drive, hell. That's just a putt, the voice in her head shot as a self-deprecating joke.

"Ok…it looks like you just missed a flight out at 11:55 to Savannah. But I think we can get you on the 4:20. I have a seat open for it. Would you like that one? It is $425.00 open pass, round-trip."

"Is there any way to get me there any earlier?"

"Hot date?" the saleslady asked.

"Very…if I don't get there soon enough." Andrea let the irony hang without explanation.

"Well…" those nails were just a'clackin' away. "Our connection is in Atlanta. But our competition to the right here has a connection in Washington Dulles that leaves at 2:52…" That sounded promising to Andrea. "…but arrives in Savannah at 10:06." The ticket lady made a swift, down-turned pout to show she understood that would not help much.

"That won't help much." Andrea gave words to the expression.

The ticket lady kept looking at the monitor and shaking her head 'no' in agreement as she sucked air through her teeth. Then a few more clickety-clacks followed with, "Our other competitor to the left here has…a flight leaving at 4:00…" That seemed even later to Andrea. "…but a short layover in Charlotte would put you in Savannah at 9:42."

"I'll take it!" she said.

"The price is $446.00 and as a courtesy I could go ahead and book that for you here if you like, but you would still need to go through their line to check in."

"That would be fine. Please and thank you."

She gave the ticket lady all of the required information and then stepped back out into the wide lobby area to think things through a little. She realized that since 9/11 security was tighter. She could easily take the gun and stun gun on the flight with her credentials. But if she got a Deputy Dog type of security person, it could take hours and phone calls to resolve.

She also knew that the NTSB had not installed bag-screening devices in all airports yet. So the decision was made to check all of her bags and just ride sans luggage.

She approached the other ticket counter and checked in with the reservations just made. In a few short hours, she would be in Charlotte and then a few more—Savannah.

October 20, 2002, 10:00 p.m. EST

As Andrea was waiting in line at the car rental counter after an uneventful flight to Savannah, Danreck was working with George on the finishing touches to the bomb.

The basement to the Bethesda Orphanage was expansive to say the least. It was not the average dank and musty cinderblock variety with a dirt floor like one would expect in the South. The architecture was far too old for that. Instead, it was more like the old livery stable style that was common in buildings with the Old Spanish influence in these parts.

Wide and squat arched windows ran all the way across the large double wooden doors. The doors themselves were not solid, but rather made of planks that had been joined together by expert craftsman hands belonging to an artisan that had not walked this mortal coil for hundreds of years.

The walls were stacked brick made from fired Georgia clay. And in keeping with the custom of the day, they had been whitewashed. There were windows set up above eye level that would allow light to come in through their frosted tinting. Tonight, no light escaped them though. Black plastic garbage bags had been taped over them in a quickly applied shielding to prevent the precious light from slipping out to signal people outside that private and sinister work was going on inside.

The white walls reflecting the low wattage fluorescent glare gave the whole place a ghostlike appearance. These special lights were chosen to avoid heat and risk of spark. Danreck and George did not long for a premature fireworks pageant with them as the main attraction.

"So why not just set the damn thing off tonight?" George said as he carefully moved the last of the large blue plastic drums into place. The expertly mixed combination was all set for the big moment.

"Patience my Yankee friend," Danreck mused as he was opening the box containing sneak fuses, MOV switches, spools of wires and various sets of electronics. "I told you. We have to keep pace with other events. The blogs and other leaks will need time to soak after tonight. Besides…I have one last promise to keep with Josephine."

"The full moon?"

"That…and the last day of the current cycle. It is rare to have such a combination. More rare than a blue moon by far!" Danreck began assembling the first of twenty micro detonators.

"Well…you can buy into all that metaphysical bullshit if you want to. But for me, I trust what I see with my own eyes!"

"Or feel with your own neck?" Danreck said as a dig.

George's hand went instinctively to the scar and not finding it realized he was still Leroy. "Yes and my neck. Reality and my belief in it have saved that very same neck many-a-time!"

Danreck looked up from his needle-nosed pliers and alligator clips for a moment. "George...there is a reason why you haven't made it into the circle. You keep shunning the Warrior's ideas and philosophy. If you outshine the master..."

"Yeah, yeah...don't give me any more of that *48 Rules* bullshit. Greene is a nut and people that spout that bullshit are nuts, too. Just because I have my own philosophy on life doesn't make me a threat to Hacquee. And looking for ways to cuddle up to your peers so you can stab them in the back just to get ahead a little is a lousy waste of our time here on this rock, and it never really pays off. You just look silly and become shallow."

Ticking his tongue and saying in a shaming tone, "Tsk, tsk George! You make it sound like we are monsters!"

"I don't give a flying fig what you think. I've always been loyal and have always pulled my share of the load." Standing back like a show model on a game show, he waved his arm at the rows and rows of drums behind him. "Do I need to say more than to show you these prizes for your trust in me?"

"Ok, ok George! You win!" he said with a laugh. "I just think it wouldn't hurt to be a little more interested in the ideas of our maker."

"I was interested fine for the first century or two. But you know...there is only so much mysticism I can take before I want to go out and get my hands dirty."

Looking back at his work, Danreck returned to wiring and said, "You are a good team member George, but damn...you could be so much more." Looking back up at George, he asked, "I mean...what would you do without me running political interference for you?"

"I hope to never find out," George said in a distant voice.

"And you never will have to," Danreck said in a reassuring voice as he went back to his work. "That is...if I don't make a clumsy mistake here and set off a spark."

George's fear returned when he realized that Danreck had begun the electronic work. It may be this twisted bastard's idea of fun to play with fire but it sure as hell wasn't his. "You know...umm...Danreck?"

Looking back up, he said in a disgruntled voice, "Yes, George?"

"Well...I mean...I have been at this Mission for two weeks now...and, well...?"

"Just get on with it," Danreck said.

"Look. It's like this. We have been lucky in not getting caught. The truck has gone largely unnoticed in the back alley. It looks like so many of the others. But it has been parked there unattended for hours tonight and that is unusual."

"Yes, George."

"And…well…I've been on *my* Mission for two weeks as well and I really need to take care of that White bitch soon. The voices in my head calling for her blood have been overwhelming lately."

"Yes, I see."

"And you are done here except for the triggers…"

"George you can leave in just a moment. Let me get the first of these in place. I want to make sure that no one can disarm this thing should anything unforeseen occur."

George was beading up sweat as Danreck continued to clip the bare ends of electrical wires to electronic devices. He knew that the fumes in this place made it a tinderbox just waiting for the right catalyst.

Danreck busied himself with great concentration as George seemingly held his breath for long minutes at a time. He connected the first detonator to the first cluster of drums and then the booby traps were added with great care.

Danreck saw the perfect opportunity so he moved the tools well away from the connections and said in a hushed and serious voice, "Shit."

George went into full-blown panic. "What's wrong? What's wrong?" he was almost yelling.

Danreck turned a smart-ass look to his longtime friend and said, "I smell shit…did you just lose some?"

George was enraged since he had just been burned in another sense of the word. "You bastard!"

"I'll have you know that both of my parents were happily married. It just so happens to other people at the time…but that is another matter entirely!" and he let out a belly laugh like he hadn't in decades. It felt good.

"Damnit, Danreck! That ain't funny!"

Looking over a barrel at George, Danreck said, "I mean it George…we are going to have to put you in Accent Detox when we get back to New York. You can't keep that up for long there!"

"Then just let me go!"

"Ok, ok George. You may leave. I have this set to where only I could take it apart without setting it off. The detonator can be set off remotely but won't allow for more than twenty-five hours to pass before BOOM!" He made a hand gesture with his uttered onomatopoeia to symbolize a large explosion.

"I will be three states away and a woman will be dead before that happens. I'll try to be in New York to watch it all on your TV. But if not, I'll catch it in a hotel room."

Danreck stood and crossed to the man he had helped hang, and had also helped save over 300 years earlier. "Travel well my friend. If the wind is at my back, I will be there to celebrate in two days."

George looked at Danreck and said, "So what do you say to a man who is about to blow up hundreds of orphans? I mean…'Break a leg' just doesn't seem to fit."

"You can just wish me luck to a Mission well completed."

"Luck then, old friend," George said and patted him on the shoulder while they shook hands. George made his exit, heading out to the truck to start it up for the long drive back to Mississippi, and Danreck returned to the remaining nineteen detonators.

October 20, 2002, 11:00 p.m. EST

Gravel and rocks spat out from under the rental's tires as Andrea skidded slightly to a stop in front of the northern administrative wing for the orphanage. She was afraid she wouldn't remember the way here, but once she made it to the bypass and began her approach from the north, some of the larger landmarks started coming back to her.

The gravel drive divided a yard that was largely peat. The deep green carpet sprouted huge trees with grey trunks, spreading tentacles of root-systems, and sprouting large, generous canopies out and up toward heaven. Their branches became the curtain rods for the large drapes of Spanish moss hanging down, swaying in the breeze. The light from the lone streetlamp mixed with the soon-to-be full moon slanting through the intertwined lace, casting bizarre and moving ghosts across building and lawn.

Stepping out of the car, Andrea was more than aware of the quietness of this place. The street traffic had died down and all that was obvious was the howling wind whose presence was visible in the shifting shadows.

The administration wing was the only two-story section. All the others were multi-floored dorms, educational facilities, and recreation centers. The architecture was ancient. Grey stucco with concrete caps worked as an inexpensive, but relatively perpetual establishment. It would have been horribly institutional and drab had it not been for the surrounding flora and fauna. But with it, the whole thing made a gothic scene for a ghastly disaster.

Andrea heard in the distance a large truck start its engine. It sounded like it was coming from the other side of the orphanage. She ran up to the front door and found it unlocked. She heard the truck brakes release with a loud blast as she reached for the old brass handle with a thumb-trigger on top that opens the door by pressing it down. She then heard the truck rumble off in the distance, shifting gears as it faded away.

The large wooden frame with the old, cut glass shot prisms of light in rainbows as she opened the door and stepped into a lobby from another time. A kind, older woman was standing behind a counter to Andrea's right. "Well…it is late to be having company…may I help you, young lady?"

"You must be Liddy," Andrea said as she stepped up to the counter, extending her hand.

Taking her hand in return, "And I'm afraid you have me at a slight disadvantage, Miss...?"

"Ellijay. Andrea Ellijay."

"Oh yes! You are the young lady that called last week. I'm glad that you stopped by. Do you want me to find Wren? He's probably just finishing his work in the rec-hall for the night. I'll just go fetch him up."

Liddy quickly disappeared through a door behind the counter.

The clock in the main entrance room hung on the wall. It was huge. The antique face allowed for a key to wind the chain, which was presently playing its way out, pulled by large brass weights behind a pendulum big enough to double as a bed-warmer. The droning *tick* followed seemingly a year later by its corresponding *toc* brought to Andrea's full attention how urgent this matter was.

There was a large Plexiglas window on the left side of the lobby looking into a clean and bright play area for toddlers. Scores of young crumb-crunchers would be playing over the colorful mats in just seven more hours or so. Currently, some older boys were walking around the room picking up toys and placing them on shelves. They were wearing the traditional cardigan with logo proudly displayed on the chest pocket. "Good to see some things never change," she observed, and then more solemnly, "I hope I'm wrong about this."

Finally, the sound of voices brought a new emotion that quickly crowded out that of her professional sense of duty and the emergency at hand. Added to the mix was the now stunning revelation that she was once again a teenager. There was a lump of excitement in her throat as she realized the voice was that of the man she spoke with at length only a few nights ago, the one she had dreamed about and danced with in her youth.

As they rounded the corner, she felt silly for imagining she was on the *Dating Game* and the host had just asked Bachelor Number 2 to come on around the partition and meet your lucky date! But that was precisely how she felt. She struggled to suppress her delight with her professionalism.

Wren came around the opening with his arms stretched out and a huge smile across his face, "Andrea! How fantastic to see you!" and the word 'you' stretched out into almost an excited scream as he picked her up off her feet and swung her around. His blue jean jacket felt so comfortable and familiar to her. It was the type hard-working men wore in these parts. It wasn't for show. It was for wear. And it was serving its purpose well as the young southern bell was transported to cloud nine in its arms.

She slowly returned to the Earth's greedy pull and touched down square in Realityville. Even though her arms had given up on the moment, her fingers stubbornly refused, still being laced behind his neck. Andrea always hated that these moments passed away far too soon, and that you couldn't stop them, or hold on to them. They slipped away into the twilight leaving little behind. She promised herself that she would try harder to capture its essence the next time she got a moment like this with Wren.

She would never get that chance again.

Her fingers relented and opted instead to grab his hand and pull him out onto the porch, "We need to talk."

Trailing behind her, he chuckled the word, "Ok…" He was led outside, looking at Miss Liddy with a *What can I do?* look on his face.

After the door was pulled-to he said, "So, to what do I owe this pleasure?"

"This isn't pleasure, Wren. I suspect a plot to harm the orphans."

Now his face became very serious. "Ok, Andrea. Let's call the authorities."

She held him in place with the hands that were still holding his, "That is the *worst* thing we can do right now. I am a professional and in this case, you and I need to check something out."

"Fine. But we will call the authorities. It is a must. What do we need to do?"

"Just show me around the place first. I think I can stop this, but a big commotion with lots of lights and sirens may put the children in harm's way," she said.

"I have to at least tell Miss Liddy. She would worry about me if I just walked off."

"Ok, but hurry," she implored.

Wren stepped in and spoke with Liddy. Then he stepped back out and said, "Follow me."

They left the porch and began walking around the grounds to the East. Andrea was somewhat pleased to see the wolf trotting along beside them. She asked Wren, "Whatever happened to that huge basement that ran under the center of the original building?"

"You mean the one we would sneak off to given half the chance during a mixer?"

Trying not to get caught back up in the memory she said, "The one in the same."

"It's been cleared out. There are some plans to maybe renovate it next year if our fundraisers are successful. But for now it's completely empty and not being used."

They walked around the East wing and came back in to the apex where all the buildings joined. There was a narrow, short driveway that led up and out to a service road around back. At the bottom of the short driveway were the large wooden, double doors she had remembered from happier times. There was a faint light emitting from a crack in the door but all of the windows where pitch.

"That's odd…" Wren said as he noticed it too.

"Wren wait," she said as she grabbed his forearm. Fishing around in her purse she positioned her free hand between her revolver and the stun gun. She was not quite sure which to have ready, but wanted to be prepared for either.

They quietly began their approach. There was an audible but muffled movement coming from within. Andrea had to steel her nerves and slow her breathing. She went back to her years of training on all the different staging grounds where cardboard bad-guys popped out. A split decision was made whether they were crooks or babysitters.

As she was breathing in through her nose and out through her mouth to stabilize her body's desire to scream and run, she noticed a faint, acrid aroma. Realizing at once that her suspicions had been correct, her hand moved around the handle of the revolver, opting for fewer chances of spark.

She looked at Wren and said, "Let me handle this."

Andrea opened the door silently and stepped inside as quietly and quickly as she could manage. There in the ghostly, pale light she saw a figure bent over some work. Around him, she saw the edges of blue drums but could not make out how many.

As she was approaching, revolver extended in front of her, the figure stopped its work and look up at the drums in front of him. Without turning around, he said in a calm and almost melodic voice, "Well, well…what have we here? Two doers-of-good failing miserably in their attempt to stop me."

Andrea wasn't sure if it was the words or the wanton apathy with which they were spoken that caused the gooseflesh to rise up on her arms, but it really didn't matter. It had a hell of an effect either way. "Step away from the barrels and put your hands in the air! Now!" she said with as much command as she could muster.

His arms went up and he slowly turned around as he said, "You mean like this?"

What happened next defied her ability to comprehend. The man in front of her became a blur to the left, then a gust of wind blew past her to the right and the man was now standing back where he was with his arms still up in the air—only now, one of them was holding a choking Wren a good six inches off the ground without any apparent strain or effort at all.

Before she could even fully understand what she was saying she yelled, "Release him now or I *will* shoot!" Andrea had the perfect bead. She could easily cap this asshole in the forehead without breaking a sweat.

Now with more bravado he said over Wren's struggling grunts and choked gasps, "I'm afraid that won't work. Besides the obvious that you cannot harm me, the spark from the gunpowder would certainly blow up all those poor orphans. Either way, your man here will be just as dead."

"I mean it dirt-bag! Drop him!"

"Why, that's impolite. I don't even know your names. Let me rectify that…" Andrea saw him re-grip Wren's neck between his thumb on one side and his ring finger and pinky on the other. His middle finger was now out of view. There was a shudder made by Wren that was both grotesque and overwhelming. The man continued his sentence as if it were not interrupted by this maneuver, "…Andrea. I am a bad man. And you two are going to die. If you pull the trigger, then the orphans will not survive long enough for Miss Liddy to make that call to the authorities. She will only do so if Wren is gone thirty minutes without word back. And it has only been five minutes or so."

Andrea's brain was working in double time. She had concluded everything she needed to approach this situation the best she could. "We can work this out. Spare us, and we will get you what you want."

"Hmm…I fancy that you will do that anyway, Security Officer Ellijay." Andrea was relieved she had not mentioned the Order to Wren. "I fear you are in over your head this time. Isn't that right, Wren?"

Wren answered in a high, shrill voice like a ventriloquist puppet might but Andrea recognized it to be his. In a bright and cheerful tone like one would expect to hear at a child's birthday party, "That's right, bad man! You are going to get everything you want because you're the boss!" His limbs were moving in the dangling way a dummy might—sick and stinted.

"And what do you think about that Wren?" He asked his puppet.

Continuing with the cheerful voice and gestures, "We think it's just swell! You always were better than the Warrior! You are the greatest of the great! We should all bow down to you instead of him!"

Andrea felt sick. She felt like she was going to vomit. Nothing had prepared her for this cruelty, this humiliation. "Put him down you bastard!"

"Now see…" the man said in a different voice, one of a perturbed judge, "Why is it that people keep questioning the mating habits of my parents today? I mean, do I have a sign on my back that says 'Kick me, my mom wasn't married when she conceived' or something?" He made mocking glances over his shoulder in both directions to see if he could find the sign.

"You are a snake!" she spat.

Just then, Wren spoke in his own voice, "Andrea! It's me! Please help me! Please, oh God, please help me!" And as she heard Wren's continuing pleas for help, Andrea became aware that there were actually two voices. The monster had his free hand up on his chin and was looking with sincere concern at Wren. His lips were moving with Wren's. He was saying precisely the same thing at the same time as Wren.

Looking back at her, the man said coldly, "Not working, is it. I mean…you could see my lips move, couldn't you? I don't think I could do it with a glass of water."

Andrea could not stand any more. She knew she only had one chance and that was to rush him. She could maybe free Wren and let him escape to warn the others. "You ass-fuck!" she screamed as she ran towards him with all of her speed.

Before she could cross half the distance between her and the man, she saw blood shoot from two holes made on either side of Wren's neck by the man's thumb and ring finger. As she got nearer, still she was aware of the clicking sounds of bone breaking. Wren's eyes rolled back in their sockets.

As Wren's body flopped to the ground from the man's outstretched and blood-drenched hand, she could see a long black hair flipping around from the tip of his middle finger, whipping at the air in jerky coils as he said, "Oh…tired of the show so soon?"

17.
12.19.9.12.6. 4583; 19 YAX, 8 CIMI — DEATH

October 21, 2002, 12:00 a.m. EST

Hitting him was like running into a brick wall. Andrea jarred with the collision.

In a flash, she felt his hand grab her arm above the elbow. He then raised his bloody right hand in front of her face, showing her the solid red palm. The little black filament from the tip of his extended middle finger was teasing the air just in front of her.

She could hear Wren sputtering bubbles in his own blood on the floor to her side. She hoped he was dead, or at least unconscious, so that he would not suffer. She was afraid that he was not.

The man said, "Tut, tut, luv. Why the concern?" his voice was meant to be calm and soothing. He told a lie from his newfound knowledge he now studied in order to increase his advantage, "Wren didn't really care for you that deeply. You were just a girl of whom he had fond memories from long ago, showing up here to tell him something was wrong…"

He twisted a confused look at her and continued while she struggled in vain to free herself from his vice-like grip. "Well now…how exactly did you come to know *something* was going on here?"

She tried to pull back from the grotesque, bloody probe that was now whipping furiously in front of her face. It brushed the tip of her nose from time to time leaving little red crosshatched reminders of Wrens wasted life-flow. Thinking fast, she said, "I heard a truck out back. It was unusual for this time on a Sunday night."

"Hmm…that very well could be it. No matter…I shall know soon enough. It is a shame we do not have much time."

Still pressing against his force, "Why? Because the *bomb* is about to explode and take you with it?"

"No," he said calmly. "Unlike you, I have all the time in the world. Hell, I even have a full day before *that* happens. But now I must track down this Liddy within the next...oh say...twenty minutes or so, and make sure that the 9-1-1 call never happens. I wouldn't want any interference." Then turning a rueful smile on, "At least not any more than you have already presented me."

He continued to push for tactical advantage, "Actually, there is a reason I would wish for more time...I would be interested in sampling some of the warm, soft goodies that Wren recalled with such fondness. There were at least three reasons you remained so prominent in his memory, if I'm correct. Too bad that delicious mouth of yours wasn't one of them...but you all can't have *that* talent, can you."

The rage in Andrea flared. She felt she had to take action, but her struggles were useless. This monster appeared to be determined to have his little fun with her next, and didn't seem to be in much of a hurry. She knew Wren was the luckier between the two of them. Because she was charging, this creature had to dispense with him quickly. She did not think she would be so lucky.

Wren gurgled. She could hear his foot sliding in spasmodic, nervous shuffles on the floor behind her. She wasn't sure if it was better or worse not being able to see his condition.

"What do you plan to do with me?"

"Not nearly as much as I would like to. You see...I am a one trick pony, and being on a current Mission prevents me from accepting...well...a gift from you."

"Why not leave me alive long enough to finish your Mission and then take me?" she bargained.

The man howled with laughter, "Do not flatter yourself. You are insignificant; not worth my time."

Just then, Andrea remembered something. The one reason she detested the Order seemed to now be her possible saving grace. "Then why not just finish me now if I'm so worthless?"

The words had no sooner left her mouth then she regretted saying them. Suddenly, she realized that he might not try to probe her brain, but just crush her instead. Further, she didn't know if the MS would only be able to kill him if he were harvesting. She was filled with doubt and remorse.

She had failed.

"Because...contrary to my mother's steadfast attempts, she could never get me to stop playing with my food."

This was a new wrinkle.

Andrea's stomach turned. She didn't know if he was being literal or just toying with her emotions. It really didn't matter; her fear and repulsion were the same. She realized now that her only chance was to get him to engage her. She tried to think of a way in the brief seconds that were left.

Wren stopped making noises all together with one last shudder.

Attempting to fill the morbid silence, "At least you will not know the other plan."

"Nice try," he said wryly.

"Search your mind...where did I come from?"

He said dismissively, "Atlanta...or north. So?" He sounded as if he were getting testy.

"Atlanta...where someone failed to kill Jenna Domnanovich just one week ago."

That registered.

She watched as the stun waved across his face. Then to twist the dagger she perfectly timed the next dig, "Josephine was close to you, wasn't she?"

Andrea was guessing about this part, but she could tell by the immediate look on his face that the arrow had found its mark.

Chasing the now obvious line, Andrea said with growing intensity, "You weren't able to protect her were you, big bad warrior? For all your strength and power, you failed her when she was most vulnerable. When she needed you the most, you weren't there." Now that she had his complete focus, she said in a purposed tempo, "And it was probably all your fault." The man's eyebrows roiled together in a tempest as he became flush with fury.

Driving in the last nail as hard as she could, she finished with flippant coolness, "You will be on the news tonight if I don't call in by 1:00 a.m."

The man's voice started at a low growl and began to build from there. The pressure around her arm became more intense; pain started ripping up and down the right side of her body. Andrea wondered if she might have overdone it.

Then in a blur, the bloody hand disappeared from her sight. There was a wet smacking sound as his palm made full contact with the back of her neck. She felt the warm ooze, which had just recently been coursing through her now expired friend's body, slowly dripping down inside her collar. The smell of the thick blood was retching.

"What are you doing?" she feigned.

"Finding out what you know!" he howled.

The sting at the base of her skull coincided with the large smile of vengeance that crossed her face. In his rage and fury, he missed it.

With unparalleled satisfaction, Andrea felt the length of his fiber-like appendage driving deep inside her head. She waited with guarded anticipation for the big connection failure. She did the best she could at controlling her thoughts; hiding the secret that awaited him like a patient landmine.

He leaned into her and she could feel his chest pressing against her breasts. The moment was becoming more and more intimate as he penetrated her mind.

There was a ringing in her ears that was faint, but getting louder. Her vision narrowed, surrounded by a dim light. All she could see was his face and then his eyes. His voice still could be heard clearly.

The grip of his right hand shifted and she felt a slight throbbing at the base of her neck. She actually could feel him insider her. The probe was moving deeper and deeper.

She realized that she was fast becoming his slave in all things physical. But there was more.

Andrea became aware of ideas flashing in images, as he sifted through her mind, looking at thought after thought. She was panicking a little that he would find out the truth before he reached the point of his own destruction.

The images began to slow.

They became more intense, and more intimate with each passing moment realized before her as a living scene she could experience. He was finding the darker things inside.

Her panic and fear grew in intensity. But at the same time something new started to emerge from the dark regions of her mind.

She was becoming warm all over.

As much as she hated it, this monster was arousing her. She focused on fighting this feeling, but the desires were becoming overwhelming. Her heart started to race, and a strange attraction was drawing her in.

She noticed warmth in his gaze, which invited her to betray her repulsion. Her physical desires were growing beyond her ability to deny them.

Just then, he stopped. She wanted now, more than anything, only to share herself with what she was starting to realize was a god. She no longer cared about the Order, or her past, or even the now cooling corpse of her memory beside her. All she wanted was to give this man her world and she didn't even know his name.

Andrea desperately wanted him to continue.

She heard his voice down the far, distant tunnel. His voice was a comfort and eased the agony of her unfulfilled desire. She knew he was about to kill her, but she found that she no longer minded.

His voice was like the sweetest melody, as she heard words that sang to her soul, "I cannot take your seed my precious one, but I will still take you to that moment if you like."

She had no ability to speak. She was gasping for breath. But she knew her communication was received. She gave him permission to take everything. The perfect voice spoke to her, saying, "The bud bursts into bloom!"

Andrea Ellijay felt both release and explosive pain, as she was knocked back three steps. She somehow regained control of her legs—just enough to prevent falling on the ground, but her vision was still foggy.

In the tunnel of her vision that was slowly expanding back out, she could first make out the legs that belonged to the once-living man named Wren. The tunnel slowly flared out even more and she could make out the rest. Pools of blood were on either side of his upper body and head—the puddle on his left was much larger. They were rich, dark crimson reminders of his life that was now poured out on the cold ground.

The man that had just been holding more than her body; had held her very soul, was on the floor beside Wren. And unlike Wren—was very much still alive. He was getting up, but looked rather wobbly.

The fog from her mind was receding along with the fog in her vision, and she immediately felt dirty for her desire to share herself with this monster, this thing, this...

"Danreck?"

The man spun around with a greater stun on his face.

She was regaining her composure rapidly, "Danreck Porter?"

He was rubbing his head as if he had a nasty bang from the concrete floor. More feebly than she could imagine, he breathlessly said, "What?...What did you say?"

He seemed somehow smaller—somehow diminished.

Now there was a surety filling her mind and a new strength began to course through her veins. She nodded as she said with realization, "You are Danreck Porter...of the Salem Porters. You were born in 1643." A look of curiously happy surprise highlighted her face.

Danreck looked at her as he slowly straightened to his full height. He was moving like an athlete after a long and arduous game—stiff and sore. "Who the hell do you think you are?" he cried with indignation.

"You became immortal in 1692. The lady who died carrying out your Mission last week was Josephine."

Danreck changed expression and position. "I am not going to put up with your insolence any longer! You will bow down to the Croatoan!" It was still strong, but his voice had lost some of its earlier majesty.

Now filled with a complete lack of restraint, and risking all, she said, "Make me."

The silence was thick. No one had ever challenged Danreck before. He felt it beneath him to grace her command with his own movement, but was driven by his rage to twist her into tiny pieces. Danreck Porter put all his energy into a swift attack and launched himself towards her.

But all that resulted was a single shaky step, and he halted.

Andrea patronized, "Ah...big bad monster is going to come make me bow down."

Danreck had been looking at his foot in confusion, but at the sound of her words, slowly looked up with a new anger and determination. He took another step. This one was more stable and sure. He followed it with another.

To Andrea, he looked like some forty-nine-year-old toddler trying to figure out this whole walking thing from scratch. It was as if gravity was playing some sort of prank on him. Just then, she registered a slight stinging itch on the tip of her right, middle finger.

Danreck was now actually making a pretty good dash at her. She figured she would be on the ground at any second from the thrust of the body-check, but she really saw no way of avoiding it. Her strength was coming back fine, but she felt a little light and figured she was near fainting.

The freight train that was now Danreck Porter blew his horn, "I'm going to rip you apart!"

The collision was severe. Danreck's full force hit Andrea as she braced for the impact. When she opened her eyes, she saw that the ground was still amazingly perpendicular to her aspect, and remained in its proper place. Of course it was a little untidy with Danreck's body splayed out in front of her. He had spun and fallen back from the impact.

Andrea watched as he got back up from a facedown position. He was mumbling something about how all this could *not* be. Then she saw it. Andrea noticed something under his nose. Offering some friendly advice she said, "You have a little something just there," and she made a motion under her own nose with her finger.

Trying to look down at his own upper lip made Danreck look even more comical to Andrea. He wiped under his nose with his left hand. Blood was on his finger. In stunned silence, he just stared at it with a look of shocked disbelief.

Andrea stared as well. There was something in her telling her that this was significant. He was bleeding. His kind didn't bleed. They were undead, immortal. If he was bleeding, then something was wrong. Something had changed. Her confidence grew with the realization.

Now it was Andrea's turn.

All those years of being shuffled from house to house, all those other orphans that picked on her, the unfair gender-gap in her profession, the disease that lay in wait in her body, a world where everyone uses everyone else, and her dead friend laying not fifteen feet away—all conspired in her being to exact the perfect revenge.

Without understanding or planning what she was about to do, Andrea approached a shocked and silenced Danreck with purposeful and strong steps. "Alright piss-head. I have had enough of you. Your number is fucking up!"

Grabbing him by the collar in both hands, she lifted him off the ground! Looking up in his perplexed and befuddled eyes she said, "Welcome back to the land of the living you ass-clown!" With this, she threw him as hard as she could.

She only expected him to hit the post three feet behind him—if he made it that far...but to her astonishment, he flew *through* the wooden support beam and into the brick wall behind that. Dust filtered down from everywhere. The ceiling gave a groan.

Looking up at the ceiling, and then over to the barrels she said, "Shit! I better not do *that* again!" Then looking over at the moaning pile in the floor she said, "But first...a little unfinished business."

Marching over to him, she saw his pathetic attempts to right himself. She really didn't understand this strange strength. In her mind, it was probably just adrenaline.

But she was going to ride it for all it was worth, baby.

"Here, let me help you up." Andrea grabbed Danreck and threw him over on the floor behind her. He was now on his back, looking up at the ceiling. A trickle of blood was running down his chin.

Andrea straddled his torso, and sat down hard on his stomach. Danreck let out a short, explosive groan. She first jiggled and then slapped his face, "Wakie, wakie."

Danreck came to, and with dizzy eyes said, "You can't kill me." Then cutting his eyes over at the barrels, "No one knows how to disarm the explosives but me."

Andrea cocked her head to the side, and putting her finger up to her chin she said in her sweetest Montgomery accent, "You mean the Sneak fuses? Why that's just a little quicksilver to be avoided while I pull out the yellow and orange wires at the same time."

Then looking down at him with fake consternation, "Why...does that bother you that little ol' me knows something a woman ain't s'pose to know?"

Then remembering how this monster had felled Wren, a deluge of anger poured over her soul. Her blows began as mighty hammers. She alternated right and left punches to his face while saying, "Well you're just,"

hit,

"gonna,"

hit,

"hafta,"

hit,

"lump it!"

With the first hit, Andrea heard bone break. With the second, she felt the jaw give completely. The third brought a tearing sound from underneath the flesh.

Surprisingly, Danreck appeared to still be conscious. She grabbed him by the collar, and with one fluid motion, she stood up and righted him at the same time. When she released him, he swiveled a little like the town drunk. She took pains to prop him back up each time he tilted a little too far to the right or left.

Andrea Ellijay became aware of a growing desire—little more than an instinct really. She reached her right hand out around his neck and pressed her middle finger into the base of his skull. She felt a burning sensation at the tip of her finger.

Danreck's eyes shot open with a sudden look of fear. He appeared to be frozen in time. His useless mouth tried to form words, but all that came out from the bloody mass was a series of muffled nasal tones and gurgles.

She leaned into him with a genuinely concerned look on her face—like a friend struggling to hear what the other was saying. "What's that my dear friend? Are you trying to say something?"

More noises. More gurgles.

"Any last words, old chum?"

With a defeated look of horror and shock, Danreck shook his head *no*. A wet smacking sound emanated from the coagulating pulp, which was all that was left of the opening below his nose.

She increased her grip around his neck and lifting him up over her head, she said, "Welcome to the land of the dead, you son-of-a-bitch!"

The last thought Danreck had as he saw the concrete floor rushing up towards his mutilated face was of his mother and how she had really taken it on the chin today. He tried to laugh at the mental pun, but the floor interrupted him.

Andrea looked down at the mess. His face would be extremely difficult for the next of kin to identify. But she didn't think that would be an issue.

Danreck's blood pooled out and blended with that of Wren's.

She stood there in the cold silence for a while…just watching the two intermingle. She wondered what it all meant. She found no answers in the carnage.

Only pain.

Eventually, she was able to move from her frozen gaze. Somehow, she knew that Danreck had told the truth. There were now at least twenty-three hours before the bomb would go off on its own volition.

But she also realized that time was ironically running short. She could now see and hear in her mind Wren talking to Liddy *before* they came out here. She saw it all through *his* eyes as if she had been there. She heard Wren say, "Liddy, I think something is wrong." Followed by Liddy saying, "My dear, shall I call 9-1-1?" then Wren said, "Not yet. Give me thirty minutes and call if I don't come back."

She heard and saw this as if she were there in his body. Everything was in first-person. Andrea didn't really understand it all, but she also didn't want Deputy Dog, that would probably be a local sheriff, running in here with wire clippers and giving them all a really big show.

With haste, she moved towards the barrels. She seemed to arrive at them faster than she thought possible for her. She said, "I'm going to have to take it easy while this gravity thing catches up with me." She figured it was all from a blow to the head or something that she couldn't remember.

Going patiently from cluster to cluster she expertly pulled the yellow and orange wires out at the same time. She thought it was odd—she remembered just setting these up not two hours before. She remembered it clear as day. She fixed up the first one and then said goodbye to her old friend, George (who was Black for some strange reason...oh yeah! *His* Mission!) and then she had started on the rest.

Back then, all but one had been completely set up before being interrupted by two petulant people, and now here she was...patiently undoing all that work.

She carefully gathered up the detonators and took them out to the back yard. She placed them as far away from the fumes as she could and still be able to keep an eye on them. Then she opened the double doors and as many windows as possible to allow the basement to expel its dangerous fumes.

She walked back down the short wide ramp into the basement and stopped at her purse. She pulled out her ID and flipped the wallet inside-out. Then she slipped the back flap in under her belt, displaying the shield prominently.

Andrea solemnly walked back over to the bloody, lifeless scene and stood there looking down at the loss of her friend, and waited for the sirens to come.

It didn't take long.

The flashing lights that bathed the upper half of the basement walls told the story that squad cars had either driven around the grounds or pulled right up the back alley to the doors.

Deputy Dogs, one and all.

They had "snuck up" on the crime scene with all the grace and silence of a rabid elephant. They seemed to have stopped at the top of the ramp, waiting until they had enough men to form a quorum. Eventually one yelled down. "This is the police. Drop your weapons and come out with your hands up."

Without taking her vacant gaze off Wren, Andrea shouted in a clear voice, "This is Agent Ellijay. We have two dead, no survivors. Send for the bomb squad and watch for sparks on your way down."

Then she thought better of it and added, "Limited presence, please."

Five officers came through the door with weapons drawn. One of them shouted at her, "Ma'am, turn around slowly, and keep your hands where I can see them!"

Andrea did the safest thing. She held her hands out and slowly turned, badge-side first. The officers seemed to relax a little when they saw the badge. But they didn't lower their guns all the way. At present, they were covering the ground five feet in front of them with an enormous amount of firepower.

"I have a service revolver and a stun gun in my purse over there. I'm unarmed. I'll come over and show you my shield."

She slowly walked over to them, realizing she was not completely out of trouble. She was wondering if she would have difficulty here with these blues. If these dunder-heads didn't recognize the credentials, they may detain her, or even take her into custody. She was just getting her introduction lined up when she heard a voice come from behind the wall of blue in front of her, "It's ok, boys. She's one of us."

This surprised Andrea a little as the owner of the voice came pushing his way through the ranks, saying, "Or at least she *used* to be, before she skipped country and became a Fed."

With some relief, Andrea recognized Brian Ortega from the GBI. She had trained with him a few times at headquarters. With this announcement, all the officers checked their arms and relaxed. Brian crossed over to Andrea and gave her a big hug. He said, "What in heaven's name happened here, Andrea?"

"I was stopping by to pay a visit to an old friend, Wren Carmichael." Then catching her mistake, she corrected herself, "Er...I mean, Wren Busby. I knew him from my childhood. He works as a counselor here.

"I was coming up the front porch to visit him at the end of his shift when I heard some strange noises from back here. It sounded like a big-rig getting ready to leave, which was odd for an orphanage this late.

"I asked Wren if they made deliveries this time of night and he told me no. So, we decided to investigate. He had Miss Liddy call 9-1-1. When we came across the scene, we found the perp getting ready to blow the orphanage sky-high with fuel oil and fertilizer bombs."

"Holy shit!" Brian said.

"The perp seemed to be hopped-up on something strong. I suspect PCP. He attacked Wren and Wren fought him the best that he could. They ended up killing each other. While they fought, I secured the detonator devices and placed them near the fence in the backyard. By the time I made it back here, they were a bloody mess."

Andrea felt her story was good enough to sell—at least for now. She felt that she needed a little more detail to make it authentic and started searching her imagination for any kind of tidbit that would add credibility.

"Is that it? Any more info?" Brian asked her patiently.

"Just that he kept yelling something about wanting to kill the Warrior. He said it was his ultimate Mission. He had to kill the Warrior." And as she said this, a name came to her mind—*Hacquee*. She quickly chose not to share this.

She was wondering over the puzzle of these before-unknown pieces of information that seemed to be floating around her brain without a home when Brian interrupted, "Well…you know the process. We're going to be here all night and most of the day. GBI will need to get involved as well as the FBI and Homeland. This will be a three-ringed circus."

"No, Brian. What we need to do is get a CSI in here, stat. They need to doc whatever they need to from the drums, and then these blues need to haul them out with the bomb squad as quickly as possible. They are safe enough for now, but I don't want to take any chances with the children."

"It's your collar, Andrea."

That reminded her. She didn't want this kind of publicity, and she sure as hell didn't want to stick around here for the coffee and doughnuts session. "I need to report in."

Andrea crossed over to her purse and as she picked it up, retrieved her satellite phone. She pressed the digitally displayed button next to the name Casper. In moments, she heard a sleepy voice answer the phone.

"Casper, we have a situation. I'm in Savannah, Georgia at the Bethesda Orphanage. One of our friends just tried to kill all the children with a bomb. We stopped him."

"Is everyone safe now Andrea? Any casualties?"

Andrea looked over to her friend from a bygone day. She was thinking about the mixer. This time in her memory, she didn't see *him*. Instead, she saw *herself*. It was as if she was in Wren's body and was on a date with herself. This was *his* memory.

The emotions that she was now feeling from this memory were base, and teenage, and sexual, but at the same time there was something else there. Beneath a strong, physical drive that she did not quite understand was something sweet and enduring. He *had* cared for her. It was a very deep and sincere…love?

Yes.

She now realized that Wren was in love with her in some innocent and naïve way all those years ago. Danreck had lied. She had to clear her throat a little to knock back the lump that was driving a desire to break down and cry.

"One," she managed to answer.

In the end, a few quick calls from Casper allowed her to leave. The story became that Brian Ortega of the GBI crossed a scene where Wren Busby had heroically encountered a terrorist that was trying to destroy the orphanage. The world was told of the lone nutter that had cried out that he was trying to defeat the Warrior.

This story spun out over and over. The annoyingly repeated thirty second video loop from the scene slaked the world's curiosity as the voice-over was reworded twenty-four times a day in high rotation on each cable news outlet.

Their need-to-know was satisfied over the next five days until the Sunday news shows could have their say. The next week, a kidnapped girl in Washington State bumped it from the headlines and relegated it to the position of a footnote on all the Year-In-Review segments on December 31.

Eventually, a statue was erected in Wren's honor. Future generations of orphans would study his dedication, perseverance and sacrifice to make a world for them that was far better than it could have been.

Late in the night, Andrea drove her car back towards the airport, but decided she had had enough for one day. Near sun-up, she pulled into a nice hotel. Hell, the nicest one she could find.

Damn the expense account, full speed ahead!

She checked-in to a nice suite, and spent an eternity in a hot bath. But she was having a difficult time relaxing. Her mind seemed to be ablaze with new information. It just wasn't working right. She would get an idea and try to track it down, only losing the trail along the way.

In frustration, she gave up and drained the water out of the tub, as the energy simultaneously seemed to drain from her body.

Sliding between the sheets of the bed, sleep would not permit her any more waking time to contemplate the tragedy and success of the day. It overtook her with blinding speed, and in a moment, she was no longer part of this world.

Andrea slept as well as could be expected. The physical exhaustion was total. But at the same time she was having repeated phases of nightmares. They were sparse at first—every three to four hours she would wake up from one. But then, as the day wore on into the night, she was waking up from a jolt in decreasing time intervals: ninety minutes, sixty, forty-five. Towards midnight, they would no longer let her sleep.

The dreams were all the same. Blurry, flashy images of people and places she did not know. There was a feeling that she had changed. She saw herself kneeling before a throne for which she had no respect. And then, with some incantation she did not understand, she would see the tip of her middle finger rupture and the horrible probe flick out, freakishly whipping at the air.

During these nightmares, she would sit bolt upright with her heart pounding out of her chest. Once she realized it was just a dream, she would find herself rocking slowly, holding her right middle finger with her left hand, rubbing the tip with her left thumb in soothing strokes.

There would be no blood, no pain, and thankfully no probe.

After a time, consciousness fully convinced her that it was just some horrible nightmare, but with that same consciousness came the retched memory that she had actually *wanted* him to take her.

She felt used and dirty and violated—horribly violated. The only thing that saved her from utter depression was the sleep that would then overtake her, and the whole cycle would start over again.

In the late of the following night, she gathered up her stuff and checked out. She hardly spoke to anyone, or noticed anything all the way through the check-in process at the airport. She did manage to text-message Ned to have a connector flight ready in Richmond. It was the one piece of traveling logistics she just couldn't handle on her own.

As the plane left the ground this time, she was beginning to realize that things *had* changed. She was not sure how, but she knew things; things the Order didn't even know.

And knowledge is power.

This time, she was leaving her old life behind completely. This time, she had the ammunition to turn the tables on *them*. And this time, she was bold enough to stand up for herself and take control.

The Order now needed her *more* than she needed them. And she fully intended to use this new leverage any way she could.

18.
12.19.9.12.7. 5417; 0 ZAC, 9 MANIK — HAND

October 22, 2002, 1:00 p.m. EST

Andrea had tried to busy herself with work during the morning hours. She managed to put together some sort of report on her computer and submit it. But she was really having difficulty.

The way she saw it, things had not gone exactly as the Order suggested they would. She thought that Danreck would have spontaneously combusted or something like that. Actually, she was thankful he had not. It could have easily triggered the very event she was trying to prevent!

Also, nobody had said *anything* about some sort of Vulcan Mind Meld. But she had all these thoughts floating around in her head from *somewhere!*

Early in the morning, during one of the plane rides home, a very scary notion started to rumble around with all the new little bits in her brain. She began the paranoid line of thought that she may be *becoming* a Croatoan. After all, she really didn't know how all this stuff worked. Her speculation was that Croatoan came from somewhere. How did she know this wasn't it?

This was the gist of her thoughts as she wrote and re-wrote her report back at home. She was really worried that she may become the very thing all of these people were here to kill. So she left a few things out and reworded a few things to hide the changes that were happening inside her until she could sort things out.

She had looked in the mirror at one point. It was one of those ethereal moments like after a big fight with a longtime lover. Things are said that you never really knew existed down deep. But once they were out in the open, they changed things.

It's like walking through a room many times a day, extremely comfortable that there is nothing over there in the dark corner. Then someone flips on a light and you realize that a Bengal tiger has been sitting there from the beginning. One doesn't quite feel so comfortable walking across that room any more.

She felt that emotion coming from the person staring back at her. Things had been revealed to her. Things she had inside that had never been shown in the light of day. There was a tiger in the corner and the lights were on. Andrea really had no idea who that was in the looking glass.

She gave herself an easy short-range goal. Giving her mind something different to think about would help her become more productive. She was a little worried about the meeting Ned had requested on her schedule. It was to be held in his office. He wanted to go over what happened two nights before.

Her greatest fear now was that they would discover she was a Croatoan and they would what? Kill her somehow? All she really knew was that it would be bad. She had to keep this from them…somehow.

She needed a little time to sort things out.

Andrea was a nervous wreck as she walked across the quad. She felt like she had a huge bull's-eye on her back and it was open hunting season. About the only way she could think to handle it was straight. Just tell them that Wren did most of the damage. That she was scared of setting off sparks. That the creature *did* jack-in to the back of her neck, and that he died in violent spasms. Let them figure out why things were different and don't volunteer anything else new!

Andrea walked into Ned's office and was somewhat surprised to see Casper there. They had been talking about something, and it was obvious by the body language and sudden silence that they did not wish to share it with her. Andrea thought that the funny thing about such happenings is that they could be talking about football or cars, but all a person thinks is *They were talking about me!* and then they desperately want to know about what.

Andrea fought the paranoia. It was not her friend in this moment. It was the tattletale stool pigeon that was trying to flip on the lights and show the tiger in the corner to the world.

"Good afternoon gentlemen!" she said with a broad smile on her face. "Looks like the rookie girl bagged her first tiger!"

Casper moved back behind Ned and leaned against the credenza-like desk. Ned gestured for her to have a seat in one of the chairs in front of his desk, while he sat in his own chair. "That was some bit of detective work you did, Agent Ellijay. We are both very proud."

Casper, feigning applause from behind added, "Yes, hear, hear! You were spot-on, and a lot of lucky young boys are extremely thankful, as is a nation that is watching the good news every two minutes on cable. You handled things smartly and expertly, Andrea. We are not reading about the carnage of hundreds or even thousands of innocents this morning. You are to be congratulated and thanked!"

"And we got one of those filthy bastards to boot," she added with pride.

"Well...that's what we wanted to talk to you about..." Ned said in a change of tone.

"What do you mean?" Andrea asked.

"Now, now...there's nothing wrong," Casper tried to interject in an attempt to *not* dampen the celebration, "Ned just has a little clarification on the matter for you."

"Yes," Ned said as he laced his fingers neatly on the desk in front of him and leaned in with purpose, "Andrea...your actions last night were extremely brave and you did save all those orphans from a mad-man...but you see, he was just that...a mad-man."

"I don't follow you," and a look of confusion joined the sound of her voice.

"He was just a *man*. He was not a Croatoan, Andrea. He was completely human."

She wanted to argue. She wanted to stand up and tell Ned he was a fucking idiot.

She had been there last night—he hadn't. She knew. He didn't. But just then, a higher level of intelligence than she had ever known before kicked in. Suddenly, she could see this conversation like a giant chess match. She had an objective and that was to gain some time and avoid suspicion while she worked out what was happening inside her. This new introduction of misinformation from Ned actually played to her favor. So, even though it was incorrect, flat wrong, she could let it stand and work to her advantage.

"How do you know this?" she asked.

"Your John Doe perp was tested by one of our people at the scene."

Now she registered a little panic. She was alone there last night. There was absolutely no way for any agent to have been there. She stepped carefully across this minefield. "I don't remember seeing an agent there..." she tested.

"Oh, he wasn't there until well after you left. That place was crazy with investigators. We just sent one of ours in before the cleanup started. He was able to test the perp, and concluded completely and accurately that he was 100% human. There were absolutely no traces of Croatoan there at all."

Andrea knew this couldn't be. She knew the truth, and she was going to sit on it. But she wanted to figure out if they were playing a game here or if they really believed it. In her mind, she charted out the shortest path to this conclusion and took the first move, "But all the pieces of evidence that clicked together before I left: the reports, the plans, the wire transfer..."

"Were all circumstantial at best."

Andrea sat there in stunned silence. He was right about that.

"I mean think about it, Andrea. You had maybe enough to get a judge to sign a search warrant. You may have been able to make a case for prob-cause at best. But a jury would have had a difficult time giving you a conviction unless you found the physical evidence. The pieces all related in some way, but there was no smoking gun. He tested human."

Now stepping in to soften the blow of Ned's bluntness, "But an excellent job of detective work, none-the-less! You really put the pieces together and then most importantly you *acted* on your instinct!" Casper looked like a football coach with all his gestures as he said this.

Andrea knew the truth, but even now, she was seeing it through a new light. Was it possible she had been wrong? She began to doubt even the new information that was in her mind. All of it could be stuff she had picked up subconsciously as she half-read all those books and reports while she was pouting about her troubles.

"Not a Croatoan," she said flatly.

"Nope," Ned punctuated, "But an excellent job and a change in you that we have been looking for."

This caught her attention. "Change?"

Casper spoke now. It was a tag-team free-for-all with these guys. It almost seemed scripted. "You put the pieces together and you acted. You were brave. Hell, you were fierce! You made decisions on your own and they were good. You weren't conservative or cautious. This is the exact quality we look for in our agents."

"It is by design," Ned added.

"By design," Andrea echoed with a serious voice.

"Yes. It's something we all went through here," Ned answered.

Now Casper, "This is how we bring up new agents, Andrea. I'm sorry that we were harsh on you. I hate that part of my job. But it's necessary to make our agents what they need to be."

"So the whole cold-hearted asshole routine was all an act?" she asked squarely.

"Well…" chuckling Casper answered, "Maybe not in Ned's case."

"Hey!" Ned objected.

"Easy, tiger." Now back to Andrea, Casper continued, "It isn't really an act. I may have been a bit gruffer than I like to be. But that is part of the entire psychological shaping." Andrea objected to these words, but she was going to keep that to herself. "We bring in a person with training in law enforcement or military special ops…those kinds of things.

"We know they have MS, they don't. We send them on some shit-assignments until a Croatoan jacks into someone with MS or until some spontaneous combustion story comes along. Then we send the rookie out to discover things for themselves.

"They become angry and indignant. We treat them harshly…"

"And they become psycho-cops and go kill the bad-guys for you without fear," she concluded for them.

"Our history proves that once they make that jump, they never go back. We can be ourselves and move on," Casper added.

"So no hard feelings!" Ned blurted out and extended his hand.

Andrea was just staring through him. She mumbled, "Everyone uses everyone."

"I'm sorry, I didn't catch that," Ned said.

Clearing her thoughts and her throat she said, "I can't say that there are no hard feelings Ned. I will work for you. I will get the bad guys. I will be aggressive. But I can't say there are no hard feelings."

"Look…" Ned started.

Feeling she now had the upper hand, "Look your own damn self! I'm going down to Savannah day-after-tomorrow and plant an old dear friend of mine in the ground, and say goodbye. You two can play your little games with the next person that comes along." Then to Casper she asked, "Is it a requirement that an agent *not* have hard feelings to work here?"

"No, Andrea. It is not a requirement," Casper answered.

"Then I have fucking hard feelings!" she yelled and slamming the desk to punctuate her point, stood up and marched off.

Ned yelled out to her, "Spend the rest of the week studying culture and customs during the Industrial Revolution of the seventeenth and eighteenth centuries!"

Casper put a hand on Ned's shoulder and said patiently, "Let her go. She'll be fine."

"I'll put it on her itinerary just to make sure she knows what to work on," Ned said in a business-like tone.

Casper smiled, shook his head and thought, *"Nedward?…Nedson?… Neddles?"*

The air outside had turned cool where forebodingly grey clouds hung low to the ground and the wind caressed the darkening trees, speaking hisses through their thinning leaves. Andrea hoped to see Sorin. She could use some advice right about now and he always seemed to have an uncanny bead on what was needed.

She turned her collar up against the cold and watched as a few leaves made a little ballet, directed by a small zephyr along the way. They spun in and out of the mix, settling down to the waving grass beside the walk.

The cold was inside her as well. She was horribly alone. There wasn't even talking to Wren to look forward to anymore. Clutching her collar at her throat, she made a fruitless attempt to lock in the heat before it escaped.

It's hard to catch something that isn't there.

All of the benches were vacant. All of the shrubs were people-less. No gardeners were rooting around in the roots. People were walking briskly to their next destination and looking forward to whatever it was that made them warm.

At one point, Andrea was walking along a path that would eventually meet another coming into it at an angle. She saw Scott walking on the other path. They would surely meet at this present clip. She accelerated her pace to get to the intersection before he did—hoping to avoid such a meeting.

Even though she found him interesting and had honestly hoped to go out with him, there was that dinner snub the other night. Plus, she really didn't feel like hanging around with any Croatoan hunters just now. Not to mention, Wren just died. The timing was all wrong to be sorting out all these crazy feelings.

Scott matched her new speed step for step. She slowed down and he slowed. He was doing this on purpose. When she got to the corner she said, "Scott. I really don't have time to talk right now. A friend of mine died back home and I need to go call about the arrangements."

Scott held up his hands in the air making a gesture to say *No problem, pass on by,* but he said, "I'm sorry to hear of your loss. Please let me know if I can do anything for you at all."

"Thanks, Scott. I really appreciate it." And her words were just as sincere sounding as they were genuine.

Continuing on in her direction, she looked home towards her townhouse. She had no sooner taken five steps than she heard Scott call out, "Wait!" then after a short pause, "Andrea."

She stopped without turning. A feeling came over Andrea that she could not quite identify. She was worried that Scott might have detected the worst in her. She was equally frightened that she might actually discover she had some feelings for him—regardless of all the risks *that* would bring. And she was terrified that he wouldn't feel the same way about her. All of these emotions were brought to a simmer by the sound of his voice, the call of her name.

She was standing there, scared to turn around, and equally scared to continue on alone. Then came his voice again, ringing true through the bluster and breeze. Softer this time but still clear and with some sense of pleading, "Andrea, please. Wait."

She realized she was trembling a little. Turning around she saw him simply standing there. He looked helpless. Sometimes a person has to reach beyond the void to find something for which they didn't even know they sought. She took a bold step back towards him and stopped. "What is it Scott?"

"I can't let it end this way. Not again."

Andrea was not sure she understood, but his voice was filled with a sincerity she had never known. Yet she knew it somehow. Her mind seemed to be awash with memories that didn't belong to her. They were borrowed memories and yet they were hers to keep. They all testified that this moment, his words, *that* look were all true.

"I am not sure I understand, Scott. What are you trying to say?"

Looking as if he were engaged in his own struggle, he took a cautious step towards her. Andrea began to suspect that he had fears as well. We are seldom aware of the novel someone else may be living, while we are in the middle of our own. Struggling to get his words right he said, "I have been dealing with my own trials. It is not fair for me to impose them on you when you have recently lost a friend."

Seeing the wounded man not but a few steps in front of her, Andrea closed the gap with one more trusting, but cautious step. "Scott, I am dealing with more than losing my friend Wren." She stopped for a moment to collect her thoughts. Then, "Have you ever struggled with not knowing who you were or what you were becoming?"

A simple "Yes," he proffered.

Then looking as if he were gathering up his courage he said, "Andrea, the other day when I told you about the Sideboard Café..."

"Yes?"

"I wanted to ask you out."

In this next, Andrea felt she could be completely honest and not so guarded, "I would have liked that. So why didn't you?"

"I was afraid how you would respond when you got to know me better."

"I'm sure I would have found you to be a great guy, Scott. You seem to have a lot of friends. What could possibly be wrong with a guy like you?"

Taking a step towards her, he said, "Just after passing up the chance to ask you out, I remembered your hair. I saw you on the jet to Atlanta. You were looking outside the window and the sun caught your hair. It looked like it was on fire. It was beautiful."

His eyes took a moment to look at her hair as if he were living the moment all over again. Andrea felt the warmth in her cheeks pressing against the cold air around her, but managed a quiet, "Thank you."

"After leaving that spot, I realized that I had made a mistake and was about to turn around and ask you to wait."

"Why didn't you?"

A look of confusion and doubt came across his face. Looking back at her with a dumb smile, he said, "I don't know, really. I just knew today that I didn't want to make that same mistake again. I didn't want to spend days kicking myself for another missed opportunity."

There are times, few though they may be, when a woman will let a man off the hook. It is the fabled leprechaun, shooting star, or northern lights. They, that are fortunate enough to see it, never forget and often spend the rest of their lives looking for another fix.

The first trip is free, man.

This was one of those moments. Andrea allowed a warm smile and said, "Then don't miss this one."

Not missing a beat Scott asked, "May I take you out this Friday night?"

"I would love that." The words were out of her mouth before she had a chance to realize the predicament that came with the bargain. She almost regretted the freedom of the moment, but as they say back home—you can't unmake a pie.

They said their goodbyes and even though they were well north of the Mason Dixon line, it took a good, long time. The words were awkward and Andrea had to root for the positive side of her thoughts just to make for a fair fight with her growing paranoia.

Eventually she made her way back to her townhouse alone. The dark clouds gathering overhead were a reminder of those gathering in her mind. She had just made a date with a Croatoan killer when she wasn't even sure who or what she was becoming. Still, there was comfort in knowing she had something to which she could look forward. That might help her get through the grizzly tasks she faced this week.

Arriving at the front of her place, she really didn't feel much like climbing in a cave and hiding from the world. She was already doing that in her mind.

Even though it was cold to the bone, she jumped in her car and just took off. Eventually the winding road found her back at the little park in the valley. It was as sad looking today in its grey cold isolation as it was happy in the brilliant color and warmth of all the people playing there just a handful of days earlier.

Andrea got out of her car and crossed the grass that was still green and slightly too long. Needing one last cutting for the season, the blades were bending over in waves as the wind made its presence known in yet another way.

She found again the concrete park picnic table and benches. She loved how fixed they were. It gave a person the impression that at least some things never change. These tables and benches would be there for years to come. And they were already ancient, weathered and steadfast.

Andrea Ellijay climbed up and sat on the table using the bench for her feet. Her mind was reeling with new thoughts. For example, she had never been particularly keen on flora or fauna. Her acquaintances back home always seemed to know the name of every tree right down to the genus and species. It was like they had held a class at some point and invited everyone but her. She didn't even know what genus or species *she* belonged to any more. How could she possibly be expected to know the trees?

And yet, here she was—naming off every single one in order. All she would have to do is look at a particular tree and wait for it to come to her. Andrea's mind would study it, inspecting every detail. She would name them off one by one.

"Shield cut leaves, white on the bottom, petioles, the piece of wood that connects the leaf to the twig, are flattened, the bark is white almost directly from the ground up, Genus: Poplar or Populus, Species: White."

She found she could go on like this forever. It preoccupied her for a time. Occasionally she would pause when she found her thoughts returning to Scott, or Wren, or Danreck the Croatoan. For that was what he was, right? He was a Croatoan. Now he was human.

Correction: Now he was dead.

She was once human. And she was still alive. What is she now? Why could she name every damn genus and species in the valley save one—her? Her frustration would build on that for a while.

Then another tree would catch her attention and the whole game would begin all over again. At a certain point, she grew tired of all the new information that was floating around in her head. What does it profit a woman to gain the entire world and yet loose herself?

She sat there and looked out at the little valley park between the two long hills, the forest thick on either side. There was a small creek that called to visitors softly as it gurgled and splashed down the small rapids caused by twigs or gathered rock. Paths crossed it at distant intervals making the waters contract and expand to pass under the little bridges.

There are times when people can become very certain of the world around them. They grow confident in their positions in life. Work becomes easier, politics become plain, and religion is the old friend we grew up with, and now revisits us in our maturity. Hell, we can even balance our own checkbooks.

And yet...

And yet we can spend hours gazing into the mirror and be totally ignorant of the person staring back at us. It is in these times that we can either accept that we have lost ourselves and begin the process of rediscovery through experimentation and exploration, or we can live in denial and pretend that everything is A-OK.

There is little immediate peace to be found in the first method and none to be found in the second. Really the only thing we can do in these moments is hang on to what we know to be real and accept that the story is not yet completely told. There is so much more ahead. And this is the beginning of hope.

For a long while, she sat there and watched the clouds flying past overhead. She sat there and listened to the autumnal voices in nature. For now, her spirit was calm and her mind was settled. She had much to think about, but thinking would come later.

After a span of this pleasant calmness, she found herself returning to the little roots she had. She decided to hold on to what she knew to be real and just accept that the story was not yet completely told.

Praying aloud for the first time she could remember in years, she said, "Lord? I know I haven't spoken to you in…well…quite some time. I remember that day the Johnson family took me to their church. I remember the words the preacher-man said and how they made me feel inside.

"He told me that if I had done anything wrong in my life, anything that would displease you, that I had sinned. And he told me that the wages of those sins was death."

Here she stopped for a moment. She was worried that she had taken all this God stuff too far. But it felt good to talk about it. And the creek and the wind didn't seem to mind. And in the end, that is why she continued. Because it just felt good.

To Andrea, this was still all the debate there was to religion. She believed it because it made her feel better to do so.

"Well? He told us all that if we confess to You and ask forgiveness and say that we believe in Your Son, that we would be saved. He told us to walk down the aisle. And I prayed that prayer and I walked down that aisle."

There was nothing miraculous in the sound of the wind weaving through the trees around her. Or maybe then again there was. Even though she believed the real her was gone, at least she no longer felt lost.

"At the time, I thought it would be the hardest thing I would ever do. But I don't think it's the hardest thing anymore."

She started to choke up. Her voice was trembling a little at that last. She wiped a few trespassing tears from her cheeks with the palm of her hand and continued, "Well? The preacher-man told me that I was now a child of God—that I wasn't an orphan any more. That I now had a Daddy and that he owned the cattle on a thousand hills.

"He told me that I had the biggest Big Brother on the block and that Your Son would take care of me. And he told me that if I ever needed anything at all, all I had to do was ask."

Andrea found courage in her own words—at least, that is from where she thought the courage came. We speak to family in a different way than we speak to acquaintances.

She was now speaking to family.

"Now here I am talking to you after all these years. My life is pretty much in a mess right now and I really have no idea what is happening to me."

It occurred to her that she really hadn't *asked* for anything as concrete as the table upon which she sat. She was only rattling off a laundry list of things that were bothering her.

Deciding to put the preacher-man's words to the test, she ventured, "Lord? Please forgive me where I have failed you. I don't want to carry this burden any longer. It is too heavy."

Then thinking more specifically what she really needed in this very moment she shouted up at the sky, "Who am I?" then after gathering her strength, "What have I become?"

There was wind, and leaves, and water answering her echo as it moved down the valley. But there was something else there as well. She was looking in the mirror of life, and was totally ignorant of the person staring back at her. There was little immediate peace to be found, but something was quieting her soul.

The soothing prompted her to continue—to ask what was really on her mind. Now softer, her quivering voice offered up what she really wanted to ask all along.

"Please—help me?"

One simple word from a now-known, still, soft voice wafted into existence almost audibly between her two ears—from the very center of her soul.

"Wait."

THE END